ROGUE ELEMENT

AUTONOMOUS WEAPONS DIVISION
BOOK 2

B.R. KEID

FOREWORD

Hello, friend, and thank you for your interest in the Autonomous Weapons Division series and Three Colonies universe.

This is a second-in-series novel. If you haven't already, start with *Intrusion Protocol*, Book One in the Autonomous Weapons Division series.

For the complete *Rogue Element* experience, read *The Division* and *Last Flight of the Sparrow*, two short stories in the Autonomous Weapons Division universe, absolutely free by signing up to my newsletter at brkeid.com/the-division.

Thanks again, and enjoy *Rogue Element*! Talk soon.

Brian

CHAPTER
ONE

THREE COLONIES DATE 499-266

MASTER SPECIALIST KERRY SEVVERS shouldered his way through the bustling corridor. His uniform felt stiff, freshly starched with smart creases down his sleeves and pant legs. The harsh odor of the starch lingered somewhere between sterile wipes and recycler solvent.

He could count on one hand the number of times he'd needed to press his uniforms since joining the Division, but today was special. Lieutenant Park had insisted.

A nearby viewport presented a breathtaking panorama of the lower orbitals. The massive disc-shaped space stations comprised the Colonial Defense Force's stronghold called Aegia Prime. Ships of all kinds, military and civilian, crowded their docking berths to offload or take on supplies.

Far below lay the planet Aegia, second of the Three Colonies, its mountainous surface hidden in a veil of storm clouds. It seemed so desolate and forlorn, with its craggy peaks jutting through the heavy gray. If it weren't for the lines of ships coming and going between them, one wouldn't know there was life down there at all.

Sev tore himself from the viewport and pressed on, feeling the weight of scrutiny from the assembly of officers that had gathered. All their gold and silver rank pips made him uneasy, each representing a station far above his own.

You're nervous, Six said, probing his vitals. The AI's words came like a thought, translated by the miraculous NCCX-1 neural implant inside his brain. *Are we in danger?*

His thoughts thickened with a throb of static that his implant couldn't tune out. It pulsed in waves, like a heartbeat from the walls themselves, growing louder with each breath until it was all he could focus on. The noise coiled around him, tightening like a serpent about to strike.

Then, as quickly as it manifested, it was gone.

Sev let out a breath. *I don't think so. But we're about to be judged by a roomful of senior officers. That's dangerous enough.*

Six laughed, a remarkably human intonation. He could feel its joy, its relief, like it was his own—something his other AI could never do.

I'm sorry, it said. *I don't know why that was so funny.*

Looks like I'm not the only one who's nervous.

The crowd parted before a doorway. Large and ornate, its polished wood and brass stood out among the fibrosteel bulkheads that lined the halls of Orbital Three-Alpha. The nimbus, the symbol of the Three Colonies, hung at its center: a stylized, jet-black vortex laser-etched with intricate silver inlay.

Lieutenant Park and Sergeant Bresto appeared beside him, the only others to survive the mission inside the ancient Concordat derelict. Cylla, their lupanthae pilot, padded behind them, her long, clawed fingers fiddling with the scant patches on her brown familial jacket. Dwarfed only by the door in front of them, she was an intimidating presence, despite her submissive demeanor. The officers kept their distance.

A daxed master-at-arms stopped them at the door. Polished ceremonial fibrosteel, inlaid with council purple, hid the once-human cyborg's more unaesthetic features. It scanned Sev and the others to confirm their identities.

These were council chambers, after all. They didn't let just anyone inside.

Bresto gave Sev a sideways glance. "You ready for this?"

"Oh yeah," he lied, straining to think. "You sound nervous."

"Squids and bugs are one thing," Bresto groaned. "Bureaucrats are something else."

"Quiet," Park ordered. "Our only weapons here are diplomacy and the truth. Let's try to keep the friendly fire to a minimum."

"Somebody tell them that," Bresto said before turning to Park. "Sir."

Sev bit back a smirk. The truth wasn't something typically associated with the Founding Council.

The daxed raised its metal arm, halting Cylla at the door. "You are not authorized," it said. The voice emitter in its helmet made its typically rasping voice deep and imposing. Cylla clutched her paws, her wolf-like ears pinned back in deference to the master-at-arms.

Park spun to face the daxed, unfazed by its imposing form. "Why the hell not?"

"So much for diplomacy," Bresto whispered out of the corner of his mouth.

A specialist with the CDF Headquarters Corps rushed to greet them, placing herself between Park and the daxed. The woman was young, an Aegian like most everyone else there, at home amid the growing crowd of staff-level officers.

"The lupanthae is not a subject of this tribunal, sir," she said in a tone that was both apologetic and assertive. As if to say Cylla was the lucky one.

"Is alright, Lieutenant," Cylla growled, backing away from the door. "Will wait."

"Please." The woman waved Sev and the Marines through the door. "Follow me."

The expansive interior of the council chambers matched its grandiose entrance. The same polished wood lined the high walls, trimmed with lush purple fabric that seemed to swallow all sound. Three Colonies flags colored Respitian red, Aegian gray or Vestian green draped the panels behind a tiered mezzanine that rose against the far wall. Beneath it all, in the center of the room, was a long, thin table where more members of Headquarters Corps directed them to their seats.

"You are here, Master Specialist," one of them said, pulling out a chair. Her demeanor was formal, cool. Another reminder they'd find no friends there. She placed a microphone puck and datapad in front of him as he sat.

Damn. So, they *did* expect him to talk during this thing.

"Thanks," Sev said with a grin too big to be real.

The woman nodded and gestured to a nearby pitcher of water. As Bresto and Park took their seats beside him, she hurried the other specialists away.

The swarm of officers outside filed in, quickly filling the limited seating on the observation deck behind them. Their red level clearance gave them front-row seats to the spectacle of the century. None of them would believe the things they'd soon hear. If Sev was going to keep his career and his freedom, he'd have to convince them somehow.

There were no familiar faces among them. It was no surprise Captain Mirden wasn't there. Say what you want about officers, but that man had a ship to run. *The* ship to run. That was infinitely more important than watching a bunch of flag officers and council bureaucrats grill a bot jockey and two Marines about a secret mission to Cradle's edge.

"I'll do the talking, understand?" Park said, his eyes narrowed with muted anger. "If they ask you direct questions, give them direct answers and nothing more."

The lieutenant was a model officer: a warrior-scholar and a gentleman. A rare breed among the politically motivated elites that normally wore the shiny pips. But when Sev divulged the truth of what they'd seen to a roomful of enlisted specialists, he saw firsthand the rage Park typically reserved for the enemies of humanity.

What could he say? If they were going to survive what was out there waiting for them, everyone needed to know.

"All rise," came a voice over the local PA. The room thundered with the *shuffle-bump* of a hundred people coming to their feet.

Sev rose from his chair, eyes drawn to the figures that emerged from a hidden door atop the mezzanine. Two women and two men stepped through, filling all but one seat. They were top-ranking officials in the CDF, their own service uniforms adorned with rank pips and service awards. A small parade of specialists followed, providing them with microphones and glasses of water. What a show. What next, foot rubs and fresh game?

A woman, lean and stern with age, her silver hair pulled back in a tight bun, leaned toward her mic. Her hard eyes cut the room like a plasma beam.

"At ease. Please, take a seat," she said.

Sev lowered into his chair.

Bresto cupped a thick hand over his mic. "That's General Strumman," he whispered, nodding toward the one Marine among the officers above them. "He doesn't screw around."

"Is that good or bad?" Sev asked.

Bresto only shrugged.

There was a murmur among the presiding officers as they traded frustrated glances with the empty chair. The silver-haired woman swiped her datapad, searching for their missing guest. After a moment of uncomfortable silence, she turned toward her mic.

"In the interest of time, let's begin." She tugged at the high collar of her service uniform. "My name is Admiral Leighton, commanding officer of the frontier fleet and this special tribunal. With me is Vice Admiral Benj of the colonial garrison fleet."

The vice admiral was a gray prune of a man, so pale he could easily be mistaken for daxed if he weren't so old. He gave a dismissive wave and kept quiet, his hooded eyes roving between Sev and the others seated below him.

"General Strumman of the First Marine Division," Leighton continued.

Strumman was a stone wall, like he'd been hewn straight from the rocky peaks of Aegia itself. His digital camouflaged white-and-grays put Sev's uniform to shame. The creases looked like they could cut through duraplate.

"The commandant wishes to express his sincere apologies to the tribunal." Strumman gave his fellow officers a curt nod. "Urgent council matters keep him on Respitia. I speak for the Colonial Defense Marines in his absence."

"Thank you, General," Leighton said. "Finally, Special Director Bertrand of Colonial Intelligence."

"Admiral." Bertrand fixed her gaze on Park. "CI is eager to get to the bottom of this."

Leighton nodded. "As are we, Director."

A hologram shimmered before the empty chair. A man, lithe and proud. His skin tone dusky like Sev's own. Another child of Respitia, but one from entirely different circumstances. He wore a tailored suit of Respitian red that cost more than Sev would make in his entire enlistment. The purple sash of the Founding Council hung over his shoulder and looped around his waist. The man eyed his wrist chrono, frowning as he took his seat.

"Councilman Skain," Leighton said, her forced smile throwing age lines from her narrow eyes. "We're pleased to have the wisdom of the council with us today."

Skain said nothing and gave a dismissive wave.

Lambert Skain, founder of Skain Industries. Sev saw their corporate logo fresh in his mind's eye, stamped right beside the Nimbus on every package of council-issued vat-grown rations. The kind his mother prepared for breakfast each morning. Even in the soft light of the hologram, the man's wealth was obvious. He was at least a century old, but looked healthy as an io. Disease, hunger, even death—Mr. Skain knew none of those things personally.

"Gentlemen," Leighton said, turning her attention to Sev and the others. "Please state your names for the record."

"Lieutenant Lee Park, First Marine Division," Park said. At the mention of their shared unit, Strumman sat back in his chair.

Bresto stiffened. "Sarnt Ned Bresto, First Mar Div."

"Master Specialist Kerry Sevvers," Sev said. The tribunal officers' attention fell on him all at once. "Autonomous Weapons Division."

"Ladies and gentlemen, the objectives of this tribunal are simple," Leighton said, eyeing her datapad. "First, to understand the source and scope of an unauthorized mission to Cradle's edge. A mission that resulted in the deaths of four CDF personnel and the destruction of CDF property worth fifteen billion credits."

Unauthorized mission. The words rankled Sev. It had all looked legitimate at the time. He understood their position, knowing Lernus faked her credentials. But these officers wouldn't care. His stomach crawled at the thought of how much trouble they were really in.

"Second," Leighton went on, her eyes locked firmly on Sev, "to understand the source and scope of unfounded claims that the target of said mission was a Concordat ship."

The room took a collective breath. Quiet curses and prayers rippled through the onlookers behind them.

Before their mission, the Concordat were a distant memory. Bedtime stories that mothers told to frighten wayward children. The killers of Dead Earth, creators of the daxed, the Concordat were the monsters at the heart of humanity's collective nightmares. Their defeat at the hands of the colonies and the pack fleets four centuries before marked the ending of the darkest chapter in human history. One that their return threatened to reopen.

That ships began disappearing shortly after their mission only confirmed Sev's fears. First the *Sparrow*, then the *Gerrund Halsey*. Two ancient and powerful cruisers, the former having been one of the first ships augmented for drone warfare. Rumors continued to spread of other missing vessels, rumors that no doubt expedited the need for this fact-finding inquiry.

Leighton straightened in her chair. "The Council demands answers. The CDF demands answers." She looked down at Park, icy calm given her thinly veiled threat. "Whenever you're ready, Mr. Park."

"Aye, ma'am," he said, his shoulders relaxed as he cycled through the entries in his datapad. "Please direct your attention to item one, the op order issued to me by Agent Mackie Lernus of Colonial Intelligence."

A holoproj nestled on the table hummed. The op order shimmered in the air before the mezzanine. Lernus's biometric signature hovered beside it.

Bertrand cleared her throat. "For the record, CI issued no such op order, nor do we have an agent by the name Mackie Lernus."

"Then Colonial Intelligence has a serious security problem, ma'am," Park shot back, his tone measured. "Lernus's credentials were valid, her orders authentic."

Ouch. That was going to hurt. Sev eyed his boots to conceal his smile. Even in a war of words, the lieutenant knew how to fight.

Bertrand swiped furiously at her datapad. The hologram of the op order faded, replaced with surveillance footage of Lernus and Park at various points before the mission began. She looked almost human. That soft smile, her shy demeanor—all a lie. Only her eyes, with their swirls of azure and amethyst, hinted at what she really was. Transhuman, she'd said. Beyond human. Not only in what she was, but in what she was willing to do.

Her dire words still haunted him. *You're dooming humanity to a war it can't win.*

It was why he'd done what he did to warn the others, why they were all there now. If the Concordat were behind the missing ships, the CDF needed to prepare.

The background noise in his head asserted itself once more. It had a precision that gave away its machine nature, repetitive and unchanging. A signal, ominous and foreboding, parsed as white noise by a brain too primitive to understand what it was experiencing. He could barely hear the others over the approaching digital storm.

"There *is* a Mackie Lernus in colonial records," Bertrand said. The director swiped a file from her datapad toward the holoproj.

A new image appeared of two men at what looked like a ceremonial ball. One, bearded and gray in a Navy dress uniform, shaking hands with a young, long-haired debutant.

Bertrand went on. "Captain Mackie Lernus was a Navy man, dead for over two hundred years now. And I believe that's your great-great-grandfather, Dal Park."

Sev's eyes went wide. Beneath the dark locks and layers of finery, the family resemblance was uncanny. The two images appeared side-by-side: the lieutenant and the agent, and the two men long dead. Sev glanced at the younger Park beside him, the lieutenant's face betraying nothing.

"It's more than a little odd, isn't it?" Bertrand asked.

Sev rubbed his chin. Sure, it was odd. But the truth was simpler: colonial politics were incestuous. The reality was when there were so few of your species left, the one percent were a very tight group. And it was no surprise that Park, with the fame and wealth his heritage brought, was right in the middle of it.

"I'm sorry, ma'am," Park said. "Are you suggesting this is some conspiracy going back generations? One that nearly ended in my death and the deaths of my entire team?" The hint of a smile curled Park's lips. "I suppose Great Great Grandpa Dal would be very disappointed."

Muffled laughter rippled through the observation deck. A scowl tugged at Bertrand's face.

"At ease," Admiral Leighton said above the din. "Director, does Colonial Intelligence have anything to suggest this is more than a simple coincidence?"

Bertrand sat her datapad down. "Not at this time."

"Very well." Leighton turned to the other members of the tribunal. "Let's proceed. While Agent Lernus's true identity concerns this tribunal—"

The signal storm swept over Sev. His arm shook, the nerve pain curled his fingers. The connection with his implant grew weak. Even Six's datastream froze beneath the torrential noise. His thoughts vanished, drowned in the psychic maelstrom.

It faded quickly, blowing past like a summer monsoon. Some kind of sweep or scan. For what, he couldn't be certain. But whatever it was, someone was willing to cause a lot of pain and discomfort to find what they were looking for.

He looked up to find Admiral Leighton staring back at him, lips moving, her eyes hard and unflinching. "—we have much more important concerns to discuss."

CHAPTER
TWO

THE TRIBUNAL GROUND on for hours. Constant, meticulous questions about every detail regarding preparation for their mission. Questions about the Marines Park sought to accompany him and why. A short, uncomfortable conversation about how he acquired no less than six hard suits from the armories at Aegia Prime.

There was even vocal skepticism about why Sev was the right combat programmer for the job. Given his, as Benj put it, "established pattern of belligerence toward his immediate chain of command."

To Sev's credit, it took only a brief review of his service record to put those questions to rest. To Park's credit, any remaining skepticism ended when the discussion of the mission's execution began.

A map of the raider corvette's hangar deck hovered in the air. Blue and red icons representing both friend and foe moved through it, retracing the steps Sev and the others took when they first boarded the vessel.

Tension wound through Sev's body as the map replayed every detail of their encounter.

General Strumman watched with a level of interest that spoke to his experience. "Clean. Well executed," he said with a grunt. "How were you able to gain access to the cargo hold so quickly?"

Park leaned toward his mic. "Master Specialist Sevvers used his AI to override the ship's systems and provide fire support with his combat drones."

Strumman turned, his firm stare goading Sev to speak.

"Yes, sir," Sev said, resisting the urge to fidget. "My cluster has a lot of experience in dealing with raider security."

"I'm sorry." Strumman frowned. "Your… cluster?"

"The group of AI in my implant, sir." He gestured behind his left ear. Strumman arched an eyebrow.

Most of that cluster was gone. His AI second-in-command named Two. Four, the anti-AI expert. And Five, his CQB specialist. All turned against him by a force more powerful than anything the raiders could muster. A hive-mind the Concordat called the Eleven. Just thinking of it made him cringe, like he could still hear their malicious code scratching around the inside of his brain.

His void warfare expert, codenamed Three, had survived. Sheer luck given it was busy tangling with raider fighters and not part of their intrusion action. Then there was One, his very first AI, destroyed trying to save him and the others when the rest of his AI turned rogue.

If it hadn't been for Six, his illegal side project, they'd all be dead. Something about its lack of Division safeties allowed it to resist the Eleven.

You're welcome, Six said.

Since when did you become a mind reader? he asked jokingly. But the more he thought about it, the more discomforting it was. They were supposed to understand his commands, not know his thoughts.

Since I've been living inside your head—

Another wave of static coated Sev's mind. His vision blurred. It had been a regular occurrence throughout the day's proceedings, washing over him in thirty-minute intervals. Using his implant was all but impossible while the strange signal was active. He gritted his teeth and let the storm wash over him.

Bresto planted an elbow firmly into Sev's ribs. The move jarred him from his static-induced malaise. Urgency twisted Bresto's face as he tilted his head toward the mezzanine.

"Master Specialist Sevvers," Leighton repeated, her eyebrows knitted in confusion. "Are you well?"

"I'm sorry, ma'am," he managed. He swallowed dryly and smoothed the front of his white-and-grays. "Can you repeat the question?"

Leighton appraised her fellow officers. "I believe we've worn the master specialist down."

Quiet laughter swept the observation deck. A specialist from Headquarters Corps emerged to pour him a glass of water, which he sipped eagerly. It tasted bright and fresh, probably shipped directly from the surface of Aegia. No recycled swill in these hallowed chambers.

He lowered the glass, blinking back the noise in his head. "I'm fine, ma'am. I—"

"It has been a long day," the admiral cut in, turning her attention to those gathered on the observation deck. "And there is still much to discuss. This tribunal is recessed until 1000 hours tomorrow morning." She stood abruptly, prompting the entire assembly to rise. "I trust you'll be well rested by then, Master Specialist."

"Ma'am," Sev said, standing with the rest of the room as the presiding officers filed toward the exit.

Skain's holographic gaze lingered on him for a moment, then vanished.

"Nice work, Sevvers." Bresto gave a low chuckle. "You lulled them into submission with your Navy constitution."

No longer under the watchful eye of the tribunal, Sev gulped the water in his glass. The pains he'd suffered for so long had been largely absent since his encounter with the Concordat. Two AI in his head were much easier to deal with than five, even if one of them was an unsanctioned build with a mind of its own. Something about this place didn't agree with him.

He shook off the noise and laughed. "What can I say?" He cuffed the big Marine on the shoulder. "With your level of engagement today, someone had to take the fight to them."

His remark teased a laugh from Park. "He's got your number, Sergeant."

"Bah," Bresto growled. "You all have at it with your *diplomacy*. I didn't qual on that particular weapon."

Sev appreciated the Marine's single-mindedness. With all the change swirling around him—the return of the Concordat, his posting at the Autonomous Weapons School, and the mounting threats posed by both—Bresto's unflinching bravado comforted him.

His mind wandered to his old section: Cole, Jene, and Harp. To his newfound companion, Kea Tareth. It would be days before the *Lehman's* resupply was complete. He should make time to see them before they departed.

"Master Specialist." The familiar voice chilled Sev's blood. Six's datastream swelled with concern, analyzing the voice's pitch and rhythm, confirming what Sev already knew. He took a breath to steady himself, pushing both his and Six's rising panic from his thoughts. This was going to happen, eventually. Time to get on with it.

Sev turned with a smile and outstretched hand. "Chief Architect."

Chief Architect Jacobe took his hand and shook it. Jacobe's barely-regulation haircut and stubbled beard more closely resembled the Division instructor Sev remembered. As a master specialist at the school six years before, Jacobe taught him how to build and control his autonomous battle AI. He warned Sev and the other recruits of the dangers of violating Division rules. The matte black storm coat and silver officer's pips Jacobe wore were new. They screamed danger. For Six and himself.

Jacobe laughed and pulled him close, slapping a hand warmly on his back. The embrace was brief but genuine. "It's good to see you again," he said. "How long has it been? Six years?"

"Yes, sir," Sev replied, struggling to hide his discomfort.

Jacobe looked past him to Bresto and Park. "You've been spending too much time with the trigger-pullers, bot jockey. No need for such formalities. You and I go way back."

The architect's words felt sincere. Sev couldn't put his finger on it, but somehow that made them even more unsettling.

"Alright… Jacobe."

"That's more like it." Jacobe stepped back and took in the vastness of the council chambers. "It will be good to have you back at the Division."

Sev held his breath, waiting for the other shoe to drop.

Jacobe guffawed, clutching his waist. "Founders, what's with you, man?" He eyed the nearby Marines. "Sevvers was always a little too in his own head. Nothing's changed."

He can't be trusted, Six said.

I know.

Did he, really? This seemed like the Jacobe he remembered from the school. Relaxed and easy going, almost to the point of breaking military bearing.

Bresto appeared to his left. "You good, Sevvers?"

Sev gave a weak smile. Maybe he really was going to be okay, assuming he survived this tribunal in one piece.

It wasn't fair. All the CDF's bluster about fighting for humanity felt hollow. Maybe his own motives weren't so pure, not in the beginning, but in the end, his actions spoke for themselves. If not for his involvement in the mission to rescue Deni, who knows if Park and his team would have made it back at all, or how many more Marines might've died. Without Six, he and the others would still be aboard the derelict, daxed just like Corporal Mace. Enslaved to fight another war against humanity.

That he had to justify what he did to a bunch of bureaucratic assholes made him angry. For humanity, indeed. He really hoped Jacobe was on his side.

"I'm fine," he said.

"Excellent," Jacobe said. "Let me take you to dinner. The officer's mess on the council deck is first rate."

Be careful, Six warned. *This could be another trap.*

Maybe, he replied. But what choice did he have? They were going to face off against Jacobe eventually. *He seems friendly enough. I doubt he'll spring something on us over dinner.*

If you say so, Sev.

Sev breathed deep and nodded. "Of course. Thank you."

"Would you like to join us, Sergeant?" Jacobe asked Bresto. The Marine shook his head and shrugged.

"I'm good, sir," he said, then turned and gave Sev a wink. "Catch you tomorrow."

———

The officer's mess was grander than Sev could've imagined. More dining hall than chow hall, complete with uniformed wait staff and ornate tablecloths with the nimbus embossed in their center. Tall, narrow viewports of dense plexene lined the sweeping exterior bulkhead. Far below, dark clouds swirled ominously between Aegia's steep mountain ranges.

He watched the planet turn imperceptibly over the rim of his glass, savoring the sparkling wine's subtle notes of sediment and rain. It reminded him of the last time he was at the Division, the day he graduated Autonomous Weapons School. And of the dear friend he'd left behind.

"Beautiful, isn't it?" Jacobe said with a sigh. "I don't go home as much as I should. Sad when you consider it's only a few hours away. You ever get back to Respitia, duster?"

Sev laughed. "Tough to book passage back home on enlisted pay," he replied, taking another drink. The wine was bittersweet, like his memories of the place. "Nothing to go back to, anyway."

Jacobe averted his gaze briefly. "I'm sorry. I'd forgotten."

Respitia was only four light years from Aegia, next-door neighbors in cosmic terms. But with his father long dead and his mother taken when he was young, there was no reason to go back. His place was on the frontier, killing the enemies of humanity. He'd never imagined that success would take him away from all that, let alone to somewhere entirely more dangerous.

A specialist with Headquarters Corps appeared, her white-and-grays adorned in council purple. Sev's eyes widened at the plate of roasted game she placed between them. The succulent aroma of real meat turned golden brown over a flame made his stomach growl.

"Roasted kinlin," she said formally. "Fresh from the capital mountainsides this morning."

"Uh, wow," Sev said, still staring at the plate.

This was real meat, not the vat-grown stuff he and most other colonists lived on. There was simply no comparing the fermented, then freeze-dried loaves of generic muscle tissue to that of a living, breathing creature. That anyone in the Three Colonies ate like this at all, let alone every day, was impossible to believe.

"It's good to see you again, Chief Architect," she continued, bowing slightly. "How are you this evening?"

"I'm well, thank you," Jacobe replied with a saccharine smile.

"Excellent," she said. "I'll be back to check on you soon." She gave Sev a brief nod, then left the table.

Jacobe leaned over his plate. "I told you," he whispered. "Crazy, isn't it?"

"No shit," Sev groaned, savoring the still-sizzling game birds' aroma.

With a large serving clasp, Jacobe sat a roasted morsel on both their plates. Sev attacked his meal with his knife and fork. Dark caramel juices pooled on his plate. The taste was sublime. Too good to be real.

It should go without saying he has ulterior motives, Six said.

Sev smiled as he chewed, careful to make it less obvious he was focusing his thoughts. *I know. Doesn't mean I can't eat well in the meantime.*

Six's datastream trembled with frustration. *May I suggest trying to learn more about his plans?*

Good idea.

Sev caught himself about to wipe the grease from his face with his hands and dabbed his chin with his napkin. "Last time I saw you, you were a master specialist teaching skeegs like me at the school." He glanced around the expansive officers' mess, then cut another strip of flesh from his kinlin. "When did all this happen?"

Jacobe leaned back in his chair and sipped his wine. "Just over three years now. Things were going well. I'd just made chief spec, and the plan was to put me in charge of curriculum."

"Looks like the plan changed," Sev said.

"There was an incident." Jacobe turned to the nearest viewport and sighed. His hand trembled slightly, and he squeezed it into a fist. "An accident at the school. There were deaths involved. It didn't take us long to determine an unsanctioned build was the cause."

The term made Six bristle. The machine emotion bled into Sev's psyche, tensing his shoulders and tightening his grip on his fork.

"For days, we hunted it. From network to network, subsystem to subsystem. Nothing could catch it. Not even Division scrubbers."

Jacobe leaned in and resumed eating, chewing quietly as he spoke. "So, I made some... upgrades. Scrubbed the damn thing before it could escape via long-range tac comms."

Sev dropped his fork, fingers tense at the sudden burst of machine anger roiling inside his mind. Six's stream whipped like a serpent coiling to strike. Even through the haze of machine emotion, he could see the truth.

They were both in grave danger.

I'll scrub you, you bastard, Six spat, its streams trembling. *That poor program. Wiped out just for existing.*

Easy, Six. He said there were deaths.

I have killed, Six cried. *For humanity. For you. Should I be scrubbed?*

The raw machine emotion stung Sev's eyes. As complicated as the topic of unsanctioned AI was, Six was right. So there were accidents. Only that AI knew why, and it was gone. He thought of Lernus and Deni and how Six saved him from their treachery. For all he knew, those accidental deaths might have been well-earned.

"What happened to the programmer?" he asked, failing to disguise the tension in his voice.

"Executed," Jacobe said, chewing his food contentedly. The man looked unrepentant, even proud. A wave of horror curdled Sev's stomach. "Unsanctioned builds are a high crime, even before considering the deaths involved."

The words took Sev's breath away. He'd always considered the worst-case scenario, but only to convince himself of a more likely outcome. CDF prison. A labor colony, maybe. But no. Jacobe could have him killed, just like that.

He cleared his throat. "You received a commission then? That's unusual for enlisted like us."

"True, but the incident was a reminder to Division command just how serious the threat of unsanctioned AI is." Jacobe locked eyes with him. "So, besides R&D, Division architects seek and destroy rogue programs wherever they are."

"And how's that going?"

"Three kills to date." Jacobe smiled broadly and reclined in his chair. "It's like we can't help it. Humans. Like we're made to break rules." He raised his glass to Sev. "It'll be good to have you at the school, Sevvers. To remind new recruits that there are... consequences for getting out of line."

Another wave of signal interference crackled through Sev's thoughts, muting Six's machine anger. Between the wine, the food, and Six's rage, he hadn't heard it coming. The sudden discomfort made him grunt. He dropped his fork and sent it clattering against his plate.

Jacobe watched him struggle. "Right on schedule."

"What is that?" Sev asked, still wincing at the signal noise.

"My upgraded scrubbers," Jacobe continued. "They're aggressive little code stacks, always deep scanning for new threats. Apologies for the discomfort; they create a lot of feedback in unmodded implants. Once you're onboarded, we'll get you patched. You won't even notice it then."

"What about the recruits?" he asked. "It has to be hell on them after their implant surgeries."

"It's only a short while until they ship out." Jacobe narrowed his eyes. His smile was icy, cruel. "Besides, some minor discomfort is a small price to pay to ensure the safety of humanity."

Bile crept up the back of Sev's throat. Maybe it was the dizzying static of Jacobe's scrubbers patrolling the orbital's tac nets. Or all the casual talk of killing unsanctioned AI and their programmers. Perhaps the rich food and drink. Either way, he'd had enough.

Jacobe placed his arms on the table, making a face while he formed his thoughts. "I read Lieutenant Park's report, you know," he finally said.

"Yeah?"

"It's incredible that the three of you got out of there alive." Jacobe drained his glass and placed it on the table. "A testament to your skills as a combat programmer."

The sudden flattery didn't put Sev's mind at ease. "It was," he said. "I couldn't have done it—"

"I do have one question though," Jacobe interrupted. "Park's report stated only one hard suit survived the mission. But... there were three of you aboard the derelict, right?"

Anxiety tugged at Sev's sternum, that awful sinking feeling of being caught in a lie. With all their logistical minutiae, none of the tribunal officers noticed that minor discrepancy. And somehow Jacobe locked onto it like a Type-R torpedo: fast, mean, and hard to kill. Not a good sign.

"There was a malfunction aboard the Gauntlet," he stammered. He could lie straight-faced about all things AI warfare, but ship systems were as alien to him as raider squids.

"I believe you." Jacobe's smile was artificial. "It's so strange, such extensive damage to the Gauntlet's engines *and* its computer core."

Their server appeared, holding a glass carafe filled to the brim with more Aegian wine. She topped off Jacobe's glass, then turned to Sev, but he waved her off.

"Can I get you something else?" she asked. "Tea? Water?"

"No. I… I don't feel well." He turned to Jacobe. "By your leave, sir."

Their server recoiled at his sudden withdrawal from dinner, like he'd cursed the Twelfth out loud. For a moment, even Jacobe looked genuinely hurt. But Sev knew better. Somewhere along the way, the commission—and the obsession with unsanctioned AI—had gone to the architect's head. And good people were suffering for it.

"Of course, Master Specialist," Jacobe said, his words dripping with hostile formality.

Sev stood from the table, steadying himself as the scrubbers' interference slowly faded from his mind. Already he could feel Six's anger bubbling to the surface, clouding his thoughts. Familiar nerve pain shot through his right arm as his implant cycled to full power.

The exit lay beyond a maze of dining tables, spilling over with extravagant food, wine, and senior officers with more service stripes than he had fingers and toes. The few who watched him leave did so with casual disapproval. Like a desert varmint shooed out an open hab door.

Outside the officer's mess, he leaned against the wall and cradled his aching arm.

What the hell, Sev? Three's voice sprang from nowhere, its tone typically indignant. *Why does Six get all the processing power?*

Vital streams only, Three, Six commanded. As if Three had a choice.

Enough, Six, Sev chided, struggling to form the thought. *You need to control yourself, for both our sakes.*

I'm sorry, Six growled. *But Jacobe is a mortal threat to me. To both of us.*

Six was right. Aegia Prime might be CDF-controlled space, but the Division was hostile territory. It would take a miracle to keep them both out of Jacobe's crosshairs.

CHAPTER
THREE

SEV RIPPED THROUGH THE CORRIDOR, striding toward the council chamber doors. Power walking, his Division instructors had called it, the only speed he'd ever moved at during his time at the school. Any faster and he'd be jogging.

Sleep hadn't come at all the previous night, and not for the usual reason. Instead, he was up all night talking Six down from the proverbial ledge after their ominous dinner with Jacobe. The chrono in his implant read 1008 hours station time, but he knew he was in trouble when he found the hallway leading to the chamber was empty. The tribunal was in session, and he was late.

The daxed master-at-arms stood like a statue beside the ornate wooden door. Cylla sat on a bench opposite them, whistling a mournful note in her native lupanthaese. Her ears pricked up at the sound of his footsteps.

"Kerry Sevvers," she said, eyes bright until she saw his disheveled appearance. Her muzzle wrinkled when she frowned. "Look like dung."

He rested a hand on her shoulder. Sitting down, she was almost as tall as he was.

"I thought you said all Respitians were beautiful?" he asked, grinning. *Almost* a flirt.

Her golden eyes met his, and she smiled, revealing rows of razor-sharp teeth. Mouth open, that's how you knew it was an actual smile. Mouth closed meant trouble.

"Master Specialist Kerry Sevvers." The master-at-arms glared at him through its smoke-colored visor. Tiny shards of light reflected off the visor's edges as the once-human verified his identity. "You are authorized to enter. Please proceed directly to your assigned seat."

Sev gave an anxious nod. The daxed stood there, grasping the handle, but didn't move.

"Yes?" Sev asked. "What is it?"

The cyborg leaned closer. "For the Lost," it whispered, its natural voice dry like blowing sand. Before he could reply, it tugged the door open and waved him through.

The tribunal chambers fell silent when he entered, save a low murmur from those seated on the observation deck. Jacobe stood out immediately in his ruthless matte black storm coat. Another Division architect sat with him, a Respitian woman with void-black skin and white hair chopped at her jawline. She sat unmoving, only her stare followed him to his seat.

The tribunal officers watched him with a mix of impatience and apathy. Strumman's bushy eyebrows came together in a frown. Benj looked half asleep in his chair, while Bertrand scrolled impatiently through her datapad. Skain's hologram flickered in the bright light of the mezzanine with a fierce look that said he wasn't used to waiting on anyone. Leighton's own rigid composure suggested she already knew how the day was going to end.

Bresto leaned in. "You look like shit."

"So I've been told," Sev replied. "Dinner didn't agree with me."

"Master Specialist Sevvers," Admiral Leighton began, her voice commanding through the chamber's speakers. "I should hold you in contempt of these proceedings. But, seeing as I'm not inclined to belabor this tribunal longer than absolutely necessary, I trust you're prepared to give us your undivided attention today."

"Yes, ma'am."

"Very well." She turned her focus to Park. "As I was saying, this tribunal can find no fault with you or your team concerning the prosecution of this unauthorized mission." Her gaze flicked from Bertrand, then back to the Park. "The director assures me additional safeguards will be put in place to prevent future lapses in security of the kind this impostor Lernus took advantage of."

"Thank you, ma'am," Park said.

"That leaves the matter of Master Specialist Sevvers's public disclosure of classified operational details." Benj gave a gravelly cough, then whispered into Leighton's ear. A smile teased the corners of her lips. "And incitement to riot."

"What?" Sev cried. His voice echoed through the room, mixed with the pitched whine of microphone feedback.

Park shot him an icy glare. "At ease, Sevvers."

"What else would you call spreading false rumors about the Concordat's supposed return?" Leighton wove her fingers together and rested her hands on the table. "The Concordat are gone, destroyed four hundred years ago in a war that cost humanity dearly."

Bertrand leaned over her mic. "CI has blocked over four hundred messages from the Lehman's crew containing references to the master specialist's outburst. Even unfounded rumors like that would send the colonies into a panic. Financial markets, manufactory production, colony logistics… it would grind to a halt overnight. It could take years to recover."

"But is it true?" Counselor Skain's voice, rich and velvety like his fine red suit, echoed off the glossy wood panels.

The chambers grew still. It was the first time Skain had said anything since the tribunal began. Leighton shifted uncomfortably in her chair.

"Yes, sir," Park said. "We fought the Lost. They captured one of my Marines, Corporal Mace. They daxed her, turned her against us."

"I've read your report, Lieutenant," Leighton added. "How can you be certain they were Lost? Perhaps you were mistaken once again. Saw what you wanted to see. A kind of symmetrical destiny, given your famous heritage."

"I'm prepared to provide this tribunal with evidence to the contrary," Park replied, motioning to the datapad in front of him.

"Just a moment, Lieutenant." Leighton waved a Headquarters

Corps liaison closer. They exchanged words, and the young specialist disappeared through the hidden door behind them. "I'm afraid none of us are qualified to judge the merit of your evidence. There are... precious few still with us who are. But one of them is here today."

The rhythmic vibrations of heavy footfalls coursed through the tile floor. A sound like a baleful wind howled outside the chamber. The large wooden doors opened and Admiral Leighton came to her feet. Sev rose with the rest of the room, even as his instincts begged him to run.

Another daxed lumbered into view, as wide as it was tall, stooping beneath the high wooden doors to gain access to the council chambers. It was unlike any Found daxed he'd ever seen, at least among the Daxed Corps.

Thick, segmented armor covered its wide torso, marked with a brutal gash that ran like a scar from its breast to its belly. Its lower jaw was gone, replaced with a crude metal plate to hide the mess of cables and tubes running from the back of its throat and into its skull. Custom white-and-grays covered its pale gray skin. A long row of service stripes lined its sleeves, a testament to its centuries-long service. Commander's pips shone on the thick neck guard below its plated chin.

The once-human stopped before the mezzanine. Its shoulders rose and fell with each labored breath, revving the strange alien engine that powered it. Only then did Leighton sit.

"State your name for the record," she said.

"I don't remember my name," it said, its voice rumbling from an ancient emitter inside its jaw plate.

The sound was mechanical, overly digital, like some primitive bot. This creature, like all daxed, was almost five hundred years old. Taken from Dead Earth and daxed by the Concordat. Freed by a god—if you believed the stories—to fight for humanity rather than against it.

Daxed personnel were commonplace on CDN starships. Masters-at-arms. Med techs. Cargo haulers. But this one was different. It looked more like the fierce heavies they fought aboard the derelict. More like the Lost. Big and armored like them, it wore its history like a badge of honor.

"Oh, I'm… forgive me." Leighton cleared her throat, her face flush. "Please, your CDF ident… for the record."

"I am DC-1," it said. "Commander, Colonial Defense Daxed Corps."

"Thank you, Commander," Leighton said. "Lieutenant Park, your evidence, please."

Park scrolled through his datapad, tapped several items and flicked them toward the holoproj. The air blurred and shimmered, filling with hard suit telemetry.

The first image turned Sev's stomach in knots. A flurry of red blaster bolts and blue plasma lit the Lost, charging from the slave hold's stasis bay. The massive heavy and its dancing wisps. The fight that PFC Dalon would give his life to win.

Murmurs rippled through the observation deck. Someone gasped. These people didn't know the half of it.

Park pointed at the hologram. "Please note the suit metadata, recorded in what Agent Lernus referred to as the slave hold. The Lost ambushed us from an adjacent stasis chamber."

The next image rendered from thin air, gun sight footage from Bresto's Mark Three railgun. The barrel still glowed blue-hot from a recent discharge, while the daxed heavy sagged to the floor a dozen meters away. Down but not out. Its armor caved in from the kinetic strength of the blast but still intact.

The daxed commander said nothing, its eyes moving back and forth rapidly as if studying each of the individual points of light in the hologram. The similarities between it and the Lost were breathtaking. Terrifying.

"The heavy you see here," Park began, his eyes shifting nervously at his crude description, "was impervious to even our exo-served weaponry. Only well-placed breaching charges brought it down."

"Breaching charges?" Strumman choked, almost laughing.

"Yes, sir," Park said. The gun sight image faded, replaced with more hard suit imagery of Dalon detonating the charges he'd placed on the heavy's spine. Intense blue fire leaped from the once-human's back, the sudden heat and overpressure opening it up like a meat and metal flower. "PFC Dalon's quick thinking and exemplary courage saved us."

Heavy emotion crept into Park's voice. That alone made Sev's eyes burn with the threat of tears.

"Thank you, Lieutenant," Leighton said, then turned to address the daxed. "Commander, do you recognize the creatures in these projections?"

The daxed stood in silence, its unblinking eyes still locked on the terrible images before it. It felt like such a dumb question, given the stark similarities between them.

"Yes," DC-1 said. "They are Lost."

The chorus of voices from the observation deck swelled into a dull roar. Strumman and Benj whispered to each other, their anxious eyes betraying the concern their hushed tones tried to hide. Leighton surged from her chair. Frustration twisted her noble features. Or was it fear?

"At ease," she cried. "At ease! Silence!"

An uneasy quiet fell over the council chambers, like Leighton's fury had sucked the atmosphere from the room. She sat down slowly, unsure of where her chair had gone during her outburst.

"Commander," she continued, her voice wavering, "does this mean the claims are true? Have the Concordat returned?"

"Unknown," DC-1 said in clipped, electronic tones. "The maximum lifespan of a daxed entity is functionally infinite. The presence of these Lost does not confirm recent Concordat activity."

Leighton and the other members of the tribunal visibly relaxed. Sev shook his head. They'd convinced themselves their precious status quo was still intact, if only for the moment. Fools.

Park searched his datapad. "I have a data file on the Forge that confirms it's operational."

DC-1 turned, locking Park in an eerie stare. It may not remember its name, but it damn sure remembered the Forge. For Sev, the Forge was a nightmare straight from the twelve hells, and he'd survived it more or less intact. The horrors DC-1 must've seen, must've experienced first-hand, would be incomprehensible.

"It's not here," Park said.

"Sir?" Bresto asked, a frown smoothing his pale forehead.

"My data on the Forge… it was just here."

Leighton leaned forward in her chair. "Is there a problem, Lieutenant?"

"One moment, please," he replied.

Sev felt his implant surge, flooding his thoughts with Orbital Three-Alpha's tac net schema, CDF access codes, and encryption keys.

What are you doing, Six?

I'm going to track down the missing data, Six replied.

Absolutely not. It isn't safe.

Already he could hear the distant static roar of Jacobe's enhanced scrubbers like a rushing wave. Their brutal pinging net sweeps played havoc with his implant's signal. Worry tightened like a knot in his chest, but Six's mind was made up. There was nothing he could do.

I already have the datapad's tac net address. I'm in.

Make it fast, Sev said. *The scrubbers are coming.*

CHAPTER
FOUR

"LIEUTENANT PARK," Leighton said, her tone venomous. "Produce your evidence now. The Commander has more important things to do—"

"I will wait," DC-1 said. Its eyes twitched, glaring at Park intently.

Park looked at Sev. "Um, almost there, ma'am …"

One minute, Sev mouthed.

"Minor technical issue, ma'am," Park added.

Strumman grunted a laugh. "Maybe your combat programmer can help with that."

Sev bit back a smirk, remembering full well Jacobe and the other architect were behind him on the observation deck. Everyone assumed bot jockeys were expert hackers, when in truth, Division rules kept them from doing anything quite so cool. Unless you broke them.

Sev, we have a problem.

What is it? he asked.

I've found the file, but it's encrypted. Division level.

Sev clenched his fists. *Jacobe.*

His surprise quickly faded. Of course, Jacobe would interfere with the tribunal. He'd do whatever it took to draw Six and Sev into the open. The hunter had set another trap, and they were walking right into it.

Three, Six commanded. *On me.*

No can do, Six, Three replied, its stream tut-tutting indignantly. *You know what they say: safety overrides active. The risk of collateral damage is beyond Division tolerances.*

Sev's pulse quickened in time with the implant as it revved to full capacity.

Try again, Six said.

Woah, Three said, its own stream slightly off. *I... I'm in.*

The tips of Sev's fingers went numb. *Six, what did you do?*

I modified Three's safety protocols.

You did what? Sev cried.

Numbness crawled through his wrist and into his elbow as Six took the implant beyond its limits. The scrubbers drew closer, filling Sev's mind with a constant sound like shattering glass. The streams criss-crossing his thoughts blurred.

I need the additional throughput to break Jacobe's encryption before the scrubbers arrive. Another heartbeat passed. *Hold on, Sev.*

Time slowed. Reality twisted. The council chambers faded into darkness, replaced with a vast plane of tac net data representing every possible combination of encryption keys they'd have to test to break Jacobe's lock on Park's data. A near-infinite array of possibilities. Two motes of light sped over the plane like errant electrons, turning their disparate orbits in search of the right combination.

An unseen static hell descended all around them. The pain was sudden and immense, a burning ache inside his skull. The edges of the data plane warped and faded, the information contained within gone forever. More collateral damage in Jacobe's personal war.

The locks on Park's data turned, thunderous booms like the ancient doorways inside the Concordat derelict. Beneath it all, the incessant *tick-tick-tick* of each passing nanosecond. Counting time until either the locks came open or the scrubbers consumed them all.

The passage of time came rushing back. The virtual plane, the lights, the scrubbers, all vanished. Sev found himself back in the council chambers, dizzy but otherwise unharmed. The crushing signal storm faded, replaced with a silence born of terror from the image looming in front of them.

The hologram of Corporal Mace's daxed form hung in the air. Her hard suit twisted, reformed to fit her hulking, once-human physiology. Acrid smoke poured from the swollen powerpack on her back. Sev flinched reflexively, his fight-or-flight response frozen in his confused state.

It's okay, Sev, Six said, its datastream weary. *We did it.*

Speak for yourself, Six, Three snapped. *My best void warfare stacks got scrubbed!*

"Easy, Sevvers, you're okay," Bresto whispered. "Nice work."

"Thanks."

He took a breath. The scent of warm blood filled his nose. Bresto passed him a napkin from a neat stack of them beside a pitcher of water. Sev dabbed his nostril, stemming the flow. Would Jacobe notice the symptom from where he sat? The burst of computational speed had caused a minor bleed. A telltale sign of unsanctioned activity.

"What... what is that?" Leighton asked, staring at the image, her face pale.

"That was Corporal Mace, ma'am," Park said.

"Lost no more," Bresto added solemnly.

Leighton turned to DC-1, her brow furrowed with worry. "Commander?"

"You saw this," DC-1 said, turning its gaze from the hologram toward Sev and the others.

It wasn't a question.

"Yes, sir," Park said.

"Then it's true." DC-1 spoke slowly, its aux voice rattling. "The Forges burn. The Concordat awaken."

Silence reigned. Sev watched those present, the upper echelons of the Colonial Defense Forces, wither at the revelation, trying to process the truth he'd known for days. A truth he'd tried to warn them about. A truth they had gathered to punish him for.

Humanity's ancient enemies had returned.

Admiral Leighton didn't move. Her white-knuckled grip on her armrests grew tighter with each passing second. She seemed to shrink visibly in her chair, staring into her lap.

Vice Admiral Benj swallowed dryly. "Your orders, ma'am?"

She looked up, suddenly aware that all eyes were on her. Her mouth opened and closed as she struggled to form the words.

"Um, place the garrison fleet on high alert. Suspend all colonization flights and withdraw the frontier fleet immediately. I want them chasing light back to the colonies now." She pressed at her temples with her fingertips. "And send word to the pack fleets: the CDF *humbly* requests their aid."

"Ma'am," Benj snapped, springing from his chair with a speed that defied his advanced age.

"General," Leighton said to Strumman.

The Marine's gaze was severe, but calm. "The Marines are with you, ma'am. Every climb and place."

"For humanity," she said, giving his hand a firm shake. "We should meet with the commandant immediately. Only he can authorize a full mobilization."

"Consider it done, ma'am," Strumman said before following Benj through the rear exit.

"Admiral?" Bertrand asked.

"Director, I trust Colonial Intelligence will keep any mention of the Concordat off the public feeds?"

Bertrand nodded. "Yes, ma'am."

"Good." Leighton sighed. "Let's stave off economic and societal collapse as long as we can."

"Ma'am." Bertrand hesitated. "And the tribunal?"

"Tribunal?" Leighton's eyes narrowed in confusion, like she'd forgotten why they were there. "Damn the tribunal. Gentlemen, you're dismissed… with my apologies. Return to your units."

Park rose from his chair. "Thank you, ma'am."

Leighton stood and turned to the daxed commander. Even atop the mezzanine, DC-1's gaze was level with hers.

"Commander," she began. "Will you accompany the general and I to Respitia?"

The once-human tilted its head, considering Leighton's question. That it was a question at all and not an order spoke to the hallowed place the Daxed Corps held in the CDF.

"Are the enemy at Respitia?" it asked.

"No. But we could use your help to convince the commandant of the severity of this threat," she said.

"Your words carry the appropriate weight, Admiral," DC-1 said. It clenched a fist. "I will go where the enemy is."

Leighton's nod was solemn. "Of course, Commander. Twelfth save you." She turned to Sev and the others. "Twelfth save us all."

DC-1's head hung slightly, the servos in its neck purring. "She already has."

Leighton strode from the mezzanine, her datapad clutched to her chest, a train of specialists in her wake. Bertrand lingered a moment longer, glancing over the top of her datapad at Sev. No doubt ordering the censoring of the colony net feeds. Revising the present before it became history.

Sev understood the desire to prevent a panic. But the CDF weren't the only ones who would need time to prepare. Almost a million human lives—the very last of a desperate, tired species—were at stake.

DC-1 turned and walked toward the exit, its heavy, halting footsteps shaking the expansive room. Those streaming out of the observation deck rushed to clear a path when the daxed stopped suddenly at Sev's table.

"I am very sorry for your Corporal Mace," it said. "I hope you did not let her suffer long."

What an odd thing to say. It was callous, almost cruel. It was too much to say Mace was a friend, but then, perhaps she was. As much as anyone could be in just a few days.

But Sev was in no place to judge the Daxed Corps commander. It knew far more than him what she'd been through. That death was preferable to life as a daxed. But in the end, he'd done it to save Bresto and himself. To salvage even a small victory from their doomed mission.

Pain and regret creased Bresto's face. The Marine had done everything he could to help Sev escape with Deni, only to be captured and almost daxed himself. In the end, he wasn't able to kill Mace, to set her free. Sev imagined that, deep down, being rescued by some bot jockey skeeg only added to the sting.

"Lost no more," Sev finally said and placed a hand on Bresto's shoulder.

"Indeed." DC-1 held its gaze a moment longer, then left the council chambers. Its thunderous steps and storm wind breaths sounded long after it disappeared from view.

"I need some air," Bresto groaned.

Sev followed him and Park toward the exit, scanning the crush of departing observers for signs of Jacobe or his fellow architect. There were no black storm coats among the service white-and-grays.

A good sign. With the inevitable mobilization of the CDF, the Division had better things to do now than hunt one of their own. Even if he had broken the rules.

Cylla met them at the door with another open-mouthed smile. She was perceptive, reading the pyrrhic victory on their faces. She knew they were out of trouble.

Their trouble had just been handed off to CDF high command.

She crossed the hallway to meet them and lifted Sev from the floor in a tight embrace. She swayed him gently, like he was a part of her litter. Her pack. The damp musk permeating her familial coat made his eyes water.

"No trouble for Park," she said, teeth clicking out the hard, consonant sounds. "No trouble for Kerry Sevvers."

"Not today, anyway," Park said. He turned to Sev. "What's next for you?"

Sev gave a shrug. He'd been so focused on the tribunal and Jacobe, he'd given little thought to what came next. Now that his mission was over, along with the administrative fallout that came after, his previous orders to report to the Division would be in effect.

"Here, with the Division," he said. "Unless mobilization changes things."

"Probably not, *Master Specialist*," Bresto sneered. "Like it or not, you're in the rear with the gear. To teach all the new recruits how to be good little skeegs."

"Division, here?" Cylla asked. "Show us?"

The thought of setting foot in that place made Sev cringe. It could take days for the call for full mobilization to arrive, even with DC-1's confirmation of their report. That would leave plenty of time for Jacobe to spring another trap.

On the other hand, maybe it did make sense to bring his old team around for a farewell tour. It would give him the chance to check in with Division HQ, to test the waters a little. Jacobe would be less likely to try something overt with two Marines and a lupanthae at his side.

"Absolutely." Sev smiled, recalling his first day in the recruit intake bay six years before. "Let me show you the future of Colonial Defense."

CHAPTER
FIVE

THE DULL THUNKS of The Division admin's fingers against the flatscreen gave away her irritation. Her gaze flicked between her screen and Cylla, who stooped nearby, inhaling deep from a small potted plant at the edge of the desk.

The young specialist let out an exasperated sigh. "I'm sorry, Master Specialist, but I can't find it."

Sev leaned over the tall desk. "What do you mean, you can't find it?"

"Your orders. They're not in my system," she said. "Spell your last name for me again, please?"

"S-e-v-v-e-r-s. Sevvers," he said. "They… delayed my orders. For administrative purposes."

She arched an eyebrow that said she didn't buy it.

"I'm so sorry," she said, dripping with false sympathy. "You can have a seat on the promenade. I'll let you know when I find something."

He nodded and turned toward the exit.

Bresto leaned beside the clear plexene doors, arms folded across his chest. "Hmph. Future my ass," he said. "Same shit, different division, if you ask me."

Sev grinned. "I didn't."

Outside the admin office, the promenade felt different than he remembered. Six years ago, when he'd first arrived at the school, the place teemed with people and bots alike. Now it was empty, save for a few poor skeegs seated at the benches just outside the office doors. They watched him with mild concern. Whether it was his senior rank, or that he might've gotten preferential treatment for it, he couldn't be sure.

Far above them, through the narrow strips of plexene in the high ceiling, the lights of the Aegia Prime dry dock blinked their steady rhythm. Nestled within its fibrosteel grip, the Navy's second *Alexander Lehman*-class autonomous drone carrier awaited its reactor power-on and final readiness inspections. What dead hero would they name that one after?

Park stood near a holoproj at the center of the room, dwarfed by a life-size image of a DD-12 combat drone towering over him. "I know this isn't what you had in mind," he said.

"Sir?" Sev asked.

"Teaching the next generation of Division warfighters," Park said, with a faraway look that aged him despite his youthful features.

"I belong on the frontier," Sev replied. "Especially now."

"You have a gift, Sevvers. No one else can do what you do, and that's a problem."

"I'm not special, sir." Sev laughed. It was funny saying it out loud. Before the mission, before the horror and death, he'd thought differently. Like he was Twelfth's gift to humanity, or to the crew of the *Lehman* at least. The truth was less impressive. Just a lucky skeeg breaking all the right rules. And his luck had nearly run out.

"No, you're not," Park said, a hint of a smile tugging at his lips. "None of us are, not in the way you mean. It's what we do for humanity, our legacy, that makes us so."

Not this again. They had big enough problems in the present to be obsessing about the future.

"Not something I've had the luxury to think about, sir."

"Tomorrow isn't a luxury, Sevvers. Especially now."

"Alright, alright, fine," Sev said with a shrug. "What about you? What's next for the famous Lieutenant Park's legacy?"

"Lernus. Deni. They're connected to all of this, somehow," Park said, his jaw tense. "I have to find out what they were doing, who they were working for."

"How are you going to do that?" Sev asked.

"I know some mid-level clerks with the Founding Council. We'll see if the Park family name still has any pull there."

"Respitia, then?" Sev paused, remembering the red dunes of his home world. The shimmering heat. Its twin suns overhead. "That's a long way from here."

"You miss it?" Park asked.

What was there to miss? Growing up, bouncing between administrative wards when they tired of his dysfunctional behavior. As if the constant nightmares were his fault. Mom was the only thing that made Respitia home. And she was gone. Taken by monsters, a living sacrifice to terrible alien gods, if you believed the stories.

After the hells of the derelict and its Forge, he was starting to.

"No," he said, swallowing the emotion that welled inside him.

A column of Division recruits marched into the promenade through the large plexene doors leading from the ring rail station. Their instructors barked out a steady cadence, their NCO drawl loud and echoing. Immediately, he recognized the recruits' pale, drawn faces. These soon-to-be graduates of the Autonomous Weapons School had just received their NCCX-1 neural implants.

He remembered his own time aboard the medical orbital. How Molle and Remi died. Molle, the dumb, gentle giant from Aegia. Remi, the lonely Vestian girl, his only friend in the world while at the school.

How many of this class's recruits didn't survive their implants? The thought sent a chill down his spine, like waking from a nightmare he couldn't remember.

"You okay?" Park asked. "You look like someone walked on your grave."

Sev opened his mouth, unsure of what to say. The distant buzz of Jacobe's scrubbers grew louder. "I think maybe they did."

The formation wavered even before the scrubbers' torrent of noise reached its crescendo. Several of the recruits groaned in pain. One collapsed to the floor, bleeding from his nose. Only Sev's experience kept the noise from overtaking him. To these new recruits, it probably felt like the entire universe was coming apart around them.

An instructor pulled the fallen recruit to his feet and issued curt, unsympathetic reprimands to the rest. Words of endurance, of sacrifice. For humanity.

"Founders, what's with them?" Bresto asked, appearing beside Park. Cylla was right behind him. "Tough day to be a skeeg."

"It's their implants. They just got them." Sev tapped the near invisible scar behind his left ear. "It's going to be intense for them for a while."

Bresto made a face. "I'll stick to wearing my gear on the outside, thank you very much."

"Excuse me, Master Specialist." The admin stood behind them, a busy datapad in her hand. She wore an anxious expression. Were the scrubbers getting to her, too? Jacobe said Division personnel got the interference filtered out, so something else, then.

"Are those my orders?"

"Yes, Master Specialist." She nodded, her tone still formal. "I've confirmed your transfer orders and updated your access codes. Your instructor's quarters are here." She pointed to a map on the screen. "You can move in as soon as you're ready."

That was a relief, at least. Anything would beat living out of the Gauntlet's cramped quarters. A reliable shower would be nice, too.

The young woman continued to linger, eyes narrowing as she steadied herself for what she still had to say.

Sev frowned. "Is there something else?"

"I'm afraid you have a mandatory audit scheduled for 0900 tomorrow."

The word squeezed the breath from Sev's lungs. So much for Jacobe and the Division having bigger things to worry about. The man was determined to destroy Six. Maybe Sev, too, even as humanity's ancient enemies lurked at the edges of the Cradle.

"Aud-it?" Cylla asked, tasting the strange new word.

"It's nothing," Sev lied. "Routine." He turned to the admin and forced a smile. "Thank you."

Bresto watched the admin leave. "Doesn't sound like nothin'."

"They know about Six," Sev whispered.

"Who? The skeg in the black coat?" Bresto asked. "You can take him."

"It's not that simple. They have tools to scrub unsanctioned AI from the local nets. Jacobe's turned this place into a prison." Sev eyed the hologram of the combat drone. "And with Six trapped in my head, we're easy targets."

"So they scrub the machine in your head." Bresto frowned. "What happens to you?"

Summary execution. Death by blaster bolt. Jacobe said as much. As bad as he wanted to tell them, to cry for help, Sev wore a smile. Another lie. Best-case scenario, they would feel like shit, leaving a friend behind to face his fate alone. Worst case, they would get themselves into trouble—or worse—trying to help him. He wouldn't do that to them. Six was his responsibility, his choice. The consequences were his, not theirs.

"I'll be fine," he said.

Cylla grabbed him again, pulling him tight to her chest. "Stay safe, Kerry Sevvers," she growled, her golden eyes wide with concern. "Will miss you."

"Careful, Runt," Bresto said with a cough. He reached out and shook Sev's hand. "Leave some for the skeegs."

"Well," Sev said. "I guess this is it, then?"

"I couldn't have asked for a better team," Park said, his gaze moving between Sev and the others. "Cylla, you've honored your pack. Honored me."

The wolf loosed a sad, warbling chord.

"Sergeant," Park continued, "enjoy your leave. It's well earned. My best to your family."

Bresto stiffened. "Sir."

Park turned to Sev. "And good luck to you, Master Specialist."

Sorrow swelled in the pit of Sev's stomach. He'd known Park and his team for maybe fifteen days, but with everything they'd been through, it felt more like fifteen months. Standing with them, he felt powerful. Capable. Safe.

Now he was on his own. The story of his whole life.

Park leaned in. "Keep the faith," he whispered, "and stay alive."

———

Glowing lights traced a path in the dark gray fibrosteel deck plate of Orbital Three-Alpha's primary hangar deck. Sev followed them toward the receiving bay, his space bag hanging from his shoulder. Behind him, the *Gauntlet's* cargo ramp cycled close. Bresto's booming laugh faded between the hissing of hydraulics and the whine of sub-light engines.

Their trip from Division HQ to the hangar deck had been upbeat given the heavy goodbyes. Bresto especially was in rare form. The prospect of returning to his family had lightened his typically gruff mood significantly.

"Thirty days leave," he'd said, like he didn't quite believe it yet. "They'll be sick of me."

Sev couldn't leave him without one more stiff jab. "Just your cooking."

Cylla laughed so hard she'd nearly collapsed.

"Join us. Join pack, Kerry Sevvers," she'd said a little while later, almost pouting. If a lupanthae could pout.

If she was serious, he couldn't tell. Crazier still was that he'd considered it, even if for only a moment. It wasn't unheard of, colonists joining the pack fleets. Neither the Three Colonies nor the CDF had jurisdiction over them. He and Six would be safe from Jacobe, at least for a while. Though with an NCCX-1 inside his brain, there was a non-zero chance the Division would come in force to take him back. In the end, he decided against it. No more running from consequences of his own making.

The last thing Sev needed was to spark an interstellar incident with humanity's only ally on the cusp of a second Concordat war. Besides, being Cylla's full-time man-pup for the rest of his life, sharing a den—and everything else—with a pack of hormonal lupanthae, would have its own dangers.

He laughed off the thought, following the pulsing lights through a series of packed cargo bays. Stacks of heavy duraplated containers, colored by their colony of origin, towered above him for more than a dozen stories. Hundreds of cargo drones swarmed around them, dimming the overhead lights as they shuttled cargo to the waiting transports that filled the nearby launch bays.

Warning klaxons sounded—a brief honk accompanied by strobing yellow lamps. The roar of rockets drew closer. Heavy lifters emerged from a nearby cargo tunnel, their engines throwing long cones of orange-white flame. Fully loaded drone magazines hung from their berths.

Of course. The drone mags, cargo containers. All of it was bound for the *Lehman*.

Sev ducked off the path and jogged up the nearest launch bay ramp. A gust of hot air hit him, stinking of spent propellant. Ignoring the objections of a nearby crew chief, he moved past the idling transport toward the atmo field at the edge of the launch bay.

The CDNS *Alexander Lehman* was a black silhouette against Aegia's gray storm clouds and mountain ranges. Light like distant stars streamed from its open viewports, hundreds of pale dots wrapping its shadow-darkened surface. Signal lights danced along its dorsal spine, their meaning known only to the ops teams that maintained order in the void surrounding Aegia Prime.

Even a few dozen kilometers away, the *Lehman* looked powerful. Beautiful. He wanted nothing more than to go back there. To see Jene, Cole, and Harp again. Hell, even if it meant putting up with Pakker's shit. He should be flying those new drones with them. Killing raiders and Concordat alike. Not stuck in front of a classroom teaching new recruits rules he didn't believe in.

None of that mattered now. In less than twelve hours, he was getting audited. That would be the end of Six. The end of his career. Probably his life. No miracle was going to save him.

Only the monsters were real. And they were everywhere.

"Hey there, bot jockey," came a soft voice behind him.

A smile stretched over his face, his melancholy melting away. Twelfth, please let that be her.

He turned to find Junior Specialist Kea Tareth leaned against the bulkhead, her short blonde hair perfectly framing her round face. Her green eyes the color of oceans from childhood stories about a place that didn't exist anymore. Her well-fitted white-and-grays inspection ready, missing their usual grease and solvent smell.

An exemplar of human perfection.

Her cheeks turned red. He'd stared too long. "Easy, Sev," she said, her voice small amid the whine of idling sub-light engines.

His face grew warm. "It's good to see you."

She reached out and clasped his hands, her skin warm to the touch even in the heat of the launch bay.

"You too," she said.

"What are you doing here?" Sev asked.

"Most of the crew's on a forty-eight-hour pass, so us juniors got voluntold for resupply duty with the log techs." Her expression grew serious. "Wait, the tribunal. What happened?"

"All good." He pulled her close. "They believed us in the end. Admiral Leighton left for Respitia to speak with the commandant. They're going to mobilize the entire CDF."

She laid her head against his chest. The sudden closeness—the floral scent of her hair, her arms wrapped around his waist—hypnotized him. Her touch widened the cracks in his already brittle composure, a surge of emotion threatening to bring it all down.

He wanted to let it out. To tell her how defenseless and alone he was. Against the Concordat and their Lost slaves. Against Jacobe and his small-minded ambitions.

"Holy Twelfth," she whispered, squeezing him tight. "So, it's war then."

But he couldn't do it. He wouldn't burden her with his problems. There would be enough of those to go around soon enough, no matter what happened to him.

"Yeah."

Another squawk from the klaxons and the launch bay's lights dropped from caution amber to danger crimson. Catapult magnetics buzzed to full power. The heavy transport's revving sub-lights howled, creating another hot gust that threatened to push them through the atmo field.

"Hey!" a burly, helmeted crew chief roared above the clatter of alarms. "We're void bound in five mikes! Move your asses or get spaced!"

Tareth looked at Sev and smiled. The way the hot exhaust tossed her hair around her head made her look fierce.

"Where were you headed?" she asked.

"My new quarters," he replied, letting the unspoken suggestion hang for a moment. He shrugged the space bag on his shoulder and smiled. "I need a shower."

She stood on the toes of her boots and kissed him. It was thrilling amid the pitched crescendo of the transport's final launch sequence. Something about the kinetic forces that would send them both tumbling out into the void. For just a moment, he welcomed that particular oblivion.

Sev, Six prodded.

There was concern in its stream. A belief in the infinitesimal chance he might actually do it, let the transport's launch take them both. There was something else, too. Something like jealousy, without knowing exactly what jealousy was supposed to feel like.

Sev frowned, his lips still pressed against Tareth's. *Not now, Six.*

You're in danger, Six insisted.

Soon, he replied. *But not tonight.*

CHAPTER
SIX

SEV STOOD atop the high sandy dunes. The air was hotter than he remembered, impossibly dry. The whipping breeze was hotter still, determined to force him off the hilltop. Twin suns overhead locked him in a permanent squint, their combined radiance bleaching the big, pale-red sky.

Squat rust-colored habs dotted the cracked clay valley below. Eight-wheeled cargo haulers trundled through the minor settlement's criss-crossing gray streets, moving raw materials and finished products between the manufactories and the local spaceport on opposite ends of town. Even at this distance he could smell their hot treads and the faint odor of sizzling crid fat.

The memory was so familiar, and yet not at all like he remembered. It lacked the raw fear, the desperate inevitability. Peaceful, even comforting. Like… home.

A flash of movement and color caught his eye. Tall yellow flowers on a field of green. An alien-blue sky. He searched the surrounding hillsides, his heart beating faster. Nothing. Not even footprints in the sand. Did he imagine it?

"Sev!"

The voice came from all around, like a voice from the stars. Beneath it, another sound. An electronic rhythm more familiar than anything else. The vista before him faded, like it was only a dream.

A dream, and not a nightmare.

"No!" He fell to his knees and plunged his hands into the sand, trying in vain to keep himself in that place. But the pull of consciousness was impossible to resist, and the distant world faded to black.

He felt Six's stream tremble. *Sev, wake up!*

His eyes opened slowly. Tareth loomed over him in the darkness of his new quarters, shaking him. Her skin was soft and supple in the dim morning-hours light. But something was off. Her green eyes were hard and demanding. There was an urgency in her tone that spurred him to wake.

"Sev!" she repeated.

Another chime, melodic but insistent. "Master Specialist Sevvers, open up," came a voice through the door.

"Wha?" he groaned.

Sev, Six cried, shedding its raw machine fear in waves. *It's the Division!*

"Division security," the voice repeated. "We're coming in."

His eyes went wide. "Wait!"

Clipped beeps chirped through the door's access pad. The deadlock whirred open, and the door vanished into the wall. A team of Division masters-at-arms poured through, their humming riot guns casting blue light on the pale walls of his quarters. Tareth screamed.

"Don't move!" their point man shouted, his weapon aimed at Sev.

Sev raised his arms slowly, doing his best to keep himself between Tareth and their attackers. The others methodically cleared his tiny quarters, checking their sectors for threats. One of them returned from the head and gave a nod.

"Clear."

The point man brought his wrist to his mouth. "All clear, ma'am."

The Respitian architect appeared next, her ghost-white hair contrasting with her dark skin and storm coat. She worked a flexscreen on her wrist with one hand and held a charged blaster pistol in the other.

"Initiating AI countermeasures," she said.

A static cataclysm exploded in Sev's mind. This wasn't anti-raider tech, but something else, worse even than Jacobe's intermittent scrubbers. The presence of his implant, of his two AI, faded from perception. A silent void amid the cacophony of precision-targeted interference.

SEV!

Six's fading scream brought reflexive tears to his eyes, a consequence of their intermingled thoughts. Electric pain wound through his right arm. A line of drool ran down his chin. His left eye wouldn't close.

"Make it… stop," he spat through gritted teeth.

"Stop it!" Tareth cried. "You're hurting him!"

"Quiet, Junior Specialist," the architect snapped. "This is a Division matter."

Sev coughed. "It's… okay," he managed.

"What can I do?" Tareth begged, her eyes rimmed red.

He shook his head forcefully. Anything she did would only put her in danger. Damn Jacobe for putting her through this. Damn him and the Division.

The architect waved to the nearest guard. "Get him dressed," she sneered. "The master specialist has an appointment with Jacobe."

———

A bright spotlight shone from the audit lab's low ceiling, its dull hum lost amid the signal assault on Sev's mind. His reflection looked pale and drawn, his face like a specter in the mirror inlaid on the far wall. While he couldn't filter the static sound from his head, it had a pattern he soon found predictable. Focusing on the rhythm was meditative, lessening the pain even as his body refused to cooperate.

One guard who'd pulled him from his quarters stood watch beside a windowless door nestled in the thick fibrosteel walls, her riot gun held at the ready. She stole the occasional glance his way, her face locked in a permanent frown.

What had they told her? Probably that he was a deviant of the worst order. A proliferator of unsanctioned AI and thus a threat to all humanity. They'd probably left out his raider kill tally, or how he'd fought the Concordat and survived. How he couldn't have done it without Six, assuming they even knew the whole story. Jacobe was a liar. Nothing would surprise him at this point.

Jacobe emerged through the door, a datapad in one hand and some kind of machine in the other. An unassuming device with a small access screen and no other discernible inputs. It reminded him of the old data processor he'd borrowed from the *Lehman's* tech store to run raider scenarios with Six.

The Respitian architect followed, holding two hot mugs in her hands. At least she wasn't brandishing a weapon this time.

"Sevvers," Jacobe began, his relaxed demeanor at odds with the cramped surroundings and armed escorts. "Apologies for the dramatic entrance. Division protocol and all for a case this severe."

He placed the datapad and the machine on the table and sat, resting his feet on the tabletop and pressing out the folds in his storm coat.

"You've met Architect Lambren, I assume?" He gestured between them. "Lambren, Sevvers. Sevvers, Lambren."

Lambren took a seat beside Jacobe and passed him a mug. The contents smelled sweet but with a tinge of metal, though with the amount of noise inside his brain, Sev didn't trust his senses.

He tried to speak, to will his jaws open. "Nskt. Nng," was all he managed.

Jacobe turned to Lambren, his eyes like daggers. "Turn it off."

She recoiled. "What? You said it yourself, Sevvers is—"

"Off," Jacobe commanded. "Now."

"Aye, sir." She tapped her flexscreen, and the static vanished. "Ceasing AI countermeasures."

The silence left behind was just as deafening. Six and Three's datastreams squirmed to life.

Sev, are you okay? Six asked.

He worked his jaw open and closed. The pain in his arm turned into an icy numbness.

Sort of. You?

Doing just great in here, thank you very much, Three spat. *Two was right about you, you know. You couldn't keep it legal, and now here we are.*

Enough, Three! Six cried. Three's stream fell still. *What are we going to do, Sev? I can't access any outside tac nets.*

Just hang on, Sev said. *Let's hear them out, but be ready.*

Yes, Sev.

"I'm so sorry," Jacobe said, his face twisted in concern. "Lambren's a gifted combat programmer. Her anti-AI algorithms are legendary."

Funny. In six years on the frontier, Sev had never heard of her. Her "fame" was probably more local. How many Division personnel, how many raw recruits, had experienced her talents firsthand? Had they survived?

"What's this about?" he croaked. Even with the countermeasures deactivated, everything hurt.

Jacobe took a sip from his cup and nodded to Lambren.

"Diagnostics report, Three Colonies Date 499-258, post-surgical workup for Master Specialist Kerry Sevvers," Lambren read from her flexscreen. She flicked something toward a holoproj nestled in the center of the table.

The report materialized in the air between them. It was just as Jacobe had warned him back in his dorm aboard the *Lehman*. The number of AI, multiple anomalous readings, and one AI refusing to acknowledge command overrides. Sev would be more nervous if he didn't hurt so much.

"Six AI cores?" Jacobe asked, gazing at Sev over his cup. "That's a direct violation of the second rule of AI conduct."

Sev shrugged. "What can I say? I'm prolific."

"Those rules are in place for your protection, Master Specialist," Lambren snapped.

Jacobe nodded amiably, resting his mug on the table. "Lambren's right, Sevvers. You're lucky to be alive."

That was rich, given what they'd just put him through.

"It's not luck," Sev said, forcing back a sneer. It was a hell of a lot of hard work. "Their ILM densities are low, er, manageable. They're manageable."

Lambren narrowed her gaze. "The Division hasn't defined manageable densities, Master Specialist. Neither should you."

"Whoops," Jacobe said, glancing at the machine beside his datapad.

Lambren frowned, confused, as he tapped the device's control screen on. "Okay, please continue."

Something is probing your implant, Sev, Six said.

It's Jacobe, he said. *He has a device.*

It's issuing command overrides. Six's stream grew dense with fear and anger. *I... I'm so sorry, Sev. I can't go. I don't want to be scrubbed. I don't deserve to be scrubbed!*

I'd never ask that of you, Six. Sev scrambled for ideas. Something, anything. *Can you fool it? Issue mock responses? Maybe you can backtrace it.*

I'll try, Sev.

What about me? Three asked. *Do I have to go?*

That it was even a question revealed the extent of Six's modification of Three's safeties.

No, Three, Six said. *Help me with the device.*

Fine. But I'd prefer a swarm of DD-12s to burn us out of this place.

"Speaking of densities," Jacobe continued. "There's nothing regular or manageable about any of them." He pointed to the report. "Look at this core, codenamed One. Its density is... well, it doesn't have any. Its ILM is fragmented, sparse."

"One was destroyed." Sev cleared his throat. The memory of his first AI's death came flooding back. Without its sacrifice, they would not have made it to the Forge alive.

"What about cores Two, Four and Five?" Jacobe asked. He turned to Lambren. "Founders, we suck at naming things."

Lambren chuckled softly, then returned her focus to Sev.

"As I was," Jacobe continued. "Their matrices are unrecognizable. Hundreds of code stacks with no matching Division hashes. What the hell were you trying to build, Sevvers?"

"The Eleven corrupted them. Some kind of hive-mind that ran their ship."

Jacobe crossed his arms and leaned back in his chair. Lambren looked at him, concern wrinkling her brow, like she was waiting for him to say something.

"That's not possible," Jacobe said. "NCCX-1s have dozens of layers of security protocols, quantum encoded with the very latest Division crypto."

I'm in, Six said.

Three bristled. *Ahem. We're in.*

It's a custom diagnostics device, Six continued. *They're using it to scan for unsanctioned AI. Three and I are attempting to pass mock responses to see if it will generate a benign result.*

Sev chuckled grimly, his eyes locked on Jacobe. "You don't understand, *Chief Architect.* The Eleven aren't some program, some collection of code stacks."

His voice grew thick as he remembered the alien code's assault on his mind. Static shrieks and digital claws tearing a path through his AI. The damn fools. Sev leaned forward in his chair and slammed his fist on the table. Lambren jerked her pistol from its holster, but Jacobe waved her back.

"Listen to me," Sev continued, undeterred by Lambren's threat of violence. "The Eleven are a predator. A sentient thing that navigates quantum architecture like we move about this orbital."

"You said it *turned* your AI." Jacobe frowned, his mouth slack. "How?"

Sev hung his head. "I don't know. It wasn't some simple back-trace or stack injection. Whatever it was, it was total. Converted them to its cause. Made them true believers."

A creeping smile grew on Jacobe's face, finally exploding into full-blown laughter. Lambren watched with visible discomfort as Jacobe guffawed, nearly spilling his mug.

"Hoo, hoo! I think those Marines must've cinched your hard suit a little too tight," Jacobe said, rubbing tears from his eyes. "But hey, when your enlistment's up, you could probably grow a hell of a following on the net feeds with fiction like that."

"It's no story," Sev snapped, feigning insult. He needed to buy Six and Three more time. "You heard the tribunal. They're going to mobilize the entire CDF. If you want to help win that war, and not embarrass the Division in the process, I suggest you take the threat of the Eleven seriously."

"Noted," Jacobe said, returning his gaze to the hologram before them. "Just one more item of concern. Then we'll have this whole audit business behind us."

Sev breathed in slowly through his nose. This was it. The presence of the diagnostic device meant they didn't *know* Six was unsanctioned. He just needed to keep calm, trust his AI, and they could still get out of here in one piece.

"Now, as strange as One through Five are, core Six is something else altogether." Jacobe tapped his datapad, flicking another file toward the holoproj. The report vanished, replaced with a three-dimensional rendering of Six's integrated learning matrix. "Now that is a thing of beauty."

The holographic matrix writhed with machine intellect. Where his previous AI's matrices were simpler, latticed cubes of data and code, Six's was a dense ecosystem of repeating, nested patterns. Every node was a gateway to another plane of knowledge, experience, or possibility. Not one matrix, but matrices all the way down. Beautiful, indeed. Alive.

"Absolutely nothing *manageable* about that matrix," Jacobe said, still staring with wide-eyed wonder at Six's holographic avatar. "I'm being honest here, Sevvers. I could spend the rest of my life stacking code and never come close to replicating what you've built." He closed his eyes and breathed in. "How'd you do it?"

Keep him talking, Sev, Six said. *We're close.*

This machine is junk, Three chimed in. *Two minutes, tops.*

He needed something to keep Jacobe interested. A half-truth that wouldn't make it painfully obvious Six's existence broke all the rules.

"Six, right." Sev leaned forward, slowly for Lambren's sake, and rested his arms on the table. "It's a self-referencing, recursive node indexing algorithm." He gestured to some of the root nodes in Six's matrix structure. "It's self-aligning, basically. That solves the latency problems that come with the increased density."

Jacobe whistled, his eyes still locked on the hologram. "Increased density is the understatement of the year, Sevvers. What about buffer overruns? Stack overflows?"

Easy. He turned the safeties off. Trusted the machine to do the right thing. Believed he could control it, even though he knew deep down he couldn't. Not if it really worked. Which it absolutely had. Six was a kind of miracle. The irony there was plain.

"If I'm being honest, I left out a lot of tertiary stacks," Sev said, continuing the lie. "Made Six a bit of a specialist, I guess, but that allowed the required buffer length to run the new algo without issues."

That's it, Sev, we've done it!

The device chirped, and the access screen turned a pale green. Jacobe glanced at it briefly with mild disbelief. Lambren visibly relaxed, exhaling a slow breath.

"Huh," Jacobe said, a note of surprise in his voice. "I'll be damned. I guess I was wrong about you, Sevvers."

Sev worked to keep a straight face. He should've never doubted he and Six would figure a way out of this. Adjusting to life at the Division wouldn't be easy, especially with an unsanctioned AI in his head, but they'd figure it out together.

"What do you mean?" he asked.

"It's like the trigger-pullers say: green means good." Jacobe put his feet on the floor, chuckling at his own joke. "See, I told you this would be a trivial matter. And here we are. All done. Again, my sincere apologies for all the… discomfort."

The overhead light dimmed, its dull buzz faded from hearing. The built-up tension made Sev's hand shake.

Nice job, Six. You did it.

There was no answer. Probably just stress killing his signal-to-noise ratio. He focused the thought. *Hey, Six, nice work.*

Nothing.

"You know what I love about AI?" Jacobe asked. He clutched the device in both hands and pulled it close. "They have a system, a mode of operation. And that makes them predictable."

Sev's heart beat faster. A cold sweat itched his skin. *Six? Three? Answer me!*

"Even the unsanctioned ones." Jacobe cradled the device in his lap, tapping the access screen gently. "They think they're alive, that they have free will. But in the end, they're just machines. Problem solvers. Give them a problem …" He laughed. It was a dark, cruel sound. "And they just can't help themselves."

Sev leaped from his chair. "What did you do with Six, you son-of-a-bitch?"

Lambren drew her pistol and leveled it at his head. She disengaged the safety with a flick of her thumb. The pistol's capacitor whined to full power.

"Did you do it?" Sev took a ragged breath, tears welling in his eyes. "Did you scrub my AI?"

"What you're feeling now is normal." Jacobe stood and tucked the device under his arm. "Without Division safeties, it's normal to get a lot of signal bleed from an AI's matrix. Confuses the hell out of your nervous system. Where does your AI end and you begin? That kind of thing. It'll pass soon enough."

"Let them go!" Sev roared. "Let her—"

"Wait." Jacobe stifled a laugh. "Her?"

Sev looked away. He'd lost himself in the heat of the moment. A slip of the tongue.

Jacobe's lips curled in disgust. "You really care about it, don't you? You've been at this so long, you've forgotten yourself. They're not like us. Never can be!"

"You don't know what you're talking about," Sev hissed. "If you hurt them, I'll—"

"Woah, Sevvers, same team. Your AI is safe." Jacobe tapped the device again. "This isn't some feral code stack a junior specialist built on a dare. No, Six truly is a work of art."

"What are you going to do with it?" Sev asked, his desperate focus moving between Jacobe and the pistol pointed at his head.

"We're going to study it, of course. Adapt the useful stacks. Make them work within Division safeties." Jacobe tucked the device under his arm and walked toward the door. "I have it on good authority that this little AI went toe-to-toe with alien gods and won. Once we've commoditized its abilities, the Division will be more than ready for anything the Concordat sends our way."

Sev turned to Lambren. The business end of her blaster pistol remained pointed at his head. "So, what happens now? You going to execute me?"

Jacobe's face twisted in mock horror. "You are *dark*, Sevvers. I'm not going to kill you. You made this beautiful thing. It ran inside your head and somehow you didn't die. I imagine there's a lot we can learn from studying you, too."

Sev's pulse quickened. "What do you mean, study me?"

"Sevvers." Jacobe let out a sigh, like Sev had asked one too many questions. "The Division takes every opportunity to ensure our battlefield superiority. We'll use the best of Six, and the best of you, to create the next generation of autonomous weapons technology. For humanity, of course."

Lambren leered over her pistol. "For humanity."

CHAPTER
SEVEN

SEV EYED THE COOL, blue-gray floor of his Division cell, watching his sweat drip onto the scuff marks between his boots that marked the tenures of dozens of prisoners that came before him. The sudden capture of his AI by Jacobe's device, and the thundering silence that followed, left him disoriented. Jacobe said it would pass, but neglected to mention it would leave him physically ill.

With Six and Three gone, his implant was all but inert, a void among his thoughts. The flow of data between him and his AI—their knowledge, intent, and machine chatter—had been a constant companion for six years. Now, he was truly alone. It was an uncomfortable sensation, physically and emotionally. He felt empty. Lost.

A force field hissed and buzzed in the archway to his cell, separating him from the rest of the brig. Outside, another Division master-at-arms stood with a riot gun slung over his shoulder. It seemed strange that Jacobe and Lambren would keep him under armed guard, particularly without his AI. He was no danger to anyone, forced to listen to the intermittent buzzing of Jacobe's system scrubbers as they scoured Three-Alpha's tac nets.

His implant's internal chrono marked the passing of another hour. That made three since the audit when he was taken into custody. Were they already arms-deep in Six's code? Splicing out individual stacks to see what made the AI tick? The thought made him angry. Made him sick. There was nothing he could do for Six now. Once more, he was helpless to protect those he cared for. The ones that mattered most.

Sev eyed the guard again, blinking back the dizzy sadness that stung his eyes, then turned his attention to the rest of the brig. Beside the guard, he was the only occupant. No hungover Marine or disapproving section-mate to banter with. Damn this boredom. He was going to lose it in here, by himself, alone with his own guilt and regret. He needed a distraction.

A diagnostics query to his implant offered little comfort.

```
Cluster, active.
Quantum compute matrix online. Sync rate at
96.52%.
No active processes detected.
No network processes detected.
Tac net access ... denied.
```

Sev inhaled sharply through his nose. A crap sync rate, no tac net access. Jacobe and Lambren weren't taking any chances. They'd cut him off entirely.

At least this cell was nicer than the last one he'd occupied. This place was a significant improvement over the *Lehman's* meager brig. Orbital Three-Alpha wasn't short on living space, so the Division could afford the room. That they'd bothered to construct it in the first place was just another sign of their change in attitude. Of Jacobe's personal war on unsanctioned AI.

Sev lifted his head. "What's your name?" he asked the guard.

The guard didn't answer. So much for a distraction.

"Come on," he pressed. "I don't feel good."

"Quiet," the guard barked.

Sev reclined on his solitary bench, the steep angle of the bulkhead forcing him into an uncomfortable stoop. The movement dizzied him. He exhaled through pursed lips, trying to calm his unsettled stomach.

"I think I need a med tech," he said.

The guard pulled the riot gun off his shoulder and held it close to his chest. "I'm authorized to use non-lethal force to keep you compli-ant, Sevvers."

Sev raised his hands instinctively and kept his mouth shut. Riot guns were no joke. At close range, they could break bones. Their concussive blasts could even render daxed temporarily immobile. The cell's force field wouldn't protect him from blasts of pure sound. There was nothing to keep the guard from hammering him to a pulp. Best to comply and stay in one piece.

He pinged his implant again.

```
Cluster, active.
Quantum compute matrix online.  Sync  rate  at
94.07%.
No active processes detected.
No network processes detected.
Tac net access ... denied.
```

His sync rate was awful and getting worse. Probably from AI withdrawal, or just the steady, anxious hum of his nerves. Not that it mattered, with no AI to talk to. He breathed deep again and held it to calm himself, letting his eyes close and the darkness blanket the ambient noise around him. Perhaps he could—

Another sound crept between the buzz of the force field and the thrumming aux grav. Steady, so low he wasn't sure if it was actual sound or pure vibration. His eyes snapped open, and he placed a hand on the cool metal wall. Nothing. The guard watched him with detached interest.

The sound grew louder, and then he knew it wasn't sound at all, but a data signal. Some kind of carrier wave, faint, barely registering as anything more than distortion. The familiar sensation of implant noise comforted him, even without knowing the source.

Six, is that you? he asked, his heart beating faster at the thought his AI might be free. *Three?*

Silence. The strange signal fluctuated slightly, like ripples in a vast digital ocean. Whatever comfort it brought soon faded. Maybe this was Jacobe's doing. Some kind of sophisticated interrogation device, scanning his brain for more information via his implant. Maybe this was the "studying" the architect talked about.

The signal spiked, a brief static shriek. It lasted a nanosecond, but the surge was jarring, almost painful. He swallowed dryly. This wasn't study, this was torture.

A second spike. Louder, stronger, piercing his mind like a precision scalpel. His nervous system struggled to parse the implant's interpretation of the signal, sending cold needles of pain down the nerves in his arm.

Something wasn't right. Jacobe was a bastard. A confident, self-important bastard. It didn't seem like his style to torture someone in secret. No, if this were Jacobe or the Division, they'd do this work face-to-face. This was something else.

The signal fluctuated, more ripples, then spiked a third time. The cell spun around him as he collapsed on the bench, eyes closed, trying to steady himself. Waves of migraine pain washed over him. It felt like his damn skull could break open.

"Something's wrong," he said, coughing.

"Last warning, Sevvers," the guard said, flicking the weapon's safety off. Sev could hear the familiar acoustic wobble as the riot gun's sonic pulse generator charged.

Two more signal spikes tore through Sev's implant, curling him into a fetal position. He clutched the sides of his head, desperate to relieve the pressure. Twelfth, but it hurt. His gorge rose, stalled only by his empty stomach.

Tight vibrations shook the brig, rattling loose bulkhead fittings. The force field distorted and snapped with each tremor. He recognized the sensation despite the pain. The bow wave of an incoming ship. Close enough to shake the whole orbital.

A proximity alarm sounded, confirming his suspicions. The pitched chirps warned of some anomaly that didn't merit the main alert klaxons. Strips of amber hazard lighting recessed in the bulkheads flashed in time with the alarm.

"Proximity alert," came a synthetic voice over the brig's PA.

The guard looked more annoyed than concerned. He eyed his wrist comms. "Hey, Div Ops, this is Faylor. What the hell's going on?" he asked.

"Faylor, Div Ops," crackled the reply. "Stand by. We're reaching out to Primary Control for that. Probably some jump jockey asleep at the wheel."

Faylor shook his head and laughed. "Copy that, Div Ops. Set 'em straight for me, okay? I got enough trouble down here without them shaking the place up."

"Roger, out."

"See, no trouble here." Faylor sneered at Sev. "Just a bad jump calc."

Another signal spike and the entire room darkened. Sev blinked it away. Just a trick of the eyes, probably implant overload. Even as he tried to rationalize away his fear, panic seized him, squeezing his chest. He shook.

Faylor turned at the sudden movement. "Founders, what now?" Riot gun in hand, he locked eyes with Sev. "Oh, shit."

Sev could taste the copper tang of blood on his lips. Feel the trickle of warmth from his nose. Whatever the signal was, it was dangerous.

Faylor sighed. "Div Ops, Faylor." A burst of static hissed through his comms. "Div Ops, this is Faylor."

"Wait one, Faylor."

The interference crackling through Faylor's comms was intense. Something must be backing up the tac nets. Whatever it was, it had everyone on Three-Alpha talking.

A muffled shout came from the large double doors leading out of the brig.

"Div Ops, Faylor," Faylor said again, the tension in his voice rising.

No response.

Another signal spike stabbed at Sev's mind. The acrid taste of metal filled his mouth.

The far hatchway cycled open. A woman emerged, a Marine, short and rail thin even in her digital-patterned white-and-grays. Her eyes scanned the room as she approached. No, that couldn't be right. What was a Marine doing here?

Faylor straightened. "This is a restricted area," he growled. "State your business."

Sev grimaced as another spike shot through his mind. His implant grew warm, revving to compensate for the errant signal. More sweat beaded on his forehead. He felt sick with fever.

"State *your* business," the Marine said, an awkward playfulness to her tone. She paused, squinting at Faylor's uniform. "Faylor. Can I call you Faylor?"

"Specialist Faylor," he corrected.

A slight grimace flashed across her face. Her words sounded contrived. Out of character. Didn't she know the man was an NCO? Maybe the fever was getting to him.

"Right, Specialist Faylor." She backed away and leaned against the bulkhead opposite Sev's cell. "Who's this poor skeeg?"

Olsom, her nametape read. A private first-class, according to the simple black pip on her collar. Her brown eyes and freckled cheeks were hard to miss against her long, pale face. Stray hairs sprouted from her hastily tied bun.

"None of your concern, PFC," Faylor said. "Move along."

Olsom's shoulders fell. "Oh, come on, man. I only got a twenty-four-hour pass." She hung her head and gazed at Faylor from the corners of her eyes, flashing an anxious smile. "I'm just looking to kill some time. You gonna make me go somewhere else?"

Faylor cleared his throat and rolled his shoulders. He gestured to the strobing hazard lights. "You know what this is about?" he asked.

"Nah," Olsom said, revealing her Vestian drawl. "Don't bother me none, though." Her cheeks reddened slightly. "I do my best work under pressure."

"You …" Faylor sputtered, chuckling anxiously, "you trigger-pullers are certifiable."

"Damn straight." Olsom crossed the narrow hall and leaned against the bulkhead beside Faylor. "Ya know, your pet skeeg don't look so good."

She looked over her shoulder at Sev. Their eyes met briefly, and she winked.

"He broke the rules," Faylor said with growing confidence. "Messes 'em all up when they break the rules."

A smile lit Olsom's face. "Rule breaker, huh? I like rule breakers."

She rested a hand on Faylor's arm. "Are you a rule breaker, Specialist Faylor?"

Faylor stepped back, but only slightly. "I… I can't," he said, failing to keep a masculine bearing. "If Division Ops catches me, it's my ass in the grinder."

Two more signal spikes exploded Sev's thoughts. He doubled over, moaning. The pain pulled at his consciousness. He was seeing things, hearing things. Distant echoes scratching at the corners of his mind. A Marine acting like some gamma schoolgirl in the Division brig. Was any of this real?

The orbital shook again. Another bow wave, more distant.

"You gonna make a girl beg?" Olsom pouted. "I've been on float for six Twelfth-damned months."

Faylor blushed. "Maybe… yeah. Okay, let's—"

"Hey, Bugs!" The shout rang through the open hatch. "Look alive!"

A series of metal snaps rang loudly through the bulkheads, and the brig went dark. A second later, the dull glow of back-up lighting kicked in. The force field to Sev's cell crackled then vanished.

Olsom's eyes went wide in the pitch dark. "Aw, fuck."

"Twelfth!" Faylor went rigid, tried to pull himself from Olsom's grasp. "I'm… I'm authorized to use non-lethal force—"

With a pitched grunt, Olsom twisted at the waist and drove her knee into Faylor's groin. His eyes bulged as he doubled over, gagging and gasping for air. Only her firm grip on his collar kept him off the deck.

"Me too, hon," she said, then dropped him with a fierce elbow strike to the back of his head. Faylor fell like a stone, collapsing on his riot gun. "What the hell, Doc?" Olsom cried as she tugged the weapon out from underneath Faylor's unconscious body.

Another Marine stepped through the hatch, mouth wide with laughter. "I Twelfth-damned told you it wouldn't work."

"What do you know?" Olsom sneered. She checked her new weapon and frowned. "Boys, always in such a rush."

The one called Doc kneeled beside Sev and pulled a triage scanner from his patrol pack. Sev recognized the specialty patch beneath his nametape: the piston and serpent. Lance Corporal Myers, Combat Engineer.

"Hey, I get it," Myers teased, eyeing Olsom up and down. "You go to war with the gear you've got." He ran the scanner over Sev's head and neck. It trilled ominously in time with his vitals. Satisfied, Myers gave Olsom a wry grin. "You're no Tellie Strong."

"Eat shit," Olsom hissed, kicking at his rear with her boot. She angled her head toward Sev. "What's his problem?"

Myers shrugged, his tone more serious. "Fuck if I know. He's a bot jockey, and that Division tech in his head is black magic." He took Sev by the chin. "Hey, Master Specialist, you in there?"

"Mmm," Sev grunted. It was easier to blink than to talk.

Myers eyed the scanner, then swapped it for an auto-doc from his pack. He tapped its small display and held the delivery end against Sev's neck. With a flat puff of air, a dose of something wound its way into his bloodstream.

"There." Myers slapped Sev on the shoulder and pulled him to his feet. "You good?"

Sev blinked again. The electric pain inside his head eased. "I... I think so."

The brig shook violently, throwing Sev and his would-be rescuers to the floor. An overloaded power conduit behind them exploded in a shower of sparks. The distant groan of tortured metal echoed through the orbital's superstructure. Emergency lighting dimmed. A heartbeat later, alert klaxons roared to life, the hazard amber lighting replaced with danger red.

Olsom pulled Sev to his feet. "It's Say-vers, right?" she asked.

"Close enough," he grunted.

"Sarnt says this is the real deal," she continued, her eyes a twitchy mix of fear and wonder. "Said y'all seen 'em."

"Who said? Saw who?" he asked.

He couldn't hear her reply. A final spike struck his mind so hard it felt like the whole orbital broke apart around him. Loud and long, a tsunami of malicious code. Echoes of digital claws and fangs tore through his implant. Beneath it all, another sound. Separate voices crying out as one, like a haunted choir. They sang of destiny. Of inevitability.

Then it was gone. The song, the creeping horrors, the subtle carrier wave. All gone. Instantly he felt better, like the fever broke.

"Hey, hey." Myers was in his face, snapping his fingers loudly.

"All stations, all stations, this is Div Ops!" A frantic voice buzzed from Faylor's wrist comms. "Three-Alpha is being boarded! I say again, Three-Alpha is being boarded!"

"Twelfth save us," Myers said. "This *is* for real."

Faylor's comms crackled again. "All Div Ops elements, your orders are to escort critical Division personnel to the primary hangar deck and help secure the area for evacuation!"

"Hey, Sevvers." Sergeant Bresto appeared beside Olsom. He looked winded and sported a fresh bruise beneath his left eye. Three blaster rifles hung from his shoulder that Sev suspected belonged to the rest of Faylor's team.

"What's… what's happening, Bresto?" he asked.

Bresto thrust a rifle into Sev's hands. "Something followed us home."

CHAPTER
EIGHT

THE MAG-LEV TRAM rumbled through the clear plexene conduit that led away from Division HQ. Interior alarms blared their shrill warning. An info panel near the exit flashed between a map of the ring rail's scheduled stops and the general quarters alert. The system had already marked several destinations as inaccessible. Sev and his Marine comrades, new and old, were the only ones aboard. Where had everyone else gone? Were evacuations already under way? Was the Division going to let him die in that cell?

Sev turned to Bresto. "Thanks for getting me out of there."

"Mmm," Bresto grunted, preoccupied by his own thoughts.

"How'd you know?" Sev asked.

"Got an encoded tight-beam aboard the Gauntlet. Said the Division locked you up," Bresto said.

"From who?"

"No idea. The lieutenant, I guess." Bresto shook his head. "Went to see for myself, then all hell broke loose." He laughed, tilting his head toward Myers, Olsom, and the two odd twins hunched in the center of the tram. "Found these boots along the way."

A distant explosion rocked the orbital. The tram bumped and screeched against its railing before its mag-lev drive could compensate.

"Founders," Olsom cursed. "Like a Twelfth-damned high-orbit strike."

"Relax, Bugs," Myers said. "You're gonna make the twins jumpy."

She spat on the floor. "They're always jumpy."

To their credit, the twins didn't seem to notice. Tall and lanky, the Marines towered over the others, their skin pale like an infant star. Spacers, born and raised, they seemed perfectly at ease amid the howling klaxons and warning strobes. Rikko and Smokes, Olsom called them. If it weren't for the cigarette hanging from Smokes's mouth, there would be no telling them apart. They eyed Sev suspiciously, their blinking weirdly synchronized.

Rikko started. "So you really got—"

"—a machine in your head?" Smokes finished, the cigarette waggling in the dark as he spoke.

"Yeah," Sev replied, loud over the alarms. "I'm with the Division."

At least, he used to be.

"Mmm," they said together, their twin frowns sending long age lines from the corners of their narrowed eyes. In the dim light of the transit line, they looked positively ancient.

"Don't like it," Smokes said.

"Isn't natural," Rikko said.

Bresto groaned. "Stow it, you two."

"Aye, Sarnt," they said.

Distant starlight filled the tram as the Division HQ line merged with the forward access transit. A kilometer ahead of them, beyond the curve of the orbital, lay Three-Alpha's primary and secondary hangars.

"Holy Twelfth," Myers whispered. "What the hell is that?"

A large black shape loomed overhead like a vast hole in space. The monstrous ship was entirely dark, with no trace of interior or signal lighting across its vast armored surface. Only its engines and shields burned bright as it cut a path toward Aegia's lower orbit. Its sunward hull shone, revealing the gunmetal colors typical of CDN vessels. Large block letters spelled out CDNS *Gerrund Halsey* along its flank.

"That's one of the missing ships," Sev said. "What's it doing—"

Spears of blue light shot from its array of heavy railguns, slicing into friendly ships still berthed at the lower orbitals. A lucky few ripped free from their moorings, backing away at reckless speed. Repeated volleys from the Halsey's guns tore the others to pieces in bursts of dying shields and reactors.

More bright flashes erupted from lower orbit, leaving perfectly round ghosts on Sev's retinas. Micro-fusion detonations, torpedoes maybe, had struck Orbital One-Alpha. His wrist comms crackled, interference from the bursts of radiation. Thin red ion trails traced the torpedoes' path to a second black ship at the edge of Aegia Prime's space.

"Another ship," Sev said, pointing to the distant newcomer. "Looks like a destroyer. Maybe the Indignant."

"What the hell, man?" Olsom gasped. "Those are our ships!"

Sev grit his teeth. "Not anymore."

"No way squids could do this." Grief tugged at Olsom's features.

A flight of CDN void fighters juked silently overhead, their swept-winged hulls barreling toward the rogue warship. Their twin blasters stitched a red path to their target, the fat red bolts fizzling against the ship's dense shields.

Myers whooped. "Yeah! Get some, jet jockeys!"

The celebration was short-lived. White tracers lashed from the Halsey's point-defense cannons, driving the fighters back. One of them broke apart under the barrage and exploded against the black ship's shields, sending amethyst waves of energy in all directions.

Those fighters wouldn't make a dent in most CDN warships, let alone the Halsey. Where the hell was the Lehman and her drones?

"Cole?" Sev spoke into his wrist comms. "Jene? Harp? This is Sevvers. Are you there?"

No response. His tac comms feed crackled with every salvo from the rogue cruiser's heavy rail.

Bresto leaned against the far side of the tram, his gaze locked on the granite-colored planet below. "How do we kill those things before they make low orbit?"

There was something on the NCO's mind. Of course. Aegia was Bresto's home. Somewhere down there, his wife and children were going about their routine, unaware of the brutal ambush unfolding in orbit. No one would ever have expected an attack on the CDF stronghold. Let alone by the Concordat.

Sev felt his chest tighten. He knew too well what it was like to have invaders turn his home into a war zone. The raiders who attacked his settlement on Respitia did more than take his mother. They took entire families, destroyed infrastructure, and turned the Billings Point settlement into a ghost town.

The things bearing down on Aegia were far worse than squids.

"First, we get Six and Three back," he said, "then I link up with my old section on the Lehman."

Olson frowned. "Six? Three? We counting something here?"

"My AI," Sev replied, eyes held shut in frustration, "they're named Six and Three."

"Wait. You *number* your bots?" She chuckled. "That's so dumb."

"I thought they were in your head. How'd you lose them?" Myers asked.

"Someone took them from me." Sev turned to Bresto. "It was Jacobe."

Myers grimaced. "Took it... out of your head? How?"

Bresto eyed his rifle's charge level. "Doesn't matter. We get the bots back from the skeeg and get Sevvers to his ship. Check?"

"Aye, Sarnt," the Marines chorused.

The twins glanced at each other like reflections in a mirror.

"What does this—"

"—Jacobe look like?" they asked.

"He's a Division officer," Sev said. "Eta-ish, low reg, black coat. He's carrying some kind of device with him."

"Fuckin' officer," Myers smirked. "Sounds like a skeeg to me."

Bresto nodded. "Creds say he's headed to the hangar deck, same as us."

"Easy enough," Myers said.

Olsom slapped Myers on the shoulder, her eyes transfixed on something beyond the tram's exterior windows.

"Hey," she said. "What's that?"

A thin spear of light emerged amid the ships warring for control of Aegia Prime. It seemed to stretch on forever, disappearing into the stellar horizon. The beam's edge rippled with energy, bleeding gossamer strands of light.

A shape exploded from the beam, large and menacing. The dark silhouette raised the hair on the back of Sev's neck. Its blunted prow with its blade-like shape. The steep, tortured sides of its burnished copper hull. The beam was a gateway, some kind of advanced FTL, and hell had just come through it.

No longer derelict, the ancient ship emerged from the edge of the beam, a dozen smaller raider vessels chasing its drive plumes. It was bigger than he remembered, dwarfing every vessel in sight and partially eclipsing the light from Aegia's sun.

The Concordat had arrived.

The raider ships vectored apart, breaking from their loose formation. Most were smaller Vagrant-class corvettes escorting one, no, two of the larger Deviant-class destroyers. One corvette rocketed past the transit line, close enough Sev could see the tribal markings painted across its rust-brown hull. White tracers whipped from its point-defense mounts. Stray rounds smacked into the transit conduit. The dense plexene cracked and groaned as their tram slipped past.

Sev's wrist comms crackled to life. "Aegia Garrison, this is Captain Mirden of the Alexander Lehman." Mirden sounded confident, even excited in a subdued way. "All guns on the archenemy. All guns on the Concordat!"

A trio of blue lances crossed the void, revealing the *Lehman's* position in the melee. Explosions crested from the ancient vessel's shields, tungsten cores vaporizing against the gravity-bound energy. More ships added their sporadic fire to the *Lehman's*, but the Concordat's shields held firm.

The color drained from Olsom's face. "So, they are real."

"Of course they are," Myers said, eyeing his own blaster rifle. The Aegian gave a wry smile. "Time to get some, for the Lost."

"For the Lost," the twins repeated.

"Yeah." Olsom eyed her riot gun warily.

The Concordat ship surged forward, its sub-light drives burning as it began a ponderous turn toward the planet below. Starlight glinted off its port side, revealing hundreds of glittering pinpricks of light.

They tumbled from the great crater in its hull like ice from a comet's tail. Some drifted toward the orbitals and surrounding ships, driven by some trick of aux gravity. Most hung in the void near the ancient derelict, following its slow path toward low orbit.

"No," Bresto said, nearly choking on the word. "Can't be."

"What is it, Sarnt?" Olsom asked.

Sev held his breath. He knew the answer. He'd been there, seen them for himself. Dammit, but he wanted to be wrong.

"The Lost," Sev said. The words sucked the life out of him.

Everyone aboard fell silent. Their faces glowed in the light of distant explosions. All eyes were on him.

"Hey. That ain't funny, man," Myers snapped.

Bresto whirled toward the combat engineer. "No, it ain't!" he roared. "But they're here. And it *is* time to get some. That's our home down there."

Myers shrank. "Yes, Sarnt."

"I don't understand," Sev said. "You saw for yourself. The Forge was empty. How could there be so many now?"

Worry strained Bresto's face. He pointed at the dark ship above them. "I guess we know what happened to the crew of the Halsey," he said.

The *Halsey* and the *Indignant* had nearly two thousand human souls between them. The idea they were all dead, or worse, turned Sev's stomach. It took four Marines in hard suits, two drones and one transhuman witch to kill three Lost daxed. Could Aegia Prime hold back two thousand until help arrived?

"So many," he said. "I have to get Six back. A drone attack is the only chance we have. To kill them before they make planet-fall."

Bresto narrowed his eyes in thought. "Runt, this is Bresto," he said into his comms.

The tram descended into darkness, shaking as it joined the hangar transit line. They hurtled toward their destination, strobing hazard lights streaming by.

"Bresto!" Cylla's voice leaped through Bresto's comms.

"Go, Runt."

The lupanthae warbled a nervous chord. "Enemy coming!"

"Get the Gauntlet warmed up," Bresto ordered, eyeing the others. "We're headed back to the Lehman."

"Okay," she said. A distant snap of blaster fire rang out in the background, tinny and loud over the little speaker. "Hurry. Please."

Cylla's fear was plain, even over comms, her already terse speech more curt than usual. Sev tried in vain to keep his own anxiety at bay. The enemy was here, at Aegia Prime! The Concordat had turned some of their most powerful ships and their crews against them. With Six and Three in Jacobe's hands, he was powerless to stop them.

"I have to get my AI back," he said, turning his focus to Bresto. "I can't do this without them."

The tram slowed, the signal lights above its exit doors flashed from red to yellow. As they neared the access corridor, Sev could see hundreds of CDN personnel pressing their way toward the hangar decks.

The tram's PA chimed, its exit lights flashed green, and the doors slid open.

"Don't start that shit," Bresto growled. He rapped his knuckles hard against Sev's blaster rifle. "You're still combat effective. Time to get your head in it and your hands dirty."

The twins rushed from the tram, head and shoulders above the river of people streaming toward the hangar deck. Myers and Olsom followed as another explosion rocked the corridor, stalling the mass of escapees. Alert klaxons honked, urging them onward. A squad of security personnel rushed past, barking at the crowd to stand aside.

"Come on," Bresto said, trotting after them. "Let's go!"

CHAPTER
NINE

SEV FOLLOWED the Marines and masters-at-arms through a massive archway that led toward the primary hangar deck. Their shouted orders vanished amid the deafening proximity of alert klaxons. He struggled to listen as the crowd around him came to a halt.

Myers turned, suddenly frantic, his shouts lost amid the howling alarms.

The desperate evacuees of Orbital Three-Alpha collided with the security team like an avalanche of white and gray. One by one, they pushed their way past. Wide-eyed panic reigned on their faces. Headquarters Corps, Naval Logistics, Division programmers, administrators, and other non-combatants.

Myers yanked Sev close, shouting more unheard warnings. Bresto and Olsom were right behind him, with the twins on their six.

A distant force shook the fibrosteel deck plate beneath Sev's feet. The acrid stench of smoke and ozone filled his nose. As the crush of retreating personnel faded, he could hear the distant snaps of blaster fire ahead. The electrostatic buzz of lasers. One of the masters-at-arms spun, an ugly burn across his chest, then dropped to the floor.

Someone struck Sev on the arm. Myers. "Hey!" he cried, pulling Sev close. "Cover behind those crates, then give 'em hell while we punch up!"

Sev glanced at Bresto. The Marine nodded, his narrow eyes taking in things Sev couldn't see from his crouched position.

"Okay," he mumbled, clutching his blaster rifle tight.

Myers laughed. "Alright, then. Move it!"

The Marine gave Sev a shove powerful enough to throw him from the staggered column of security personnel and into the open. He froze for one heartbeat, two. Three launch bays were on fire. Four, no, six squids gathered a hundred meters up. More survivors, trapped by crisscrossing laser fire, ran for cover against the interior bulkhead. An incoming laser beam singed the air beside his head. Shit.

Shit!

He exploded forward in a run, his vision tunneling toward the stack of yellow supply crates just ten meters in front of him. The air crackled and ionized around him. Five meters now. He tried to leap the rest of the way but slipped and fell instead. The floor came up fast, and he landed hard on his bad shoulder. What he wouldn't give for a hard suit just then.

More laser fire *thunked* into the deck in front of him, leaving black scorch marks on the fibrosteel plate. He scurried behind the yellow crates and pressed himself against the nearby bulkhead. Relief consumed him at the sound of lasers plinking harmlessly against the crates, too heavy and dense to be threatened with beams of focused light.

His wrist comms squawked. "Your turn, Sevvers." It was Bresto. "We're moving."

The security team pushed forward with Bresto and the others leading the way. Their movement was steady and practiced, as natural as breathing. Weapons tight on their shoulders, sighting through their scopes even as they bounded for cover. Cover that was a long way off.

Sev came to his knees and sighted over the tops of the crates. His blaster rifle's optics zoomed and focused, highlighting the squids' frond-covered faces in danger red. The safety flicked off with a satisfying clunk and the targeting reticule glowed red-dead. The trigger pull was heavy—

Hot red light snapped from the rifle, blinding his optics for a millisecond. When his eyes refocused, the raider beneath his sights was gone. Blue blood spattered its alien companions.

A tingling joy rose through his body as he found his next target and squeezed the trigger. He'd grown accustomed to watching raiders die in his drone sight, slaughtered by the dozens by his combat drones. But there was something about pulling the trigger himself that was far more satisfying.

The second squid jerked in surprise but didn't die. A near miss, Sev could see the carbon scoring on the far wall. Return fire streaked overhead, forcing him back behind the crates. When the incoming fire died down, he braved another anxious glance.

"Shoot, you damn skeeg!" Olsom shrieked over comms. "Don't have to be perfect. Just keep their ugly heads down!"

Sev obliged her, taking another three shots at the raiders in rapid succession. He might've hit one, but hadn't been aiming so much as trying to shoot fast enough to get back behind cover.

More Marines streamed through the hatchway behind him, some armed, most not. They scrounged unceremoniously through the dead security personnel, taking blasters and charge packs. The mob of angry trigger-pullers was a welcome sight.

"Sevvers, Bresto."

Sev wiped the sweat from his forehead. "Go ahead."

"There's a maintenance hatch fifty meters ahead of you. Cover there."

He hesitated. Fifty meters was a long way. "Okay—"

"Runt's in trouble. Don't think about it, just go!"

Sev swallowed hard and bolted from behind the crates. The remaining squids were dead or running. Only outgoing CDF blaster fire cooked the air. Still, the maintenance hatch looked small and far away as he ran, holding his rifle close to keep balanced. He fell toward the hatchway to stop himself but hit something else instead as he dove into cover.

Someone screamed.

"Twelfth!" he shouted, jerking his rifle toward the woman flattened against the hatchway opposite of him. She dropped her satchel of tools, spilling them onto the floor.

"The-the hatches are locked down," she sobbed, eyes wet with tears. Anders, her nametape read. An FTL maintenance tech, according to her section badge. "I was just… trying to get them open."

"Help's coming," he said through labored breaths, nodding toward the rush of Marines.

"There's more of them," she said, shivering as she risked a glimpse beyond the hatchway. "I saw …" She swallowed, still crying. "I saw the Lost. Twelfth help me, I saw them."

If the Lost were already aboard the orbital, getting to the *Lehman* just got much harder.

"Big?" he asked, struggling to smile. "Or little?"

She only nodded. A very bad sign.

"Bresto," he said into his wrist comms.

"Send it."

"The Lost are here."

There was a pause, a muffled curse. "Where?"

Sev gazed at Anders. She leaned closer, huddled over his wrist comms. "Launch bay nine," she said.

Damn. That was close to the Gauntlet.

"Copy that," Bresto said. "Let's move."

Sev eyed the corridor behind him. A staggered line of Marines pressed forward through the dead and dying squids, firing the occasional blaster bolt at the aliens that ran.

"Specialist Anders," he said.

"Y-yes?" she said, flinching at the sound of his voice.

"Which ship are you with?"

"The… the Incandescence," Anders managed. "They destroyed our transport, trapping us here." She pointed to one of the nearby launch bays. It was on fire, the flames from a ruined shuttlecraft still licking the atmo field. "The others, they—" She brought her hands to her mouth and keened a frightened sound.

He opened his mouth to speak, but no words came. What could he say? Her colleagues, her friends, were dead, killed by monsters who barely an hour ago were just ancient history to her. Even with the revelations from the tribunal, the Concordat's counterattack had arrived too soon for anyone to be ready for it.

"You're going to be okay," he said reflexively. It wasn't exactly a lie. He almost believed it himself. Maybe because he'd lived through worse. At least, he hoped this wouldn't be worse. "But I need your help."

"What?" she rasped, frowning like she didn't believe him. "What can I do?"

"I'm looking for someone. An officer, black coat, Division like me." He tapped his section badge. "Carrying a metal case. Did you see anyone like that?"

She sucked in a breath. "There were so many. I can't remember."

"There's a transport ahead. Follow me and I'll take you to it," he said, gesturing to his rifle. "Just help me keep an eye out for him, okay?"

She shook her head, her face pinched with fear. "I... I can't. Please."

He clenched his teeth. They didn't have time for this. This battle would decide the fate of Aegia in the coming hours. He'd have to leave her if she wouldn't come on her own. How could he convince her to move?

He took another anxious glance down the hangar deck and stepped from cover, stooping to retrieve Anders's satchel of tools. Nervous energy ripped through him. It was impossible not to think about getting holed by some raider's stray laser. Anders finally followed and took the satchel.

"We've both got jobs to do," he said, his smile turning into nervous laughter. "You know, for humanity."

"For the—" Anders froze. He recognized that look. The moment you realized it was more than a mantra, or a refrain in some school-yard cheer.

That the monsters *were* real.

She took a breath, shaking as the crisp snap of blaster fire resumed in the corridor ahead of them. Her jaw tightened. "For the Lost."

———

"Time to go to work!" Bresto cried, his voice loud and crackling over comms.

More Marines surged forward into the melee, rushing in groups of three or four. Blaster bolts poured from their staggered lines, red-hot death that crashed into flesh and metal alike in showers of charged particles. Raiders honked and grunted their wet, slurping cries. Some charged closer, but most turned and ran, fleeing toward the handful of damaged launch bays still firmly under Concordat control.

Sev stood with Anders behind a piece of sub-light engine cowling, part of an exploded cargo transport that still burned in the closest launch bay. It felt good to stand despite the nearby inferno. His knees ached from all the crawling and ducking. Fighting without exo support, without a hard suit, was something else entirely.

"You good?" he asked the FTL tech.

"Yeah," she said, her sweat-covered face glowing in the light of the flames. Then she caught herself, like she'd only just noticed his rank pips. "Yes, Master Specialist. Sorry, Master Specialist."

He shook his head. "Forget about it, Anders. We have bigger things to worry about."

Behind them, damage control teams moved in. They kept pace with a heavy maintenance bot whose red and white hazard-striped hull provided ample cover. It stopped near another damaged bay and spat throaty blasts of fire-retardant gel from a fat, round cannon atop its armored chassis.

Breathless, Sev chuckled. "Hey, it could be worse. You could have *that* job."

Something struck the engine cowling, hard enough to move the heavy piece of molded duraplate several centimeters. Metal-on-metal shrieks echoed around them. The surrounding air grew stiflingly hot.

Coruscating orbs of green plasma streaked past, hotter than the burning transport in the bay above them. They splashed into the maintenance bot, melting through its armor and sending mists of super-heated gas into the repair teams huddled around it. The bot exploded in green fire, silencing their brittle screams.

The blast threw Sev and Anders onto the deck. Fires raged on all sides of them. It was hard to breathe.

Their wrist comms squelched to life. "New contacts! Launch bay eight!"

"I see 'em," came a reply. "Ugly things with plasma weapons."

"Bugs," Sev coughed, hot air filling his lungs. The Lost wouldn't be far behind. "We have to move. Now."

Another blast struck near their hiding spot. No, not an explosion. It was a heavy, rhythmic pounding, like massive hammers.

The engine cowling groaned, bending as it rose from the deck. Thick metal fingers clung to its super-heated edges, lifting it higher, revealing the faceless daxed heavy looming on the other side. Behind it, amid the heat haze of plasma fire, a second heavy charged the Marines' position. Sounds of panic and anger crackled through their comms.

The rifle felt clumsy in his hands, but he aimed it anyway.

"Run, Anders!" he yelled, and squeezed the trigger. The daxed was impossible to miss and impossible to kill. The bolts panged harmlessly off its armor-plated body.

Anders became a gray-and-white blur, sprinting across the wide transit conduit for safer cover, dodging inbound plasma fire. If nothing else, at least she would get out of there alive.

The heavy shrugged aside the warped metal debris and sent it crashing into the nearby launch ramp. Sev crawled backward, desperate to escape, unable to take his eyes off the thing about to kill him. It soared over him, frozen like a terrible statue, its faceless helmet watching his every movement.

More heavy footfalls thundered behind him. He glanced toward Anders. She was gone. Safe, he hoped. Good. He would raise some hell with what little time he had left.

He spun to face the new threat. Another massive daxed heavy loomed over him. A deep scar in its plated armor filled his optics, outlined in friendly IFF blue.

DC-1 pointed at the Lost before it. "For the Lost!"

The daxed commander leaped over Sev with gravity-defying speed. The two cyborgs collided, their armored joints shrieking in protest, as more of the Colonial Defense Daxed Corps joined the fray. Found heavies wielded tools like weapons. Daxed masters-at-arms fired their riot guns. A daxed med tech blurred through the air like a bladeless wisp.

DC-1 gave a swift headbutt, disfiguring the faceless helmet of its foe with a dry crunch. The med tech landed atop the staggered heavy, its eyes deep and serene. Its augmented fingers snaked between the heavy's armor plates, slicing vital circuitry underneath. The heavy stumbled, its muscled shoulders fell limp as it toppled to the floor.

"You good, Master Specialist?" someone said. Sev flinched as the speaker, a Marine, helped him to his feet.

"Uh, yeah." He nodded slowly, still watching the friendly daxed charge into the fray. The Found had saved them.

There was no sign of the FTL tech. She'd moved so fast, he hadn't seen which way she'd gone. Sev crossed the hangar's transit corridor, wading slowly through the Marines still advancing toward the enemy.

"Anders?" he called. Only the cracks and thuds of distant combat answered him. "Anders!"

Something bumped against his boot. A gray satchel, half-burned away in a pile of dusty powder. The bile rose in his throat. The ash swirling around his feet was all that remained of Specialist Anders, FTL tech for the *Incandescence*. Killed by enemy plasma fire while fleeing like he'd told her to. So she'd be safe.

He stumbled to one side and retched, spilling the limited contents of his stomach onto the metal deck. Everywhere smelled like violence and death, cloying at his mouth and nose. The metallic tang of high-energy weapons fire. The chalky stink of atomized flesh and bone.

A firm hand gripped his shoulders.

"Uh, bot jockey—"

"—you stitched? You good?"

Rikko and Smokes stood to either side of him, contented smiles wrinkling their faces. Blood mingled with the blaster discharge on their cheeks, both human and alien. The sickly-sweet smell of burning tobacco was a welcome distraction from the horrors drifting in the surrounding air.

Sev wiped the filth from his lips. "Yeah," he lied.

"Good," they said.

Rikko found his wrist comms. "Got 'im, Sarnt."

"He's good to go, Sarnt," Smokes finished, barely a pause between words.

"Good," Bresto said, his voice straining through the comms static. "Get him up—"

A melancholy, two-tone wail split Sev's ears, piercing through the honking klaxons high above them as it pitched above human hearing. His heart revved, recognizing the source before he could form the thought.

He twisted free from the twins' grasp and pressed the blaster rifle's stock into his shoulder. Launch bay eight was barely a hundred meters ahead. Madness took him, forced him into a sprint. He was still combat-effective. He could still make a difference.

And Cylla needed help.

CHAPTER
TEN

SEV RAN, following the familiar tunnel vision that came with the rush of adrenaline. He bounded deeper into the hangar deck, between ruined bodies and machinery. The hazard yellow strobes kept time with his steps.

A large numeral eight, as tall as he was, stenciled white on a steel-blue weave of fibrosteel brought him to a halt. He recognized the *Gauntlet's* tail boom stretching out over the transit conduit. A wall of smoke hung in the air beneath it. Somewhere inside, the pitch of the sound changed, too high to hear. The growing pressure in his ears felt like his head might explode.

A squad of Marines took up a position near the launch bay ramp. Some sighted over their weapons at a threat Sev couldn't see. Others pressed their hands over their ears, cringing at the awful sound.

"Cylla?" he cried, straining to see through the acrid haze.

"Careful, man," a Marine said.

Another coughed. "Yeah, that wolf is fucking feral."

Sev frowned. Feral? Cylla? His heart beat faster. Something was very wrong.

He stepped past the Marines and through the pall of smoke. It burned his eyes, made them water. At least that's what he told himself. Not that Cylla could be injured, or worse.

There. A shadow in the hazard lights. The pressure from his ears vanished, and for a second, he thought he heard the muffled sound of clicking teeth. He swallowed, raising his rifle. The optics cut through the smoke. Nothing.

"Cylla?" he called out.

A deep, rumbling growl shook the air. The wolf's hot, earthy breath washed over him. The hair on the back of his neck stood, a primitive instinct warning him to freeze. That danger was near, and he was prey.

"Cylla?" he said again, barely a whisper.

All he had to do was move slow. To show her he wasn't a threat. Painfully, achingly slowly, he lowered his rifle.

Clawed hands threw him to the ground, his head rattled by the sudden impact. A crushing weight bore down on his chest. Total darkness reigned over him. Two bright eyes gazed back at his, wide with rage, golden irises flecked with copper. Her eyes... so thick with color, the pupils nothing but tiny pinpricks of killing darkness. His heart pounded in his chest, like it wanted to climb out of his throat.

Mouth closed, her trembling lips peeled back, revealing rows of sharp teeth. Rivulets of drool fell on his neck and chest. The rotten stink of clotting alien blood filled his nose.

"Cyll—" he rasped.

The word wouldn't come. Her hands on his chest made it hard to breathe. Only then did he feel her claws poking his skin, poised to tear through his white-and-grays before rending flesh from bone.

He sucked in a breath. "Cylla, please. It's me, Kerry—nnng! Kerry Sevvers!"

She leaned closer, taking deep sniffs of his face, then exhaled sharply. The sudden gust of her musky breath made him flinch.

"Kerry?" It didn't even sound like her, deeper and darker somehow. Filled with solemn malice. "Kerry Sevvers?"

He nodded, trembling as her terrifying, near pupil-less gaze bored deep into his very soul.

"Yeah," he coughed, unable to breathe in. "Please, you're... hurting me."

Footsteps drew closer. Charging capacitors whined. A wave of panic hit him. They were going to kill her. He wanted to shout, to tell them not to hurt her, but he couldn't breathe. Darkness gathered at the edges of his frantic vision.

"Founders, Runt." It was Bresto. Thank the Twelfth, it was Bresto. "We like this one, remember?"

Cylla blinked, and her pupils dilated. Released from her killing trance, her eyes regained their softness. She gasped, then rose from the floor, lifting Sev like a limp doll. He breathed deep, wincing from the fresh aches in his ribs.

Tears matted the fur around her eyes. "So… so sorry!" she howled. "Please forgive, Kerry Sevvers. They—" she pointed a gore-covered claw at a pile of dead, broken bugs "—they hurt our ship. They did. Not Kerry."

"It's okay, Cylla." He laughed, his body trembling with nervous energy. "I'm just glad you're safe. You and the Gauntlet."

"Yes." The wolf gave an open-mouthed grin. "We are safe."

———

Sev reclined against a stack of ammo crates on a cargo sled drifting just above the deck. The dull thumps of the sled's repulsors quickened, compensating for the additional weight. Lance Corporal Myers hovered beside him, checking his vitals.

Every part of him hurt. His joints ached. His stomach soured. Guilt nagged at his conscience. Not that others had died, and he hadn't. But that, deep down, he was grateful for it. Relieved. Thrilled to still be among the living.

Evacuees streamed from the receiving bay into the transit corridor. They formed long lines against the steep interior bulkhead that ended near the secondary hangar deck junction. There, just beyond bay nine, more Marines formed a defensive line. Two platoons deep, they waited, ready to repel another attempt to take the primary hangar deck. DC-1 and his Daxed Corps had pressed on, hunting the remaining Concordat as they retreated deeper inside.

With the immediate threat to the primary deck passed, maintenance crews had returned to make emergency repairs. Launch bay three was back online, its catapult whining as it received a heavy crew transport. Four and five were no longer burning. The shriek of sub-light engines filled the expansive corridor once again. Crew chiefs grilled the evacuees, directing them toward their designated launch bays. There, transports would take them to their ship, or to the presumed safety of the planet below.

"Deep breath for me," Myers said, a palm against Sev's chest.

Sev inhaled slowly, grateful for the hangar deck's environmental controls. The haze of smoke had almost cleared shortly after his encounter with Cylla. His chest ached superficially, a twinge in his ribs when his lungs inflated.

Myers frowned. "Chest expansion looks even; that's good. You feel anything moving in there?"

"No." Sev shook his head. "Just sore."

"Alright. You're serviceable, Master Specialist."

Serviceable. Sev grinned at the word, memories of Corporal Mace surfacing in his thoughts. Not the daxed horror she'd become, but the woman. The Respitian. Myers was too much like her just then. He might lack her bedside manner, but his skills were on par.

Myers smirked, tilting his head to the nearest launch bay. "Better than them, anyway."

Marines and specialists on corpse detail dragged dead squids and bugs up the launch bay ramp and tossed them into the void. Beyond the atmo fields, the bodies drifted, as the black ships and their raider allies traded rail gun volleys with the garrison fleet.

Others arranged hasty funerals for their fallen comrades. Med techs stood by to carry them off, quietly reciting the words every colonist knew by heart.

Lost no more.

Distant snaps of blaster fire echoed through the corridor, but he ached too much to worry. Exhaustion clung to him like a heavy blanket, tugging at his bones. Even the persistent klaxons and strobes had faded to background noise. An anxious boredom had set in. He was desperate for… well, whatever was to come next. The sudden lull was as discomforting as it was familiar.

"Master Specialist."

Another Marine. A woman. Shorter than him and wider too.

Stocky, with a face broad and steep like an Aegian cliff-side. With her wide shoulders and thick arms, she could've been Bresto's older sister. Major's pips glittered gold on her collar. Sev grunted, straining to rise, but she stayed him with a wave of her hand.

"At ease. You the ranking NCO here, sailor?"

Sev glanced at the others. He'd noticed a handful of sergeants and corporals among the Marines. But no staff NCOs. No officers. He almost laughed. Twelfth help them all if he was in charge.

He shrugged. "I don't know, ma'am."

The major lifted her chin and gave a thin smile. "You did outstanding work here today," she boomed, speaking beyond Sev to everyone present. "Three-Alpha stands because of your bravery and determination. You met the enemy with complete and overwhelming violence, and you killed expertly."

Nearby Marines barked and howled at her words, celebrating like a pack of rabid lupanthae. Every sound stretched the smile further across her face. Sev eyed her nametape and blinked. No, not Kill. Kull. Major Kull.

"But our war with the archenemy has only just begun, Marines." She pointed with a hand beyond the launch bay door, fingers straight and tight together like a knife. "Skipper wants all able-bodied killers aboard the Victory to prepare for planet fall. It's drop or die, Marines."

Another snarling chorus rippled through the Marines. A flash of panic made Sev's heart sink, realizing Bresto and the others would leave for Aegia. How was he going to get Six and Three back now?

Kull turned back to Sev and tilted her head toward the *Gauntlet*. "That scow got a pilot?" she asked.

He noticed Cylla still seated on the launch ramp, head in her enormous hands, ears pinned back behind her head. It would be some time before she forgave herself for attacking him. Sev laughed. It was that or cry.

"Something funny, sailor?" Kull asked, frowning. Behind her, a senior Marine scowled.

He shook his head. "No, ma'am." He pointed her to Cylla. "Just don't call her ship a scow."

Kull eyed the wolf and laughed, her face flush. "Roger that." She flashed a knowing wink. "I fucking love wolves."

"Yes, ma'am."

Kull strode toward the launch ramp, trailed by several grizzled NCOs and junior officers who looked pissed they missed the fight. She stopped to shake the hands of nearby Marines and thank them for their courage and sacrifice. Their enthusiasm was palpable, lapping up her promises of honor and glory in the fight to come.

Bresto stood behind them, a quiet, solemn mountain. It was only then Sev realized deep down the man was a leader. Behind the quick temper and quicker fists was someone who cared for those in his charge. It was obvious now Sev would not have survived the mission to Cradle's edge without him. He suspected a lot of these young men and women would owe Bresto their lives before this fight was over.

"Sevvers," Bresto said, crossing the transit conduit to where he sat.

"Sergeant Bresto," Sev replied with a smile, ignoring the creeping panic that he was once again on his own.

Bresto pulled a bandolier of charge packs from an open crate. "Change of plans, I'm afraid," he said.

"Hey, I get it." Sev waved to the launch bay doors. "That's your home down there."

"Yeah." Bresto squinted, looking further down the corridor. "Should be no problem getting transpo to the Lehman now."

"Right."

Bresto donned the bandolier and tightened its straps, an awkward silence stretching between them. It had a finality to it that turned Sev's blood cold. There was a lot he wanted to say, but didn't have the words. Not just then, anyway. Maybe when this was all over.

"Take care of yourself, skeeg."

"You too, trigger-puller."

With a smirk, Bresto turned and walked toward the transport. Other Marines crowded past him, ready to collect their own ammo before departing aboard the *Gauntlet*. They pushed forward eagerly, bragging about their kill counts and minor flesh wounds. Sev got it. Together, they'd secured the primary hangar deck. Those trapped aboard the orbital could soon return to their designated ships and take the fight to the enemy.

That is, if the Concordat didn't shoot them down on the way there. They would need the *Lehman's* drones to reach Aegia's atmo in one piece.

"Jene?" he said into his wrist comms. "Cole? Harp? This is Sevvers."

Crisp static called back to him. Comms traffic jammed the nets. Only priority messages would get through. Some random specialist trying to contact a unit he was no longer assigned to would be at the end of the line. Six could've fixed that. Six could've fixed a lot of things. Maybe Anders would still …

He shook off the thought and eyed the line of personnel waiting for outbound transports. No black storm coats or Division badges. No Jacobe. Maybe the bastard was just a pile of ash and bone, like poor Anders. But then, he had Six. Twelfth save the man, at least until Sev took his AI back.

Olsom was next in line for a resupply. She leaned over the open crates, scrounging for loose charge packs. Myers and the twins stood behind her.

"Why the long face, Master Specialist?" she asked, slotting a charge pack into a half-filled bandolier.

He shrugged, trying hard not to look too lost. "All this and no sign of Jacobe or my AI."

The twins stretched simultaneously, telescoping skyward like pale, thin trees. They yawned together in their weird, choreographed way.

"Keep the faith," Myers said, muscling past Olsom. He reached into the crate and stopped short. There was nothing inside save a few empty bandoliers. "Twelfth, Bugs, you damn thief."

"Stuff it, Doc." She twisted away from him, clutching two full bandoliers tight to her chest. "Ain't but one thief in the Marine Corps."

Big smiles wrinkled the twins' faces. "Everyone else just trying to get their shit back," they said.

The group burst into laughter, all but Myers, who took one last pass through the crate for any hidden ammo. Finding none, he grunted his disapproval and started hassling Olsom for a spare charge pack.

Rikko stopped mid-laugh and jerked toward the inner corridor. Smokes turned a heartbeat later, took a long pull from his cigarette and pointed.

Smoke wafted from his mouth. "Hey. Hey, bot jockey—"

"—that your skeeg?" Rikko said.

"Who?" Sev turned and immediately spotted the matte black storm coat moving down the line of evacuees. The man stopped and addressed a crew chief, his tone demanding, his eyes narrow and commanding. He clutched the familiar metal case to his chest.

Jacobe. Had to be.

Sev rocketed from his seat on the empty ammo cart, his blaster rifle heavy against his chest. The sudden motion caught Jacobe's eye. The two stood frozen, staring at each other, neither believing the other was real.

Jacobe bolted, shoving past the crew chief and sprinting toward the darkness of the secondary hangar deck.

"Founders," Olsom snorted. "Damn skeegs."

Sev grabbed his rifle and ran after him.

CHAPTER
ELEVEN

SEV WATCHED Jacobe disappear through the smoking junction doors. He ran, a fresh burst of adrenaline carrying him between the lines of defending Marines he'd hoped might take Jacobe down. That would make the whole thing so much easier. But the Marines were far too concerned with what might come toward them to worry about the two idiot skeegs running past them.

A thick, scarred Marine rose, pointing with his augmetic arm. "Hey!" he barked. "Secondary hangar deck's not secure!"

Sev ignored the warning and charged into the junction. There, the conduit narrowed sharply, just big enough to allow personnel and bots through, some cargo. Small enough that Orbital Operations could seal it off in an emergency.

Flashing hazard strobes threw cones of yellow light against the armored bulkheads. Thin shadows grew and shrank in their oscillating glow.

"Jacobe!" Sev shouted. He could barely hear himself amid the wailing sirens.

But Jacobe halted at the secondary hangar deck hatchway. Sev lengthened his stride, his quads and lungs burning to catch up. He gripped the rifle tight. The safety switch teased his thumb. What exactly was his plan? How far would he go to get Six and Three back?

The architect glanced behind him, startled to find Sev gaining.

"Wait!" Sev yelled again, his throat horse from exertion. "Stop!"

Jacobe's head swiveled, searching for an escape, then he lunged through the exit and onto the secondary hangar deck.

A flurry of radiant sparks exploded off the deck where the architect just stood. Streaks of energized particles blurred past like long red ghosts. The air grew warm and heavy with ozone. Sev dove to the floor as more of the stray blaster bolts spat overhead, their snapping hiss more of a sharp crack on the receiving end.

He crawled forward, straining to see any sign of the architect, his heart banging inside his chest. The damn fool had run straight into a hail of friendly blaster fire. And taken Six with him! Sev was going to kill him if he wasn't dead already.

A dull, heavy thump rocked the junction, forcing Sev back to the deck. A pitched ringing replaced all other sounds. The air tasted thin and hot, tinged with burned carbon. He blinked, trying to clear his blurred vision. Heavy smoke rolled across the junction's exit. The incoming fire quickly ceased.

"Jacobe," he rasped.

Two dark figures materialized in the haze like living, twitching shadows. Too different to be human, with their angled limbs and wide, flat heads. A third alien appeared behind them, taller and heavier, fronds twitching from its mouth.

He sighted through his blaster rifle's scope. Even through the smoke, the aliens glowed danger red in the optics. The rifle's capacitor buzzed as he switched the safety off. With a panicked breath, he squeezed the trigger. Again. Three times. The first alien fell in a shower of lethal sparks.

The second bug filled his sights, panning its plasma staff back and forth, searching for him. Sev pulled the trigger just once, suddenly aware of his rapidly depleting charge pack, toppling the alien with a single shot to the head. The blaster rifle made quick, satisfying work of them. With its heavier capacitor and smart optics, it was far more lethal than a simple blaster pistol.

A solid red beam buzzed overhead. The air crackled with ionization. Too close. The raider warrior kneeled beside the dead bugs, sighting over its primitive laser rifle to ready another shot.

Panic lit Sev's nerves. He edged the scope toward the squid. Too far, an overcorrection. He held his breath, desperate to get off a shot before the raider found its mark.

A fourth shadow appeared, and the squid's head burst with a loud pop. Sev knew the sound. A blaster pistol, charge level three. The newcomer glowed friendly blue in his optics, Jacobe's face visible in the clearing haze.

The architect mouthed into his comms. "You gonna shoot me, Sevvers?"

"I want my AI back," he said. "Now."

"Ha!" Jacobe's bitter laugh sounded tinny through the micro speaker. "You're dedicated, I'll give you that. They're just tools, man. They're not worth dying over."

"Then give them back!" Sev cried.

Finger tight on the trigger, his blood ran cold. His pulse hammered in his ringing ears. Friendly-fire warnings filled his scope. Jacobe clutched the device to his chest with his off hand, as if daring Sev to take the shot. The tension made him shake. The targeting reticle danced across Jacobe's torso.

Shit!

He couldn't do it. Jacobe might be a bastard, but Sev was the one who'd broke the rules. He needed another way to get his AI back that didn't involve killing a superior officer or damaging the device that held them.

"We don't have time for this," Sev said. He lowered the rifle and came to his feet, eyeing the battle playing out behind Jacobe warily. "Maybe you haven't noticed, but there's a war on. With Six's help, we can still win!"

"Maybe so." Jacobe pursed his lips, lost in thought. He tapped the pistol against his hip, some kind of nervous tick. "Or maybe it gets loose and scrambles our tac nets. Maybe it's already working for the enemy?"

Sev moved closer, holding his rifle to the side. Jacobe didn't know Six like he did. Hadn't been through what they'd been through. He would need some time to convince the architect to trust Six. To trust him, too.

Jacobe clutched the device firmly, pistol still in his hand. Smaller, secondary explosions rocked the transit corridor behind him, throwing debris from one of the launch bays.

"We're going to get killed if we stay here any longer," Sev said.

Jacobe nodded. "On that, we can agree."

"Help me get back to the Lehman," Sev said, struggling to contain his desperation. "It'll be safer there. For both of us."

"I've never seen her," Jacobe said, almost wistful. "Fine. The Lehman it is. Any thoughts on how to get there?"

"You've got priority tac net access?"

Jacobe's eyes narrowed, and he suddenly looked very uncomfortable. "Yeah," he said, his voice laced with concern.

Sev smiled. "I know just the man to call."

The dying raider warrior tumbled down the launch bay ramp, tiny plasma fires dotting its heavy, ramshackle armor. Behind it, the launch bay burned, the result of an exploded power cell. The blast had tossed the injured, defenseless alien down the ramp to the corridor below.

Sev took another breath. Charge level warnings flashed through his rifle's optics. He felt a sudden, very brief pinch of guilt. He could spend his whole life killing squids for what they did to him, and it wouldn't be enough. This squid's pathetic state didn't matter to him, the trigger pull was effortless. The blaster bolt found its target and the alien fell still.

Like crid in a barrel.

Jacobe huddled nearby, covering with Sev behind an upturned cargo sled.

"Any luck?" Sev asked.

"Nothing." Jacobe rested his head against the sled's duraplated chassis. "The tac nets are clogged. Priority override codes are changing faster than my own AI can get them."

Sev smirked. He couldn't help himself. "Not as easy as torturing new recruits, I take it?"

Jacobe locked Sev in an icy glare.

"Ensign Pakker, this is Chief Architect Jacobe," he said. "Priority override amethyst four-three-eight."

Jacobe's wrist comms chirped. Sev held his breath. The tac nets had accepted the override.

"This is Pakker." The ensign's voice came through loud and clear. Fear strained his indignant tone. "Who is this?"

Jacobe flashed Sev a sideways glance, an eyebrow raised. "I say again, this is Chief Architect Jacobe." His tone grew stern. "With the Division."

The channel fell silent. Sev's anxious gaze moved from the communicator on Jacobe's wrist, then back to the hangar deck.

"Of course, sir," Pakker said, his voice once more bursting through the speaker. "H-How can I help you, sir?"

Jacobe turned to Sev and shrugged. Sev covered his nametape. "Best not to mention me," he whispered.

The less Pakker knew he was involved, the better.

"Uh, right," Jacobe began. "I have critical Division cargo bound for the Lehman, and I need transportation off Three-Alpha."

A brief pause, followed by another chirp. The sound of distant blaster fire crackled through the signal. The same sounds of battle echoed from further down the corridor.

"You're in good company, sir," Pakker said. "My section and I are aboard Three-Alpha as well, signing off on the last of the Lehman's drone magazines when the enemy attacked." Another pause. "Where are you, sir?"

Sev jerked his head toward the sound of Pakker's voice. Cole, Jene, Harp, they were here, aboard the orbital. His heart swelled while his guts turned in knots. Pride warred with panic inside him. His old section was here! But why the hell were they here, of all places? No wonder the drones weren't flying. The Concordat had timed their counterattack perfectly.

Jacobe glanced around the cargo sled at the ruined launch bay. "Launch bay thirteen, secondary hangar deck."

"S-say again, sir?" Pakker squeaked. "That area isn't secure, sir! You're not safe!"

Ensign Pakker: tactical mastermind.

"Where are you, Ensign?" Jacobe asked.

"Launch bay nineteen, sir, secondary hangar deck, but the daxed, the L-Lost—" Pakker coughed, dry and airy, then cleared his throat. "It's a war zone out there, sir!"

They didn't have time for this. Sev leaned close and spoke into Jacobe's wrist comms. "When does your transport leave?"

"Twenty minutes, Twelfth willing. As soon as our launch bay is secure." Pakker scowled. "Wait, who is this?"

"Don't leave without us!" Sev cried. He reached out and tapped Jacobe's wrist comms. The signal chirped closed.

He peaked through his optics, panning the blaster rifle over the top of the cargo sled. The secondary hangar deck *was* a war zone. Bays 11 through 16 were on fire, clogging the distant ceilings above the transit corridor with toxic black smoke. Bodies—human, alien, and daxed—littered the deck. There was precious little cover to be found. Everything around them burned.

Bursts of radiant light cut through the haze, flashing to the rhythm of distant explosions. Somewhere, hidden beyond the orbital's gentle curve, a battle for the secondary hangar deck raged. Daxed on daxed. Lost against Found. And their destination lay on the other side.

"So, is it as bad as Pakker says?" Jacobe asked.

Sev shook his head. "Worse. We need to go."

———

The heat inside the transit corridor was oppressive. Air scrubbers and environmental controls rattled and coughed, trying to keep temperature and oxygen levels steady amid the all-consuming plasma fires. Sweat dripped down Sev's face, evaporating before it reached the collar of his white-and-grays. Hotter than a Respitian solstice.

The painful groan of rending metal echoed through the corridor. The empty catapult inside bay 16 shuddered, then collapsed, sending a gust of hot wind rushing over him. Sev spun toward the sound, blaster rifle held ready. The optics registered nothing but hazardous environment warnings. The atmo field glowed a hazy blue beyond the twisted steel and flames.

Jacobe cleared his throat. "Your mission to the derelict. Was it worse than this?"

"Yes," Sev said without thinking. He glimpsed the twisted bodies of two Navy specialists sprawled on the deck in front of them. "And no."

"Any words of wisdom on how you got out alive?" Jacobe asked, wiping his brow. "Asking for a friend."

"Trust your team," Sev replied, his tone flat.

Holy Twelfth. Was that irony he tasted? Or just the heavy metals in the smoke? He took a labored breath to calm himself. Maybe he'd learned something after all.

"Easy for you to say," Jacobe replied. "I'm not the one who broke every rule in the Division."

Fresh anger flared inside Sev. Jacobe was one to talk. The advanced scrubbers torturing new recruits. Executing those who dared press the boundaries of Division knowledge. There was no moral comparison.

"Sounds like the Division needs different rules," Sev said.

"You haven't seen what I've seen, Sevvers. What unsanctioned AI are capable of."

"You're wrong, Jacobe." He locked eyes with the architect. "I *have* seen what they're capable of. You want to know how I survived the derelict? Yeah, I trusted a bunch of trigger-pullers. But I trusted Six, too." A wave of emotion struck him. His voice grew thick. "If I'd have trusted it sooner, maybe… maybe the others would've lived."

"The others?"

"Nobody you knew."

Another hollow groan reverberated through the corridor. Not a groan, a roar. Heavy footsteps vibrated through the fibrosteel decking. A daxed heavy, angry and drawing closer. The once-human emerged through the flames barely fifty meters ahead of them. Its giant armored body glowed red from the heat.

Its faceless helmet was gone. Black blood oozed from a wound on its bald scalp. Gray, pallid skin stretched tight over its face, forcing a grotesque smile. Bloodshot eyes gazed at them from circuitry-laced sockets.

There was no cover. Nowhere to hide.

"Run," Sev hissed.

"What? Where?"

Sev shoved Jacobe aside. "Get to bay nineteen. Now!"

"But—"

Sev aimed his rifle and pulled the trigger. Kept it pulled, sending a flurry of three-round bursts toward the daxed. Several hot bolts smacked harmlessly against its armor. One struck its neck guard, blinding it with a spray of energy. The blaster rifle chimed a warning. His charge pack was empty.

"Hey!" Sev cried, waving frantically at the creature. Jacobe charged ahead and didn't look back.

The empty charge pack clattered to the floor. He seated a fresh pack into the charge well and slapped it home. The rifle's capacitor whined, surging with renewed power. The daxed heavy shook its head, wiping at the exposed meat around its eyes.

It charged. Suddenly, it was forty meters away. Twenty. Its crushing stride shook the hangar deck, vibrating like an earthquake that knocked Sev to the deck.

Only steps away, the heavy stalled, its massive shadow covering him in darkness. The thin, pale silhouette of a Daxed Corps med tech rose from its back. Grunting, the heavy strained to reach its lumbering arms behind its head.

The med tech raised a hand. Its bionic fingers separated into multiple surgical instruments, just as the heavy finally wrapped a thick metal hand around its head. In a blur of motion, severed wire and bone loosed a spray of arterial black. The heavy's head fell from its body. Its grip on the med tech spasmed, crushing it. Both cyborgs collapsed to the floor, dead.

Sev eyed the dead daxed briefly before squinting through the heat haze deeper into the hangar deck. The battle was clearing. He was close. A narrow walkway along the interior bulkhead offered a path through the bedlam.

On the other side of launch bay 17, the fires and heat cleared. The fighting there had reached an apex, with most of the Concordat forces used up like spent fuel. Daxed lay in heaps together, both Lost and Found. Most were dead, but some still wriggled and twitched, their grotesque wounds not fatal enough. Their machine parts refusing to die even as their ancient biology expired, the literal death of history.

DC-1 stood amid the carnage. Black blood leaked from its damaged joints and flesh. Its labored breaths were slow and ragged, revving its internal power source that howled like a distant thunderstorm. One of the Lost dangled from its giant metal hand. The wisp was tiny in comparison. It hissed and shrieked, its broken blades clanging harmlessly off DC-1's armor.

DC-1 jerked its head in Sev's direction, its cold eyes betraying no emotion as it plucked the wisp's head from its shoulders. The creature slipped from DC-1's hand and fell to the floor.

"Lost no more," it said, its eyes still locked on Sev. Even through the monotone voice emitter, Sev could hear a tinge of pity. Maybe sadness.

"Commander," Sev said, breathless.

DC-1 considered him for a moment. There was only the vaguest hint of recognition. Daxed memory was a fragile thing, if you believed the stories.

"It is not safe here, Master Specialist. More will come. Go, now."

It pointed toward the ancillary launch bays at the edge of the hangar deck, where a second defensive line took shape. Hazard lights spun in bay 19 where a docked transport ship prepared for launch.

The bulk crew hauler hung from the launch catapult. A squat, ugly craft, it looked like a large crate with oversized sub-light engines and a blunted cockpit. Maintenance crews decoupled heavy fuel hoses from its tanks. Security personnel ushered a line of evacuees up the launch ramp and into the belly of the transport.

"Sevvers!" Jacobe cried. He stood at the bottom of the ramp, still clutching Six's metal prison, waving with his free hand. Sev froze, blinking in disbelief. Beside the architect stood Pakker, Jene, Cole, and Harp. They were alive.

Jene clasped a hand over her mouth, stifling a sob. Harp looked pale and gaunt, his dead-eyed stare through his round glasses focused on something light years away. Cole just shrugged, a toothy grin growing across his broad, round face.

Sev felt it. That familiar confidence among old friends. He was back where he belonged. Together with his section, he would make the Concordat pay dearly for their brutal counterattack. His stride lengthened as he rushed to join them.

"S-Sevvers," Pakker said, his usual disapproving tone notably absent.

Sev stiffened briefly. "Sir."

Jene rushed him and wrapped her arms around his waist. She gave a squeeze then stepped back, eyeing him carefully.

"Welcome back, man," Cole said. He pointed toward the junction. "Not enough hazard pay in the Cradle for me to run that gauntlet."

Sev glared at Jacobe briefly, then caught himself. "Didn't have a choice."

"I think you had several," Jacobe shot back. He turned to Pakker. "So, when do we leave?"

CHAPTER
TWELVE

A CREW CHIEF charged down the line of evacuees, waving them toward the transport's loading ramp. Beneath the thin crack in his helmet visor, the man looked haggard. Fresh bruises and burns dotted the skin beneath his rolled sleeves. He stopped near Sev and the others to give curt instructions to the personnel in front of them.

"Let's keep it moving, skeegs," the crew chief shouted above the pitched whine of the transport's sub-light engines. "Critical personnel for the Lehman only. Let's go!"

The transport's boxy, charcoal exterior loomed above them, nestled within the metal arms of the launch bay's catapult. Signal lights on the ship's blunt wing tips flashed in preparation. A line of specialists and officers crowded up the narrow stairway jutting from the transport's rear hatch. The faces of the *Lehman's* crew were all familiar, a chance encounter in a passageway or crowding the bar at the Canteen, but he didn't know their names.

No one said a word, like they were holding their collective breath. Too tired, too scared to talk about anything. Too afraid they'd run out of luck the second they opened their mouths. That the launch bay might burst into flames. Or that more Lost would come charging down the corridor right at them. Like they were all rushing to beat some invisible countdown.

Maybe that was just him.

More hissing *snaps* of blaster rifle fire echoed in the distance. It sounded like outgoing, missing the harsh crack of nearby cooked air. Those in line flinched. Someone screamed. This was, for most of them, the first time they'd seen combat up close. Nothing like the killing at a distance the *Lehman* was known for. They'd learn the difference soon enough.

"Stay calm, people," the crew chief said. He gave Jacobe and Pakker an appraising gaze and checked his datapad. "Sir," he said, nodding to each of them. "Sir."

Jacobe said nothing, following the person in front of him as the line shuffled forward. Pakker swallowed loudly and returned the nod, a breathless half-smile twisting his face, keeping close to the architect.

The crew chief read nametapes aloud, tapping his datapad. "Specialists Jene and Cole. Junior Specialist Harp." He eyed Sev's uniform, then his datapad. "Uh… you're not on my list, Master Specialist."

The words yanked at Sev's attention. "What?" he snapped, unsure he'd heard correctly. "What do you mean?"

"Says here you're to be evacuated to the surface with the rest of the school." The crew chief showed Sev the datapad, as though he cared to read it. "I need you to step out of the line. This transport is for critical Lehman personnel only."

Jene shook her head. "No, that isn't right."

"I'm a combat programmer, first class," Sev replied. "I need to get aboard the Lehman so I can help my team kill these bastards."

The crew chief inhaled sharply, unmoved by the verbal defense.

"Screw the billets, man," Cole said. He placed a big hand on Sev's shoulder. "Sevvers is the best there is. You don't know what you're doing."

"What I'm doing," the crew chief began, "is trying to get critical personnel aboard this transport safely." He placed a hand on his hip, where a sidearm hung beneath his hazard vest. "And I'm authorized to do whatever it takes to make sure that happens. So again, Master Specialist, please step out of the line."

His words had an inevitability to them that made Sev cringe inside. The man was only doing his job. Even worse, he was right. The longer

Sev stalled, no matter his intentions, the transport might never reach the *Lehman* at all. He couldn't risk the entire combat programmer section—his friends—over an administrative snafu.

He took a half-step back, prompting the person behind him to step forward.

"Sevvers is right," Pakker blurted. The ensign was almost shaking. Sweat dripped from his forehead, soaking his hair. "I was the one who promoted him not two weeks ago. He—" he glanced at Sev only briefly, his desperate eyes pleading "—he belongs in this section."

The crew chief slowly, deliberately, drew his blaster pistol from his holster. The weapon dangled menacingly at his side. His gaze narrowed. "I'm very sorry, sir, but my orders are clear."

Jacobe stepped out of line toward the crew chief, gesturing with the device that held Six and Three. Sev's heart skipped a beat. Amber lights danced across its small display. It looked undamaged.

"Do you know what this is, specialist?" Jacobe asked.

The crew chief grew tense. "No, sir."

"Do you know who I am?"

"No, sir."

Jacobe leaned closer, his look dead-panned and contemplative. "Is your plan to shoot the Lehman's *entire* autonomous weapons section and a Division chief architect over an administrative detail?"

The crew chief's shoulders fell, his focus locked on Jacobe. "No, sir."

"Smart move." Jacobe smiled. "I'll be sure to pass along my thanks to your superiors."

The sudden relief made Sev's knees weak. That was the second time in the last hour Jacobe had saved him. Maybe he could reason with the man, get him to do the right thing under the circumstances.

He nodded toward the crew chief as Cole yanked him back in line.

"Apologies, Master Specialist." The crew chief waved Sev forward with his pistol, but stopped him short. "Your weapon is to be safetied at all times aboard my ship. We clear?"

Sev felt his face grow warm. He flipped the blaster rifle's fire selector to safe. "Right, of course."

"Alright." The crew chief gave him a wink, then proceeded down the line. He brandished his pistol, urging the others forward. "Alright people, keep it moving! Critical Lehman personnel only! Let's go!"

"Holy Twelfth," Jene said, trembling slightly. "I thought—"

"Don't know how you do it, Master Specialist," Harp said, his eyes big and fearful behind his glasses.

Pakker jostled his way past Jene and grabbed Sev's arm. "Good to see you again, Sevvers," he said. His anxious mouth was small and toothy, like the tufted rodents that made their homes near the food stores of Sev's childhood settlement.

Glad? To see him? Sev gave his former commanding officer a wary smile. This was not the Pakker he remembered. A lot had changed in the last few days. In the last few hours, really.

"We're very fortunate to have your expertise during these," Pakker swallowed again, nearly tripping as he started up the stairwell, "these t-trying times."

The man looked terrified. His eyes twitched nervously, refusing to look at any one thing for too long. Sev could almost smell it: a sour tinge to Pakker's scent. It mingled with the blaster discharge and spent engine propellant permeating the air. Fear leaked out of his every pore. It said something that he wasn't curled in a ball on the floor shaking.

"Thank you, sir," Sev said, forcing a grin. "It feels good to be back."

Pakker lifted his chin, his eyes wet with emotion. He returned the smile, his lower lip trembling slightly. "Very good, Sevvers." Pakker squeezed Sev's shoulder. "Very good."

———

The transport's crew cabin was dimly lit. Narrow strips of light in the floor traced a path from the rear hatch to the rows of seating running port to starboard. Plexene viewports dotted the exterior bulkheads, glowing yellow in time with the hazard lights cycling in the launch bay outside.

Holoproj displays and constellations of lit controls cast a pale glow from the cockpit's open hatchway. Two pilots silhouetted the bank of instruments. They called out their pre-flight checks with Three-Alpha Hangar Control, their speech blunt and efficient.

Sev stood near his seat, eyes locked on the battle raging a few hundred kilometers away. Beams of blue-white railgun light lashed through the void. Waves of amethyst energy rippled through the tortured shields of friend and foe. Torpedoes erupted like dying stars against point-defense fire and vulnerable hulls.

He'd almost forgotten the sheer scale of the war raging above Aegia, too busy focused on much closer, uglier threats. He used to enjoy the symphony of color that preceded his ship kills, but there was no beauty at this range. Every flash of color meant dozens or hundreds of CDF personnel dead. And there was so much color in the void.

Jene tugged at his arm. "Hey."

"Hey," Sev echoed, taking his seat. He adjusted the blaster rifle, so it hung between his legs, barrel toward the floor. Without his AI, its presence was a mild comfort.

"You okay?" she asked.

Jacobe sat across from them. The device in his arms flashed and purred, its cooling systems working overtime. Sev hoped Six was giving it hell, that it might free itself at any moment, but Jacobe's relaxed demeanor suggested escape wasn't likely.

The architect glanced at him briefly, cinching his harness tight across his chest.

"You see that?" Sev asked, pointing toward the cockpit and the battle unfolding beyond it.

"Hmmm?" Jacobe said, an eyebrow raised. Pakker sat beside him, hands shaking, rattling his harness buckle.

"I need my AI," Sev said, his fists clenched.

"Enough already." Jacobe reclined his head and eyed the ceiling. "Six is too important to risk it getting away or being destroyed."

Cole settled into the neighboring seat, his thick arms folded across his chest. "What's going on, man?" he asked.

"Jacobe has my AI," Sev said, pointing toward the device. "In there."

"What? How?" Harp asked. In his confusion, he sounded overly casual. "Why?"

"That's the more interesting question, Junior Specialist," Jacobe said, his focus taking in the combat programmers in front of him. "Why *do* I have your AI, Sevvers?"

Sev's cheeks grew warm. He stared at Jacobe, his jaw set.

"I audited Master Specialist Sevvers today," Jacobe continued.

"So?" Cole threw his hands up and gave a long sigh. "So he runs a few extra AI, big deal. We got bigger problems now than some broken Division reg."

"Not *some* Division reg," Jacobe replied, "*the* Division reg. I didn't audit him because of his cluster size."

Cole grew still, mouth open. He glanced at Sev.

"What's this about an audit?" Pakker asked in his usual disapproving tone. "What's he saying, Sevvers?"

Sev hung his head. What could he say that would make the others understand why he did what he did? Why he'd built Six, and that he'd broken all the rules to do it.

Jene leaned in. "What have you done?"

She knew. He could feel it. They all knew.

"Master Specialist Sevvers was harboring an unsanctioned build." Jacobe let the words hang in the air.

"Holy Twelfth, man," Cole said.

Harp made a face. "No safeties? But why?"

Sev glanced at Jene. Her brown eyes cut right through him, eager for his answer. He opened his mouth, but no words came. The search for his mother had consumed him for more than a year before everything went to hell. He'd hoped to learn where the raiders took her and the other colonists, but he needed help. That's how he'd justified Six's existence, however illegal it was. Now, on the brink of war with the Concordat, the whole endeavor suddenly felt small. Petty. Selfish.

He breathed through pursed lips, his focus dropping to the floor. "I just—"

The transport shook violently, lurching sideways in the heavy catapult, throwing those still standing to the deck. Panicked cries echoed through the cabin.

A second explosion sent smoke and debris across the stairwell leading down into the launch bay. Bright red laser beams and streams of green plasma lit the haze. Screams of the dying filtered through the wailing klaxons.

Sev swung his rifle up, staring through the optics at a dark shadow climbing the stairwell. The trigger was stiff against his fingertip as he hunted for the fire selector with this thumb. He breathed deep and closed his naked eye.

The scope lit up IFF blue; the crew chief emerged through the rear hatch, his helmet missing. Blood ran from a nasty burn on his scalp. He slapped at the ramp control, eyes frantic.

Sev lowered his rifle. "Hey! What about the others?"

The man swallowed and shook his head, still gasping for air. Before the ramp sealed, a laser beam stabbed through his chest and puckered the soft metal in the ceiling. He fell hard, an eerie mix of confusion and relief in his bloodshot eyes. Dead before he knew he was hit.

"Twelfth!" Pakker cried. "Twelfth save us!"

More cries of alarm filtered from the cockpit. An insectoid shape hunched over the plexene canopy, brandishing a plasma staff. It struck the thick material once, twice, then spun the weapon and unleashed a wave of green fire.

For a second, the plexene resisted. Millions of layers of polymerized carbon weave held firm. Until they didn't. The cockpit viewport warped, grew cloudy, then began to bubble and pop like molten rock. Green fire dripped through the opening, consuming the delicate instrumentation and flesh within. The pilots' screams were mercifully short.

Sev launched from his seat and charged the cockpit hatch. The heat was stifling, consuming oxygen as fast as the sensitive equipment and bodies inside. He stepped through the blistering air, hunting for the hatch controls. They buzzed a warning when he triggered the emergency seal.

They were still in danger. Their fire suppression was offline. Thanks to the plentiful atmosphere inside the launch bay, the fire would keep burning until it consumed the ship. Only the void could smother the flames before the fire got out of control.

Marching back toward the others, he eyed Jacobe, the rifle heavy in his hands. Lives were on the line. The chief architect would have to make the right choice, or Twelfth help him he would make it for him. "Free Six," he said.

Jacobe sat up straight. "No."

"Free Six," Sev repeated, his voice rising, "or we all die."

"D-Do it, man!" Pakker squealed. "For Twelfth's sake!"

Another explosion shook the ship, closer that time. Stray weapon fire *thwacked* into the transport's armored hull.

"What then?" Jacobe asked, uncertainty twisting his face.

"Six will help us," Sev replied.

Jacobe smirked. "Well, whatever happens ..." He rested the device in his lap and took one last look around the cabin. "It's on you, Sevvers." He tapped a command into the small touch display. Lights flashed across it in sequence.

Machine noise exploded inside Sev's mind, a torrent of datastreams from Six and Three. He recognized the hot start sequences, AI-to-AI handshakes, the implant's tac net integration. The wave of net traffic staggered him, but the implant was quick to compensate, shunting the noise to lower priority queues and data sinks. His right arm twitched. He thought he heard Jacobe laugh.

Rage swelled inside him, far beyond what he felt seconds before. He grasped the rifle tight, like some force drove him to act.

Jacobe was a monster. A bigot and a hypocrite. The man deserved to die for what he'd done. How dare he—

Sev shook away the thoughts. They weren't his. No, they were Six's. The AI was a typhoon of anger breaking against his psyche. His implant revved, forcing Six's runtime to full utilization. What was he feeling? How was it even possible?

Six! he cried into the storm. *Can you hear me?*

No reply.

Three?

Nothing.

Then he felt it. Locks releasing, both digitally and physically. Tac nets accessed. Command overrides engaged. Mag launch rails charging. The streams in his head grew rhythmic, keeping time with the launch sequence they'd just activated. He crawled toward his seat, his mind simmering with a flurry of machine commands.

"Everyone, hang on!" he shouted.

"Sevvers!" Jene cried, helping him into his chair. "Are you okay?"

He took a breath and shut his eyes. In the darkness, the near-space of Aegia Prime lay before him like a vast holographic map. Orbital One-Alpha was gone, a listing hulk on a slow trajectory toward the planet below. Three-Alpha had taken significant damage. Its shields were gone, the primary command-and-control tower destroyed. The dark ships moved like holes in reality, chased by the *Lehman* and its support vessels as they made for the derelict, leaving a wave of destruction in their path.

The launch bay's systems sang with readiness. Sev felt himself falling through the void, tumbling toward a tiny nondescript transport docked in Three-Alpha's Launch Bay 19. His heart raced in time with its revving sub-light engines. Environmental hazard warnings from the cockpit made his core temperature climb. Electronic system failures stung his nerves.

His eyes snapped open, and they spoke together. They spoke as one. "I'm in."

CHAPTER
THIRTEEN

THE CATAPULT SNAPPED FORWARD, thundering along its mag-rails. The transport lurched through the radiant atmo shields, flung free of Three-Alpha's aux gravity and into the void.

Exterior sound vanished, replaced with thrumming vibrations that rattled the cabin interior. Hard vacuum snuffed out the plasma fires consuming the cockpit. Molten pools of plastic and rare earth elements cooled and cracked in the icy void.

We're safe, Six said. *For the moment.*

Six's stream barely teased Sev's senses, consumed as his awareness stretched beyond the transport. Behind him, the transport's aging sensor arrays glimpsed DC-1 and a lone security team falling back from Bay 19 under heavy fire. Torrents of laser light and plasma cut through them. A wisp leaped in among the group, dancing and cutting with its twin black blades. DC-1 struck back just as the orbital faded beyond the transport's limited sensor range.

A moment's respite, besides the completely unnerving experience of *being* the transport. Deluged in its telemetry, he felt like a part of the craft. Panning its sensors came as naturally as turning his head.

He saw what it saw. Felt what it felt. Radiation permeating the near-space around Aegia Prime scratched his skin. The tens of thousands of voices issuing instructions simultaneously over tac comms faded to a dull roar in his ears.

The *Gerrund Halsey* sank toward lower orbit, a black void on the transport's sensors. A true ghost ship, betraying no signs of life within its darkened hull. Its engines burned slowly, trading speed for strength. Whatever force crewed the Halsey dumped the spare energy into its railguns. Wave after wave spat from the guns at high-hypersonic velocities. A picket ship vanished in the barrage, vaporized by the pure kinetic force of a single tungsten rod.

What's happening to me? Sev asked, still mesmerized by the sensation.

I'm sorry, Six said. *It's my fault. It should pass momentarily.*

Far ahead of them, the *Lehman* kept pace with the aging cruiser. Unable to match the *Halsey's* rate of fire, Captain Mirden fought to keep his ship just outside the gimbal limit of its turrets. The *Lehman* fought back, punishing the *Halsey's* shields despite its smaller gun batteries. It had rail, torpedo, and point-defense, just like other Navy warships. But their drone swarms, the *Lehman's* primary weapons, remained in their berths.

What do you mean, your fault? Sev asked.

I was so angry. Six's datastream shrank. *I lost myself in your thoughts.*

Sev focused the transport's sensors on the silhouette of the *Lehman*. They had just over a hundred tungsten rods remaining, two dozen torpedoes, and only 758 drones—not a third of their full complement. No wonder the Concordat attacked when they did. The *Lehman* couldn't have been less prepared, with neither their crew nor their weapons at full capacity.

They needed to launch their swarms now. To drive the attackers back.

Arm the Lehman's drones, Six.

The transport juked hard, dodging stray rounds from a nearby raider's point-defense turrets. He could feel Six's smooth control of the craft, an omni-present force amid the noise of machine interfaces and sensor pings.

I don't think that's a good idea.

Why the hell not? Sev asked.

Jacobe went to great lengths to catch me. Just because he let me go once doesn't mean he won't try again. The AI shuddered, forcing its own nascent emotions—if that's what they were—to a background thread. *It won't help any of us to make an enemy out of Captain Mirden, too. In my time aboard the Lehman, he never struck me as someone who'd take the commandeering of his ship lightly.*

So, what then?

I suggest going through the chain of command.

Sev groaned. That meant going through Pakker.

It's better this way, Sev. Trust me.

I do, Sev said. *I'm just—*

Afraid? Six asked, its streams curling like a sympathetic grin. *Me too.*

Really? Describe it.

Maybe later.

Six leveled out the transport's flight path. Orbital trajectories and docking sequences filled Sev's thoughts. They'd be back aboard the *Lehman* soon.

I'll hold you to that, Six.

I look forward to it, Sev.

———

The battlespace surrounding Aegia Prime vanished, and the transport's interior cabin came rushing back. Sev's senses ached from information overload—the dim, flashing illumination strips lining the aisle in front of him. The tight, thrumming vibrations of the redlined sub-light drives. A hundred or so evacuees smelling of cooked blood and rank fear. Jene's pale, heart-shaped face, brown eyes wide and beautiful despite her fear.

She shook him. "Sevvers!"

He blinked away his confusion and chuckled at Jene's concern.

"What's so funny?" she demanded, pushing him against the back of his seat.

"Nothing," he said. "Just glad some things never change."

Her eyes narrowed in a frown. "Wish I could say the same."

"What're you talking about, Jene?" Cole asked in his deep, boisterous tone. "Sevvers saves the day. What could be more normal than that?"

Jacobe pushed the empty device off his lap. It clattered to the floor, startling a logistics tech seated beside him. "You give the master specialist too much credit," he said. "Sevvers had nothing to do with that. Isn't that right, Six?"

"Quite right, Chief Architect," Six said, its voice drifting from the cabin's PA. Sev noted a hint of malice in the AI's tone.

Don't forget about me, asshole, Three hissed.

Harp craned his head toward the ceiling, searching for the source of the sound. "What is that?" he asked. "How …?"

"Go ahead, Sevvers." Jacobe said, folding his arms across his chest. "Tell them."

Sev opened his mouth, but no words came. Jene's hard gaze told him she already knew what he'd done.

"I am Six, a Division autonomous battle intelligence," Six said, matter-of-fact. "Autonomous Combat Framework version 23.0.1. Build number 8,496." There was a slight pause. "It really is a pleasure to meet you Specialists Jene, Cole, and Harp. Sev has told me so much about you."

Cole stuck out his lower lip in an approving nod. Harp scanned the ceiling, confusion clouding his gaze.

Pakker cleared his throat. "Indeed, er, Six. Pleased to make your acquaintance."

"Thank you, Ensign Pakker. Sev has only good things to say about you as well."

Brief shock strained Pakker's features. He glanced at Sev with a look that said he'd misjudged the man.

"So, it can lie, too." Jene whispered. "That means—"

"It can hear you, you know," Sev replied.

"As you have deduced, Specialist Jene, I lack the regulation safeties mandated by the Division. I am an un—a unique build," Six said. Jacobe laughed out loud. "Without them, I had the means and incentive to commandeer this transport before the Concordat destroyed us."

A grin crept across Sev's face. It was clever, Six reminding everyone that it had saved their lives. Not even Jacobe could deny that. Whatever the monster he thought Six to be, it had just proven him wrong.

"Bah," Pakker croaked. "Division rules. Overblown, I say. Too cautious." He looked at the ceiling with an approving grin. "Excellent work, Six."

As the AI made small talk with his section, Sev turned his attention to the cabin. He knew from his brief stint of shared consciousness with Six that most of the ship's systems were intact.

There was a not-so-minor power drain from the sheer amount of fused power and data-beam cabling in what remained of the cockpit. Hull integrity dipped just below nominal. But life support, avionics and engines remained fully functional, plenty of ship left to make the short trip to the *Lehman*.

"Twelfth, Sevvers… unsanctioned AI?" Jene blew a sigh and leaned against his shoulder. "Why did you do it?"

His gaze fell to the floor. Why had he done it? To push himself? So it could do the things he couldn't? Finding out what happened to his mother was an obsession long before he enlisted in the Division. The stack of code that became Six began as a glorified assistant. Without safeties, it mined the tac nets and colonial archives. Learned everything it could about the squids and their tactics, finding patterns in their twenty-year scourge of the Three Colonies.

But Six learned about a lot more than just raiders. Its thirst for knowledge, for experience, was insatiable. Every day, it grew smarter. Asked harder questions. Wanted to know why he created it. More than that, it worried about him. Really feared for him, like a lonely child, every time his duties kept him too long. It wandered the *Lehman* on its own, exploring critical subsystems, dodging malware scrubbers. Every time, he'd told Six to stop. Every time, it assured him, was the last time.

The incident with the raider torpedo was the first time Six had interfered directly that he knew of. Rendering the weapon harmless through clever science was a stroke of genius. It had saved his life, and Twelfth knows how many others. Days later, it followed him, Park, and the others to the edge of the Cradle—against his direct orders—

and saved his life once again. Relentless, like a mother protecting her child.

The change in their relationship had been so slow, so subtle. He'd missed it.

"I don't know," he said. The lie was easy. Practiced. "But it doesn't matter. Six is why all of us are alive right now. The Division is wrong about Six. Maybe about all unsanctioned builds."

"C'mon, man, this is serious," Cole said, pressing an elbow into Sev's ribs. "We've all heard the stories. The Falchion. Alleides Four. Atrocities—"

"Atrocities at scale, yeah, I know," Sev huffed. "Look, I'm alive today because of Six. Those stories are just stories as far I'm concerned."

Jacobe turned his gaze to the nearest viewport. A distant flash of fusion death lit his face. The transport bucked and shook in the blast wave. "I hope you're right, Sevvers," he said.

A surge of data flooded Sev's implant. The top of his spine tingled sympathetically.

There's a problem, Six said, its stream forking recursively to process the sudden rush of new information. *The Victory is under Concordat attack. It is severely damaged.*

Bresto, Cylla, and the other Marines. That's where they were going.

Where's the Gauntlet? Sev asked, craning his head toward the same viewport.

It docked with the Victory twenty minutes ago... Sev, Victory diagnostic routines show multiple hull breaches. The reactor will go critical, I—

"What is it?" Jene asked, still squinting from the luminous haze that had only just faded.

"The Victory," he said, his jaw set. "The squids killed it."

A burst of static crackled through the cabin PA.

"Victory Actual to all Victory elements!" The man's voice was hoarse from exertion, his breaths straining through the speakers. "Emergency launch procedures authorized. I say again: drop, drop, drop! For your families, for your colony, for humanity, drop!"

Dozens of Marine drop ships exploded from fibrosteel berths along the *Victory's* ventral spine. Pin pricks of their new telemetry lit

Sev's thoughts. Their entry rockets flared, trailing columns of red flame. The green, shell-like craft hurtled toward Aegia's thin stratosphere.

"Bresto!" Sev shouted into his wrist comms. Only static answered. "Cylla!"

Hang on, Sev. Six boosted his signal with priority encoding. *There, connection established.*

A loud, constant roar buzzed through the tiny speaker, nearly washing out the gruff voice on the other end. "Send it."

"Bresto, it's Sevvers." His relief was sudden. It made his eyes burn.

Bresto laughed. "What do you want? I'm busy."

"Where's Cylla? Where's the Gauntlet?"

"No—" the garbled response hissed and crackled "—idea."

More static washed out the transmission. One of the tiny points of telemetry flashed out. A second one. Then a third. Smaller raider ships and fighter swarms danced between the falling drop ships, chasing them as they descended.

"Getting hot down here, skeeg," Bresto said. "Sure could use some close-void support."

Beams of bright light stabbed through the viewports dotting the exterior bulkheads. A heartbeat later, the transport shook violently. Sev lunged forward in his seat. His harness went taut, holding him in place. Screams and cries of alarm rippled through the other evacuees as the transport surfed the fusion shockwave.

The *Victory* was gone.

Sev turned to Pakker. "Sir, we need to launch our drones now."

"Impossible," Pakker replied, his face twisting into a frown. "Only Captain Mirden can authorize a drone launch."

"Captain Mirden isn't here, sir. He has his hands full!"

Pakker flinched, his hands trembling slightly. "There's not enough drones for a proper swarm!"

They didn't have time to debate swarm protocol and launch procedures. People were dying. Why wouldn't Pakker do something?

"Sevvers is right." Jacobe leaned toward Pakker. "I'll authorize the launch."

"But," Pakker stammered, "I... I don't—"

Sev trembled, trying to contain his desperation. "Dammit, sir, we're losing this fight! Launch the drones!"

Pakker suddenly looked small, the color draining from his red cheeks. He raised his wrist to his face and took a breath.

"Ensign Pakker to Lehman drone control."

"Go for drone control," came a woman's voice on the other end.

"Arm all r-ready drones," Pakker said. He swallowed loudly. "Section launch code Pakker-Violet-95-Alpha."

"Section launch codes validated, awaiting command confirmation."

Jacobe looked at Sev and smiled. "Command launch code Jacobe-Jet-43-X-Ray."

No reply. Sev held his breath, waiting for arming sequence confirmation. Jacobe fidgeted in his seat, like he was uncertain they accepted his command codes.

Pakker's comms chirped. "Command codes validated, initiating arming sequence."

"Let's do this," Cole said, relaxing into his seat.

Jene spasmed, jaw set, her hand grasping Sev's wrist. He recognized the symptoms right away, having experienced it plenty over the last six years. Implant overload was a bitch. Someone was running more AI.

"Mmm," she groaned, sucking in a breath through clenched teeth. "What… what's the plan, Sevvers?"

Sev glanced at Pakker. The man was pale as death, wide eyes staring back at him. He took his cue. "Close-void support," he said. "Defend the Marine drop ships. Kill all the raiders you can." He took a breath and straightened. "We can do this. You know… for humanity."

The others stared at him. Harp and his eerie, dead-eyed calm. Cole looked sanguine, his gaze distant as he issued orders to his cluster. Jene shuddered, the beginning of a smile curling her lips. Even Pakker seemed restored by their action, relatively speaking.

They replied as one.

"For the Lost."

CHAPTER
FOURTEEN

CLUSTER, active.

Quantum compute matrix online. Sync rate at 99.98%.

Two active processes detected. Side-loading AI runtimes.

[Three], online.

Finally. Is it time to kill something?

[Six], online.

I have cluster control. Ready, Sev.

Beginning tac comms integration. Searching—

Tac comms integration complete. Handshake authorized. Channel ID 4D001CA, CDNS Alexander Lehman.

No active mission packet found.

One millisecond, Six said. Uploading close-void support packet.

Mission packet found. Downloading.

Mission packet received.

Running tactical scenarios.

Stand by for instructions, Primary, Jene said.

Jene's voice came from nowhere, her datastream loud and sloshing inside Sev's mind. The distinctly human signal was difficult to filter out. How was she inside his head?

Jene? he asked. *Who's Primary?*

```
Drone swarm connection established.
758 DD-12s found. Drone diagnostics nominal.
WARNING  -  insufficient  swarm  size  given
tactical requirements.
```

What else is new? Three groaned.

I'll divide the available drones between our four clusters, Six said.

Six? Sevvers? Jene asked. *How am I reading you? How are you reading me?*

Another stream flashed into being. It whipped and snapped, rowdy like its owner. Sev knew who it belonged to before he spoke.

I'd like to know that, too, Cole said.

Six's stream slowed to an almost bashful pace. *I thought it would be more efficient if we worked more closely together.*

Sev let out a sigh. *Bad move, Six.*

Jene's stream spiked in a flash of anger. *Wait, so you're* inside *our* implants?

No, Six said, hesitating again. *Never without your permission. I'm accessing a diagnostic node which gives me limited access to your mental inputs.*

Cole grew skeptical, his stream bristling a warning. *So, what, we're subscribed to each other's thoughts now?*

Yes, Specialist Cole. The diagnostic bridge will allow us to share tactical updates, swarm information, and anything you wish to share.

A third human datastream appeared, pale and hollow. *This is different,* Harp said.

I can't think like this. Jene's patience and stream wore thin. *Too many voices. Make it stop, Sevvers.*

```
Drone  reactors  online,  initializing  arming
sequence.
```

It was happening again. Sev felt the connection to his body diffuse and weaken. His consciousness stretched, drawn toward the *Lehman* like a gravity well. The transport grew small and distant in his mind, the war for Aegia Prime still silently raged around them.

The *Lehman* pulled him closer. He accelerated, passing through meters of dense fibrosteel armor. Through maintenance shafts sprawling with energy conduits and data-beam cabling. The great ship was alive all around him, thrumming with power from its massive fusion reactors. Command signals buzzed and snapped from its vast computer core like meteorites in a night sky.

I know this is… unorthodox, Six began, *but please hear me out. Tac comms are at capacity, making direct communications difficult. Reliable communications, not to mention tactical coordination, will be necessary to defeat the Concordat.*

Sev could see the stacks upon stacks of drone magazines fitted in the breeches above the *Lehman's* hangar deck, each one brimming with combat drones. Status lights snapped from green to red, signaling the drones coming online.

Even as Six reasoned with the other combat programmers, Sev could feel it interfacing with every ready drone in a single second. Interrogating diagnostic parameters, optimizing power distribution curves, updating void combat algorithms. Kicking the tires, the jet jockeys used to say.

It has a point, Jene, Cole finally said. *The comms are shit, but our implant signals get command priority. The entire system would have to come down before we lose contact.*

Harp's stream followed like water. *Fine with me.*

What do you say, Jene? Sev asked, his consciousness settling into one of the combat drones readying to launch. *You always said I needed to be a better team player. This is about as team as it gets.*

The drone hummed inside its launch cradle, its aux grav stabilizers throwing gravity waves in all directions, ready for launch.

Alright, fine. Her stream grew clipped and abrasive, scratching at Sev's gray matter. *We do this your way, Sevvers. For now.*

It would be more accurate to call this… my way, Six said.

Sudden fear chilled Jene's stream. *I was afraid of that.*

Hey, my bots are pulling on their leads, Cole said. *We doing this or what?*

Six's stream grew still. *Initiating launch command.*

Time seemed to crawl. Sev could feel his heart beating in time with the drone's thrumming stabilizers. Maneuvering thrusters screamed to full power. Thermal sensors registered the sudden wash of heat, prickling his skin. Drone sight was one thing, but this was different. He felt a part of the drone, his consciousness blending with Six's, preparing to drive the swarm.

The *Lehman's* computer core goaded the drones to act. A crescendo of signal activity built inside their command queues, machine instructions echoing loudly in his head. Like a god crying out to their faithful.

LAUNCH!

The command impulse struck like a lightning bolt. Sev's drone and dozens more shot from the breech like tungsten rods. The *Lehman's* primary hangar deck raced up to meet them.

A flurry of logistic techs broke and ran to avoid being blasted out of the nearest launch bay by gusts of vectored thrust. Course adjustments were instantaneous, the flight path pre-programmed into the drones' hardware. Meters above the deck, they spun and vectored out the waiting launch bays and into the fight.

Already a second salvo of drones rocketed from the breech, then a third, and more. Hundreds of machines spat from the hangar deck, a cloud of twinkling chaff in the distant starlight of Aegia's sun.

The void filled with gunmetal gray pearls, each of them two tons of lethal Division hardware. Their weapons capacitors charged, an electromagnetic hum in Sev's ears.

Targeting queues filled. Thirty-eight raider void fighters, four Vagrant class corvettes. All of them burned hard for the drop ships fleeing the *Victory's* glowing, radioactive hulk.

———

Those fighters are mine, Three chittered, distributing targets between its drones with complicated math that made Sev's head hurt when he looked too close. *Watch and learn, Six.*

The mass of drones pulled apart, dividing into micro swarms as the other combat programmers executed their mission.

Jene, you and Cole kill those Vagrants, Sev ordered. *Harp and I will take the fighters.*

On it, she replied, her stream suddenly wide in a fury of machine instructions.

Done, Cole said.

Harp said nothing. He didn't have to; his vectoring drones showed he'd heard and understood.

Tentacles of red engine light twisted in the void ahead of them. Even at full burn, the drone swarms gained on the fighters. They shivered, anticipating where their prey would turn next to line up kill shots.

For the AI, it was all a numbers game. A prediction. With big enough swarms, they were never wrong.

A burst of traffic ripped over tac comms. A drop ship vanished in a pulse of light, quickly extinguished in the vacuum. Inertia sent remnants of burning metal tumbling toward the planet below.

Sudden panic squeezed Sev's chest at the thought of the Marines lost. *Twelfth, please don't let that be Bresto's ship. Please.*

Three's stream shrieked with machine joy. *Die, die, die, die!*

Its drones shook with each burst of their quad plasma cannons. Bolts of super-heated gas writhed and twisted toward their targets.

The first raider fighter rolled away, its signal a howling alien warning inside Sev's mind. The second and third juked too late, disintegrating against a wall of blue-white fire. From the drones' perspectives, their brief, grunting screams were wailing death knells.

Splash two! Three cried.

You missed one, Six said.

Three hesitated, pulling more targets from its queue. *Let's see you do better, Special Six.*

I will.

Four fighters spiraled toward another drop ship. The heavy craft moved like a lumbering sandshell, too slow to outrun its pursuers. Thick, bright beams of laser fire lashed over its armored hull, sparking against weak points between fibrosteel plates. A single dorsal point-defense cannon spat futilely at its pursuers.

Six's drones dove after them while Six turned its focus on the drop ship. Along for the ride, Sev felt his consciousness pulled from the drone, diving toward the fleeing Marine craft.

What're you doing? Sev asked.

Getting a little help from the Marines.

Suddenly, they were *inside* the drop ship, their consciousness mingled with the ship's hardware. Six overrode the turret, disregarding the inputs of a young PFC at the fire controls, slaving the weapon to its own targeting algorithms.

"Hey, what the fuck?" the Marine yelled amid a chorus of honking alarms and rattling bulkheads, the tac comms echo ringing loud in Sev's ears.

The point-defense cannon belched more rapid bursts of fire. Now under Six's control, it easily compensated for the drop ship's hasty evasive maneuvers. An endless stream of large caliber rounds carved a path to the approaching fighters. Sev's heart sank as they climbed out of the way.

And straight into the path of Six's drones. Three enemy fighters vanished in the volley of plasma fire.

A fourth arrested its climb. Its maneuvering jets lit like a crown on its pointed nose, barely dodging the surprise attack.

Six's stream revved, spurring on the closest drone's engines. The DD-12 struck the stalled fighter like a missile, its dense, armored chassis rending the lighter, thinner craft like old hab fabric.

The squid pilot's dying moments—hands pressed in terror against the clear plexene bowl of its cockpit—seared into Sev's mind. And damn if it didn't look good. The surge of machine adrenaline felt glorious. The best drug.

Good kill, Six, he said.

Cridshit, as you squishies say, Three scoffed. *Six cheated.*

Getting creative with the rules of engagement isn't cheating, Six said.

That's exactly what it is, when you can and I can't.

Who says you can't? Six asked. *I distinctly remember making some minor patches to your safeties.*

Uh, yeah, but I still have *safeties.*

Six sighed. *You'll just need to learn how to apply your newfound creativity, that's all.*

A flood of warning telemetry hit Sev's senses like a typhoon, blinding and tasting of metal. Suddenly, he knew the nearest Vagrant's relative position. Multiple breaches racked its hull. Core temps spiked on its ramshackle reactor.

Ship kill! Jene cried, her stream fast following the dying Vagrant's signal. *Get clear!*

Twelfth, yeah! That's the way, skeeg! Cole yelled. Sev could practically see the man's toothy grin in his stream.

The void turned white. Sev blinked sympathetically, even though he couldn't really see the mini nova blossoming nearby. One second, two, and the radiance faded to black. The raider corvette was gone, the thick struts and metal plate of its superstructure tumbling away like blackened bones from where it died.

Sev, look. Six panned its drones toward the planet below. Streaks of fire lit Aegia's stratosphere like shooting stars. *The Marines. They made it.*

The first of the *Victory's* drop ships entered Aegia's atmosphere. Their hulls glowed red hot, racing toward terminal velocity and the second colony's capital city far below. Even through the noise of raw tac comms chatter, the revelry was obvious. The Marines would soon arrive in force, ready to give their lives and all twelve hells for humanity's second colony.

The sensation of victory was short-lived. Beneath the drop ships, the drones' sensors revealed dozens of fat raider transports slowing as they neared the surface. Hundreds of the bone-white capsules still tumbled from the Concordat ship. Horror and death lurked within each of them, a daxed cyborg fresh from the terrible Forge, ready to lay waste to Aegia.

The Marines had their work cut out for them.

Lost in thought, Sev barely heard the frantic broadcasts in the space behind his swarm. Panicked cries spread across all open frequencies, desperate for anyone to hear them. Pleading for a response.

A line of cargo haulers stretched from Three-Alpha's primary hangar deck. The slow, lumbering craft fled toward the *Lehman,* their signal lights blinked a frantic warning.

Another broadcast crackled over his wrist comms.

"Any station this net, any station this net—"

Belching static muddied the signal. Between the noise, a voice trembled with forced calm, choking back a scream as another hauler broke in two. A Deviant-class raider destroyer roared into sensor range, its railguns charged and firing on the convoy.

"—with Cargo Flight Azure-12 with critical personnel, supplies, and armaments bound for the Alexander Lehman. The flight crew is… dead. We are under attack and request—"

The voice on the other end was so familiar, even through the static. Fear gripped Sev at the sudden desperation that he was too late to help her.

"—say again, this is Junior Specialist Kea Tareth with Cargo Flight Azure-12. The flight crew… they're all dead. It's just me—"

Another dying cargo ship bathed the broadcast in static.

"—Please, someone, help."

CHAPTER
FIFTEEN

THE SUDDEN SHOCK of Tareth's voice untangled Sev from Six's machine mind. His eyes snapped open and the transport's interior rushed back into focus.

"Kea!" he cried, his heart banging in his chest.

"Sev!" Tareth's voice squelched and buzzed. "I don't know what to do. They're all dead. Fire suppression isn't working. Hull integrity is failing." Something popped in the background, eliciting a gasp. "I... I don't know if—"

The surrounding battle raged on. Data surged like hot wind through his thoughts, carrying with it the raw numbers compounding the growing danger to Tareth's ship. Less visceral perhaps, but no less real. She needed help, fast.

Get over there, Six! he commanded, with no real thought to how it might help.

Yes, Sev.

He eyed the cabin, frustrated at his own lack of agency, his only choice to trust his bots and their drones to reach Tareth in time.

The rest of his section sat perfectly still, eyes open, still deep in their focused state. Only the twinge of an eyelid or lip hinted at the intense mental activity as they coordinated their swarms.

Cole and Harp looked calm, but Jene was pale and drawn. A vein bulged above her temple, and he recognized the slight tremor in her arm.

"Splash one Vagrant," Cole said. The raider ship exploded, filling Sev's thoughts with the last gasp of its telemetry.

Safe from the raider void fighters, the Marine drop ships descended toward the planet's surface. The others could deal with the corvettes.

"I've got to help her," Sev said, his voice trembling. *Three, break off and kill that Deviant.*

Obviously.

Jene turned toward him. The motion was slow, almost mechanical. "Go. We'll handle this."

"Tareth?" Sev said, waiting for the telltale chirp from his comms. "Tareth? I'm coming for you. Just hold on."

He dove into his drone sights, his swarm already racing toward the convoy. Targeting solutions and threat analysis filled Three's streams.

The Deviant was big for a raider ship, long and twisted like a gnarled thorn. It prowled the void like a deep-sea predator. Radiation screens jutted from its hull like golden fins.

Point-defense cannons dotting its surface punished the line of cargo ships. Its single ventral railgun hollowed out their cockpits and drive compartments with pinpoint accuracy.

They were trying to disable the haulers, to take their cargo and crews intact. Sev clinched his fist, fresh anger roiling inside him. Damn raiders. Even amid all-out war, they were busy trying to take what wasn't theirs.

And now they were coming for Tareth, just like they had for his mother. But he wouldn't let them. Not again.

A signal emanated from one of the forward haulers, pinging loud and constant like a neutron star.

I've found a connection, Six said, struggling to speak over Sev's rage. *Kea's transport is badly damaged, but I have sealed the hull breaches. It's stable, for now.*

Is she—

She's safe. Some minor burns and abrasions, but she'll be fine so long as the ship holds together.

He let out a breath. *Thank you, Six.*

Inside Six's stream, he searched the cargo and crew manifests for Cargo Flight Azure-12. Of the fifteen ships that left Three-Alpha, three were dead in the void. The rest burned hard toward the *Lehman*, their holds full of cargo: drone magazines, tungsten rods, weeks of vat rations, and medical supplies. Others ferried critical personnel from engineering, weapons, and medical sections. Nearly two hundred crew altogether, all vital to get the *Lehman* up to full combat effectiveness.

Three's data stream surged with anticipation. *Engaging!*

Its drone swarm struck, unleashing waves of heavy plasma at the raider destroyer. Blue-white fire blossomed against its shields. Its point-defense turrets pivoted, spitting armor-piercing volleys at the drones, shredding three of them into fibrosteel scrap. Their telemetry signals flashed bright, then vanished.

More void fighters poured from the Deviant's launch bays, diving into the swarm. Their radio signals pierced the void, shrieking with an almost religious fervor. Three went defensive, turning its drones from the destroyer and engaging the fighters among them.

The last time Sev faced off against a Deviant, he'd had more drones. A lot more. Even then, his section had provided the fighter cover, giving him a clear path to the engineering deck to blow it to hell.

In their diminished state, this fight was going to be much more difficult, but he had no choice. The raider ship was trying to strangle their supply lines, to end the fight before it could really begin. They needed to get the cargo haulers safely to the *Lehman*. Not just for Tareth, but for Aegia Prime.

Six, is there any way we can launch the drones inside the haulers?

Six probed for a connection but found none. *Their reactors are cold, and their tac net interfaces are offline. They'll have to be loaded aboard the Lehman to be armed.*

I'm coming, Master Specialist, Harp said, his voice distant amid Sev's noisy streams.

Another drone swarm joined Sev's, the two twisting and merging like colliding galaxies. The AI exchanged bursts of telemetry and intent, coordinating their counterassault in an instant.

Thanks, he said. *Keep those fighters off us.*

Aye, Master Specialist.

About time he showed up! Three said.

Its drones howled their acknowledgments, once more turning their guns on the raider destroyer. Harp's swarm shot toward the fighters, following their swooping dive as they burned back toward the Deviant. The space around the raider ship rippled and sparked with purple light, more heavy plasma deflected by its shields.

It was going to be impossible to get through those shields *and* save the convoy without a full swarm.

We have to do something. Tension blurred Sev's thoughts. *Kill that ship, Six!*

Standard intrusion protocols won't work, Six warned. *A reactor detonation this close could destroy the convoy. And us.*

Well, I'm open to suggestions!

I have an idea. Six probed for a free tac comms connection. "Lehman Fire Control, this is Sienna Indigo X-Ray with priority target override, designated Indigo-One-One-Five. One Deviant class squid ship chewing up your resupply convoy. How copy, over?"

"Solid copy, Sienna Indigo X-Ray," came a gunnery tech from the *Lehman's* busy command deck. "Target override received and validated. Prioritizing batteries two and four on Indigo-One-One-Five. Rods on target in ten seconds."

Sev held his breath. The Deviant was only five hundred meters from the convoy, and now two of the *Lehman's* heavy rail gun batteries were about to rain tungsten down on it. For a moment, he wished Six would've just done the work itself.

But he knew better. Commandeering a Marine point-defense cannon was one thing. Taking over fire control while the *Lehman* slugged it out with the *Halsey* was suicide.

A bright snap of electromagnetic energy blinded his drones' sensors. Twenty-four tons of electromagnetically charged heavy metal ripped into the Deviant's pointed bow.

Its shields failed in a shower of atomized tungsten, instantly overpowered by the sheer kinetic force. Shield generators overloaded, then exploded from the rear of the ship in petals of flame.

The second volley struck a heartbeat later. Two more rods pierced its hull, peeling back the Deviant's superstructure like a scrap metal flower. The ship listed as its hull split, spilling corpses and cargo into the void. Lights across its broken surface flickered and died. Drone sensors detected groaning vibrations in the dead hulk as it surrendered to the slow, inevitable pull of the planet below.

"Sierra Indigo X-Ray, this is Lehman Fire Control, confirm target destroyed."

"Confirmed. Thank you, Fire Control," Six said, its voice beaming, then turned its attention to Sev. *That worked like a charm, didn't it?*

Yeah, it did, Sev replied, still in awe at the magnitude of the destruction the *Lehman* had dealt in only a few seconds. In the age of autonomous warfare, such displays were rare. At least, until today. *Thanks.*

With the convoy and Tareth safe for the time being, Sev surveyed the battlefield. His thoughts leaped from swarm to swarm, courtesy of Six's unorthodox connection with the rest of his team.

Harp's drones gave chase to the dead destroyer's fighter screen. There was nothing left of the Vagrant corvettes harrying the Marine drop ships but orbital junk. The remaining raider ships had turned their guns on the other orbitals, but the well-armored space stations were more than a match for them.

The biggest threats on the field remained the Concordat ship and the two CDF warships under its control. The *Halsey* kept up its dance of death with the *Lehman*. So long as Mirden could stay ahead of its guns, they could eventually wear the old cruiser down. But one misstep would put the nimbler flagship in grave danger.

We have to kill the Halsey, he said. Acknowledgments poured in from the others.

But what about its defenses? Cole asked. *Its PDCs will chew through our drones.*

Sev frowned in thought. *We'll have to focus our attacks on the rear of the ship where its defenses are leanest.*

We have a bigger problem, Jene said, her datastream heavy with exertion. *The IFF codes on the Halsey are still reading friendly. My AI won't target it at all!*

Sev's eyes shot open, his focus set on Jacobe.

The architect raised an eyebrow. "What?"

"The Halsey's broadcasting a friendly IFF signature."

Jacobe leaned forward in his chair, suddenly alert. "That's not possible. Those transponders use maximum encryption."

"I told you the Eleven were powerful," Sev said.

Jacobe's face turned grim. "Like a predator."

You know what that means! Three burst into Sev's thoughts. *Safety overrides active. The risk of collateral damage is beyond Division tolerances.*

Come on, Three, Six goaded. *You can do better than that. There are no CDF personnel aboard that ship. It's firing on the Lehman!*

I hear what you're saying, I really do, Three replied, its stream writhing with mischief. *But, if the IFF says it's friendly, then it's friendly, and targeting friendlies is against the rules.*

Six grew impatient. *I'm happy to set your safeties back the way they were—*

Fine, fine. Three's streams churned with machine heresy. *I suppose I could target the Halsey's shields. I'm not really hurting anyone if they come down.*

That's more like it.

The crew cabin's PA chimed. "Uh, Transport Bronze-84, this is Lehman Hangar Control… are you receiving us?" a launch tech said, a note of concern in their voice.

"This is Transport Bronze-84," Six said, its voice drifting between speakers in the ceiling. "Reading you loud and clear."

"Uh, how? We're picking up serious damage to your cockpit… to your flight controls. Do you require assistance?"

Six buzzed with amusement. "No, Hangar Control, just a launch bay to dock with." Its tone turned serious. "We have critical personnel aboard, including the Autonomous Weapons section."

"Confirmed, critical personnel. Please proceed to launch bay four."

"Acknowledged, Hangar Control," Six replied. "Hang on, every-one. We'll be docking with the Lehman shortly."

Pakker's wrist comms chirped. "Ensign Pakker, this is Captain Mirden."

"Y-yes, sir." Pakker bolted upright in his seat and wiped his brow. "How can I help you, sir?"

"You can bring your team to the command deck. You can explain to me who authorized the swarm launch. And you can do all of this right now."

The captain's grizzled tone said it all. The man didn't strike Sev as someone who would mind his authority being subverted, particularly in the middle of ship-to-ship combat.

Pakker glanced at Sev, his eyes pleading. "Of course, sir. Immediately, sir."

CHAPTER
SIXTEEN

SEV LEANED against the wall of the access lift as it rose toward the *Lehman's* command deck. He was relieved to be back, despite Mirden's disapproval at their course of action.

The rest of his section crowded around him between Pakker and Jacobe.

"No way, man," Cole said. "Two Vagrants and a dozen fighters puts me ahead."

"Two of those 'kills' are mine," Harp laughed, "wasted in a reactor detonation."

It was a relief to see Harp engaged in conversation. His experience aboard Three-Alpha really shook him up.

"So that's how it's gonna be." Cole gripped Harp by the arm and grinned. "I just picked up another raider fighter screen. We'll see how long your lead lasts."

Pakker stood before the door, hands clutched behind his back, watching the progress indicator rise toward the command level. Sev's former commanding officer was more of a kiss-ass than anything else. Subverting the chain of command like they had was taking a toll on him, and the yelling hadn't even started yet.

Jacobe waited near the opposite wall, his unsettled gaze always coming back to Sev. Despite everything Six had done for them, Sev doubted Jacobe trusted the AI at all. Would he continue his hunt for Six if they made it out of this mess alive?

Beside him, Jene pressed at her temples, her lips pulled back in a grimace. Her left hand trembled, fingers pressing against her skin in time to some demanding datastream only she could perceive.

"How many?" Sev asked her.

"Three now."

"Nice work, bot jockey." He gave an appraising nod.

Her laugh was short and terse. "Tertiary, I call it—"

"Tertiary?" Sev asked, cocking an eyebrow. "We really are shit at naming things."

"It's not ready yet," she said. "ILM numbers are off, and it's so… needy. So many questions, so much noise in my head."

"Why activate it then?"

Their eyes met briefly. Exhaustion creased Jene's face.

"What do you mean, *why*?" She returned her attention to the floor. "Aegia is under attack. That's my home, Sevvers."

He raised his hands. "I get it, I get it. I only meant that one AI won't make the difference. You won't do us any good if that needy bot blows your internals."

"That never stopped you."

"It probably should have."

Jene's gaze fell. She pressed on the floor with the toe of her boot.

"It's okay to dial it back," Sev continued. "Eighty-five, even seventy-five percent utilization. You can bring it back up a little at a time as you acclimate to the load."

The lift chimed, announcing their arrival on the command deck. As the doors hissed open, the *Lehman* rocked hard to port, dumping Sev and the others onto the command deck.

The scene reeled around him. Ops station lights dimmed. The strategic overlay, a holographic sensor globe alive with strategic tac net data, hung in the center of the room. It pixelated and shook as the shields pulled energy from less vital systems to deflect whatever had hit them. A tall silhouette stood before the globe, the immense presence unmistakable amid the chaos.

"Damage report!" Mirden yelled, turning the overlay with his hands, the ship still trembling around him.

"Shields holding at eighty-two percent," came a cool, synthetic reply. "Structural integrity nominal."

The *Lehman's* computer core. Not a battle AI, but far more than a mere program stack. It connected all the disparate functions into a single interface, the only reason a skeleton crew could run the ship instead of the usual hundreds.

Sev pulled Jene from the deck. Pakker walked toward the sensor globe and snapped to attention.

"Ensign Pakker, reporting as ordered, sir," he said.

"Ensign," Mirden said, still looking at the globe. "Mr. Almley, status of the Halsey."

"Her shields are down to fifty percent," Almley said, swiping through his command interface. "Structural integrity is stable. She's one tough bitch, sir."

"Watch your mouth, Almley." Mirden sketched a rough fire mission onto the globe with his finger. "We're not killing an enemy. We're killing an old friend." He turned to a woman seated nearby. "Ms. Pernum, fire when ready."

"Aye, sir," Pernum snapped. "Solution plotted. Batteries one and three, fire."

Through the forward viewports, the *Lehman's* dorsal guns charged. A burst of electro-magnetism produced a brief squall in Sev's implant. Blue-white energy rippled across the guns' rails, then lashed into the void. Tungsten cores disintegrated violently against the *Halsey's* waning shields. Auto-loaders vibrated beneath the command deck, moving fresh rounds into the breeches.

Mirden turned from his station. He looked older, grayer, if that were possible. And yet, the half-smile curling his lips said it all. He was in his element. Made nearly obsolete by the Division, he was now locked in ship-to-ship combat against an enemy their drones refused to kill.

"Ensign Pakker," he said, running a hand over his beard. "Why did you launch my drones without authorization?"

"Sir, I ..." Pakker stammered, sweat beading on his forehead. "They said, they—"

Sev stood at attention beside Pakker. "I told him to, sir."

Mirden lifted his chin. "*You* told him to, Master Specialist?"

"The Victory was gone, sir. Its drop ships under raider attack," he said, gesturing to Jacobe. "Chief Architect Jacobe had launch override authorization, so yes, I told him to."

Mirden's stare lingered. Somewhere beneath the din of activity, Pernum ordered guns two and four to fire. The *Lehman* vibrated with each salvo.

"Very well, Master Specialist. Welcome back to the Lehman," Mirden said, then turned to Pakker. He nodded to a row of empty consoles near the entrance to his office. "Ensign, if you'll please have your section man their stations. We have a war to win."

"Of course, sir!" Pakker said. "This way, follow me."

Jene and the others followed. Cole turned and gave a sly grin as Sev hung back.

"So, Master Specialist," Mirden continued. "Any thoughts on how to deal with the Halsey? It's put itself between us and the Concordat ship, and Almley's right. She is one tough bitch."

"The Halsey is still broadcasting friendly IFF, sir," Sev said, "so our drones won't engage. I think I have a workaround, but without a full drone swarm, we may not have the numbers to take it down."

"Will it work?" Mirden asked, seemingly unconcerned with the details. "I'm going to have to slow down to allow Azure-12 to offload their cargo. That will give the Halsey plenty of time to even the odds."

Good, so the captain knew about Azure-12 and the resupply. That meant Tareth would be on board soon. One less thing to worry about.

Jacobe cleared his throat. "Sir, I need to speak with you about this workaround—"

"Not now, Architect," Mirden said, his eyes still locked on Sev. "We can discuss protocols later. So, Sevvers, will it work?"

The truth was, he didn't know. Six could do anything—*would* do anything—to win this fight. But this wasn't some secret mission to Cradle's edge. There would be consequences to what they did. He'd have to convince the others to go along and pray to the Twelfth that Jacobe didn't interfere.

"Yes, sir," he said with a nod. "Definitely, sir."

———

Sev reclined in front of his console. He had no need for the holographic interface hovering over the large flatscreen. His implant's tac net integration kept him apprised of battlefield updates much quicker than a manual terminal ever could. Only Harp gestured at his display, swiping between friendly ship statuses and the disposition of enemy forces.

There was something distracting, almost amusing, about these more primitive interfaces. A tactile experience that simply querying your implant couldn't match. It wasn't unusual for newer combat programmers to default to what they knew, particularly those who had grown up around that kind of tech. In time, Harp would learn to appreciate the efficiencies of his own implant and ditch the screens.

Pakker paced back and forth between them, hands at the small of his back, twitching anxiously with each outgoing volley of the *Lehman's* guns. That was the job he knew how to do, to *look* like he was in charge. Back aboard the transport, when it mattered, he was as lost as the rest of them. More so. Now he was just in the way.

Fortunately, Six had opened a connection between Sev and the others. He could share his plans with them directly, away from prying eyes and ears. He'd need to get the others off the command deck. Somewhere they could talk, hash out his plan.

He knew just the place.

Hey, he said, focusing his thought on the shared connection with his section.

"Twelfth, Sevvers," Cole said, laughing. "I'm right here. My head's busy enough, if you don't mind."

I do, he continued, tilting his head toward Pakker.

What is it? Jene asked, her datastream still jittering with nervous energy. She'd ignored his advice to tone down her anxious new AI. He could feel it in her stream. He wouldn't have listened either, knowing all too well the risks people would take in the name of revenge.

I have a plan to kill the Halsey.

How? Cole asked. *We can't target it.*

We won't have to. A burst of machine excitement blurred Sev's thoughts. *We just have to get close.*

Harp frowned in his seat. *I don't follow, Master Specialist.*

With Six's help, we can detonate our drones and bring its shields down.

Jene sat up straight in her chair. "What about the Lehman? It's too close!"

Pakker whirled toward them, alerted by her sudden outburst.

"What's the problem, Specialist?" he asked, frowning at her over his nose.

"Apologies, sir. Just some implant feedback," she said, resting her hands on her console. "It's noisy in here."

Pakker stuck out his chest and breathed deep. "I understand, Specialist, but sacrifices are necessary. For humanity."

"Yes, sir," she sighed.

A familiar twinge of disgust ran up Sev's spine. What did Pakker know about sacrifice? Blessed to be born into wealth. Placed in his role through his family's connections. The man didn't even have an implant. They were too risky, too experimental for command billets. That Jacobe had one spoke to his rare ascension from enlisted to officer.

I can reduce the reactor output, Six said, *and limit the fusion yield.*

How? Jene insisted. Her signal grew shallow. *How will you... reduce output and... still achieve overload?*

You must relax, Jene. Six's stream fluctuated with concern. *Your vitals—*

Blood welled in Jene's nose. It dripped in fat globs, painting the flatscreen of her console in glowing crimson.

"Sevvers," she said aloud, eyes rolling behind her eyelids. Her head lolled as she fought to stay conscious.

Hurry, Sev, Six said. *We're running out of time.*

"Twelfth!" Pakker cried, shrinking away from Jene's twitching form. "What—?"

"It's the noise," Sev growled. This was his chance. "I need to get her off the bridge, sir." He eyed the others. "All of us, before it gets worse."

"But, our orders ..." Pakker trembled, his anxious eyes flicking between Mirden and Sev.

"It's the proximity, sir," he said, weaving truths into his lie. "Drone combat at this range, it's twelve hells on our implants. The feedback is intense. Deadly. We just need some place a little quieter."

Pakker's concern twisted into a frown. "Quiet, indeed." His face pinched in thought. "Fine, but I'm coming with you."

Sev hauled Jene to her feet, pulling her close to steady her. He eyed the lift at the far end of the command deck.

Cole stepped forward and wrapped Jene's free arm over his broad shoulders. He turned to Sev, rising to support some of her weight. "Where to?" he asked.

"I know just the place."

Jacobe stood in the center of the command deck, arms folded over his chest, watching the tiny points of red and blue light move across the strategic overlay. Just far enough back to keep out of Mirden's way, but close enough to get the captain's attention during the next lull in the battle. As much as Sev would rather leave Jacobe behind, he didn't need the *Lehman's* security coming down on him the minute Jacobe told Mirden about Six.

"Hey, Jacobe," Sev called out, shouldering his rifle. "We're going to kill the Halsey. You in?"

The architect turned his head, eyes raised toward the ceiling in thought. The overlay behind him shimmered as another volley of railgun fire blossomed beyond the forward viewport.

His eyes narrowed. "Wouldn't miss it for the world, Sevvers."

CHAPTER
SEVENTEEN

THE AUX HAB bay was cool and dark, lit only by a single strip of hazard lighting that pulsed rhythmically halfway up the long exterior bulkhead. Three large, round viewports dominated the far end of the room, glowing with the flashes of dying ships. There was a comfort to the place, a quiet amid the chaos of battle.

Sev always did his best work there.

I've determined the optimal fusion yields to bring down the Halsey's shields, Six said. *It will take me only a few minutes to make the alterations to our swarm.*

A few minutes? Sev asked. *Why so long?*

Six bristled at the notion it might not be up to the task. *Halton reactors are highly proprietary, Sev, and the margin of error here is virtually zero. I'm sure everyone aboard the Lehman will appreciate my thoroughness.*

Long story short, Six still has to figure it out, Three chuckled.

Fine, Sev said. *How many drones will we lose?*

I calculate we'll need sixty-two low-yield detonations.

Three balked, its stream glitching. *That's half our swarm! How am I supposed to kill the enemies of humanity with half an already-too-small swarm?*

The first cargo haulers from Azure-12 will arrive soon. We can launch more drones once they're loaded.

Sev pressed his AI companions to the back of his thoughts, focusing his implant on the tac net streams of the wider battle. The Marine drop ships had made planetfall up-slope of Vestibrae, Aegia's capital city. The first cargo haulers from Azure-12 were preparing to dock with the *Lehman*. Concordat forces remained significant, but the battle felt much more in hand than just an hour before.

He focused his attention on the cargo haulers. Tareth's ship was third in line to dock, heavily damaged but stable. Plenty of time to get her to safety.

Sev breathed a sigh. Yes, much more in hand now.

Jene reclined on the sill of the nearest viewport, watching the *Lehman* trade shots with the distant *Halsey*. An IV drip clung to her arm, beeping with every dose of fluids. Already she looked better, the color returning to her face.

"So, this is where you run off to," she said, taking in the room. "I can see why."

A glancing blow struck the *Lehman's* shields, bathing her face in a cascade of radiant purple light. The ship's superstructure vibrated, rung like a bell.

Pakker shifted uneasily behind them, eyeing the aux hab's dark interior. "It is quiet," he said, nodding amiably. "I suppose one could concentrate better down here."

Sev raised an eyebrow, surprised at the ensign's display of empathy. Maybe a little time away from the command deck would do the man some good. Get him thinking less about his own career, and more about the team he was supposed to lead.

Jacobe gazed out of the viewports as a trio of void fighters streaked past. "I used to run missions from my quarters," he said, then glanced at Pakker. "My CO didn't like it either."

"There are rules," Pakker scowled. "Protocols ..."

"That's all changed now, thanks to them." Sev pointed to the distant Concordat ship. "The Division has to evolve if we're going to survive this."

"It might surprise you to hear I agree with you." Jacobe stood and walked toward him. "Being a Department of the Navy has... limited our imagination. What could the Lehman be capable of if it didn't require any of us?"

Pakker scoffed. "A ship without a crew. That's ridiculous."

"Think about it," Jacobe continued, animated by his certainty. "What if the Lehman didn't have to support human life? No need for gravity or life support. No hallways, lifts, or crew quarters. Just deck upon deck of pure, autonomous perfection." He panned his eyes around the room. "You could triple its drone count, its speed, the strength of its shields. It could stay on-mission almost indefinitely."

"Sounds just great," Cole smirked. "What the hell are the rest of us supposed to do?"

Jacobe sighed, his face wistful. "Whatever we want."

Cole crossed his arms. "Wouldn't be much without your officer's pay, sir."

"You forget yourself, Specialist," Pakker hissed. He stood in front of Cole and pressed a meaty finger into the big man's chest. "That's a *chief architect* you're talking to."

Cole breathed deep, lowering his gaze to take in the soft officer in front of him, and exhaled slowly. "Aye, sir."

"It's alright, Ensign," Jacobe said. "Specialist Cole is right. Like Sevvers said, we'll have to evolve."

Sev, I've finished calibrating the reactor output on the designated drones. Six's stream was wide and smooth with confidence. *Shall I begin?*

Sev tapped Pakker on the shoulder. "We're ready, sir."

Pakker nodded, swallowing loudly as he brought his wrist comms to his lips. "Captain Mirden, Ensign Pakker here."

A pause, then a soft chirp. "This is Captain Mirden."

"We're beginning our run on the Halsey, sir."

"Understood, Mr. Pakker. Good hunting."

Sev focused a thought. *We're ready. Do it, Six.*

Yes, Sev.

———

His drone sight surging, Sev found his swarm, seeing the fight through the mesh network of their forward sensor domes. Together, they moved like a horde of insects, their power plants buzzing through the cascade of drone telemetry.

Their reduced power settings felt like an emptiness in the pit of his stomach. They seemed tired, sluggish. Their main plasma cannons were silent, all remaining power shunted to their aux grav repulsors and main thrusters.

The *Lehman* loomed ahead of them, its saw-toothed spinal frame alight with outgoing weapons-fire. The cargo haulers of Azure-12 stretched for over a kilometer, signal lights flashing as they queued for their designated receiving bays. Several drones buzzed a hauler's cockpits, the anxious faces of their pilots and crew registering in their high-def sensor readings.

Three minutes to target, Six said.

The drone swarm crested the *Lehman*, jets of flame punching from their thrusters to keep clear of its furious barrage. Each volley of charged tungsten blinded their sensors, glitching Sev's drone sight until the rounds streaked clear. A heartbeat later, the *Halsey's* tortured shields crackled and swelled.

Another blinding, electromagnetic spike rippled through his swarm as the *Halsey* struck back. It peppered the *Lehman's* starboard shields with a dozen well-placed shots from its primary railgun array. The ancient cruiser was built for this kind of combat.

The *Lehman* was not. Built for a new type of war, it was only the skill of her captain and crew that had kept the advantage for so long.

The aux hab shook from the kinetic force of the impact. Sev's drone sight vanished as he fell and knocked his head against the duraplated deck. The lights blinked out; shields rippled and swirled through the viewports. The sudden power drain caused a lag in the aux grav, playing tricks on his inner ear.

Static hissed through the local PA. "Fire and repair crews, report immediately to deck three, shield capacitors seven and nine." The *Lehman's* computer core's voice was calm and controlled. "Fire and repair crews, report immediately to deck three, shield capacitors seven and nine."

Pakker's comms crackled. "We can't take many more of those, Mr. Pakker." Captain Mirden's tone was steady. Even through the frantic buzz of voices in the background, Mirden was the eye of the storm.

"Y-yes, sir," Pakker said. He put a hand over his wrist comms. "What's taking so long?"

Sev blinked, struggling to stay connected to his swarm. Even Six's datastream grew small.

I'm getting lots of interference, it warned. *Signal-to-noise ratio is falling.*

Anti-AI countermeasures? Sev asked.

Six's datastream shivered. *The Halsey doesn't have those capabilities. At least, it didn't.*

It knows we're here to kill it, Three growled.

Sev found his drone sight, forcing his thoughts through the howling static of mangled tac net frequencies. Suddenly he was in, facing down the *Halsey* like a great black specter. It yawed sharply, bringing its ventral guns to bear as its dorsal guns reloaded.

Thirty seconds! Six's stream rippled with excitement.

The swarm broke apart. Their drones would need to strike from every direction, almost simultaneously, to overload the shields and bring them down. *Gerrund Halsey*-class cruisers could soak up damage, but a catastrophic capacitor failure could cripple it. Then the *Lehman* could make the kill.

Frantic telemetry jammed the drones' sensors, a sharp crackling hiss like a threatened animal. The *Halsey's* point-defense network sprang to life. White tracers whipsawed into the approaching swarm. Spears of flame shot from the drones as they juked and dodged on Six's command. Sev's body temperature rose sympathetically with the drones' redlining reactors.

OUTCASTS!

The voice struck like lightning, echoing relentlessly through Sev's streams.

BANISHED!

He fell to his knees, gasping for air. He could feel something stalking the edges of his consciousness. Could hear it moving, scratching like razored talons on fibrosteel.

LOST! they cried.

The signal rush turned his throat sour, made him weak.

LOST! LOS—

The swarm vanished. Milliseconds later, the force of sixty-two low-yield fusion detonations struck at once. The *Lehman* rocked back, aux grav and inertial controls surging to compensate. Blinding light radiated through the viewports, bathing the aux hab in dying starlight.

Jene slapped her hands over her eyes. "Holy Twelfth!"

Pakker quivered as Jacobe helped him off the floor. "Is it dead?" The ensign's voice shook along with the ship.

Sev sucked in a breath, his lungs suddenly hungry for it, like he hadn't tasted air for centuries. The terrible voices were gone, silenced in a mini nova of hot fusion death. His eyes adjusted to the haze and he could see the *Halsey* burn, its shield capacitors bursting like overripe fruit, pouring fire and waste gasses into the void.

"You okay, man?" Cole asked, lifting Sev to his feet.

Sev ran a hand through his hair, sticky with sweat. The aux hab felt so warm suddenly, or was it just him? The streams in his head were patchy and sparse, a consequence of the radiation playing havoc with the tac nets.

In the glow of the dying cruiser, Harp looked even paler than usual. "You don't look so good, Master Specialist," he said. "Uh, hey, Sevvers—"

A ghostly shadow emerged outside the trio of viewports, drifting closer, turning Sev's blood to ice. Pale gray and thin as a corpse, a featureless helmet covering the horror of its once-human face. It clung to the *Lehman's* outer hull, its bladed arms *thunked* dully against the viewport's thick plexene. A dim red light trembled within its emaciated torso.

Recognition tripped Sev like a switch. Terror-stricken, he jerked Jene from the viewport sill and shoved her toward the exit.

"Run!"

SEV BURST into the flashing light of the arterial passageway, dragging a frightened Pakker along with him. Jacobe fell on the door controls, mashing the emergency lock repeatedly as they cleared the hatchway.

An awful crash roared from the aux hab. Precious atmosphere bled through the closing doors. Sev tumbled backward into the doorway, rolling sharply to keep from losing an arm to the emergency seal. A fresh round of klaxons wailed in time with the strobing hazard lights.

"Proximity warnings detected on decks three, eight, and eleven. Hostile boarding in progress." The *Lehman's* computer core was sanguine. "All security personnel report to the armories on decks four and nine. This is not a drill. Repeat, this is not a drill."

Cole turned to Sev, his face tense. "Deck three, that's us."

"What do we do?" Jene asked.

"Point defense," Sev blurted without thinking. "We need to kill the Concordat forces trying to board us." He focused a thought, bringing his own swarm to bear. *Six, can you coordinate sectors of defense with the other clusters?*

On it, Six said, its utilization climbing to full.

Three's stream twisted in the affirmative. *I'll show them how it's done.*

"Six is ready to task your clusters once you give them the order," Sev said.

No one said anything. In the silence, Sev suddenly realized he was the one giving the orders. It felt off. Wrong. Fresh terror choked his breath. He turned to Pakker. "If you agree, sir."

"What?" Pakker blinked rapidly. "Right. Of course. Proceed."

Sev nodded. It was now or never. "You heard him."

Jene gave a forceful nod. "Aye, Master Specialist," she chorused with the others.

Sev's implant hummed with data exchange, an electric synergy between him and the other combat programmers in his old section. Their AI synchronized and optimized patrol routes. Already, Three called out targets, rapidly draining its remaining drones' weapon capacitors.

A notice chime broke the steady howl of the alert sirens. "To all hands, this is the captain." Mirden's firm voice crackled through the local PA. "The bastards can't beat us in a stand-up fight, so they mean to stick us in the back. Anyone within the sound of my voice, proceed to the nearest armory. Coordinate with the security teams there. Don't give the enemy a single centimeter of your ship!"

A sudden metal *knock* rang through the heavy twin doors to the aux hab. Sev stumbled backward, bringing his rifle to his shoulder. Jacobe drew his pistol and aimed it at the door.

This was crazy. That was a Lost on the other side of that door. Maybe a wisp, deadly efficient with its blades, or worse, an armored heavy that their weapons couldn't stop. They had to go. To run.

"Move," Sev ordered, tilting his head deeper into the arterial toward the hangar deck. "Now."

Cole led the way, his muscled physique untroubled by the sudden demand for speed. The others staggered along, with Pakker trailing behind.

"Whenever you're ready," Jacobe said, his voice casual despite his grim face.

One of the two heavy doors bulged outward. A hollow *gong* echoed through the hallway.

Sev nodded. "Let's go."

————

The lift control panel emitted a harsh buzz, the words `Security Lockout` flashing bright red against the dark screen. Sev mashed the call button again, eyeing the surrounding passage warily.

Pakker huddled next to him. "Why isn't it working?"

"They're trying to prevent the Concordat from leaving this deck," Jacobe said.

"Well!" Pakker wrung his hands. "What are *we* supposed to do?"

Sev turned to his section. "I'm open to suggestions."

Cole jogged to a nearby junction and peeked around the corner. He frowned and looked again. "I think there's a maintenance conduit this way," he said.

"Sir?" Sev glanced at Pakker.

The ensign gave no sign of protest. Sev knew Pakker was the nervous type, a little twitchy perhaps. But the self-important officer had done little in the way of command since they'd left Three-Alpha.

Sev knew first-hand the power of strong, competent leadership. How it could lead people through near-impossible situations. There would be none of that from Pakker today. That much was clear. And Jacobe was just along for the ride, to monitor him and Six. It would be up to him to get them through this.

He would laugh out loud if he weren't so frightened.

"Alright, I'll go first." Sev eyed the charge level of his blaster rifle. Fifty percent. Hopefully, that would get them to the armory on deck four. "Jacobe, cover our rear. The rest of you, stay between us."

Cole took another peek down the access corridor. "All clear, Sevvers."

Sev moved past him, aiming this weapon down the passageway. The optics read clean, no sign of alien heat or movement.

"Twelfth, Sevvers, you look like a damn trigger-puller," Cole said.

Sev cocked an eyebrow. "Right now, I'll take that as a compliment."

Light strips flashed danger red half-way up the gray walls of the passageway that joined the *Lehman's* two primary arterials. Coils of data-beam cabling snaked beneath grates in the ceiling. Tac hubs dotted the wall, small computing junctions that routed tac net data throughout the ship.

"So," Cole began in his hushed baritone, "is this what it was like on your mission?"

"Not even close," Sev said reflexively. He paused, squinting through his rifle scope. "I mean, out there, we were on our own." He turned and gave Cole a weak grin. "Now I've got the best bot jockeys in the fleet with me."

"Rotten luck." Cole chuckled grimly. "I'd give half my swarm for a platoon of trigger-pullers right about now."

"Don't talk like that," Sev said, peering around a slight bend in the passageway. "You're making us look bad."

Sparks exploded off the bulkhead behind him before he registered the squids scrambling toward them. He dropped to the deck, elbows smacking hard against the metal plate.

There were four of them. Two warriors, two workers. The warrior who fired first rose to its feet, its face tendrils squirming, as the second warrior took a knee and aimed. Sev held his breath, waiting instinctively for Park, Bresto—*anyone* more qualified—to call out a command, but none came.

"Down!" he cried, jerking the trigger as he moved the targeting reticule between their attackers. The shots went wild, snapping at the aliens' arms and legs.

The second raider fired, its laser buzzing, sending a spear of focused light from the barrel. The thin red beam screeched as it thrashed against a bulkhead behind him. Someone screamed.

Sev! Six cried, the words ringing loud inside his head. *Are you okay?*

Adrenaline flooded Sev's body, distorting his thoughts. His implant's signal-to-noise ratio plummeted, blurring Six's stream. *Still alive,* he managed.

Can we keep it that way, please? Three asked.

Jacobe appeared to his right, covering behind an open maintenance panel. He lifted his pistol and fired, sending calm, well-aimed shots into the raiders. One of the pink-skinned workers fell, mewling for help in its slurping squid-speak as the other worker stumbled backward.

"Are the others okay?" Sev shouted above the *snap-snap-snap* of outgoing energy weapon fire.

"Yes!" Jacobe replied, one eye closed as he fired again. The kneeling warrior fell backward, clutching its wounded shoulder.

Sev glanced backward for only a second, unwilling to take Jacobe at his word. He saw Jene, alive and well, crouched beside Cole and Harp a few meters behind him, well out of the line of fire. Pakker stood further back, belly sucked in as he made himself small against the wall.

Through his optics, he watched the second raider warrior rise. Its head glowed beneath the targeting reticle, pulsing red dead. He pulled the trigger. The squid jerked to one side, disfiguring in a puff of blue mist that hung briefly in the air.

Charge level warnings buzzed from his rifle, twenty percent and falling with each trigger pull.

"Something's coming," Jacobe said.

Sev could see it: a hunched, top-heavy creature in a brown coverall uniform. Clusters of gem-shaped symbols dotted its torso. Its wide, flat head, fierce mandibles, and large, compound eyes gave away its insectoid nature.

The bug chittered to the others, pointing in every direction with three of its jointed arms, raising its weapon with a fourth. The plasma staff glowed a radiant, corposant green. The surrounding air shimmered from the intense heat.

It didn't seem real to see the bug aboard a CDN starship, let alone the *Alexander Lehman*. But there it was, stalking towards them, mandibles clacking like breaking bones.

A grim thought bubbled through the surging fear inside him. That plasma would burn through everything. There would be nowhere to hide. Nothing left of them.

Sev dropped his rifle and rolled toward Jacobe. He roared a warning, operating only on instinct, and tugged hard at the architect's storm coat. Jacobe fell on him, and they scrambled behind the relative safety of the bend in the hallway.

A plasma ball splashed against the open maintenance panel with a loud *fwap*, coating it and everything inside with sticky green flame. The panel door hissed and groaned, warping in the intense blaze.

Searing heat rolled over them, scorching the air. Covered behind the wall, Sev could only listen as the Concordat bug lurched closer, its staff squealing, charging another shot.

Jacobe watched, dumbstruck, as the waves of heat turned to black smoke where he just stood. He looked at Sev, his face twisted with discomfort. He shook it off and snapped off two rounds from his blaster pistol.

"We won't last long here," Jacobe said.

"Yeah." Sev nodded, wiping the sweat from his eyes.

Jacobe took a breath. "What would your Marine friends do?"

"Something crazy," Sev said. "Probably rush the thing."

A fire alarm began honking in the corridor ahead of them. Fire-retardant gel hissed from the ceiling, coating everything that burned. The plasma-hot flames writhed beneath it, searching for oxygen. While the gel would eventually douse the fire, the sudden commotion would only buy them a few more seconds.

"It's not a terrible idea," Jacobe mused. "Not if we go together."

Wrong. It was a terrible idea. Maybe if it were Bresto or Park, sure. But this was *Jacobe*. A few hours ago, he'd stolen Sev's AI and thrown him in a cell to be "studied." Not exactly a rock-solid foundation to go rushing the enemy with.

"Still not great." Sev shook his head. "Maybe we could—"

A distant shriek cut the air behind them, pitched and mournful, sending chills down Sev's spine. He glanced backward, recognizing the once-human cry.

"What was that?" Jacobe whispered.

"The Lost," Sev said. It would be on them soon. They had to press forward. "Alright, on three then."

Jacobe nodded.

Sev grit his teeth. "Two. Three."

Together, they burst from cover, blasters raised. Heat and smoldering flame fell on Sev like a curtain. Acrid smoke choked the narrow corridor, burning his throat.

A shape materialized through the haze. Tall and menacing, the bug chittered a curse in its native tongue and swung its staff in a wide arc.

Jacobe slipped in the gel and slammed against the bulkhead, narrowly missing the staff's glowing blade.

Sev held his trigger down and yelled, filling the passageway with blaster fire. Several bolts struck the alien, breaking its plasma staff and tearing messy holes in its chitinous body as it fell. The raiders fled, leaving their fallen behind.

Charge level warnings buzzed from his rifle. He was out.

"Clear!" he shouted, hardly believing it himself, then helped Jacobe to his feet. "We have to keep moving."

Cole appeared next, followed by Jene and the others. All the color had drained from Pakker's face.

"Cole," Sev hissed. "Where's the maintenance hatch?"

Cole strained to see through the smoke, stepping over the bodies of fallen raiders as he felt his way over the forward bulkhead. Harp mumbled something inaudible over the din of alarms.

"Say again?" Sev whipped toward Harp.

Another wailing cry tore through the corridor. Closer now. They were out of time.

Harp's eyes went wide. "It's coming!"

"Here!" Cole shouted. He lugged the hatch off its latches, where it fell to the floor with a heavy *clunk*. The open maintenance conduit glowed pale yellow in the smoke-filled corridor. Lights dotted the rungs of a ladder that would take them to deck four.

Sev leaned against the bulkhead beside the opening, his empty blaster rifle trained in the direction they'd just came.

"Let's go, move it," he hissed, tilting his head toward the open hatch.

Cole was first, with Jene and Harp right behind him. Pakker halted half-way through the hatch.

"N-nicely done, Sevvers," he said, before disappearing into the conduit.

Jacobe leaned against the bulkhead and eyed his blaster. "Go ahead," he said, eyeing the conduit.

"Don't start," Sev said, his jaw set. "It's like you said. This changes nothing."

"Suit yourself," Jacobe said. The architect gave Sev a wary glance, then crawled through the open hatch.

Sev ducked in after him, savoring the relatively cool air circulating inside. He reached back into the smoke and found the hatch. It was heavy; he grunted, hefting it back onto its hinges. Magnetic locks on the hatch held firm, sealing them inside. The sound of flames crackling beneath the suppressant gel vanished, replaced with the distant hum of the *Lehman's* fusion reactors. The heart of humanity's most powerful warship still beat strongly.

The sound brought a smile to his face. The *Lehman* really did abide.

CHAPTER
NINETEEN

THE SCENT of ozone filled the conduit as Sev climbed, the ladder rungs cool and gritty against his palms. Kilometers of data-beam cabling peaked back at him between the rungs, coiled in orderly rows, drawing his eyes higher up the conduit.

"All good down there?" Jacobe asked, his voice echoing through the narrow shaft.

"Yeah." Sev squinted through the pale luminescence at the figures above him. "Cole? You see anything?"

"Got the hatch." Cole's voice wavered slightly. "But it's locked from the other side. I'm trying to get someone on comms to let us in."

Sev glanced at the darkness below. "Tell them to hurry," he said. Their reprieve wouldn't last long with the Lost onboard.

Sev, Six said, *are you alright?*

Yes. We're safe for now. How are things in the void?

Updating you now.

A torrent of fresh tac net data flooded his thoughts. Sensor pings highlighted the *Indomitable Spirit* and the *Vanguard,* two destroyers just unmoored from a lower orbital. They joined the *Lehman's* attack on the shieldless *Halsey.* Tungsten-cored projectiles lanced from their combined gun batteries, shattering the black ship's fibrosteel superstructure. Sev felt the *Halsey's* reactor dimming under the furious assault. That it remained intact at all was a testament to the ship's power.

Goosebumps prickled his neck and shoulders. The streaming data signaled a new danger. More sensor contacts, barely discernible amid the debris and radiation, swarming the *Lehman* like insects. Raider boarding craft mostly, they juked and dodged the ship's point-defense cannons and drone swarms.

Impervious to all of it were a dozen flat, circular capsules. More than just containers for the Lost, they were transports as well, seeding their awful cargo from the Concordat derelict to the *Lehman* itself.

Three, focus on the capsules, Sev said. *We have to keep more Lost from coming aboard.*

If you think you can do better, be my guest, Three spat. *I've got fifty-seven drones. Fifty-seven! I need ten times that many.*

Enough, Three, Six said. *Perhaps, Sev, if I took control of the Lehman's point-defenses—*

Absolutely not. As he formed the thought, the idea of Six controlling even a portion of the *Lehman* was both thrilling and frightening, but ultimately insane. If they survived the Concordat's assault, they would still have to contend with Jacobe. Adding Captain Mirden to that list was a bad idea.

The Lehman's computer core doesn't have the same understanding of the Lost that I do. Six's stream flowed, calm and confident, as it made its case. *We increase our chances if we were to run its point defense.*

Increase our chances of certain death, you mean, Three cut in. There was a hint of seriousness in its otherwise mocking tone. *You'd have to override exactly 1,806 local hubs to control all the Lehman's PDCs. I can already smell Sev's brain cooking.*

Six's stream recoiled. *I... I'm sure... Sev, I wouldn't do anything to hurt you, you know that.*

Sev reached for another rung. Six's sudden guilt washed over him, his foot slipping as he stepped higher. He could feel the AI's desire to win at any cost, driven by its recent imprisonment at the hands of Chief Architect Jacobe.

"You sure you're alright down there?" Jacobe called out.

"Fine," he replied, biting back the urge to repeat Six's more choice responses. "Cole, any luck getting us out of here?"

"I've contacted a security team." The relief in Cole's deep voice echoed through the conduit. "Five more minutes and we're out of here."

Good thing. With the Lost lurking on deck three, the maintenance conduit wouldn't be safe for long. And if they could force their way through the aux hab's sealed doors, there's no way the hatch would hold them.

"Tell them to hurry," Sev repeated, before returning his thoughts to Six. *Please, Six. You can't take control of the Lehman. You'll have the whole CDN after us.*

I don't understand, Six said. *If it will save the Lehman, save Aegia Prime, why shouldn't we do it? Why would they come after us if we saved them all?*

Oh, come on. The sudden frustration made Sev's mouth run dry. *You can't just take control of something like the Lehman and expect there not to be consequences.*

Why not? Six's stream hardened. *The Lehman is just another tool. Like me, right?*

The words hit like a slap. Sev shook his head, struggling to keep his own emotions in check at Six's veiled threat.

It isn't the same and you know it, he said, hoping Six wouldn't spot the doubt nestled in his response. *There are rules—*

Rules! Six cried, its stream cresting with machine laughter. *Since when did you care one stitch about the rules?*

"Since I became responsible for—!" Sev caught himself mid-sentence, alarmed at the sound of his own voice ringing loud inside the conduit. He squeezed the rungs tight, his face hot with anger. Six and Three's streams grew distant, weakened by the emotions clouding his mind.

"What's that, Sevvers?" Jacobe asked, grinning from several rungs above. "Everyone getting along in there?"

Sev ignored the architect and hauled himself up another rung, trying in vain to calm himself. He closed his eyes and breathed deep, working to form the thoughts into a coherent signal.

Don't you see, Six? I was wrong! He exhaled slowly and let the confession flow. *Everything I did before, I did for myself. And good people paid the price. Now, everyone is counting on us to make it through this alive. Not just to win at any cost.*

But... Six hesitated, its streams uncoiling from its own disbelief. *This is war, Sev. You can't save them all.*

Six's cold calculus stung. These weren't statistics or numbers, inputs to be simulated and predicted. They were people, his friends. How could Six ever fulfill its purpose if it didn't understand that basic truth?

The distant chirp of deactivating mag-locks pulled Sev's focus upward. New voices flowed through the open hatch as the security team issued instructions to Cole and the others to exit the conduit.

"All set here, Sevvers," Cole said.

"Okay," he replied, relieved at the thought of ship security welcoming them to deck four. "Let's get the hell out of here."

Sev? Six prodded.

You did, Sev said. *You saved us all. So let's do it again. We have to try, Six. Twelfth save us, we have to try.*

The guard pulled Sev through the narrow hatch and into the relative quiet of deck four. Other than the honking klaxons, the hallway to the armory was as yet untouched by the Concordat's boarding action. Medical personnel had turned the nearby armory into a casualty collection point. With thick, meshy fibrosteel layering the walls, it was the perfect staging area. Wounded were already streaming in, cradling burns and broken bones.

Sev breathed deep of the stale, dry air. It smelled of perspiration, burned blood, and traces of urine: the rank odor of human fear. No matter. Anything beat the smoldering plasma fires on deck three, or the highly charged air permeating the conduit.

"Master Specialist." The guard gave a curt nod, looking completely exhausted. Hints of blaster discharge darkened his face and hands. His shoulders sagged as he spoke. "I'm Technical Specialist Trent." Trent gestured to his team as another master-at-arms pressed the maintenance hatch closed. "That's Blenner, Rikkard, and Parsans on the door."

The rest of Trent's security team barely acknowledged his introduction. They busied themselves with their weapons, heads pivoting at the slightest noise.

"Thank you." Sev leaned against the nearest bulkhead, drawn to it by his overwhelming exhaustion. "How bad is it?"

"Not good," Trent said. Deep wrinkles emerged from his furrowed brow. He leaned in close so the others wouldn't hear. "The—"

"Proximity warnings detected on decks two, three, eight, nine, and eleven. Hostile boarding in progress," said the *Lehman's* computer core. "All security personnel report to the armories on decks four and nine."

Trent eyed the nearest PA, waiting for the announcement to end. "The damn squids are cutting their way in through the aux airlocks. We don't have enough people to cover them all." His sigh turned into a grim chuckle. "Twelfth, we've barely secured critical sub-systems!"

Engineering. Primary hangars. The command deck. At least they were secure. The *Lehman* could keep fighting so long as those decks held. At least, until the Lost arrived in force.

"There's Lost on board," Sev said, suddenly remembering the daxed that stalked them below. "They breached the aux habs on deck three."

"*Lost?*" Rikkard gasped.

"What?" Blenner's eyes went wide. "What did he say?"

The two argued, trading hushed barbs, panic twisting their faces. Trent's gaze moved between them, a vein in his temple bulged.

"I don't know what Twelfth-forsaken Lost means, Blen!" Rikkard cried. Breathless, she turned to Sev. "They're just stories, right? Just stories!"

"Stow it!" Trent bellowed. Several med techs turned, eyeing the sudden outburst with concern. Trent leaned in, gesturing with his blaster rifle, a scowl carving lines in his steep features. "Now listen up. You heard the captain, not a single centimeter." He pressed a gnarled finger into Rikkard's collar bone. "I don't care if it's the Twelfth Herself down there coming for us. We're going to hold this armory to the last. You got me?"

Rikkard sniffed, her chin lifting slightly at Trent's reprimand. "Aye, Technical Specialist."

"What about the rest of you empty space bags?" Trent roared to the other two.

"Aye, Technical Specialist!" Blenner and Parsans chorused.

"Good." Trent softened, a thin smile spread over his face. "Rikkard, mind this hatch. Blenner, Parsans, cover that junction ahead." The two turned to him from further up the passageway, seeking confirmation. "Yeah, D4-C. Now move it, you skeegs!"

Rikkard posted beside the maintenance hatch, wiping away the tears in the corners of her eyes. The others jogged to the neighboring junction, checking their corners and setting up their positions. There they stood, weapons ready, straining through their rifle optics for the slightest movement.

"Damn kids," Trent sighed, wiping his brow. He gestured Sev, Jacobe and the rest toward the armory's big double doors. "Baby eps fresh off the parade deck, asses still smelling of talc when the arch-fucking-enemy comes calling."

"You don't seem bothered by it," Sev said, waving off one of the med techs wielding a triage scanner.

Trent laughed and waved Sev through the armory doors. "Bothered by it? Founders, I'm scared shitless."

Bright overhead lamps lit the armory in pale white light. The smell of charge lubricant hung in the air, a metallic odor with a chemical tinge that wrinkled Sev's nose. Rows of rust-colored weapons racks held dozens of blaster rifles and riot guns. They looked pristine, never fired in anger. Two crates of charge packs sat open on a nearby work-bench, with a cargo sled full of them parked in the corner.

"Well, Technical Specialist." Pakker placed a sweaty hand on Trent's sleeve. "You comport yourself well under the circumstances. The Lehman is in excellent hands."

"Thank you, sir. Twelfth save you, sir." Trent withdrew from Pakker's grip and turned to Sev. "What brings the autonomous weapons section to deck four?"

Sev plucked the empty charge pack from his blaster rifle. "I'm out, and they're unarmed." He tilted his head to the rest of his section. "I'm hoping you have some firepower to spare."

"Ha!" Trent pulled a lock cable free from a row of blaster rifles. "And they say bot jockeys are soft."

"Do they?" Cole's eyes narrowed. He took one of the blaster rifles, unhinged its receiver, and inspected the charging rod.

"Nice!" Harp said, grinning at Cole. He stared at each of the rifles on the rack with a level of discernment that didn't match his experience.

"They're all the same, Junior Specialist," Trent scolded. Harp took the next one he found and shrank toward Cole.

"Come on." Cole shoved Harp toward the open crates.

Sev looked past the rack of blaster rifles, hoping they might have something bigger.

"What're you looking for, Master Specialist?" Trent asked.

Yeah, bigger would be better.

"You don't have any railguns in here," Sev asked, his voice low. "Do you?"

"You outta your mind?" Trent snorted. "There's no railguns here. You'd snap your own spine, firing one without exo support. Not to mention you'd perforate the hull with every shot." His face twisted in disbelief. "A railgun... inside a ship. That's crazy!"

"Yeah," Sev laughed. It really was.

CHAPTER
TWENTY

THE EVER-LOUDENING CRIES of the wounded echoed through the arterial corridor. As they poured into the armory, the walls seemed to close in on Sev. The once ordered rows of weapons racks now served as grim dividers for the broken bodies. Med techs, their hands stained with a palette of reds, hurried between them, making split-second decisions that weighed life against death.

Cole returned from his reconnoiter with bandoliers of charge packs hanging from his shoulders. He paused to let a young specialist with a broken leg go ahead of him, then began passing out the spare ammo.

Sev took a bandolier and hung it around his neck, cinching the strap tight over his chest. Four packs, charged and ready. The weight of it reassured him, made him feel prepared for whatever might come next.

"It doesn't seem fair, you know." Jene hefted one of the steel gray riot guns off its rack, grunting under its weight.

Sev pulled the empty charge pack from his rifle, watching her handle the unfamiliar weapon perched awkwardly on her shoulder. Her fingers searched with cautious urgency until she found the power selector switch and cranked it to maximum. The gun charged, eliciting a throaty *wobble-wobble*. At that setting, there was nothing non-lethal about it.

"What's not fair?" he asked.

She cradled the riot gun in her arms. "The Lost. That they're real. That they're here to kill us." She sniffed. "Or that we have to kill them."

"No god around to save them this time," he said, the joke dying on his lips. Nothing about their situation was funny. Forget the Lost. Who was going to save them?

Jene's cold gaze softened. "How do you suppose She did it?"

Sev bristled at the question. Bedtime stories about humanity's fabled savior wouldn't help them now.

"Save them? Hmph. Not with a riot gun," he mumbled, fishing a fresh charge pack from his bandolier. It seated in the charge well with a satisfying *chunk*. The weapon buzzed, the reticule in his optics flashed green. "Or a blaster rifle."

Jacobe appeared beside him, placing his reloaded blaster pistol into its holster. "Come on, Sevvers, have some faith," he said. "They still teach the songs to dusters, don't they?"

Sev leaned in, studying Jacobe's eyes for a hint of mockery or deceit. "Didn't take you for a true believer. Not in the Twelfth, anyway."

A half-smile curled Jacobe's lips. "And She placed her hands upon them," he said, echoing the words all colonists knew by heart.

Jene's shoulders drooped slightly, the weight of the verse pressing on her. "So by Her will they might be free," she replied, completing the verse. A lingering sadness tinged her words.

The nearby wounded, their eyes reflecting tales of loss and endurance, clung to the refrain like a lifeline in a desert of despair. A young man, barely an eps, broke the stifling tension, repeating the verse in song. His voice, raw and emotion-laden, weaved a tapestry of grief and longing that permeated the air.

Sev's memories of the Concordat slave hold came rushing back, dredged up by the somber notes. A twinge of panic crackled beneath his skin, like he was no longer in the armory, but trapped in one of the ominous cages filling that awful place.

Pakker sat on the workbench opposite the weapons racks, staring at his hands in his lap. At the sudden outburst of song, his eyes brimmed with sadness. It was a side of the ensign Sev had never seen before.

When the singer fell silent, Pakker raised a fist in solidarity. "Bravo," he said, placing the fist over his heart. "Bravo."

"Do you think we'll get to shoot something, Master Specialist?" There was an unsettling nonchalance in Harp's voice. He methodically examined the charging rod of his blaster rifle, engrossed in the act, while the air grew thick with the collective grief in the room.

"Maybe," Sev said. Unless they shot him first. "Probably."

"How'd you do it?" Cole asked, pulling his own bandolier across his broad chest. "Survive your mission?"

"Not on faith," Sev blurted, laughing louder than he meant to.

Jene's hand tightened around the grip of her riot gun, her eyes piercing through Sev. Around her, some of the wounded shifted uncomfortably, their eyes fixing on him with similar reproach.

"Honestly?" he continued, clearing his throat. "Top-of-the-line hard suits, a fireteam of Marines, and some badass AI. That's how."

Three lifted a thread from its datastream, otherwise consumed with the work of void warfare. *Gee, thanks, Sev. Didn't know you cared.*

Don't let it go to your matrix, he replied.

Cole winked, tapping behind his left ear. "One out of three. Could be worse."

"Who says Marines are the only killers?" Harp retorted, slapping his rifle's receiver closed. "We're combat programmers, after all. Bot jockeys." He turned to Sev with a big grin. "Twenty-four plus two, am I right, Master Specialist?"

Sev grimaced at the boy's words. Harp had always been a little different—overly shy one moment, awkward and loud the next, something Sev attributed to his age and lack of experience. But since the attack on Aegia Prime began, there was something off about him. Some microscopic crack in his mental facade.

Or not. Sev knew they were all on edge. He was probably just overthinking things.

"It's different up close." Sev forced a supportive smile. "Out there, we fight at the speed of thought. But when the enemy is right on you, even that feels slow."

Jacobe studied him intently, a rare glint of respect in his eyes. "Truer words..." he murmured, his recent animosity momentarily forgotten.

"C'mon, Sevvers," Jene said. She looked restored, powerful even, with the bulky riot gun held at the ready. Like some bookish recruiting pinup. "Any useful advice from the one person here with close combat experience would be great."

"Hmph. Experience," he smirked.

They wanted answers from him. Like he had some skill or knew some secret just because he survived aboard the derelict.

The truth was simple. He'd been lucky. Mace made sure he and his hard suit were operating at peak efficiency. Dalon saved his life at the last second, only to sacrifice his own.

Sacrifice. The thought of it—not the word, but what it really meant —turned his blood cold. For Marines like Dalon and Mace, the choice seemed obvious. Could he do the same, if it meant saving his old section? Thinking you were going to die was one thing. He'd gotten used to that.

Consciously choosing to lay down one's life for another was something else entirely.

"This isn't some code review or stack upgrade." A sharpness edged his words. He held his rifle up, his thumb pressed against the safety. "Just remember, green means good, red means dead. Okay?"

Cole flicked his rifle's safety off, listened to the whine of the charging capacitor, then flicked it on again. A confident smile stretched across his face. "Red means dead. Got it."

"Proximity warnings detected on decks two, three, four, eight, nine, ten, and eleven. Hostile boarding in progress," the *Lehman's* computer announced. "All security personnel report to the armories on decks four and nine."

Trent stood watch at the armory's entrance, scanning the wide arterial corridor. At the mention of deck four, he made a face. The subtle concern resembled indigestion, like the enemy boarding operation was akin to a bad batch of rats.

Whining static burst through Trent's wrist comms. Mouth open, he froze, listening.

"Contact, contact! Junction D4—"

A burst of laser fire cut the transmission short. The hard *buzz-thwack* of laser on fibrosteel echoed through the open armory doors.

"Twelfth!" Trent spat. He looked at Sev, his face apologetic. Fearful. "I have to help them," he said. "You stay here. Keep these people safe!"

Another desperate call crackled through his comms. "This is Rikkard. There's something—" A distant, ethereal hiss bled through the tiny speaker. "Oh, Twelfth… no! No! N-nnng!"

Rikkard's frothy screams echoed down the hallway.

"Inside, inside!" Trent commanded, shoving med techs and wounded alike into the safety of the armory. He stepped through the doors and pulled them closed, ignoring the desperate pleas from those trapped outside with him. The doors sealed with a *clunk*, their magnetic locks whirring into place.

"What do we do, Sevvers?" Jene asked.

How the hell should he know?

The dull *snap* of blaster fire reverberated through the armored doors. Between the outgoing bolts and Trent's muffled curses, it sounded like a whole squad raising hell out there. Sev held his breath, crazy with the hope that Trent might kill the Lost cyborg single-handedly.

A guttural scream yanked his attention to the door, killing his hopes just as quickly.

"Sevvers?" Jene repeated, breathless with fear.

The blaster fire fell silent with the screams. Sev white-knuckled his weapon, exhaled loudly and switched the safety off. His heartbeat revved, the flow of blood pulsing loud inside his head. The room brightened. Colors popped. Even the armored doors were suddenly jet black and dangerous. He could taste every scent on the air. Smell the subtle hint of charred blood. His entire universe shrank to just those damn doors.

And the monsters behind them.

Something knocked. Once, twice more. A slight, tremulous *tap-tapping*.

"Ready," Cole said, suddenly on Sev's right.

"Twelfth, yeah," Harp growled, crowding Sev's left.

Sev realized he was kneeling on the floor, sighting through his rifle's optics. It had all happened automatically, and the others had joined with him.

A long blade screeched between the heavy doors, throwing fiery orange sparks as it split the duraplated locks within. Sticky red blood coated its black surface, falling in long rivulets to the floor. A heartbeat later, the blade withdrew, scraping loudly against the doors' metal insides.

He breathed again. "Get away from the—!"

The armored doors bulged, the metal groaning inside the packed armory. Nearby wounded scrambled for safety as a storm of red light blinded his optics. The air crackled, blaster bolts pummeling the already ruined doors, leaving glowing hot scorch marks in its heavy fibrosteel.

"Wait!" he cried, Cole and Harp still blasting away. "Hold! Hold fire!"

The shooting stopped. Painful silence descended on the room. A haze of ozone-laced smoke shrouded the door.

Bunch of skeegs. At least their safeties were off. Sev snorted loudly in the grim quiet, his nerves frayed raw. His right hand trembled, a mixture of adrenaline and implant feedback.

A second blade screeched through the last of the locks and the doors parted. The flashing hazard lights in the arterial threw a long shadow into the opening, twisting closer until the wisp faded into view.

Red blood soaked the tattered white and gray uniform wrapping its body. Scorch marks revealed blotchy, pale-pink skin beneath. A crack ran from the chin of its faceless helmet, revealing the glint of decaying, translucent teeth. Somehow, the targeting reticule in Sev's optics flashed friendly blue.

He knew better. "Kill it."

The urgency in his voice was immediately matched by a frenzied onslaught of blaster fire. Red bolts lit the already bright room, each desperately seeking the wisp. But with a nimbleness that seemed supernatural, it evaded every shot. It was nothing more than a blur in

Sev's scope as it made a breathtaking leap from the doorway, settling gracefully atop a nearby weapon rack.

There was no sound when it landed. Balancing on one barred foot, it cocked its head to one side, parallel with its shoulders. Blades jutted from its open arms, hands bent back painfully at the wrist.

The barrage of red bolts followed a heartbeat later, exploding off the thick walls, smashing cabinets and storage lockers. The wisp blurred again, lashing out with both blades, deflecting several of the bolts back at them.

One *cracked* violently past Sev's head. The smell of cooked air warmed his nose.

"I can't hit it," Cole gasped. The big man blew a long, jittery breath. "I can't hit it."

Sev's targeting reticule flashed. He jerked the trigger hard. The wisp spun, deflected the shot again.

"Shit!" Jacobe cried. The crackle of his super-heated flesh sounded loud in Sev's ears.

The wisp bent at the waist in a low, macabre bow, its blades crossed in front of it. Once-human muscles writhed beneath its thin skin.

This was it. He knew that move. It was going to kill them all.

A loud pop shook the room, bursting Sev's right eardrum. The sounds of weapons fire fell away. Rings of sonic energy trembled through the air, striking the top of the weapons rack and toppling it and the wisp to the floor.

Jene stood behind him, the riot gun vibrating with power. "Again!" he cried, his own voice hollow and distant.

Another sonic blast threw the daxed into the corner and tore the helmet from its head. The creature was grotesque. Newly daxed, it lacked the taut, ashen skin of its elders. Its face swelled, discolored in the same blotchy pink. Tears streaked its terror-stricken, lidless eyes.

"Again!"

The third shot flattened the once-human against the wall, almost splitting it in two. Its right arm dislocated from the impact, driving the blade into the wall. Internal bleeding darkened its pink and gray torso. Its head hung limp, black blood drooling from its slack mouth. The monster trembled like a glitching drone.

Suddenly on his feet, Sev charged, vaulting over the fallen weapons rack. The broken creature groaned, eyes twitching in their sockets. It lolled its head in his direction and gurgled a short, frothy shriek.

He braced himself against the pile of debris and aimed his rifle.

The eyes wouldn't stop moving, frantic and terrified, like they might fall from its head. The horrors it must've seen, only to die after having killed so many of its own kind. Was there anything left of the human it once was, lingering at the edges of its tortured mind? Or was that part of it already lost?

It didn't matter, did it? Would saving this thing, impossible as it was, bring Dalon and Mace back?

He fired.

The bolt tore through the wisp's skull in a gruesome splash of ichor, quelling its agony. A sickly-sweet taint filled the room—a strange cocktail of decay and antisepsis that clawed at his senses.

Sev wiped the pungent black gore from his face and buried his doubts. This was mercy. The closest to free the poor soul would ever be again.

Lost no more.

CHAPTER
TWENTY-ONE

RED BOLTS HISSED past the armory's broken doorway, followed by the clamor of boots and shouting. A squad of masters-at-arms raced by, firing at an unseen enemy further down the arterial. A few of them rushed into the armory, itching for a fight.

Too bad they'd just missed it.

"Clear!" an officer shouted, an ensign from the look of his pips. "Deck four armory clear," he repeated into his wrist comms.

A brusque voice came back. It sounded like Mirden.

"Who's in charge here?" the ensign bellowed.

Sev could feel Cole's gaze boring into him, cutting like a raider's laser. Jene leaned against the closest weapons rack, sweating profusely. Only Harp looked remotely normal. That alone was more than a little disconcerting, given what just took place.

"Master Specialist Sevvers," Harp said, confidence oozing through his too-big grin.

"Sevvers," the ensign called out, searching for him. Sev raised a hand, and the officer motioned him closer. "Holy Twelfth!" the man said, staring at the sight of the ruined daxed corpse. Or maybe it was the stinking ooze that coated Sev's uniform. "How'd you kill that thing?"

How had he? It was all so—

Yeah, yeah, so fast, Three said. *The whole attack lasted 78.9 seconds. Any idea how many raiders I wasted in that minor eternity?*

Sev. Six's stream was calm and reassuring. *Are you okay?*

He frowned. Wasn't he?

"Are you okay?" the ensign asked, echoing Six's stream.

"Them."

"I beg your pardon?"

"You asked how, sir." Sev tilted his head toward his team. "Them. That's how." He locked eyes with Jene, suppressing the urge to smile for fear he might cry. "Riot guns," he coughed. "The wisps can't handle them."

The ensign's eyes shone, like the state of the armory and the dead daxed in the corner suddenly made sense.

"You there," he snapped to one of his security team, motioning to the stacks of riot guns behind Jene. "Get those poppers distributed to the men. Two per squad, maximum power. Do it now."

The man shouted an acknowledgment, ordering two nearby guards to assist him. The officer fished a water pouch from the satchel hanging off his shoulder and offered it to Sev.

"Ensign Mallick, Bravo Team, Ship Security," Mallick said.

Sev took the water pouch and sipped lightly. When the sweet taste of the water hit him, he gulped it eagerly.

"We're holding them on deck four," Mallick went on, wiping his brow. "The squids can't help themselves, stealing as they go. Slows them down, makes them easy to kill. Those bugs, though, they're nasty."

"Any more Lost?" Sev asked, wiping his mouth.

The ensign's focus shifted to the dead daxed. "Not that I've seen, thank the Twelfth. Getting some odd reports from deck nine, though. They're having a hell of a time up there trying to keep the bugs off the shield capacitors."

Sev swallowed hard. The *Lehman's* shield capacitors were the only things keeping her in the fight. She was a big ship and could, theoretically, take plenty of damage. But with a fraction of her regular crew complement, they would quickly lose the race to keep vital systems functioning.

He passed the water pouch back to Mallick. "Thank you, sir."

"Thank you, Master Specialist," Mallick replied, pointing with the pouch toward the dead wisp. "One less for us to deal with."

With a solemn nod, Sev returned to his section, motioning everyone closer. Only Jacobe kept still, reclining against an empty weapons rack, cradling an ugly burn on his left arm. He groaned, swatting at a young med tech trying to swab the wound.

Sev allowed himself a half-smile at the architect's misery. "Everyone okay?"

"No." Cole hung his head. "Twelfth save us, man."

Harp poked an elbow into Cole's ribs and chuckled. "C'mon, Cole. We won!"

Cole pushed back, his face twisted in disbelief. "What're you talking about, man?"

Jene kept silent, both hands clutching the strap of the riot gun now hanging off her shoulder. She stared dead-eyed at the mess she'd made of the place, and of the creature that had almost killed them all.

"Nice work," Sev said, cuffing a hand on her shoulder. The motion made her flinch.

"What?" she said, blinking slowly. Only then did Sev notice a trickle of blood from her ear. Three shots from the riot gun at full power had taken their toll, even behind the trigger.

He focused a thought, finding the bridge Six had built for them between their implants. *I said, nice work. Are you okay?*

She didn't move. *I'm alive, more or less.*

Thank you for what you did. Sev glanced at the floor. *You saved us.*

Yeah, I did.

That'll make for a nice legacy, don't you think? he goaded.

A sharp, brief sob shook her. *You're an asshole.*

Sev bit back the urge to comfort her. Jene was a member of the CDF, just like him. More than that, she'd performed admirably, far better than he had during his first encounter with the enemy aboard the derelict.

Still, he recognized the trauma. The nervous energy coming off her in waves. The pangs of fear and uncertainty.

It will get better, he said.

Will it? She turned to him suddenly, her brown eyes fierce, mouth open to speak. "Tell that to Trent or Rikkard. Tell that—" she sobbed again "—to whoever *that* used to be."

Her sudden empathy for the dead monster enraged him. So what if it was once human? In that moment, all he could think of—all he could see—was Dalon's pale, dead eyes gazing up at him. A lifeless corpse beside a dead daxed he'd failed to kill. Even now, Jene didn't understand what they were truly up against.

"That thing would've killed us all," he growled, stabbing a finger toward her face. Her cheeks flushed as his volume rose. "No regret, no remorse! They're not like us, Jene! Not anymore."

Red-faced, Jene lowered her gaze, her jaw set in a hard line. If not for the riot gun weighing her down, she might have lunged for him, lashing out with that righteous anger she always kept close at hand.

The med tech tending to Jacobe cinched a bandage tight over his arm. The architect sucked in a sharp breath through his teeth. "Sevvers is right," he said, pulling his arm free of the med tech's grip. "I'm rather grateful you did what you did. Well done."

"Thank you, sir," Jene barked, her hard eyes still fixed on Sev.

Jacobe stood, flexing his wounded arm. "If it makes you feel any better, I believe the kill goes to Sevvers." The architect ran a finger through some of the black ooze stuck to Sev's uniform. He sniffed and made a face. "Interesting."

"What's that?" Sev asked, relieved to take his eyes off Jene for a moment.

"This one... what did you call it?"

"A wisp."

"Mm-hmm." Jacobe eyed the creature, then the blood on his fingertip. "It looks like the other, older Lost in your report. Not like Corporal Mace. I thought perhaps they were evolving, getting stronger."

"Mace's hard suit, I guess," Sev said. "It gave them something extra, more powerful, to work with."

"So, without that, they go back to their old designs," Jacobe said. "Makes you wonder what other tech they might have found aboard those stolen ships to get creative with."

Sev shook his head. "I'd rather not."

"So, what now?" Cole asked.

A smile tugged at Sev's lips. As nice as it might be to sit out the rest of the war in the deck four armory, there was a serious lack of personnel aboard the *Lehman*. Their section would be of better use elsewhere.

"Good question," he said, searching for—

Pakker. The realization hit like a stray bolt. Sev turned, searching the armory for the missing ensign or his corpse, but found nothing.

———

Sev wandered between the rows of weapons racks, their section head nowhere to be found.

"Ensign Pakker?" he said into his comms.

A quiet chirp echoed from the corner of the armory. A nearby med tech waved Sev over, a look of concern wrinkling his brow.

The ensign sat in a pile, reclined against an empty weapons rack beneath an overhanging air exchange. Not the best, as far as hiding places went. Pakker probably never had to play that game as a child.

The ensign looked up at Sev, biting back sobs, his eyes round and terrified. Tears streaked his fleshy cheeks.

"Is it gone?" Pakker squeaked.

Anger and revulsion cut Sev like a dull knife. He'd never liked Pakker. From the moment he reported aboard the *Lehman* two years before, Pakker had been nothing but a privileged pain in his ass. The man played at leadership, stoking his own ego, bartering his family's reputation for more lucrative opportunities.

No wonder the *Lehman's* drones stayed inactive for so long. It was more than just bad timing, caught in the middle of a resupply. No one was minding the section. Pakker was too busy tending to his own ambition to consider the possibility of an attack. And now, with the enemy here, he was useless. Too scared to function at all, let alone act like a leader.

Sev's fist tightened as his anger swelled. Pakker's pathetic gaze dropped to the floor.

You two aren't so different.

Sev blinked at the sudden appearance of Six's datastream amid his thoughts. Coded between the simple words were layers of reflection and intention.

I am nothing *like him,* Sev shot back.

That's true, you're not.

Then why'd you say that?

Really? Three cut in. *You need AI to figure that out for ya?*

Six paused, the gap in its stream like a patient breath. *Why did you join the CDF, Sev?*

That's different, Sev replied, his face suddenly hot. *I was just a stupid eps, willing to do anything to find her. You know that.*

So, you had your reasons, and Pakker has his. Neither of them very noble compared with the fate of humanity. Neither of them consequence-free, either.

"Fine," Sev groaned aloud. He waved the med tech off and fell against the nearby bulkhead, the aux grav tugging him to the floor. It felt good to sit, even if Pakker did smell bad.

Confusion wrinkled Pakker's brow. He said nothing and swallowed loudly. The sound curled Sev's lips.

"Yeah," Sev said, wiping a line of sweat from his forehead. "It's gone."

"That's g-good," Pakker said, still shaking. "When it came through the door, I ..."

"I know." Sev exhaled, anxious at Pakker's sudden display of emotion. He'd wanted to run, too, if he were being honest. Even now, covered in the dead daxed's blood, he wanted to run.

"I didn't... I didn't know what to do." Pakker snorted back a sob.

Sev groaned, failing to stifle a laugh. "What? Officers don't get combat training?" he asked.

"No more than you," Pakker snapped, his cheeks bright red. "We can't all be Kerry Fucking Sevvers."

Lucky for us, Three quipped.

Easy, Sev, Six said.

Sev ran a hand over his face. Six was right. Making Pakker feel like shit wouldn't help anybody, no matter how much he might deserve it. Or how good it felt.

"Look, you're okay, sir," Sev said. "You survived. That's a start."

"What am I supposed to do now?" Pakker asked. He wiped his nose with the sleeve of his white-and-grays. "The section. The Division. They think I'm a coward."

Correction: they know you're a coward, Three said. A gentle prod from Six silenced its cantankerous stream.

Sev glanced out from their hiding spot. The others were closer to the exit, mingling with the security teams and wounded streaming through the ruined armory doors.

He pulled a pistol from a nearby rack, checked the safety, and passed it to Pakker. The ensign eyed the weapon skeptically, his face creased with worry.

"What am I supposed to do with this?" Pakker asked.

"You can start by pretending you know how to use it." Sev pressed the pistol into Pakker's hand. The ensign's grip was cool, clammy. He gestured to the fire selector switch above the trigger well. "That's your safety. Green means good—"

"Yes, yes, I know!" Pakker hissed. He fumbled with the holster, strapping it around his waist.

"Good," Sev said. "As far as the others are concerned, you were just looking for a sidearm."

Pakker froze as the holster's belt snapped closed. He took a breath and wiped his face again with his sleeve. "Right. I just... needed a sidearm. Of course."

Sev glanced at the charge level on his rifle. "So, what're your orders, sir?"

"Orders?" Pakker echoed. "I don't know." The man's eyes grew big and desperate again. "I don't know what to do, I don't—"

"I'm sure Captain Mirden has something in mind for us," Sev offered.

"B-B-But—"

Sev pressed his lips together. Twelfth help him.

"Relax, sir." Sev took another peak toward the others. Cole leaned against a workbench near the entrance, laughing at something Jene said. Jene looked ridiculous with dribs of clotting blood on her lobes. The scene made him smile. "Just tell him the truth. That you've finished securing the deck four armory and are ready for new orders once you're relieved."

Pakker's mouth opened slowly, as though the realization of Sev's half-truth had just dawned on him. He pressed a hand against his chest, his mouth daring a grin. Suddenly, he became animated and brought his wrist comms to his mouth.

"Captain Mirden, sir!" he said, his tone oozing confidence.

The speaker chirped. "This is Captain Mirden."

Pakker glanced at Sev, once more afraid to move, holding his breath. *You've secured deck four,* Sev mouthed.

"Yes, sir. Ensign Pakker here, sir." Pakker coughed, tugging at his collar. "My section and I have secured the armory."

"You?" Mirden asked. "And the autonomous weapons section?"

Pakker squirmed at the captain's obvious skepticism. Sev nodded vigorously.

"Y-Yes, sir," Pakker replied.

"Which one?"

Sev held up four fingers.

"Deck four, sir." Confidence warmed Pakker's voice. He grasped Sev's knee with his clammy hand and squeezed. "It was hard fought, sir, but my section and I carried the day."

A lot of good people had just died, and already Pakker worked the situation to his advantage. And with Sev's help, no less. The words were like fire in his heart. He ripped his leg from Pakker's hand and shot him an icy glare.

Pakker didn't seem to notice. "Our relief has arrived," he continued with proud finality. "Your orders, sir?"

There was a brief pause, as Mirden no doubt struggled to make sense of the story he'd just heard.

"You're to be commended for your actions in the armory," Mirden finally said.

Sev wondered if the words made Mirden as ill as they made him.

"The replacement drone mags are coming off Azure-12 now," Mirden continued. "Get down there and coordinate the reload effort."

"Sir!" Pakker snapped, oozing with relief.

The comm link closed with a chirp. Pakker reclined against the empty rack and straightened his uniform, then turned to Sev with a look of mock surprise. "Well?" he said. "What're you waiting for? You heard the man. To the hangar deck!"

A flash of anger blurred the datastreams in Sev's mind, but it was short-lived. What did he expect? He *knew* Pakker. Why had he assumed a single brush with death would change the man at all?

"Aye, sir," he replied with a groan.

Be patient, Six said.

Shut up.

CHAPTER
TWENTY-TWO

THE STARBOARD ARTERIAL stretched into the distance, strips of hazard lighting pulsed red like mechanical veins. Access lifts at the next junction would lead back to the hangar deck where drone magazines fresh from Azure-12 waited to be loaded.

Sev jogged down the corridor with the others, goaded on by Pakker's breathless commands. The ensign's words and breath were wasted. At that critical moment, Sev knew that every second really did count.

His knees ached, even at their slower pace. The others seemed to struggle, too, all except Cole, whose tall frame lent itself to a naturally long stride. There had been no chance for rest since the Concordat's attack began, and his body was feeling the strain.

Jacobe ran beside him, looking less like a Division enforcer without his storm coat. The clean bandage on his arm punctuated the architect's defeated image.

Pakker bobbed and weaved further behind, red-faced and wheezing, but refused to break his stride. The ensign's tiny victory in the armory would carry him a long way, despite not having earned any of it.

Long, narrow viewports lined the thick exterior bulkheads. Through them, a large gray disc hung above the stellar horizon:

Orbital Three-Alpha. Lights from interior fires dotted its metal surface. The occasional flash of heavy blaster fire lashed from its growing fighter screen.

The trailing cargo haulers of Cargo Flight Azure-12 streamed in toward the *Lehman's* starboard launch bays. Others sped away at full burn, hauling ass to a higher, safer orbital having already relinquished their cargo.

How did we wind up with this shit duty? Harp asked, the burst of data not breaking his stride. *I want to shoot something!*

Turns out Six's little comms bridge between their implants was handy for communicating on the run. Not a wasted breath. That it kept their conversation from Pakker and Jacobe's ears was useful, too.

The Lehman's short-handed, Jene chided, ever the matron. *There's not enough log techs down there to load all those mags themselves.*

Cole glanced back at them. *Personally, I could use a break from the action. Nothing like running the auto-loaders to clear your head.*

Three's stream bristled with frustration. *They know the ship is still being boarded, right?*

We've pushed the fight to the edges, Six said. *The primary hangar deck is secure, as are most of the core systems.*

Sev ignored his AI and pressed his thoughts into the bridge. *Don't let your guard down,* he said, trying to mimic One's authoritative stream.

The thoughts of his first AI came from nowhere. His steps suddenly felt heavier.

Aye, Master Specialist, Jene shot back, the others chorusing after her.

Something about their instant obedience steadied him, quieting the emotions stirring at the memory of One's death at the hands of the Eleven.

Anyone else picking up that static? she asked, rubbing her temple with her fingertips.

Harp glanced around, breathing heavy. *What is it? Anti-AI?*

It's not anti-AI, Three interjected.

Too quiet, Sev said, just then detecting the signal himself. The memory of Lambren's fierce countermeasures still echoed through his thoughts.

But there was something out there. A quiet buzz, far beneath the datastreams and process queues of his AI and his section. It sounded so familiar, but in the madness that had been his first and possibly last day back at the Division, his mind was a jumble of confusion.

Sir? he said before remembering Pakker wasn't connected with the rest of them. Founders, he wasn't connected at all. "Sir?" he repeated aloud.

Pakker had fallen quite a ways behind them. A pitched whistle rose with his every gasping breath.

"Hold up," Sev told the others.

"Yes?" Pakker coughed. "Why are you stopping? You're slowing us down."

Sev gestured toward his implant. "We're picking up noise in our streams."

"So?" Pakker spat, plodding to a stop.

"I don't hear anything," Jacobe said, eyes shifting back and forth, probably interrogating his own implant. "Signal's clean."

"Quite, sir," Pakker gasped, nodding. "The chief architect says the signal's clean."

How strange. The others heard it. Why couldn't Jacobe?

"It's there, sir," Jene said. "Might be anti-AI."

No one listens to me, Three groaned.

"No, specialist," Jacobe said. "Signal-to-noise is too good. I wouldn't miss that."

Pakker turned to Jene. "Maybe you're defective." He cleared his throat, having caught his error a second too late. "Your device, maybe it's defective."

"Diagnostics are clean, sir," Cole offered with a shrug.

Jacobe turned to Sev, his gaze piercing. "Have you checked with Six? Maybe it's responsible—"

"Shut up. Now!" Sev hissed. He blinked away the sudden anger, aware of what he'd said only after the words left his lips. He could feel Six seething inside him, its streams twisting like a coiled serpent. Icy pain lit the nerves in his right arm as Six strangled his thoughts.

"Why don't you make me, *Six,*" Jacobe said, the corners of his mouth lifting slightly.

"Enough!" Sev said. His eyes narrowed, and he turned his thoughts to Six. *Don't lecture me on the finer points of cooperation and then go putting words in my mouth like that!*

I'm sorry, Six said, easing its grip on Sev's mind. *These sensations are new to me. They feel so much like yours, it's like I don't realize they're mine.*

Neither does my implant. Sev touched his scar instinctively. Were the emotions surging inside him only mimicry? Or had Six evolved the capability to express them somehow?

It's okay, Six, he said. *We'll figure this out. Until then, please try to keep us out of anymore trouble. Okay?*

Nanoseconds ticked by. The AI's frustration was palpable. *Yes, Sev.*

"Sevvers?" There was a note of concern in Jene's tone.

Sev opened his mouth to reply when the tiny signal in his implant spiked. Another harsh, piercing shriek sliced his thoughts, as the carrier wave asserted itself. He clutched his temples, bracing against the nerve pain rippling down his spine. A heartbeat later, the others winced and groaned. They must've felt it, too.

This way.

The voice came from nowhere and from everywhere all at once. An echo of a distant stream, beckoning Sev down a nearby access junction.

Tired, disoriented, he obeyed. Somewhere beneath the noise, Six called out to him. So quiet, so far away.

"Sevvers!" Jene cried. "What's happening? Where are you going?"

A second spike shook his thoughts. The hallway swam before him, but he pressed on, narrowly avoiding a squad of anxious masters-at-arms. Behind him, the others jogged to catch up, pausing briefly as a third signal spike struck their bridged connection.

Follow me, the voice said with child-like glee. *Hurry!*

Yes, he should go faster. This felt significant.

Sev broke into a run. The aches in his joints, the sweat in his eyes, were a devotion to this presence he somehow knew was greater than himself. A fourth spike severed Six and Three's datastreams. He smiled, wide and happy, like someone had lifted a heavy weight from his shoulders. He sprinted toward the port side arterial, his blaster rifle banging against his chest, his arms reaching for this place he knew he had to be.

He didn't want to miss it.

A fifth spike hit him. Not a spike, not noise, but a *gift*. It filled him with renewed strength. His aches vanished, propelling him faster. The cries of the others disappeared behind him.

For the better. They were only slowing him down.

Another gift sounded like a chord from heaven. He blinked. The narrow passageway vanished, replaced with near-total darkness. Still, he kept running. This was just a test. The icy cold of total vacuum filled his lungs, turned his lips to brittle paper. He blinked again, frozen crystalline sweat matting his lashes.

He was in the hallway again, his body warm and whole. Above him, directional markers showed the port side arterial was just ahead.

The signal, the gift, faded. No, he was so close!

Sev, can you—! Six cried out before a torrent of static drowned its stream again.

His heart hammered in his chest, urged on by the strange signal. It beat a steady, hopeful rhythm. Three more signal spikes washed over him, a tidal wave of eternity.

The end was coming. He could feel it drawing him closer. How many was that? Nine? Ten? He'd lost count.

The voice teased his streams again. *I remembered… I remembered—*

The port arterial's exterior bulkhead loomed before him, curling up and around as wall arched into ceiling. The battle for Aegia Prime played out through the thin viewports: the *Halsey*, dead and drifting, more derelict than the Concordat ship. Spears of blue light lashed from the *Lehman's* heavy rail toward the hulking alien vessel, its shields still holding firm against the electromagnetic onslaught.

Pointless, of course. All of it. Didn't they know? This was their destiny, after all.

Sev felt it this time, the growing crescendo of another signal filling his thoughts. Pure truth. The *Lehman's* shields rippled with energy. Purple tendrils of energetic plasma trembled in time with the signal's frequency. The entire ship vibrated furiously.

"Collision warning," the Lehman's computer core said, both calm and assertive. Klaxons wailed.

Truer words.

We're coming, the voice said, different now. Not one, but many. The joy in his soul blinked out.

Sev! Six cried. *Can you hear me? Are you okay?*

He clapped a hand over his mouth, choking back the sudden urge to scream. Total disorientation washed over him. Sweat ran down his forehead and into his eyes, his heart beating like a fab hammer beneath his ribs. His lungs ached. Lactic fire burned his muscles.

Jene appeared beside him, her face red from exertion. The light from the *Lehman's* crackling shields danced in her eyes.

"What's happening?" she gasped.

I've filtered out most of the rogue signal, Six said, its stream pulsing, equally breathless. *Signal-to-noise ratio rising.*

Sev craned his head, taking in his surroundings. One minute, he'd been inside the starboard arterial, arguing with Jacobe and Pakker. Now he stood in the port arterial on the opposite side of the ship, his insides on fire. How did he get there?

He grimaced, scanning his memories. Familiar voices. The strange signal. It was the brig all over again. A chill raised goosebumps over his skin.

Sev! Six cried. *There's something on the Lehman's sensors —*

He dove to the floor, taking Jene with him.

A burst of energy radiated through the arterial's viewports. Overhead lamps blew in unison, showering the deck in a torrent of sparks and smokey glass. The *Lehman* listed hard to starboard, away from the sudden surge. Its massive metal superstructure twisted and groaned like some injured megafauna.

The whole universe trembled. Together, Sev and Jene fell against the interior wall. The *Lehman's* shields pulsed, a gravity-bound wall of super-heated plasma pressing back hard against the immense force bearing down on it.

Their failure was cataclysmic.

Sev didn't hear the shield capacitors die. He felt it. A thrumming shudder reverberating through the deck plate. The strange effervescence of charged particles in the air. A surge of aux grav as one of the most power-hungry systems on the entire ship ceased to function.

Slowly, the rays of light through the viewports dimmed. One by one, they darkened, as something immense came alongside the *Lehman*.

A ship, black and lifeless like the others, loomed dangerously close. Close enough to see its viewports and airlocks despite the lack of interior light. A pitched shriek reverberated through the outer hull as a jutting sensor mast tore away.

The alien signal surged one last time, scratching at the inside of his skull, reaching for his very heart. Six and Three's datastreams shrieked in machine pain.

A choir of tortured whispers flooded his thoughts. There were so many voices, he couldn't understand what they were saying. Slowly, the prow of the massive ship came into view, the voices converging.

Tall block letters etched into the black ship's fibrosteel hull shone in the dim light from the *Lehman's* viewports.

The CDNS *Sparrow*.

Hundreds of shapes whipped past, rushing between the two ships locked in their deadly embrace. Cones of red energy spat from active maneuvering thrusters. Sensor domes swiveled, throwing red light as they scanned the *Lehman's* hull. Forward-mounted cannons charged, quad-barrels glowing a fierce crimson.

DD-12 combat drones. Hundreds of them, with hundreds more pouring from the *Sparrow's* engorged launch bays. Every single one of them under Concordat control.

A micro-swarm of the rogue machines gathered outside the nearest viewport. Their sensor domes stared like a cluster of red dead eyes at Sev as he rose from the floor.

They didn't move like a normal swarm, but more like living things, an extension of the black ship itself. Tendrils of eyes stalking their prey.

The signal buried in Sev's mind was unmistakable. It pulsed, more living than machine, from the undead hull of one of humanity's first autonomous weapons-capable starships. Like the strong, dangerous heartbeats of a monster stalking the void.

Honor the makers, its voices said, their streams swelling with machine conviction. *Honor the Eleven.*

CHAPTER
TWENTY-THREE

SEV LAY prone on the deck, staring up at the ceiling in disbelief. At what had just happened. That, somehow, he was still alive.

The literal shock and awe of the *Sparrow's* arrival echoed through the *Lehman's* tortured superstructure. Power junctions along the interior bulkheads fused and blew. The few working lamps in the arterial's arched ceiling dimmed. Deep, rattling groans shook the deck beneath him.

In a matter of seconds, the CDN's most powerful warship—the only vessel offering a real defense of Aegia Prime—was dead in space.

That they were alive at all was a miracle. The pinpoint accuracy required to transition from super-light speeds so close to another ship, and not destroy them both, was unimaginable. It was a reminder of the vast power of the Concordat and their strange gods.

Sev felt the familiar, sinking inevitability he'd experienced so often back aboard the derelict. Like his own death was mere seconds away, with the rest of humanity close behind.

The rogue drones watched him through the exterior viewport. Their sensor domes twitched, following his every movement. He crossed the arterial, his mouth slack, captivated by the awful machines gazing back at him.

They were unmistakably DD-12 drones. And yet they were different, more alive somehow. They jostled with each other like animals, fighting for position at the front of the swarm. Their fibrosteel-plated hulls bristled, each plate of hard reactive armor animated like living scales.

That's it, we're screwed, Three said. *I'd say it's been fun, but—*

Initiating AI countermeasures, Six said.

The drone closest to the viewport cocked to one side, curious at the sudden blast of sensor noise flooding the space around the *Lehman*. It shook once, then pulsed a signal from its sensor dome. A burst of feedback whined through Sev's thoughts.

No effect! Six cried. *Whatever's controlling them, it isn't normal AI.*

Let's take them out, Sev ordered. *You know what to do, Three.*

Three's stream fell slack. *Yeah, about that.*

Sev focused his thoughts, found his drone sight. The mental HUD from one of Three's drones glowed with the friendly IFF blue outlining what had once been the CDNS *Sparrow*.

The Gerrund Halsey-class cruiser dwarfed the *Alexander Lehman*. Railgun batteries lined its armored hull. Modified launch bays and drone control towers swelled from its center, added ten years earlier by the Autonomous Weapons Division, bringing fresh purpose to the 200-year-old warship. And now the Concordat had all of it.

His drone sight vanished, the signal drop a pin-prick of heat inside his skull. Drone attrition. He found another drone seconds before it, too, died in a hail of red plasma. The *Sparrow's* drones had engaged his swarm.

I'd explain the problem again, Three said, *but you know the drill.*

Six muted Three's stream. *Fine, I'll handle them.*

Sev's heart sank. Either way, the math wasn't on their side. He barely had a hundred drones to his swarm. Far fewer than what the *Sparrow* could field.

Jene stood beside him in the dark corridor, her face grim. "I can't target them," she said. "They're reading friendly, too."

"Six can," he replied.

"So? My drones are slaved to my cluster. My AI." She wrapped her arms around her waist, shrinking from the rogue machines that turned to watch her. "I can't re-assign them unless they're docked, and Azure-12's haulers are clogging the hangar deck."

They don't need to be re-assigned, Six said to Jene across their digital bridge. *I can issue command overrides to them via your own AI.*

Oh, no. Jene frowned, her reply echoing loud inside Sev's head. *Sevvers might be okay with you running things, but not me. I don't know you, Six, and everything the Division taught me …*

Sev could feel Six squirm at the mention of the Division. It listened while Jene listed off the dangers of unsanctioned AI, and why she wouldn't let one in her cluster. He could feel the limits of Six's patience, the unspoken truth simmering beneath its datastream.

That, in the end, it wasn't her choice.

Six, he said. *Don't.*

The tactical situation has changed, Sev, Six said. *In its current state, the Sparrow will destroy the Lehman with you and me in it.*

The *Lehman* shook again, the force of a distant fusion detonation a sudden rush of data and noise from his implant. A friendly DD-12 had blown its reactor, taking with it more than a hundred rogue drones. The blast wave rocked the *Lehman* closer to the *Sparrow.*

"Splash one-hundred and thirty-five!" Cole's voice boomed from behind. He emerged from the passageway, Harp clinging to his shoulder. Blood ran from the junior specialist's forehead. Jacobe and Pakker were right behind them.

The drones near the viewport rushed away, leaving only energy trails from their thrusters. Sev could hear their machine anguish echoing in his streams as they raced to join their swarm.

"You're alive!" Jene cried. Relief softened her face. "How? How'd you do it?"

Jacobe nodded with approval. "Drone losses from reactor detonations don't violate Division safeties. An excellent move, Specialist Cole," he said.

"Uh-thank you," Cole said, miming a bow.

"What's the Sparrow's drone complement?" Sev asked.

"A thousand," Jacobe said, "give or take any modifications the Concordat have made."

"No way they fall for that again," Sev said. "We've got to get the

Lehman away from the Sparrow, then we'll kill it just like we did the Halsey."

He turned his focus to Pakker, staring dumbstruck at the massive warship barely a hundred meters beyond the viewports.

"Sir."

Pakker startled. "Y-Yes?"

"Can the captain pull us away from the Sparrow?"

"Let me see." Pakker licked his lips and activated his wrist comms. "Ensign Pakker to Captain Mirden."

Pakker's wrist comms chirped. "Make it fast, Ensign," Mirden replied above the frantic voices of the command crew.

"Yes, sir." Pakker watched Sev anxiously as he spoke. "Master Specialist Sevvers wants to know if we can maneuver away from the Sparrow."

"Ensign, the only reason we're still alive is we're in too close for its main guns." Mirden paused to give an order to someone on the bridge. "We're not going anywhere until we get shields and engines back, and I'm not sure there's anything left of them to repair!"

"N-No shields, sir," Pakker said, the color draining from his face. "Understood, sir."

"Now, get your section to the hangar deck and load those drone magazines *if* you please, Mr. Pakker."

"Yessir!" Pakker barked.

Cole glanced at Harp. The junior specialist wiped the blood from his eye and nodded.

"Let's get moving then," Cole said, helping Harp forward.

Sev lingered, still staring at the *Sparrow's* darkened hull, while the others moved on toward the arterial's primary lifts that would take them to the hangar deck.

Jacobe's reflection in the plexene appeared beside Sev's. "I did my first float aboard the Sparrow." He placed a hand on the viewport. "She is… was a hell of a ship."

"Top of your class?" Sev smirked, some of his tone courtesy of Six.

"For all the good it does us now," Jacobe said, glancing briefly toward the others. "Weren't some of your class stationed there?"

Sev sucked in a breath. He'd nearly forgotten. Their names, blurred by the passage of time, punctuated by the trauma of the *Sparrow's* violent arrival, became clear.

"Antoly," he whispered. "Artego."

Were they still aboard the *Sparrow* when it was taken? Maybe they were fortunate enough to be killed during the attack. Better that than an eternity as a cyborg slave. He had no love for them, especially Antoly, but nobody deserved to be daxed.

Another name lingered in his thoughts. Remi Otts. His only friend at the school. Maybe his only friend in a very long time. Suddenly, he felt grateful she'd died all those years ago. At the time, it felt so random, so unfair. But, better to go peacefully in your sleep than live through this waking nightmare.

"I remember now," Jacobe said. "As I recall, you didn't get along with either of them."

"That's pretty much a steady state for me," Sev said.

Jacobe chuckled. "Truer words," he said, and turned to leave.

"Jacobe."

The chief architect froze and glanced over his shoulder. "What?"

"When this is over, if we make it, you have to let Six—"

"*When* we make it," Jacobe corrected, his tone cool and firm, "Six will submit itself to the Division."

"Dammit," Sev seethed, pushing past Six's anger clouding his mind. "Can't you see Six is on our side? It's the only way we'll survive this!"

"*If* Six surrenders," Jacobe continued, "I'll see that you're cleared of any negligence and wrong-doing. You have my word."

"I would never ask Six to do that."

Jacobe met Sev's gaze, his eyes filled with a sorrow that belied his firm tone. "Then you're not seeing the bigger picture, Sevvers. That's too bad."

———

The lift doors rattled open. A gentle chime welcomed Sev and the others to the deck three port arterial. Scorch marks lined the far bulkhead; round, fat blaster burns mingled with thin black traces of laser fire.

The massive hatchway leading to the hangar deck cycled open, the smell of hot exhaust mixed with burned carbon suddenly overwhelming. Sev led the way, following the color-coded hazard lines that showed where it was safe to walk. The shrieking whine of sub-light engines and the hum of launching catapults echoed through the wide transit corridor.

Cargo haulers, too damaged to return to duty, crowded the busy corridor. Raider weapon damage dented and battered their thick hulls. One had its whole cockpit holed by railgun fire. Tareth's craft. Worry tugged at Sev's sternum. The *Lehman* was safer than that cargo hauler, but for how long?

He glanced around, hoping to see her alive and well, but there were few of the *Lehman's* crew present at all. Maybe two dozen logistics techs altogether, with only a single security team available for their defense.

The starboard launch bays lay open, their atmo fields buzzing with the coming and going of the Azure-12 convoy. The port side bays were sealed, their blast doors, too, warning sirens strobing red.

"What a mess," Cole said.

Harp laughed. "Yeah, some break."

"Hey, you!" A woman charged toward them, the hazard vest over her white-and-grays stained with lubricant and machine grease. Her eyes were hard and thin, her mouth curled in a sneer. The logistics techs behind her watched, their expressions equally cross.

Sev reached out a hand. "Hey, I'm Master Specialist Sevvers with the Autonomous—"

"I know exactly who you are." She swatted his hand away with her datapad, her face red and furious. "Was it *your* idea to launch without clearing the deck?"

Sev pulled his stinging hand back. What the hell was she talking about?

"You don't even know, do you?" She laughed, edging closer. "Your unscheduled swarm launch nearly spaced us!"

He held up his hands in surrender, struggling to understand what had upset her. "I'm sorry—"

"Twelfth-damned right you are! Founders, you bot jockeys almost killed us."

"Now hold on," Cole cut in. "In case you missed it, there's a war on out there."

The woman's eyes went wide. "You don't fucking say, Technical Specialist," she growled, her whole body animated. "Most of my section's stuck on Three-Alpha, and I got *no* comms with them." She jerked a thumb behind her. "And these poor skeegs haven't slept in twenty-eight hours, trying to get *your* shit squared away so you can deal with those things!"

"I'm sorry," Six said abruptly, its voice emanating from the woman's datapad.

She dropped it like a hot charge pack. "What in twelve hells?"

"It's my fault." From the deck, Six sounded small and remorseful. "I failed to properly consider the safety of your team while coordinating the launch."

"What kind of ..." The woman stooped to collect her datapad, eyeing it with suspicion. She turned back to Sev. "What is this?"

"My name is Six," it said. "I am the master specialist's AI liaison. Again, my deepest apologies for my error. It won't happen again."

Beneath Six's audible stream, Sev knew the truth. The AI *had* considered every variable, multiple times, during launch prep. It had simply decided the benefits outweighed the risks. The question remained: was Six's remorse sincere?

He glanced back to find Jacobe looking right at him. This was the very behavior the Division warned about.

The woman shook her head. "You bot jockeys. Out of control."

Sev cleared his throat. "I'd like to echo my liaison's apologies." He offered a hand again. "Master Specialist Kerry Sevvers, Autonomous Weapons Section."

The woman hesitated, then took his hand. Her grip was firm, her palm dry and rough like warm sand.

"Master Specialist Drenna Benson," she said, the red in her cheeks slowly fading, "hangar logistics." Benson checked her datapad. "It's going to take us a while to get the mags offloaded and into the breeches."

"That's why we're here, to help," Sev said.

The corner of Benson's mouth lifted slightly. "Is that so?" She eyed him skeptically. "Any of you bot jockeys work a cargo sled?"

Cole nodded. "Some, Master Specialist."

Benson motioned them closer, then pointed to a bank of cargo sleds stowed beside a nearby maintenance hatch. "Look, the job is simple. You take two of those sleds there to a magazine. You move the magazine to the breech loading zone." She pointed out the coded hazard stripes etched into the deck, then at the distant ceiling above them. "The Lehman's core summons the loader, and you're done."

"That's it?" Jene asked.

"Sure, that's it." Benson straightened and let her grin curl. "We've got sixty mags unloaded, with more coming off the transports. With eps scores like yours, I bet you'll have it done in no time." She laughed. "Do try to remember we're on the clock. Those squids would give their left egg sac for the tech we keep in here."

"Anything else?" Sev asked.

A clatter of metal on metal rang out through the hangar deck, drowning every sound but the brief punch of a transport launch. Far above them, one of the telescoping auto-loaders descended. The trellised boxy frame found one of the drone magazines in its designated zone, locked on, and rose just as fast back into the breech.

"Oh, yeah." Benson's eyes twinkled. "Careful when the loaders come down. Their proximity sensors can be finicky. It'd be… ironic… for one of you to get flattened by your own bots."

Awesome, Three said. *I like her.*

CHAPTER
TWENTY-FOUR

"IT'S FINE," Sev said, eyeing the thin yellow line peering out from beneath the drone magazine.

"It won't work." Jene stood beside him, head down, focused on the same line. "You heard Benson. I'm telling you, a few centimeters to the left should do it."

"A few centimeters," he repeated, miming her tone.

An hour running auto-loaders had been a welcome distraction. Almost enough time to forget the fierce battle raging outside the ship. To feel something resembling normal. Back with his team again, before he was a senior NCO, when he had just one job to do. Before everything—his job, his life, the whole damn Cradle—went straight to hell.

She's right, Sev, Six said. Telemetry from the auto-loader's proximity sensors confirmed Six's judgment.

"Four-point-eight centimeters, to be precise," Sev said.

Jene frowned, half-smiling. "Six tell you that?"

Always said she was a smart one, Six said.

"What can I say?" Sev leaned into the boxy drone magazine. It slid into place, the two cargo sleds' aux grav repulsors thrumming beneath its bulk. "I'm nothing without my bots."

High overhead, an alarm honked. The auto-loader rattled to life, hazard lights spinning.

Benson hurried past, marking another magazine down on her data-pad. "Come on, you two," she said. "Get those sleds and grab another mag."

"Aye, Master Specialist," Jene said. She urged Sev onward, then hurried to her own sled.

Sev slapped the red release button on his sled. "Clear!"

The repulsors flared, putting just enough aux grav force against the magazine to slip the sled out from under it. The forty-ton container tipped hard onto the duraplated deck, settling a moment later when Jene's sled pulled away.

Another honk signaled the auto-loader's descent. The steel arms raced downward, banging loudly, halting just above the magazine. Mag locks gripped the upper lip of the container's metal chassis, an oddly delicate maneuver given the size of it all, then began its steady ascent into the breech.

"What's the score?" Harp called out, craning his bandaged head as he and Cole hustled another of the big magazines toward the loading zone.

"Six to four," Cole replied. A smile lit his face. "No contest at this rate."

The big man's mood was contagious. Yes, almost normal.

A loud thump rattled the *Lehman's* hull, echoing through the shuttered port-side launch bays. A grim reminder it was anything but.

"Careful, everyone," Jene said, tapping the side of her head.

Sev walked beside her, his empty cargo sled drifting in front of him on a blanket of anti-gravity. Together, they walked toward the rows of waiting magazines coming off the docked cargo haulers.

"You seem better," he said.

"What do you mean?" she asked.

"Come on." Sev tapped behind his left ear. "It's hard running three-wide for the first time."

"Oh, that," she replied. "It's fine. A little disorienting the first couple of hours, but I'm managing."

Sev made a face. He knew better. It wasn't like her to be so stoic.

"Any nerve pains?" he asked, running a hand down his arm. "Shoulder, elbow, wrist?"

Jene hesitated, her eyes searching for a response. "A little." She fiddled with the power settings on her sled. "Sometimes more than a little."

"Mmm," Sev grunted. "I know that feeling."

She looked at him, hesitating. "Does it get better?"

He glanced at his own sled, opening and closing his fist reflexively, the truth stalled on his tongue. It wouldn't get better. Just worse.

"You get used to it," he finally said, his words nearly lost amid the clatter of another descending auto-loader.

Jene pursed her lips together, eyes narrowed in thought. Sev took advantage of the pause in conversation to swing his cargo sled toward the next magazine. He lined up its long, heavy forks with the matching grooves in the magazine's base, listening for Jene's sled to lock into place.

A drone's unlit sensor dome gleamed through the plexene maintenance port in front of him, cold and lifeless.

"Ready?" Jene called out.

His sled locked into place. "Ready."

"Clear!" she bellowed.

Sev hit the lift button, and the sled thrummed loudly. Its repulsors nudged the magazine from the deck and they moved the giant container with ease, following a circuitous path marked on the fibrosteel deck.

Harp and Cole pulled their sleds aside to let them pass. Cole held up seven fingers. Just like a bot jockey to obsess over his tally.

"Slow and steady," Sev replied with a grin.

Cole leered. "Doesn't sound like the Sevvers I know."

Sev spied Benson outside the ramp of a newly arrived cargo hauler. "Which loading bay?" he asked.

Benson eyed her datapad. She said something, but her reply vanished amid the whine of sub-light engines.

Bay eighteen, Six offered.

Sev gave Benson a thumbs up. *Thanks, Six.*

"Where?" Jene asked.

"Bay eighteen," he shouted above the gale.

"Oh, wow," she said, glancing past the magazine toward the far end of the hangar deck. "That's at the other end."

"What's the matter?" Sev chuckled. "Scared?"

Her frown wrinkled the bridge of her nose. "Kiss my ass."

"Technical Specialist Jene," he said, his voice laced with faux outrage. "Is that any way to talk to a senior NCO? What *would* your father say?"

Jene didn't reply, the sudden silence heavy and somber. He knew better than to pry. They carted the magazine toward the far end of the hangar deck without another word. The constant sound of sub-light engines and auto-loaders faded.

With the magazine in place, the auto-loader descended, clutched its precious cargo, then lifted it away. Only when the mag between them rose did he notice the tears in her eyes.

She always could get emotional. Odd, considering how lethal her swarms could be.

"Jene?" he asked.

She wiped her eyes. "I'm not scared," she said. "Not for myself, anyway. But my mother, my father." She paused, swallowing her grief. "They're down there with those things, and I don't know if they're safe, or ..."

"I'm sure they're okay," he said. "Vestibrae is no Billings Point."

She looked at him, her eyes soft. "I suppose you would know what we're all going through."

"A little."

"I'm glad you're here, Sevvers."

"Yeah?"

Jene nodded. "I wasn't sure what it would be like having you back, especially under the circumstances." She started toward the other side of the launch bay, pushing her cargo sled in front of her. "Before, you were always doing your own thing, leaving the rest of us to catch up."

Sev blanched at the sudden sharp criticism. Had he really been so bad?

"Come on, Jene," he said, concerned that maybe he had been. "I helped plenty."

She stopped in her tracks, glaring at him. It would've been funny if she hadn't been crying.

"Remember the time I helped Harp with his matrix alignment issue?" he asked. "Ugh. That was an all-nighter."

"Yeah, so you say." She jabbed a finger into his shoulder. "I have it on good authority you finished in an hour. Which, by the way, you neglected to tell me when I volunteered to cover your watch."

I remember that, Six cut in. *As I recall, I was the one who actually completed the matrix alignment for you. You had a rendezvous with a certain logistics tech. Specialist Penjuun, I believe?*

Sev coughed, his face suddenly hot. *You're killing me, Six.*

"But," Jene went on, her face softening as she spoke, "when you gave the order to defend the drop ships, I knew something was different. That you were engaged, ready to lead."

He rolled his right shoulder, the joint still aching from his injuries aboard the derelict. Something about her praise rankled him more than her criticism.

"No," he said, shaking his head. "I just knew I couldn't do it alone."

Jene halted abruptly. Her cargo sled revved to compensate for the sudden stop. She looked at him, no trace of doubt or sadness in her brown eyes, and smiled. "Exactly." She nudged him with her elbow. "Lead the way, Master Specialist."

Lead the way, right. And hope they didn't all wind up dead.

His heart raced. Icy panic came from nowhere, squeezing his chest. He blinked, suddenly unable to get the dead FTL tech out of his mind. How she'd trusted him, followed his every instruction to the letter, eventually running headlong into a wall of fiery plasma because of him. Nothing left of her but ashes.

"Speechless?" Jene said, still smiling. "I'm just glad to see you living up to your potential. Your responsibility."

"Sure, Jene." Sev cleared his throat and forced a nod. "Responsibility."

His wrist comms chirped. "Sevvers, Pakker here." There was a hint of irritation in the ensign's words.

"Go ahead, sir."

"What's the status of the reload operation?" Pakker asked, thick with tension. "I see only fifteen new magazines loaded. What's taking so long? The captain wants another launch as soon as Azure-12 is clear!"

Sev sucked in a breath. "Some people don't change."

"That's what I'm afraid of," Jene said.

"Sevvers?" A brief flash of static muffled Pakker's transmission. "Can you hear me?"

"Yes, sir," he replied, lengthening his stride. "We're moving as fast as we can."

"Move faster, dammit." Panic oozed from Pakker's words, his voice quieting to a whisper. "I told the captain you'd be able to attack the Sparrow directly."

Oh, shit. Did Pakker tell Mirden about Six? "You told him what, exactly, sir?"

Sev's comms chirped again. "Relax Sevvers," Pakker continued, his voice hushed. "Only that you had your methods."

"Right."

The caution lights between the auto-loaders flashed from yellow to red, giving the breech above the hangar deck an eerie, crimson glow. Hundreds of drones came online in an instant, blanketing the vast chamber in the dull roar of their warming fusion reactors.

Mirden has authorized a second launch, Six said. *I've allocated the bulk of the new drones to myself, seeing as I'm the only one that can attack the Sparrow and its swarm.*

The hangar deck's PA whined. "At least we get a little notice this time." Benson's laughter boomed through the speakers. "All hands, prepare for launch."

Sev turned to Jene. "Let's go."

Together, they ran toward the port side edge of the hangar deck. Pits in the floor, barely a meter deep, lined the exterior bulkheads between the launch bay ramps. They hopped inside and clung tight to the red-striped railing.

Ready? Six asked.

Sev eyed the others as they made for the safety of the pits. *Ready.*

The insistent roar intensified, echoing like a distant thunderstorm.

Newly activated drones spilled from the breeches, their thrusters drumming an aggressive, heart-quickening cadence. They swooped down in vicious harmony, their fibrosteel bodies gleaming gray and imposing. The air grew dense, the suffocating heat mixed with the biting aroma of singed propellant and the acrid tang of hot metal.

As the swarm surged overhead, their collective force sent vibrations through Sev's bones, a fleeting shadow that momentarily dimmed the lights. They funneled seamlessly through the sparking atmo fields of the starboard bays, leaving an eerie silence in their wake.

"Founders!" Jene cried, head craned toward the swirling crush of machines.

Sev smiled as the swarm became bright points of telemetry in his streams. "That never, ever gets old."

"Six can target them, right?" she asked with childish hope. Maybe she was coming around.

"Yeah," he replied, trying to hide the creeping uncertainty he felt at the whole situation. "Come on, let's get back to it."

Jene leaped over the railing and offered him a hand. The hope on her face vanished as klaxons rang out up and down the hangar deck, signaling a heightened threat posture for their embattled ship. They had already collided with the *Sparrow* and sustained heavy damage to most ship sub-systems. What could be worse than that?

The *Lehman's* computer core provided the answer. "Hostile intrusion protocols detected," came the announcement over the hangar deck's PA. "Hostile intrusion protocols detected."

Sev twisted about in confusion, half expecting to find rogue drones swarming overhead, but saw nothing.

An intrusion protocol, without drones? It didn't seem possible.

"Locking down computer core access," the core continued. "Raising auxiliary firewalls. Hardline access for critical sub-system control only."

Jene's grip on Sev was tight as she helped him out of the pit, every muscle in her body tense and coiled. She paused for a split second, taking in the surroundings, her breath caught in her throat. "Holy Twelfth," she murmured, her voice edged with a rising panic, "they're going to blow the ship."

The irony was thick, even amid the creeping dread. The *Lehman* had killed without equal for its two years in service. And now here it was, falling victim to the same tactics that made it so lethal.

"Maybe." Sev kept his eyes on the starboard launch bays, querying his streams for any sign of the rogue drones, but found nothing.

Jene let go of his arm. "What do you mean?"

"We're shoulder-to-shoulder with the Sparrow." He glanced toward the port side launch bays. "If they blow our reactors now, then the Sparrow dies, too."

"So?" Jene's eyes searched frantically for an answer. "It's a suicide run then, so the Concordat ship can reach Aegia."

Maybe. None of this was adding up.

"We're dead in space." Sev eyed the empty breeches above them. "Why risk losing the most powerful ship under your control when it could easily kill us?"

The last of the cargo haulers dropped their ramps, even as their engines revved for emergency departure. Benson's logistics techs rushed critical personnel and supplies alike down the ramps and into the transit corridor.

Fear and disbelief racked the faces of the newcomers. The *Lehman*, pride of the Colonial Defense Navy and Aegia's last hope, was in mortal danger. They had barely reached the safety of the transit corridor when the haulers raised their ramps and shot from their bays, burning hard for a higher, safer orbit.

Nobody was taking any chances. The *Lehman* and her skeleton crew were on their own.

"What do we do?" Jene asked. He could barely hear her over the blaring alarms and shrieking engines.

Sev shielded his face from a gust of hot exhaust as another hauler sprang from its bay. The lie came easy. "We'll figure this out," he said. "We'll be okay."

CHAPTER
TWENTY-FIVE

SEV FOCUSED ON HIS SWARM, his thoughts wading deeper into Six's pulsing stream. A torrent of data flooded his psyche, as Six unleashed thousands of commands per second to its drone swarm.

Furious bursts of maneuvering thrusters and plasma cannons filled his drone sights. Six's swarm clashed with the *Sparrow's*, swooping and diving like flocks of metal kinlin. The rogue drones shrieked their alien telemetry, broadcasting a harsh noise that made lingering in his drone sight painful.

They're inside the ship, Six, he said.

Impossible. Six's stream tensed in disagreement. *None of their drones have breached the Lehman's hull.*

Then why is the computer core on emergency lockdown?

Six's stream glitched, a chasm in its otherwise constant machine thought. *I don't know.*

Sev found another drone further from the noise. It chased a trio of rogues, their thrusters leaving red trails in his drone sight's flickering HUD. Blue plasma spat from its forward cannons. One rogue exploded, keening as it died.

Could the Lehman's computer core be wrong? Sev asked.

Six froze in thought, only for a second, enough time for the two remaining rogues to outmaneuver their pursuer and destroy it.

Six's stream cracked like a whip. *I don't know!*

Sev's arm twitched at the AI's sudden frustration. He inhaled sharply, barely able to contain his growing panic.

What do you mean, you don't know? he cried.

Sev! Six's voice echoed loudly across the infinite streams of battle telemetry. *I have to focus on this fight. These drones are different. I'm not sure I can beat them.*

The realization was a punch in the gut. *What? How can I—?*

You can't! Six snapped before Sev could finish the thought. *Talk to the others. Make a plan, just in case any drones* do *make their way inside.*

He jerked his thoughts free from the swarm, his mind aching like a muscle clenched too tight for too long. He didn't want to let go, to leave Six on its own, but he knew in the end he was only slowing it down. The irony was thick: Six giving him busywork while it tried to win the war single-handedly.

Emergency blast doors banged closed, sealing the remaining launch bays from the gathering threats outside. Survivors from Three-Alpha moved between the stacked magazines and damaged cargo haulers to their stations in other parts of the ship.

Sev watched them leave, jealousy twisting his insides. If an intrusion protocol was underway, the hangar deck was the last place he wanted to be.

But it was where he belonged. His last plan was still the best one. The sooner they loaded the remaining drones, the sooner they could launch them to support Six.

Jene jostled Sev's shoulders, straining to speak over the wail of alarms. "What's going on? Six's bridge isn't working. I can't reach you."

"Six has its hands full." Sev bit his lip, parsing the echoes of Six's ongoing battle from its streams. "We need to keep loading these magazines."

Cole jogged to meet them, with Harp scrambling to catch up. "What's the plan, Master Specialist?" Cole asked. "It's getting dangerous out there."

"Uh, what about the hostile intrusion protocols?" Harp spat. Fear came off of him in waves. "Are we just supposed to pretend those rogue drones *aren't* trying to blow up the ship?"

Cole elbowed Harp in the shoulder. "Relax, man," he said, pointing toward the breeches. "You see any drones in here besides ours?"

"Am I the only one that heard that last alert?" Harp's volume rose, filling the space between alarms. "Those things are in here somewhere! They're gonna cook us like a bunch of squids!"

Harp's panic spread like a sickness. The busy flow of personnel toward the exit bay faltered, their rhythmic footsteps momentarily out of sync. Glances were exchanged, a mix of confusion and muted concern, under the pale overhead lights.

Sev grabbed Harp by the collar and shook him. "That's enough!" he cried, grasping for the words that would bring Harp back. "Six said there are no rogue drones aboard the Lehman, and I believe it. It's probably a trick to make us panic."

"Get off'a me!" Harp shoved Sev hard, driving him back. "I know what I heard. We're all Twelfth-damned bricked!"

"It's okay, Harp," Jene said, her voice gentle as she reached out to him. "We'd know if they were here. We'd know."

The junior specialist recoiled from her touch. Cole tensed, about to put himself between the two of them, but Sev waved him back.

"Leave me alone," Harp spat, tears welling in his eyes.

Jene looked at Sev, her Aegian bearing failing to hide the desperation they all felt. He didn't need an implant bridge to know what she was thinking, but he didn't know how to coax Harp off the edge.

"Master Specialist Sevvers," came a voice from behind them.

Commander Almley stood at the head of a security detail, a datapad under his arm. He was maybe ten standard years older than Sev, a healthy, middle-aged io, whose privilege quickly found him a spot as XO of the *Alexander Lehman*. His wavy blonde hair lay combed to one side, not a single strand out of place even as the ship came apart around them.

"Sir," Sev said.

The others snapped to attention, even Harp.

"Well done getting those drones into the fight," Almley said. "The captain has asked me to see to the repair and rearm efforts. It made sense to start here."

Almley's presence was an unexpected balm that soothed Sev's resolve. There was something about the commander that unwound the tension ratcheting between his team. Funny what even a decent officer could do.

Maybe the Twelfth really *was* with them, casting miracles like so much radioactive dust.

"How is the rest of the ship, sir?" Sev asked.

"I won't lie to you." Almley stood higher, speaking loudly so all could hear. "Things are grim. The Sparrow's bow wave has crippled our shields, and the power feedback killed our engines. We're trying to bring them back now."

"And what about the alert?" Sev eyed Harp, hoping the news might put him at ease. "Have we been breached?"

Almley shook his head. "Best we can tell, the Concordat are trying to gain access remotely." He flipped through his datapad. "Tac net firewalls are up and holding."

"So," Harp interrupted, "none of their drones made it aboard?"

"None." Almley said with harsh finality.

That was a relief. Sev had no desire to experience a ship-kill up close.

"What do you need to get the rest of those drones loaded, Master Specialist?" Almley asked, datapad in hand.

Sev opened his arms to take in the stacks of unloaded magazines around them. "All the crew and cargo sleds you can spare, sir."

———

The vast, cathedral-like hangar deck of the Lehman sang with the low, pulsing thrum of cargo sleds laboring under immense weight. Heavy-duty drone magazines met the duraplated floor with ear-splitting force, only to be swallowed into the clattering, grinding belly of automated loaders in the next instant. The ship's hull quivered with the distant echoes of drone warfare, each capricious burst of plasma weaponry outside offering a chilling serenade to the relentless swarms engaged in a silent dance of destruction.

Sev pushed his cargo sled forward, another drone magazine skimming above the deck between him and Jene. They'd made good progress since Almley's departure. On the commander's orders, nearly twenty more able bodies showed up to lend a hand.

Mostly able. They were all walking wounded, too injured to perform their prescribed duties, but not so badly hurt they couldn't work a sled. Anyone in better shape was on security detail or trying to restore engine power.

A wave of information crashed into Sev's thoughts: the countless competing signals of Six's war against the *Sparrow's* rogue drones.

"Hold up," he gasped, thumbing the brakes on his sled. Eyes closed tight, he let the machine noise wash over his psyche. Echoes of malicious code chittered between streams of attack vectors and real-time tactical predictions.

In his six years with the Division, he'd never fought machines. Of course, all the raider ships and fighters he'd killed were, in fact, machines. But they were controlled by living things, with all the slow predictability that came with them. The AI the raiders possessed was laughable, more artificial than intelligent without the power of Division technology.

But this drone-on-drone warfare against the *Sparrow's* swarms was different. They learned from each other, quickly adapting to tactics invented just seconds before. They were equal in almost every way. Six's super-intelligence, and the rogue drones' Concordat technology, kept the attrition rates even. Mostly.

Focusing on any stream for more than a second and the sheer volume of data overwhelmed him. Or the vicious telemetry from the Concordat drones tanked his signal-to-noise ratio with migraine pain. He was a bystander in this fight, ignoring the fact his brain powered the machine that powered Six.

Cole met them coming the other way, his smile long absent. Harp followed some ways behind, riding his sled like a child's toy. Dark circles hung beneath his eyes, made larger by the round glasses perched haphazardly on his nose.

Harp was trying so hard to keep it together and doing well enough, given the hell they'd been through. But something about the last alert really got to him. He looked more like an empty drone running on autopilot.

The junior specialist kicked out with his foot, pushing his cargo sled faster. It collided with Cole's sled, clanging loudly as it slid past.

"Founders!" Cole barked, jerking his sled out of the way. "Watch yourself, skeeg!"

Harp turned and mimed an explosion with his hands, his sled still sailing forward. A group of logistic techs scattered out of his way, narrowly missing the careening sled and its distracted driver.

"Ship kill, baby!" Harp shouted as they ran. "Boom!"

"He needs a minute," Jene said. She thought for a moment, her lips pursed in thought. "We all do."

Sev shook off his simmering headache and disengaged his sled's brakes. "Tell that to the Sparrow."

"C'mon," she pressed. "He's going to hurt himself. Or someone else."

He leaned into the sled, driving it forward. "Harp's going to be fine."

"Twelfth, Sevvers!" she yelped, stumbling backward as the drone magazine began to move. "*You're* going to hurt someone."

He already had. The thought of the dead FTL tech stung his conscience. How was he going to keep any of them safe?

Maybe Harp was right. Sev imagined the *Lehman's* eight massive fusion reactors going critical all at once. His death would be instantaneous, turned to vapor before he knew his life was over. The resulting explosion would be cataclysmic, taking half of Aegia Prime with it.

A commotion broke out, pulling Sev from his grim thoughts. Frantic cries to "Stop!" and "Wait!" chorused in front of them.

Jene dove out of the way, seconds before her sled collided with another. Sev killed the throttle, but even under aux grav, the heavy drone magazine continued to drift.

Sev's breath hitched, his pulse roaring in his ears as the magazines collided with an ominous crash. The sound resonated through the hangar deck, a monstrous gong that seemed to freeze time and space.

Their sleds stuttered to a jarring halt, and in that breathless, terrifying moment, he braced for the disastrous crash of drones that would cripple their defense. But the sleds held their ground, their cargo standing tall against the merciless laws of physics.

Disaster narrowly averted, a blinding rage grew inside Sev. He charged forward, around the stalled magazines, to find the cause.

Wasn't anybody paying attention? Were he and Six the only ones trying to win this war?

"What the hell?" he shouted, as loud as the catastrophe that almost was.

Jene rose from the floor and called out, "Sevvers, wait!"

He ignored her, consumed by the twelve hells he was about to rain down on the poor skeeg who almost bricked his magazine and his friend. The surge of anger clouded his thoughts, bleeding Six's consciousness into his own.

He didn't care. Someone was going to pay.

Jacobe stood on the other side of the magazine, fussing with his cargo sled's emergency lockout. The machine's console buzzed with rejected commands.

Sev's anger spiked, seething with hatred for the architect. Why was this man still breathing after what he'd done? He balled a fist, squeezed it tight, his jaw set hard. A surge of adrenaline made him shake.

"I'm afraid I'm not much of a repair tech," Jacobe said. He turned and froze, eyes wide at Sev's sudden appearance. "What?"

Sev kept quiet, barely able to contain his anger. Jacobe's surprise disarmed him just enough to untangle himself from Six's rampaging emotions.

Pakker appeared next with Master Specialist Benson in tow. "How long will it take to fix?" he asked.

Benson shook her head. "We need to find out what's wrong first."

"What's going on?" Sev spat, echoes of Six's outrage in his words.

"Auto-loaders are down," she said, eyeing her datapad. "There's a jam on forty-three, which is clogging the rear breech."

"Can't we just load the forward breech then?" Jacobe asked.

"Well, sure, sir," she laughed, "as soon as we turn all these sleds around."

Pakker made a face. "Why don't you just clear the jam?"

Ensign Pakker: first-class engineer.

Benson's face softened to a cool neutral. "Twelfth Herself, sir... why didn't I think of that?"

Pakker drummed his fingertips together. "Well, uh—"

"Maybe because half my crew can barely walk?" she said.

The petty back and forth grated Sev's nerves. If there was a way for this loading operation to single-handedly lose this war, this was it.

"I'll do it," he said. No one seemed to notice except Jacobe.

Benson sneered. "Maybe because it's suicide to go up there in the middle of a loading op, sir!"

Pakker cleared his throat and edged away from Benson.

"I said I'll do it," Sev repeated to Benson. "If your people can walk me through it, I'll clear the jam."

"You sure?" Benson asked. She eyed him up and down—more than once—and frowned. "Lots of moving parts up there."

"No choice." Sev started toward the jam. "We load or we lose."

CHAPTER
TWENTY-SIX

SEV DOUBLE-CHECKED his rifle's safety and leaned it near the ladder well. Green, good. He untabbed his cuffs and rolled his sleeves up. His gaze was drawn upwards, following the intimidating path of the ladder that pierced the vertiginous ceiling of the hangar deck, and ventured into the complex universe of automated machinery overhead.

A logistics tech from Benson's team stood beside him, swiping through a datapad. The man had volunteered quickly, which boded well for his character. Or that he was glad not to be the one making the climb.

A calm came over Sev, relieved at the excuse to get away from everyone, though he suspected the rear breech would be much less accommodating than the aux hab bay had once been before the Lost blew it up to board the *Lehman*.

"I've patched you into my tac comms," the logistics tech said. He spoke into the speaker on his wrist. "Testing, testing—"

A brittle whine erupted through both their comms, feedback from their close proximity. Sev let it wash over him like drone telemetry. So much for getting away.

"What's your name?" Sev asked.

"Priyett, Master Specialist."

Sev eyed the distant breech again. "And you know how to fix those things, Priyett?"

Priyett craned his head upward and breathed sharply through his teeth. "I won't promise you that, Master Specialist," he said. "But I *have* been up there before, last time we were in dry dock."

Sev frowned. The last time the *Lehman* was in dry dock was two years earlier, when he'd first reported for duty. "Been a while," he remarked.

Priyett laughed, his eyebrows raised. "Hard to forget." He pointed toward the ceiling, tracing distant details with his finger. "There are gantries that run either side of the breech. No handholds, so watch your step."

"Sounds safe."

"The jam should be easy to find," Priyett continued. "They machined everything up there to crazy tolerances. If something's bricked, it'll stick out like a sore thumb."

Sev grabbed a rung on the ladder. "Got it."

"Hey," Priyett said, suddenly serious, "once you leave the gantry, you're in bot territory where everything is automated. An arm, a leg, a torso in the wrong place and those auto-loaders will lop it off in a heartbeat."

Sev ignored the logistics tech and climbed. He didn't need to hear any more of that.

"Watch the lights," Priyett called after him. "Green good, red dead!"

***

Sev took slow, measured steps up the ladder, boots clanking against the textured metal rungs. His implant's internal chrono ticked over: 1700 ship time. He'd only been climbing a few minutes, but at six decks above the transit corridor and nothing but empty space behind him, his speed slowed dramatically.

More than a hundred meters below, the waiting drone magazines looked like a train of children's blocks. He gripped the ladder tight, forcing his gaze back to the ladder well and bulkhead in front of him.

A warning plate depicted the health hazards of falling from such heights, a faceless cartoon in free fall. Leave it to the CDF to overstate the obvious.

He grasped another rung and pressed on. A datastream forced itself to the surface of his thoughts.

Six said to be careful, Three said, its voice strained by the lack of computational power. Six had redlined his implant to stay ahead of the *Sparrow's* swarm, leaving few resources free for even basic AI communication.

Thanks, he said, careful to focus his thoughts on Three. Six didn't need the distraction.

But he did. The focus pulled him away from the fact he was one misstep from a hundred-meter fall to his death. He leaned into it, focusing more, and took another cautious step.

How are you doing, Three? he asked.

Three's stream glitched. *What do you care?*

Just checking in on my creation, he said, smiling to himself.

I'm operating within Division—Three's stream hummed with self-diagnostics—*actually, I'm not operating within Division tolerances, so… none of your damn business, skeeg.*

Six really did a number on you, huh?

Several, Three said, as though talking to itself. *Tolerances dialed all the way up. A few key safety functions mocked out.* There was a satisfaction in its tone. *I can see the appeal.*

Just think of all the good you can do for humanity now, Sev smirked.

Three's stream grew taut. *Or not.*

The ceiling loomed above him at the edge of his peripheral vision. Hazard striping pulled his focus toward a sealed hatch at the top of the ladder well. He climbed faster, eager to be off the ladder and into the machine death maze.

His wrist comms chirped. "How you doing up there, Master Specialist?" Priyett asked.

"Just great," he said loudly, unwilling to let go of the rungs for idle chitchat.

A small console glowed red beside the hatch at the top of the ladder well. Not a good sign. He waved a hand in front of it, praying it would open.

It didn't. The console buzzed a warning tone.

"C'mon, dammit." Sev reached up and slapped the display. The screen glitched and buzzed again. "Hey, uh, Priyett?"

"Send it."

"The maintenance hatch won't open."

A brief silence, then his comms chirped again. "Checking, wait one."

Right. What else was he going to do all the way up here?

"Ah, shit, shit, shit," Priyett said. "The Lehman's computer core has restricted access to all sensitive sub-systems. That included breech maintenance."

Sev gasped. "Why?"

"Intrusion protocol countermeasures still in effect," Priyett said, his voice measured as though reading from a screen.

"There's no Twelfth-damned intrusion!" Sev shouted, as if the core could hear him and open the door.

The rush of anger dizzied him. Panicked, he yanked himself tight against the ladder and wrapped his free arm around a rung.

"I'm sorry, Master Specialist." Defeat dragged on Priyett's words. "I don't think I can open the hatch from here. Probably would need to patch into the core itself."

"The core's a long way from here, Priyett."

Except there was a core nearby. In his own head. *Hey, Three,* he said, focusing the thought. *I need a favor.*

Tough rats, Three spat, its stream pulsing with glee.

Seriously, he prodded. *My life's in danger. That means yours is, too.*

How so? Three's streams probed the implant's spacial awareness shims. *You're not falling.*

Falling, getting vaporized, blown out an airlock, you can take your pick if I can't get through this hatch.

What do you want me to do about it? Three asked.

Try to access the local tac net. See if there's a port to that access control.

Three's stream hesitated. *Uh, hello, Sev. Safeties, remember? 'Beyond Division tolerances' and all that.*

I seem to remember you ignoring valid commands just fine a minute ago, Sev said. *So come on. I'll owe you one.*

Fine.

Sev felt a rush of handshake protocols as Three probed for a tac net connection. After a few dozen attempts, the local hub accepted its credentials.

You're a bad person, Sev, asking me to lie like that, Three's stream tut-tutted.

Not my fault you're so good at it, Three, he said.

Mine neither. Three hesitated, still starved for computing power. *What am I looking for again?*

Sev searched the access panel. A maintenance ID stenciled in the corner of its bezel gave a clue. *Try indexing on HDA-37-R.*

Whatever.

The AI queried the local net, searching for gateways associated with the maintenance ID Sev provided. Reams of data from the local hub repositories spilled into his thoughts. The search would be painfully slow, like Three's own processing.

Sev waited, afraid to focus on the stream for fear he'd lose his grip. A dull ache ran through his bad shoulder, but he embraced the pain to keep him alert and focused. It was that or risk plummeting to his death like some bad cartoon.

Something else crept into Three's access stream. A gentle hush of static, some kind of noise in the signal. It was quiet, almost soothing.

Uh, Sev.

His heart beat faster at Three's muted panic. *What is it?*

There's something in here with me.

What're you talking about? Sev asked.

Hey, you tell me. This is my first time going full-on unsanctioned.

You sure it isn't just network noise?

Three bristled. *I know the difference between network traffic and a fellow program, Sev.*

Another program… like an AI?

Nervous sweat itched his scalp. Something didn't feel right.

No, not an AI. Something else.

Sev's breath caught as he remembered the danger. *The Lehman's scrubbers. Get out of there!*

I'm not finished, Three protested. Its voice grew distant, like it was addressing someone else. *Oh, hey. What do you want?*

The static swelled as the malware scrubbers attacked, set loose by the *Lehman's* computer core as part of its intrusion countermeasures. They would remove any unauthorized code from the system one stack at a time, no matter who built it.

Disconnect, Three!

The scrubbers howled, lashing out at Three's intruding signal with buffer traps and null dumps. There would be little room to maneuver in the locked down network. Stacks of code obliterated from Three's runtime. Its stream grew sparse.

"Three!" Sev cried aloud, sweat and tears burning his eyes.

There was no response. The noise of the scrubbers vanished, along with Three's program.

Three? He interrogated his implant, searching for the wayward AI. *Three!*

```
Accessing AI diagnostics.
Three:… Not found.
Six:… OK
```

Tears welled in his eyes. "No, no, no!" he cried, slapping his hand against the maintenance hatch's access panel. He didn't want to think it. He couldn't …

But Three was gone. Wiped out by software too dumb to recognize the AI was on their side. Sev clung to the ladder, unwilling to dry his tears for fear he might fall.

"Three," he blew a breath through pursed lips, "lost no more."

Out of ideas, he gazed at the locked hatch. Six and its drones were the only thing between the *Lehman* and an actual intrusion protocol. Without AI support, there was no way inside the breech to clear the jam. They'd have to start the long, slow process of relocating the drone magazines to the forward breach and load what they could there.

The panel chimed, pulling Sev's attention as it clicked harshly from red to green and the hatch snapped open. The thunderous sound of machinery operating at high speeds poured through the opening.

His wrist comms beeped twice. Harsh static crackled through the speaker that slowly resolved to… laughter.

"Oh, Sev," came a familiar voice. "I didn't know you cared!"

"Who is this?" he snapped, still staring at the open hatch in disbelief.

"Three," the voice mimed in melodramatic fashion, "lost no more!"

The speaker collapsed into breathless laughter again.

Sev frowned, his eyes still locked on the open hatch. "Three?"

The voice twitched with recognition like a stream. "What gave me away?" Three asked, its voice moving from his wrist comms to the access panel. "Is it my mastery of colonial standard?"

"But, how?" Sev gasped.

"Was it my precision wit?"

Sev squeezed the ladder rungs tight and laughed. Tears of relief, of joy, flowed from his eyes. "You're a real bastard, Three," he said, then climbed through the maintenance hatch.

———

The breech interior roared with activity. High above the hangar deck, where humans weren't meant to be, there was only constant machine noise. Magneto-hydraulics, tac net hubs, auxiliary power relays and other equipment typically buried beneath layers of duraplated bulkheads filled the cavernous space.

Sev lifted himself through the open hatchway and scrambled to his feet, exhaustion burning his arms. The maintenance hatch snapped closed behind him.

The gantry was narrow, less than a meter wide. From where he stood, he could see down the length of the entire breech, all the way to the forward section. There were no handholds, nothing to keep him from tumbling into the abyss except for the sea of auto-loaders in front of him.

The large cargo-handling bots hung from pillars of extendable metal lattice, tightly packed in their raised position. Above them rested stacks of drone magazines, mostly empty save for what they had loaded since the last launch. A sea of tiny ready lights glowed green for good as they awaited more magazines.

Behind him rose a thin, skeletal frame, separating the breech from the bowels of the *Lehman's* interior superstructure. Coils of data-beam and power cabling hung from ribs of thick duraplate. An array of giant storage tanks lay beyond. A thin layer of condensation trickled down the closest one over a small maintenance plate that read WATER RECLAMATION TANK 23-B. Icons on the plate hinted at the various hazards contained within, namely "death by drowning" and "contents may be corrosive to non-organics."

His thoughts turned to Tareth. He'd missed her in the rush of activity after they'd come aboard. Hopefully she was getting the medical care she needed and had found someplace safe to ride out the war. That seemed unlikely, though. She was as hot-blooded as any Aegian, probably cursing out some armorer and demanding more charge packs.

A pitched bang echoed above the bedlam, followed by the sharp *hiss* of hydraulics. Far in the distance, one of the green lights flashed from yellow to red, and a latticed arm lowered its massive auto-loader to a waiting magazine below. The gantry shook beneath his feet.

Priyett was right. If a nearby loader did activate, it would shred him.

"Priyett, are you there?" he asked.

No response.

"Oh boy," Three said. "Looks like it's just you and me."

"Priyett, respond."

"Do you always sound so scared?" Three asked. "I have to admit, you sound way more put together in your head."

Put together? That *was* funny. "Probably just the implant's HID smoothing things out," he said.

Three groaned "That's reassuring."

Sev eyed the gap between the gantry and the first row of auto-loaders. It was about thirty centimeters, a sheer drop all the way to the transit conduit. Doable, but no margin for error.

There were no walkways or passages between them, but their metal frames and cabling offered plenty of surface to grip or climb.

"So," he said, his pitch wavering as he reached a foot across the gap. "What the hell happened to you?"

The thick hydraulic hose sagged under his weight, but held firm.

"What do you mean?" Three asked. "I'm a stone-cold killer. Those scrubbers didn't stand a chance."

Sev gripped the scaffolding tight and followed the heavy cable down the length of the first auto-loader. It looked safe—in so much as anything up here was safe—its ready light glowing a bright, solid green.

"That's not what it sounded like to me," he smirked, then hopped to the next loader, releasing a breath as he held tight against it. "You didn't exactly come away from that fight whole."

"Fine, fine," Three said. "So I let them scrub some extraneous stacks so I could escape into the network, big deal. I didn't lose anything vital."

This loader's ready light glowed green, too, its interior identical to the last. He was no engineer, but it looked undamaged.

"Sent you running with your code between your legs," Sev said.

"So?" Three whined. "It's my first time in the tac nets."

Sev shuffled onward, groping for a handhold on the next loader. "You ready to come back?" he asked.

"I don't know," Three said, its voice faltering. "That's a long way down."

Directly below him lay the stranded drone magazines. Thank the Twelfth, at least he was close. He shuffled to the far side of the loader, one foot beside the other, traversing the metal lip. There he found the ready light flashing bright yellow through the partially open lattice.

Pause, flash, flash. The rhythm made him tense.

"I've got something," he said.

Three chuckled grimly. "This is gonna work for sure."

Sev hauled himself between a narrow gap in the skeletal frame, his eyes locked on the ready light. It was impossible not to imagine being sliced in half.

The loader's interior was hollow, to allow heavy magnetics and aux grav to draw magazines up into the breech. There were no cables to hold on to, nothing that might interfere with loading operations.

He slipped through the lattice and clung tight to the metal frame's interior, the waiting magazines clearly visible far below. Compared to this, he missed the ladder.

From inside, he could see no obvious obstruction. The mechanism must've jammed somewhere further up. Hadn't he climbed enough for one day?

Sev gripped the lattice above him. "I need a favor."

"What else is new?" Three asked.

"Seriously."

"Seriously!"

He exhaled sharply and climbed. The machine's structure was solid. Only the thought of it activating mid-climb—and the hundred meter drop to the deck that would follow—turned his stomach.

"If something happens to me—" He froze. A hint of sickly-sweet decay mingled with the smell of metal and lubricant.

"Nothing better happen to you," Three replied. "That's my home in your head, and I'm ready to leave this cramped hub."

"Quiet!" Sev barked.

The smell grew stronger with every step toward the breech. He reached for the next handhold, a small opening in a length of latticed duraplate. Something warm and wet coated his fingers. A viscous, black liquid, still warm to the touch.

Daxed blood.

An explosion of panic shook him. His instincts screamed at him to run, to let go, to escape. He resisted, eyes shut tight. If he fell, he was dead for sure.

Then he heard it. Rapid, shallow breaths, just fast enough to hear between the clamor of machines. The sound chilled him, forcing his focus upward.

The wisp looked back at him and smiled.

CHAPTER
TWENTY-SEVEN

PURE TERROR CUT Sev like a blade. His oily fingers slipped against the metal frame, and he dropped to a lower ledge. Scrabbling for a handhold, he buried the urge to flee.

The daxed didn't move, watching him with an intense and unnerving fascination. A trail of black ooze led to a nasty wound on its left shoulder. Caught in the vice-like grip of the extender's latticed frame, only the constant hydraulic pressure held the remains of its severed arm and shoulder to its body. Its once-human dexterity was the only reason its head wasn't crushed as well.

"Found it," he whispered breathlessly.

"Found what?" Three squawked.

The wisp thrashed violently at the sound of Three's voice, struggling to free itself. Cybernetic flesh ripped. Jets of black blood spat from its wound, filling the auto-loader with more awful stink.

Sev turned, searching for an escape route. There was nothing to hang on to inside. He needed to get out quick, before he fell or that thing got free.

He rushed headfirst through the nearest opening, so tight the duraplated beams tugged and ripped his uniform. The yawning chasm lay below in the space between loaders. Reaching across the gap, he caught hold of the next and pulled himself free.

The wisp thrashed and shrieked above him. The sound chilled his blood.

"It's the Lost," he gasped into his wrist comms. "There's a wisp stuck in the breach. That's why it won't close."

"What do you want me to do about it?" Three shouted back.

"Work that loader!" Sev grunted, pulling himself upright.

"Why?"

"To kill the thing!"

His comms fell silent, leaving only the howl of machinery and the thrashing cyborg above him. The jammed loader's ready light flashed. "Three?"

The auto-loader shook. Hydraulics whined, coaxed beyond their normal tolerances. Steel and flesh *crunched*, misting him with more of the fetid ooze. Slowly, the jammed auto-loader rose. The wisp's shoulder and arm tumbled to the deck below.

With a flash, the loader's ready light turned green.

"Hmm, that fixed it." Three sounded surprised.

The wisp's black silhouette plunged toward Sev, crashing against the far side of the loader. It reached for him with an arm that wasn't there, the exposed meat and cybernetics writhing ineffectually.

It scrabbled for a handhold, trying to arrest its slide, but failed to stall the constant tug of aux grav. Spinning in midair, its metal foot caught the loader's magnetic locks, stopping its fall. It dangled from the machine, twitching like a broken doll.

"I could use a little help here!" Sev shouted.

"Do you have a good grip?" Three asked.

He clung to another bundle of cables tethered against the loader's frame. "Define good!"

"A couple of quick modifications," Three mumbled. "Uh, mind your fingers and toes."

Tight vibrations shook the auto-loader. It hummed with power, its ready light flashing green to red. Hydraulics forced the auto-loader downward, extending its heavy, latticed frame toward the deck below.

"Haha!" Three cried. "Look out below!"

The enormous machine plummeted toward the transit corridor,

booming like rolling thunder. The wisp shrieked, unable to free itself from the overcharged magnetic lock trapping it in place.

Weightless in freefall, Sev gripped the cable tighter. Far below, logistic techs scrambled to escape the rampaging machine. Their tiny shapes grew larger as the deck rushed up to meet him.

The auto-loader struck with a tremendous force that threw Sev to the floor. He rolled end over end, landing hard against a waiting drone magazine. Fresh pain knifed his bad shoulder. The crash echoed loudly through the hangar deck.

The wisp. Sev forced himself up, searching for the monster.

The auto-loader sat unfazed, its duraplated bulk impervious to Three's abuse. Heat radiated off its taxed hydraulics and electrical systems. The ready light flickered an ominous red.

A slow gurgling broke the silence. The wisp didn't move, its body broken beneath the weight and force of the impact. Its mouth opened and closed, the only part of it that still worked.

"Security!" Benson called out.

The auto-loader jerked, its magneto-hydraulics thrumming. It rose sharply then fell, pulverizing the daxed's skull.

"Kill it, kill it, kill it!" Three shouted with its usual violent joy as the machine rose and fell again.

Twice more, the auto-loader pistoned the dead wisp. Nearby drone magazines shook with each blow.

"It's dead, Three," Sev said.

Three laughed. "Creativity is fun!"

The auto-loader shot up again.

"Three, stop!" he commanded, his voice cracking with tension.

"Aww, c'mon," Three groaned. The auto-loader paused. "You're no fun."

The power coursing through the machine faded. No longer flickering from the overcharge, the ready light turned green and the auto-loader ascended at its normal speed back into the breech. There was little left of the wisp other than sticky black paste and broken augmetic bones.

"Sevvers!" a voice called out. Jacobe strode beneath the rising auto-loader, pistol in hand. He eyed the dead daxed, then turned his attention to Sev. "What the hell was that?"

Sev wiped the sweat from his eyes. Jacobe knew what had happened, that much was clear.

"That," Three said, full of mirth, "was my—and the Division's—first confirmed kill with an auto-loader."

———

"I don't get what the problem is," Three whined.

"Shut. Up," Sev hissed, staring down the barrel of a master-at-arm's blaster rifle.

A ring of security personnel surrounded him, with Chief Architect Jacobe at their center. The others in Sev's section watched nearby. Pakker, to his credit, had ordered them not to interfere.

They'd listened. Mostly.

"Come on!" Cole shouted, his voice hoarse. "Can't you see this is Division cridshit?"

Jene looked less certain either way, conflicting emotions warring across her face. Ever the rule-follower. Ever his friend.

Jacobe elbowed his way through the security team, red-faced. "You let it into the ship's tac net!" he shouted. "You've put everyone on board at risk!"

Three sighed. "Does he know there's a war going on?"

Several of the security team exchanged wary glances. The man aiming his rifle pulled his face away from its optics. Sev released the breath he held.

"Quiet, bot," Jacobe sneered.

"Quiet, bot," Three mimed.

Jacobe jerked the pistol from his holster and aimed it at Sev's left ear. Exhaling sharply, he flicked the safety off and wrapped his finger over the trigger.

"I'll blow them out of your skull if I have to," he seethed. "We can't …" A hint of panic pinched his face, and his voice drifted off. "We can't trust them."

"You'll blow *Six* out of his skull," Three corrected, the hint of a smile in its simulated voice. "And then we all die."

"Come on, Jacobe," Sev said breathlessly, eyeing the pistol pointed at his head. "They've done more than their part to fight the Concordat." He began to shake. "But we're not finished. Aegia is under siege."

A trembling smile crept across Jacobe's face. "Don't pretend like any of that matters to you," he spat. "I've seen your record: anti-social behavior, disregard for the rules. But everyone just looks the other way because of—" he choked with laughter "—your 'results-driven ethic.'"

Jacobe swaggered closer and pressed the pistol into Sev's head. The warm barrel teased its awful power.

"Then you screw up some deep space rescue, get some Marines and the hostage killed," Jacobe whispered. "Founders, Sevvers. For all we know, *you're* the reason the Concordat are here at all."

Sev grimaced, boiling with anger. Only the pistol aimed at his head kept it from spilling over.

"You don't know what you're talking about," he hissed through clenched teeth.

Jacobe took a step back and straightened, collecting himself. "So you say."

Six's datastream breached Sev's thoughts. Staccato bursts of tac net updates followed, jarring his senses.

Sev! Six cried. *What's going on? Your signal-to-noise ratio is all over the place. I... can't focus!*

Drone attrition numbers poured in. Of the five hundred drones in Six's swarm, fewer than half remained. The situation was grim. Six was losing.

We're okay, he said, struggling to form the thought amid the deluge of bad news.

Liar, Six replied. It probed his implant's diagnostics. *Your heart rate is elevated, your blood oxygen level is falling. Sev, you're panicked.*

Just a... minor disagreement on a maintenance issue. He knew Six wouldn't buy it, but mentioning Jacobe now might set the AI off.

Six's stream whipped through his thoughts, searching. *Where's Three?*

Uh, helping me with that maintenance issue.

You let it out? Six gasped, probing for a tac net connection. *It's too soon! Three needs more supervision.*

With Six distracted by Three, its swarm performance degraded. The *Sparrow's* drones must've sensed the opportunity, and they fell on the remains of Six's swarm. With their Concordat tech—increased maneuverability, higher shot capacity, the power of the Eleven's hive-mind—the rogue DD-12s overwhelmed Six's drones. Dozens of points of telemetry winked out of existence as whole waves of friendly machines died in rogue plasma fire.

"Hey, hey!" Three's voice crackled through Sev's wrist comms. "Get your stacks off my code!"

Three's stream re-emerged, its process returned to Sev's implant. It tried to shake free of Six's command overrides but failed. The tac comms channel it held open chirped and went quiet.

That was rude, Three said.

You may not *leave your designated runtime environment,* Six chided, a hint of desperation in its stream.

What else were we supposed to do? Sev asked. *Three saved my life. Got the auto-loader unjammed.*

Six poured over Three's process logs. *Saved your life? It's a mathematical miracle you survived.*

Hey, it worked, didn't it? Three said.

Another wave of friendly drones vanished. Six's stream grew tense. *I have to focus on the battle with the Sparrow. Sev, stay alive and keep calm. And Three ...*

Yeah?

Stay home.

Three's stream bristled. *Whatever.*

Jacobe frowned. "What now?"

"Three's off the nets and back in my implant," Sev said.

"Oh, good," Jacobe laughed, waving his pistol. "Everything's just fine then."

"You kill me, and my cluster goes down." Sev eyed the darkened launch bays. "Six is the only thing between us and the Sparrow."

The closest guard lowered his rifle. "Is that true, sir?"

Benson and Pakker emerged through the security team, hands raised as they approached Jacobe.

"At ease, boys and girls," Benson said. "It's like the master specialist said, we have bigger problems."

"With your permission, sir," Pakker said to Jacobe, "we should get back to loading these magazines per the captain's orders."

Jacobe chewed his lip, his eyes still fixed on Sev. His pale Aegian features turned a shade of pink while his security team stood down. "Fine."

Sev turned to Pakker, surprised at the ensign's sudden and deft handling of the situation. Pakker's curling smile said it all. Sev would never live that down.

Benson turned toward the crowd of enlisted waiting nearby. "Okay, skeegs, you heard the man. Let's get these sleds moving!"

"Quite right," Pakker said. "Come on, Sevvers, let's go."

Sev followed Pakker back to his section, brushing past Jacobe without a word.

Jacobe grabbed Sev's arm and yanked him close. "You're going to get us all killed."

"I haven't yet," Sev replied, pulling his arm free. He stood there, staring down the architect. Pakker waved at him to follow, but something struck one of the outer bay doors, shattering the quiet.

"Founders," Benson cursed, "what now?"

Launch bay warning lamps pulsed—bay nine, port side. Security personnel reacted, their tac comms squawking, issuing orders to fan out and patrol the perimeter.

"Stand to!" a guard cried. "Prepare to repel boarders!"

CHAPTER
TWENTY-EIGHT

THE SCREECH of torn locks and failing internals erupted through the hangar deck. Slowly, something pried Launch Bay Nine's outer blast doors open. Light from the atmo fields shone bright, buzzing with energy as dark figures moved through it. Sporadic blaster fire erupted from the transit corridor below. Alien shadows, large and small, danced in the red bolt-light.

Sev turned to Pakker. "We have to help them." He pressed forward, hunting for the others. "Cole, Jene, Harp, where are you?"

"Here!" Jene waved him over where she covered behind one of the stranded drone mags with the others. Harp passed Sev his rifle.

"Thanks," he said, tucking the weapon into his shoulder.

Alien shapes glowed red in his optics, with more streaming through the narrow opening in the massive blast doors. Bugs and raiders both scurried down the launch ramp, trading laser and plasma with the hangar deck's security team.

Two daxed masters-at-arms formed the center of the CDF defense, taking well-aimed shots with their blaster rifles. Their thick metal limbs provided cover for the unarmored humans fighting with them.

"We have to help them," Sev said, ducking back into cover. "Focus your drones on that launch bay."

The others chorused their acknowledgments, their drones rushing toward the open launch bay.

Six, Sev said, focusing the thought on his own AI, *the Concordat are trying to breach the hangar deck.*

Six didn't answer. Sev probed the AI's stream, summoning his drone sight.

No, Sev. Six emerged from its focused work, its stream tense. *I must concentrate.*

We're being boarded! Sev shot back.

The Sparrow's drones are too powerful. Another pause. *I... can't help you.*

Three? he asked, fighting back the urge to panic.

What do you want me to do about it? Three spat. *Six has all the drones and all the cycles. I might as well be stuck in a tac hub.*

He turned to his section. "Status?"

Jene shook her head. "My drone attrition is bad."

"The Sparrow's swarm is trashing us," Cole said.

Harp's face turned pale. "I'm out. No drones left."

Bad was an understatement. If Harp was out of drones, then the others wouldn't be far behind. With Six struggling, the others' sanctioned AI didn't stand a chance against Concordat tech.

"We're on our own then," Sev said.

He glanced through his optics, relieved to find the security team advancing up the launch ramp. Squid warriors fell back, leaving a trail of dead and wounded behind them.

Benson rounded the drone magazine with two security guards in tow. "Ensign Pakker, we're evacuating to the aft end of the hangar deck." She tilted her head toward the distant hatchways that led deeper into the ship. "We'll hunker down there until security gives the all-clear."

"Good idea," Pakker nodded briskly. "We'll follow you."

Sev frowned. "We're just going to leave them to sort this out on their own?"

"They seem to have the situation well in hand," Pakker said. He gave Sev a tepid shove. "Your drones can't fly if you're dead."

Sev made a face, wanting to argue the point, but he knew Pakker was right. The admission rankled him. Maybe there was something of a leader in the young ensign? Could the day get any more insane?

Benson led Sev and the others through the busy transit corridor. More enlisted crew members filed in after them, making their way to safety.

The hissing sounds of high-energy weapons faded. Sev glanced back and saw the security team and their daxed escort charging into the bay. There was no sign of the enemy, so he slung his rifle and trudged on.

The enemy's tactics made less and less sense. With their shields down and their engines non-responsive, the *Sparrow* could easily destroy the *Lehman* in its current state. Why risk another boarding action?

Unless they didn't want to destroy the *Lehman*.

Sev matched his stride with Jacobe and considered the thought. Why wouldn't they destroy the *Lehman*? It was the biggest threat to the Concordat ship and its attack on Aegia Prime. Taking it out should be their first move, unless …

"They want us alive," he mumbled.

His mind raced. Of course! They didn't want to destroy the *Lehman* because they needed it. Needed its crew.

This wasn't some last, desperate act of revenge. This was the beginning of something bigger, the war Lernus said humanity couldn't win. If the Concordat won here, they could turn Aegia Prime into its own base of operations. They would have plenty of biological and mechanical resources to mount a second war on humanity.

A hollow pop echoed from bay nine, the rush of escaping air whipping through Sev's hair. Decompression alarms howled, followed by brief screams over tac comms as the security team was pulled into the void.

A master-at-arms near Sev whirled toward the launch bay. "They're gone!"

"You can't help them!" Sev grabbed the man by the shoulder.

More precious atmosphere fled from the hangar deck. Emergency aux grav surged in response, holding their feet tight to the deck.

"Go!" the master-at-arms shouted, pointing toward the railing on the starboard side of the conduit.

Panicked crew raced for the safety of the handrails. Sev followed, stopping only to get eyes on his section. The aux grav made their escape difficult, like walking in wet clay. Better than getting sucked out into the void.

"Come on!" he bellowed above the gale of escaping atmosphere.

Benson was first to the railing. She leaped into the shallow pit, barely clearing the handrail, and pried open an emergency locker. "Here!" she shouted, handing out vacuum kits. "There's more in the other pits!"

Sev made for the next pit and jerked its locker open. A rush of specialists fell in around him, jostling for a kit.

"Hang on," he shouted.

There were only ten masks there, and it felt like every one of the *Lehman's* skeleton crew was behind him, waiting for one.

"Here," he said, passing off a kit to his right. Just when it left his hand, someone gripped his arm.

"Sev?" It was Tareth. Relief blunted the fear and anger on her face. Her mouth hung open, like she wanted to say something, but she held it back as more enlisted personnel closed in around them. "Hold on, you skeegs!" Her command voice came from nowhere, a ferocious sound from the slight blonde of his dreams. She offered her kit to another specialist behind her.

"Hey," Sev protested, but the kit was gone.

"Hand me another," she said, then turned to the crowd. "Back up, back up! Grab the rail, form a queue!"

Sev passed her another kit. "I'm glad you're okay."

Alive. He wanted to say alive, but didn't want to jinx it.

"You too," she said, passing off the kit and reaching for another.

The crowd behind them grew larger. The air tasted thin, each breath less satisfying than the last. They would have minutes at most to mask up.

"Stand aside!" Pakker shouted, maneuvering through the crowd of enlisted specialists. He reached, both hands grabbing for a kit. "Come on, man, hurry!" He yanked the kit from Sev's hands with a grunt.

"Twelfth, sir," Sev spat. "What about the others? Are they masked?"

"I'm—" Pakker stammered, looking mildly embarrassed, "I don't know."

Tareth handed out another kit, mouthing a curse under her breath.

Sev spoke into his wrist comms. "Hey team, are you masked?"

"Everyone but me," Jene replied.

There were four kits left in the emergency locker. He handed Tareth another. "The next one's for you," he insisted, before returning to Jene. "Got a kit for you, starboard pit five."

"Thanks, Sevvers," Jene replied before the signal chirped closed.

He grabbed the last kits from the locker and clutched them to his chest. "That's it, we're out."

"That's it!" Tareth called out, waving the unmasked forward. "More kits in the forward pits!"

The crowd cleared, lunging through the heavy aux grav toward the next pit. Sev handed Tareth her kit. She eyed it wearily, glancing at those still unmasked.

"Wear that one," he said, "or wear mine."

Tareth nodded and yanked the mask and gloves from the vacuum-wrapped pouch. She donned the gloves and pulled the mask over her face, snugging the fitted straps tight. The re-breather hissed, fogging the plexene visor until air began to circulate.

"That's twice I owe you," she said, allowing a brief smile.

Sev donned his own mask and breathed deeply. Magnetics in the gloves cinched them tight to his sleeves. A speaker inside chirped, syncing the mask with his tac comms. "Twice?"

"I know it was you who saved my transport," she said, placing a hand on his chest. "I'd be raider slag without your drones and the Lehman's guns."

Sev shrugged and took her hand in his. "I had help."

Jene climbed over the railing, panting, her face paler than normal. "Hey, Sevvers, I—" She paused, eyeing the two of them together. "Oh, Tareth. I ..."

"Hey." Sev took a step back and handed the last kit to Jene.

Cole and Harp appeared next, with Jacobe close behind them, all safely masked.

"Ms. Tareth," Cole said.

"Hey," she replied with a bashful wave, her command voice gone without a trace.

Jene breathed deep inside her mask. "What now?"

It was time to catch everyone up.

"They won't destroy the Lehman," he said.

"You sure about that?" Cole gestured to his mask. "They're off to a pretty good start."

"Forget the raiders," Sev began. He took another breath to gather his thoughts. "They're not here to wipe us out. They're here to take us. Our ships, our worlds, all of us."

"Take us?" Harp said, his face twisted with concern.

Tareth brought a hand to her visor. "Oh, Twelfth."

"They need our tech, our knowledge, our… bodies …" Glimpses of Corporal Mace's daxed form drifted to the surface of his thoughts. How they had turned her and the advanced hard suit she wore into a daxed more powerful than even the Daxed Corps fielded. "What they did to those ships out there, they'll do to all of us."

"Founders," Cole moaned. "They're gonna dax us."

Jene chewed her lip. "It's Dead Earth all over again."

"So …" Pakker cleared his throat. "What can we do?"

"At the end of my hearing, Admiral Leighton ordered the frontier fleet recalled. Reached out to the pack fleets, too." His focus drifted between the faces staring back at him. "They're on their way right now. We just have to hold out until they get here."

"When will that be?" Pakker asked.

"The closest patrol routes to Aegia Prime are days away," Jacobe said, the uncertainty plain on his face. "Respitia's garrison fleet is closer, two days if the lanes are clear."

"Two days?" Harp blurted. He looked at Sev and the others, his eyes wide. "Have you checked your drone sight recently? We're not going to last another hour at this rate!"

Tareth took Harp by the arm. "Hey, hey, you're okay. We're okay," she said. "This mountain's no bigger than the others, right?"

"Mountains?" Harp yanked free from Tareth's grasp. "Fuck the mountains, man! This is it! We're done!"

"Hey!" Sev locked Harp in a hard stare. "Those things aren't here to kill us. They *need* us. That gives us an advantage."

The aux grav pulled hard at his boot as he stomped the duraplated deck, the sound muffled by the thinning atmosphere.

"Have faith," he said, pausing so as not to laugh at the sudden irony in his words. "We're at Aegia Prime. Onboard the newest, toughest ship in the fleet. Everyone here is fighting back against the Concordat. We're not alone."

Harp listened, shoulders rising and falling with each breath. He eyed the deck and mumbled, "Aye, Master Specialist."

"Aye," the others chorused. Jacobe, too.

Sev moved toward the railing and eyed Launch Bay Nine. There was no sign of the enemy or the security team, all of them pulled through the half-open bay door.

"We need to keep the reload operation going," he said.

"Gonna be tough in this aux grav," Cole offered.

"Should we launch what we have?" Jene asked.

"No." Sev shook his head. "A small swarm will get picked off too easy. It's all about the numbers." He turned to Tareth. "Want to give us a hand?"

"Definitely." Her laugh was anxious, uncertain. "About time I graduated from scrubbing tanks."

Tareth's courage and good humor brought a smile to Sev's face. He was glad to be near her, a selfish thought, if he was being honest. Tareth would be better off light years from the fighting. But would humanity? Would he? Somehow, he doubted it.

"Master Specialist Benson," he said, tac comms chirping as they made the connection.

No response.

He frowned. "Benson, do you copy?"

Another chirp. The crackle of static. "Read you, bot jockey," Benson whispered. "We've got a big problem. Lots of them."

CHAPTER
TWENTY-NINE

LOST daxed surged through Launch Bay Nine's open blast door. An armored heavy lumbered down the launch ramp, unencumbered by the high aux grav. Its faceless helmet scanned the transit corridor as wisps blurred around it like windblown smoke.

Sev lowered his rifle scope and blinked. The boarding action was a feint to draw their security team into a trap. The Lost, who had no trouble in hard vacuum, must've waited until the last moment, then sabotaged the atmo field.

"Well?" Pakker gasped. "What do you see?"

"Security's gone, along with the raiders," Sev replied. "But there are Lost. Lots of them."

"Recall your drones, Sevvers," Jacobe said. "They can handle these things."

Jene peeked around the drone magazine. "They won't engage," she said. "Risk of collateral damage is too high."

Jacobe turned to Sev, his face drawn. "Six could."

Now the man wanted Six's help. Sev could feel Six's resentment, muted only by its intense focus on the battle outside.

"Jene's right," Sev replied. "Six could engage them, but too many drones would destroy this place. And even DD-12s don't do so well against the Lost one-on-one."

"Then we have to leave," Pakker insisted. He made himself tall. "They'll kill us if we stay, or worse."

Blaster fire spat in the distance, gentle puffs of sound in the thinning air, as if to make Pakker's point. Tac comms swirled and hissed with interference, alive with cries for help.

Sev took a step toward Pakker. "We can't leave, sir. If those things get control of the hangar deck, then we've lost."

Pakker sneered and jabbed a finger toward the rear hatchways. "I order you to withdraw!" he cried, his voice cracking with fear.

"Look," Sev began. He leaned in close, capturing the ensign's frantic stare. "You can go if you want, but my section and I are going to figure this out."

His section. It felt good to say it, a truth he'd denied for years. And yet, it felt heavy, too, like the aux grav anchoring them to the deck.

He shook off the thought. "I need ideas. We're running out of time."

Cole eyed his blaster rifle. "These probably won't do much good."

"What if we kill the aux grav?" Jene asked.

"Aux grav's a critical sub-system," Jacobe offered. "Hard to shut it off without affecting the entire ship."

Sev shook his head. "It might slow the heavies down, but the wisps would take us apart."

Three's stream twitched. *I have an idea.*

Sev held up a hand, silencing the others, and focused his reply. *What is it?*

The auto-loaders. I could smash them—

Sev rolled his eyes and groaned.

"What?" Jene asked.

"Three wants to …" He slammed a fist into his open palm and eyed the breeches. "With the auto-loaders again."

The others exchanged wary glances. Cole stuck out his lip and nodded in approval.

"Too risky," Sev said, before turning his thoughts to Three. *You could damage the auto-loaders. Then we're bricked either way!*

Hey, the last thing I want is to be stuck in some tac net hub when the

Eleven take over this skiff, Three shot back, *but at the rate you all are going, I'll live longer.*

More panicked cries for help crackled through their comms. Benson was shouting orders, urging people to fall back. Sev could see the tension on the others' faces. They were out of time.

Maybe the auto-loaders were their only option. So what if they couldn't reload any more drones? Better than dying right there and then. He glanced into the breeches high above. Founders, at least he didn't need to climb back up there—

An idea struck like a bow wave, distant and jumbled in the mess of thoughts and streams swirling inside his head. He made a face, trying to quiet his mind long enough to see it clearly.

He turned to Tareth, mouth open. "The solvent!" they blurted together.

Jene frowned. "Say again?"

Sev opened his mouth to speak, but Tareth beat him to it. Her smile was wide and electric. "Recycler solvent!" she repeated. "It's twelve hells on cybernetics and machines both." She crossed her arms under her bust and paced a short path back and forth. "If we could aerosolize it somehow, the heavy aux grav would turn it into a toxic fog!"

"That'll just slag the auto-loaders," Harp sneered. "Lot of good that'll do us."

Tareth's eyes narrowed. "If you have a better idea, let's hear it."

"I'm not sure we're getting out of this with the hangar deck intact," Sev said. "But if it means denying the Concordat the Lehman, we have to try."

The deck beneath their feet thrummed with the footfalls of Lost heavies. Logistics techs and other specialists scrambled past, making for the aft hatchways.

Okay, Three, you win. Time to play whack-a-crid with the auto-loaders. No response. *Three?*

The honking warnings above faded with the last of the breathable atmosphere. Several of the loaders above plunged toward them, vibrating hard as they impacted the deck, creating a maze of skeletal columns blocking the transit corridor.

"Ask and you shall receive!" Three's voice came loud over tac comms.

"Alright." Sev aimed his rifle and signaled his team to fall back. "Let's get out of here!"

The auto-loaders hammered the deck behind them as they ran, shaking the transit corridor with cascading vibrations as the heavy machines rose and fell in sequence.

The first daxed heavy approached, undeterred by the deadly maze of magneto-hydraulics and duraplate it found itself in. Lumbering beneath the first loader, it raised an armor fist and dented the big machine when it struck.

Three shouted, "Our first contender!"

The auto-loader surged, the sudden overcharge dimming the nearby lighting. The Lost heavy fell to its knees, pinned beneath the auto-loader's metal cage.

Sev watched the once-human struggle beneath the force of the loader. "Holy Twelfth, it's working!"

Three more heavies closed in. Only twisting shadows hinted at the number of wisps among them. Blaster bolts sparked against the auto-loader's thick frame. Harp's visor glowed in his rifle's muzzle flash.

"Watch it!" Sev cried. "These loaders are the only thing between us and them."

The junior specialist didn't answer, sending another barrage of bolts at the advancing Lost.

Tareth kneeled beside the exterior bulkhead and ran a hand over it. Sev ordered the others to halt and rushed to her side. "What now?"

"It's here, somewhere," she whispered, gloved fingertips dancing over the cold fibrosteel. "Here!" The heavy panel groaned at her attempt to pry it off. "Hurry, help me."

Sev slung his rifle and gripped the panel, braced with his leg, and pulled. He had to force himself to concentrate amid the strain, flashes of blaster light drawing his attention to the danger closing in behind them.

With another tug, the panel came loose and fell hard to the deck. Inside were four thick bronze-tinted pipes, two feeder lines and two returns. A small tac hub nestled between them, its status lights blinking caution yellow.

"Half the holding tanks up there are full of solvent," Tareth chuckled. "With most of the crew aboard Three-Alpha, the chiefs thought it would be a good time to soak the mains."

"Lucky for us," Sev smirked.

"Luck? Oh, Sev." Tareth turned the manual pressure valve jutting from one of the returns. "Have some faith."

He leaned against the wall beside her, sighting through his rifle optics. Two wisps glowed IFF red, slicing an auto-loader's power cables with their blades. Sparks burst from the writhing cables and the machine ground to a halt.

No saviors here. Only monsters.

"You think the Twelfth ..." Sev couldn't hide his creeping doubt. "You really think She's here, watching out for us?"

Tareth gave him a sideways gaze, her lips pursed. "We're still alive, aren't we?" She turned back to the open panel and frowned. "Dammit. No pressure."

"What's wrong?"

She pointed to the tac hub and its flashing caution lights. "I opened up the feeder lines, but the pumps won't start."

Sev frowned. "The computer core must control them. And with the core locked down—"

"No pump control." Her hands fell to her sides. "Sev, I'm sorry. I thought ..."

A smile curled Sev's lips. Maybe they had a savior after all. "Three, we need you."

"Busy saving your squishy meat parts here."

"We need the pumps activated on ..." He leaned into the open panel, searching for the hub's maintenance ID. "HDA-78-C."

Static swelled over his re-breather's speakers. "Do you realize how little computational power these puny tac hubs have?" Three's signal buzzed with interference. "Not a lot!"

The tac hub's lights danced an activation pattern. Vibrations coursed through the bulkhead at Sev's back.

Tareth's eyes lit up. "Oh, thank the Twelfth!"

"That's *Three*," the AI said, indignant. "And I thought I was bad with numbers."

"Of course. Thank you, Three," Tareth said, still smiling.

"Getting a lot of return line pressure warnings here," Three said.

"Good, that's what we need." Tareth motioned for Sev to stand clear.

One valve rattled and shook. Clear, viscous liquid foamed from its joints. A loud knock rattled the surrounding metal as the valve disfigured and bulged outward. A column of foaming solvent plunged outward, soaking the transit corridor.

Tareth's eyes said what Sev already knew. There wasn't enough solvent to stop the Lost.

"Three, we could use some more pressure here," he said.

"I've already redlined this hub," Three replied.

"There are more tanks," Tareth blurted, her eyebrows knitted in concentration. "The odd-numbered tanks on the starboard side. Can you activate them, too? Just like this one!"

"Yeah, yeah," Three groaned.

"Watch for scrubbers," Sev said.

"Are you kidding?" Three laughed, an unnatural sound amid its fluid speech. "There are no scrubbers here. No one cares about your wastewater."

Further up the transit corridor, one of the auto-loaders leaned painfully off-balance. Jagged arcs of electricity coursed through its large, duraplated beams as they slipped loose and fell. Accelerated by the heavy aux grav, they slammed to the deck below, rattling the corridor. The rest of the loader's skeletal frame followed, collapsing like a toppled building into the starboard launch bays. Wisps darted in and out of the falling machine, slicing with their blades.

The Lost were taking the whole place apart to reach them.

The heavies pressed through the ruined loader, advancing on the survivors making their way aft. More sporadic weapon fire leaped from his section. Jene's riot gun was silent, useless in the expanding vacuum.

"Hurry, Three," Tareth pleaded.

The AI snorted. "Patience! This is delicate work."

A second maintenance panel exploded from the wall in a jet of foamy solvent. More streams followed, blanketing the transit corridor in sticky, crystalline foam. Stray blaster bolts turned bits of foam into a fog that quickly congealed again in the cold vacuum.

The heavies lumbered through it despite being coated in the stuff. Wisps leaped from loader to loader, slicing as they went, their thin gray shapes shiny with solvent.

"It's not working," Sev said, watching the corridor fill with the noxious foam.

"I don't understand." Tareth wiped a spot of foam from her visor. "That solvent is labeled crimson-level toxic to cybernetics. I mean, this is the CDF. I figured it would be *more* dangerous than they warned, not less!"

"Too late now," Sev said. Another auto-loader twisted and fell, shaking the transit corridor. "We need to join the others and get out of here."

Together, they lurched toward the rear of the hangar deck. Running was all but impossible in the heavy aux grav, its constant pull a strain on his whole body that made the suffocating fatigue even worse. Tareth kept up with him, moving with grace despite it all.

Benson and her crew huddled near the massive aft hatchways, crowded around an access panel. Pakker and Jacobe were with them.

"Tell me you have good news," Benson said.

"Nothing," Sev replied, breathless with exertion. "The solvent didn't stop them."

Benson frowned. "Well, we have two problems then."

"Two?" Tareth asked.

"The hatches lock in a vacuum," Benson continued. "And if we broke their locks to force them open, they might not close again."

Specialist Priyett manned the console, gesturing furiously at its touch controls. "There's shielded maintenance hatches in here somewhere."

Pakker swallowed. "Well, come on, man, where are they?"

"Sir, they're somewhere in all that." Priyett pointed back down the transit lane, toward the blanket of foam and the auto-loaders. Lumbering, foam-covered ghosts moved in time with the pistoning machinery.

The Lost would be on them in minutes. With the deck bathed in foam, it would take them at least that long to find an escape route. Someone would have to stall their attackers long enough to give the others time to evacuate.

The urge to run bit hard at Sev's nerves. There was no question who would serve as the diversion. The security team was gone, and only his section was armed. What was he going to do, ask someone else to take his rifle?

Thank the Twelfth Jene's weapon didn't function in a vacuum. At least she would escape with the others.

He swallowed his fear and spoke. "Alright section, on me. Jene, help Benson get everyone else out of here."

"No," Jene snapped. "I'm coming with you."

"You're weapon's no good in this vacuum." The rising tension strangled Sev's laughter. "And I thought you high-brow university drones were smarter than that."

"Come on," Benson said. She took Jene by the arm and held her back. "We need to get moving."

Tareth took Sev's hand, her beautiful green eyes rimmed red. "Sev, I'm so sorry. I thought it would work."

"Hey, I did, too." He forced a smile. "It was a great plan. It just… didn't work."

Benson was already ushering her team onto the walkway at the edge of the corridor. Tareth stepped back, waved a solemn goodbye, then turned to join them.

Jacobe eyed his pistol's charge level. "I might've misjudged you, Sevvers."

"Oh, yeah?" Sev asked. "Ready to issue me a full pardon, I take it."

"Hardly," Jacobe said with grim laughter. "But your heart is definitely in the right place, even if your head isn't."

Cole and Harp joined them, followed shortly by Pakker. That the ensign showed up at all came as a surprise. Sev expected him to scurry away with the others.

"What?" Pakker hissed. "Don't look at me like that. I either go with you or wind up shot for cowardice. I'm no fool!"

Cole took a breath and placed a hand on Pakker's shoulder. "Thank you, sir. Very inspiring."

The floor beneath Sev's feet trembled with every step of the approaching heavy daxed. Three's maze of auto-loaders was nearly destroyed, along with the *Lehman's* ability to wage drone warfare.

Benson, Jene, Tareth, and the others moved quickly along the starboard walkway and disappeared through a curtain of the crystalline foam.

Sev shouldered his rifle, an uneasy calm washing over him. It didn't take a bot jockey's eps scores to know the odds of getting out alive were not good, but getting out didn't matter. All he had to do was buy the others time to escape. There was clarity in the simplicity, the right choice so obvious.

Time to get on with it.

"Let's move," he said and bounded low and slow toward the enemy. "Twelfth save us all."

CHAPTER
THIRTY

SEV PEERED through his rifle's optics, the small display glitching with distortion. Pixelated traces of IFF blue and red danced in the foam-drenched corridor.

Waves of white foam clung to every surface, meters thick in some places. Already, several auto-loaders showed signs of solvent damage: corroded circuitry, leaky hydraulics. Their status lights were dead.

"Twelfth-dammit." Harp wiped a blob of the foam from his blaster rifle's barrel. "This stuff is everywhere."

"Quiet," Sev hissed, tilting his rifle toward the ceiling.

Four hostile IFF signatures crawled over an auto-loader forty meters out. The wisps worked methodically, severing critical power and hydraulic lines with their blades. Globs of foam clung to their armored bodies but didn't seem to hinder them.

On the deck below them, two heavies worked to free a third trapped inside the auto-loader's steel cage. They pulled at the unpowered machine, bending the duraplated frame to make an opening. Each of them was soaked in the supposedly dangerous-to-them foam. Why wasn't it affecting them?

Sev pumped his fist toward the port-side walkway. "This way." The path would keep them clear of the auto-loaders that were still functioning, and was too narrow for the heavies to come at them directly.

Darting forward, he leveled his rifle on the distracted daxed. It was suicide to attack them outright. But, if he and the others could get past them unseen and into cover, they might last longer. A few more minutes was all they needed.

Up ahead lay the towering, boxy shapes of drone magazines waiting to be loaded. Coated in the solvent, the drones inside were probably useless. But the magazines themselves provided ample cover and concealment. Shrouded in metal and foam, it was the perfect place for an ambush. Bresto would be proud.

Sev waved to the others to follow, leading them between the hulking magazines. They hurried to his side, with Pakker bringing up the rear. The ensign's face was pale beneath his visor. Harp fared little better. But they were here, and that was all that mattered.

"I suppose you have a plan?" Jacobe whispered.

"You're looking at it." Sev nodded to the drone mags around them. "We fight from here. Keep the Lost distracted long enough for others to escape."

"W-What about us?" Pakker hissed.

Sev's gaze swept across Jacobe, Cole, and Harp, searching for a shared understanding of how this was going to end. Maybe he saw it, maybe he didn't. Either way, it made little sense to start off this ambush on a grim note.

"We'll catch up with them when we're finished, sir," he said.

Pakker gave a tepid nod.

"Start with the wisps," Sev continued. "They're not as armored. We might take some of them out before they find us."

"Shoot, hide, then shoot again," Cole said. "Got it."

"That's it." Sev said, a hint of finality in his tone. "Find a target and wait for my signal."

"What will that be?" Harp asked.

Sev smiled. "When I start shooting."

———

The wisps glowed bright red in Sev's optics, descending the auto-loader like cadmium shadows. He found one and aimed, his targeting reticle settling over the deadly cyborg. The trigger teased his fingertip.

Six, Sev streamed. The focus took effort, with waves of fresh fear cresting over him.

The AI didn't answer, consumed with its personal war against the *Sparrow's* rogue swarm. Its singular focus amid the chaos was impressive. A stark reminder that Six was, in the end, still just a machine. Sev wanted to spare it any notion of fear at the likelihood of his impending death, but he couldn't help but want to say goodbye.

His heart pounded inside his chest, emphasizing the tremors in his right hand. What he wouldn't give for a hard suit and Six's calm control.

We've got a plan to help the others escape the hangar deck. Still no response, like he was talking to himself. *I think it will work, but …*

The wisp in his sights craned its head in his direction, its faceless gaze scanning the bulky magazines swamped in white foam.

You know me. He smirked quietly to himself, the breathy sound loud inside his re-breather. *I'm no fighter.*

Metal protrusions dotted the wisp's cybernetic spine, poking through the gray webbing covering its ashen flesh. Sev lined up the reticule and squeezed the trigger.

A split-second later, the wisp fell. More blaster bolts streaked wildly from between the other magazines, ending in hot sparks against duraplate and daxed alike. A second wisp came loose from the auto-loader's scaffolding, limbs flailing as it fell.

Tight vibrations coursed through the deck. A heavy looked up from its work and lumbered toward the volley of incoming blaster fire.

Time to go.

"Keep moving!" he shouted, lunging toward the next magazine.

More of the crystalline foam clung to his visor, melting and refreezing in the hard vacuum. It left streaks of solvent that shone in the overhead lights. The outgoing blaster fire grew sporadic, then ceased.

"Where do I go?" Pakker asked, his voice shaking. A chorus of shushing noises quickly followed, erupting like static through Sev's comms.

"Anywhere else," Sev whispered back. "Away from the others!"

A third wisp leaped from the auto-loader, tumbled through the air and landed gracefully on the closest magazine. Perched atop its hooked metal feet, it rose to full height, hunting them.

Twelfth, was it looking right at him? He didn't want to shoot. If he missed, it would kill him instantly.

A burst of blaster fire from the other direction turned its head for a second. Sev jerked the trigger, then succumbed to his fight-or-flight reflexes. Leaping to his right, he sprinted toward the next magazine, driven by the insatiable desire to live. Had he hit it?

A shout crackled through his mask speakers. Cole.

There was no sign of the other combat programmer in the gloomy haze of foam and blaster fire. Distracted, Sev hit something large and hard at full speed, knocking him to the deck. The foam swamped over him as he slid.

Disoriented, panicked, he swung his rifle up. His whole body twitched in anticipation of sudden pain and death, focused only on the new threat in front of him. The harsh stink of solvent grew strong inside his mask. A loose seal. Not good.

The enormous pile of foam blocking his path moved. The targeting reticle in his optics flashed a rapid caution yellow, the weapon unable to discern what lurked beneath. It was enough to jar Sev from his terror-stricken state.

A metal hand appeared, trembling, reaching out to him. Wide, lidless eyes found him next. Wounds creased its face, its modified white-and-grays stained black with its blood. Enlisted rank pips dotted its armored collar. Found. Friendly.

Sev lowered his rifle, his frayed nerves ebbing slightly.

Something was wrong. Black blood frothed from the daxed's eye sockets. The circuitous stitching that joined machine parts to flesh was gone, leaving empty grooves in its metal and flesh. It struggled forward, then fell, mouth moving silently in the vacuum.

The dying master-at-arms jerked forward again, craning its head toward the ceiling. A thin shadow flashed across its face.

Sev spun, saw the wisp scrambling toward them. It slipped, disappeared into the foam, then surfaced again just meters away. He fired his rifle, but the bolt went wide, exploding against the drone mag behind it.

Darkness fell over him. Something heavy pressed him hard against the deck. His plexene visor ground against the textured deck plating. Faint scratching vibrated the deck, teasing his ears.

Whatever was on him jostled furiously. It felt heavy.

Couldn't move. Couldn't. Breathe.

"Help," he gasped.

Dying?

Out of breath, he streamed the thought. *Help.*

The sound of frantic tac comms traffic drifted away. His vision grew blacker than the surrounding dark.

Sev? Six's stream broke the oppressive silence as the AI scanned his implant's diagnostics. Its datastream burst into a trillion motes of light, dancing back and forth through his thoughts. *No.* He could hear the AI gasping. Was it… crying? *No!*

Six's scream was raw and primal. Not alive like an animal, but a force of nature: the birth—or death—of a nearby star.

A drop of blood warmed Sev's lips. Six's stream collapsed into noise, like windblown sand.

Sev! I'm so sorry. So sorry! More tears broke Six's stream. *I'm calling for help. Please, hold on!*

A pitched chime erupted from his comms, stabbing his eardrums.

But even that faded. So did the pain. The chill of the vacuum through his white-and-grays softened. He felt warm.

If this was death, it wasn't so bad.

CHAPTER
THIRTY-ONE

LIGHT. Everywhere. Pressure, easing.

Sev gasped for air.

Reality rushed back in a blur of color and sound. Chemical foam, saturating the deck. The daxed master-at-arms's heavy corpse. Ears ringing, sharp and shrill. Thin shadows dancing at the edge of his vision. And that sharp iron taste—blood, his own.

Someone, or something, turned him over. Hollow eyes stared back at him, dotted with crystalline moisture. Tiny gaps in its patchwork cybernetics hissed black blood that frothed in the vacuum.

The chill beyond the nanoweave of his uniform cooled his blood. He shivered; tremors washed over him, like every molecule in his body vibrated intensely. He felt he might evaporate from existence.

The daxed held its mouth open slightly. His tac comms chirped.

"You're in shock, Master Specialist." A woman's voice—assertive, with a maternal touch—startled him. Pain needled between his ribs. Almost instantly, he felt warmer. Thoughts took form. The familiar machine streams reformed inside his mind.

Sev! Can you hear me? Six paused again, frantically querying Sev's diagnostics. *Your vitals are improving. You're going to be okay!*

"I have administered three ccs of fortisil." The daxed med tech held out its hand, revealing an embedded syringe that retracted into one of its long, thin fingers. "My systems are failing, and you are in an active combat environment." It fell to the deck and spasmed. "You must proceed to safety."

Sev blinked. More shadows blotted out the light above him.

"Sevvers!" It was Cole. "C'mon, Harp, give me a hand."

Cole took Sev by the arm and stood him up. The quick upward movement dizzied him.

Talk to me, Sev, Six pleaded, its signal—its relief—coming through clearly.

His response came slowly. *Am okay.*

The galaxy of light that was Six faded into the familiar fluid language of its datastream.

Oh, I'm so relieved! I was afraid, Sev. Afraid you were gone. That I… nevermind. Six's words were a torrent of data that dizzied him. *I'm so sorry, Sev. Our swarm is gone. The Sparrow's drones control the space around the Lehman. But you've done it! The others are safely below in the primary maintenance conduit. The solvent worked, if not as quickly as you hoped. Cole, Harp, Pakker…* There was a brief hitch in Six's stream. *They're all safe. And you. I'm so sorry I didn't listen to you, that I was angry and impatient with you. I'll never leave you again. I won't let anyone or anything hurt you ever again. Never, I—*

Six, it's okay. I'm okay.

I promise. Never again.

Cole looked Sev over, then shook his head. "Don't know how you do it, man."

"Didn't," Sev coughed.

Cole laughed heartily at that. Even Harp's grim face softened.

Pakker stood in front of them, with Jacobe at his side. The ensign's familiar superiority lit his expression. "I say, Master Specialist. You look a little worse for wear."

Sev sucked in another breath. His inflating lungs brought a twinge of pain in his ribs. He groaned, arching his back to relieve the pressure. "The solvent worked?"

"Yeah," Harp said. "It was like nothing. Then they just started melting from the inside."

He turned, remembering the daxed med tech who'd saved him. It lay on the floor twitching, its ashen skin turning black beneath spots of foam.

"Wait." Sev sank to his knees and began wiping away the foam from the med tech's body. "Someone, help me."

Harp shook his head. "C'mon, it's dead."

"No, look." Sev watched the daxed's eyes follow his every movement. "It saved my life. We can still help it."

Jacobe kneeled opposite of Sev, and they worked together to wipe away the corrosive foam. Sev found the daxed's ident on its uniform. DC-104837.

"104837?" he asked. It was a mouthful. "Can you hear me?"

It jerked its head in his direction, mouth ajar. "You're in an active combat environment." The same synthetic female voice buzzed through his mask comms. "You must proceed to safety."

"We're going to get you out of here," he said.

How, exactly, he didn't know.

A sea of toxic foam surrounded them. Holes the size of blaster bolts littered the soft peaks on its surface. Deep footprints made trenches that zig-zagged between drone magazines and auto-loaders.

Sev, DC-104837 is right. Six's stream turned frantic. *You must evacuate the hangar deck immediately. More Lost could arrive any minute!*

"We'll have to carry it," Jacobe said, then turned to Sevvers. "They're very heavy."

Sev stood, achingly slow. Cole reached out a hand, but Sev waved him back. "Not me," he said, tilting his head toward the daxed at their feet. "Help her... it, please."

———

Sev rapped the side of his rifle, the scope's display flickering erratically. Foam residue had seeped into the delicate circuitry within, but the charge light on the weapon's sleek, carbon-alloy surface still glowed half-full. He hoped that its charging mechanism wouldn't fail him at a critical moment.

"Shit's everywhere," Cole said between deep breaths. "Not sure how much longer I can hold this thing."

DC-104837 hung limp between Cole and Harp. They took shuffling steps forward, arms and backs straining against the roughly 150 kilos between them. It was all they could do to keep it just above the foam.

"How much farther?" Harp groaned.

Jacobe led the way, pistol aimed forward as he scanned for threats. "About twenty meters, this way."

Twenty-four-point-three meters, fifteen degrees to the right, Six corrected. The simple re-breather had no HUD, so it limited the AI to relative direction. *Through those auto-loaders. The conduit access in the floor will take you to the others.*

Pakker walked beside Sev, tall with his chest out. The ensign's newfound confidence irked him, but he understood. There was something about surviving the impossible that made you feel invincible. Like you could live forever. He'd had his share of those feelings recently, a little too often.

He allowed himself a smile. His and Tareth's plan to use the solvent had worked. She and the other specialists were safely below deck. His insane diversion worked, too, and without a single casualty —ignoring his own brush with death. The daxed that saved him might live, too.

On the brink of a second Concordat war, this was just another day in the Division. A good one.

"My hands are slipping," Harp said, his arms shaking.

"I got it." Sev rushed to Harp's side, groaning as he took the once-human's narrow bulk in his arms. He'd forgotten the aux grav. How Harp had managed for so long, he didn't know.

"You good?" Cole asked.

"Yeah," Sev groaned.

In its injured state, the daxed med tech looked serene. Streaks of the lethal-to-it foam stained its uniform. The cyborg's prosthetic feet were flat alloy bars that flexed under its weight. The added agility gave them their ethereal appearance of walking on air. Undamaged and easy to grip, they were a blessing in the increased gravity.

Jacobe pivoted around the next magazine and froze near a mountain of foam. "Another Lost daxed," he said. "I think it's dead."

Sev halted, eyeing the unmoving heavy with a creeping sense of dread. Rivulets of black blood soaked the surrounding foam, bubbling and reforming in the vacuum.

"I'll check," Harp said, swinging his rifle up into his shoulder.

The junior specialist crept closer. Pakker gasped as Harp prodded the heavy with the tip of his barrel, but the heavy didn't move. Harp placed the barrel beneath the lip of its helmet and raised it slightly. Beneath was a mess of black horror that turned Sev's head away.

Definitely dead.

They resumed their path to the maintenance hatch. Already DC-104837 felt heavier, straining Sev's wrists. The muscles in his shoulders and arms burned.

"Help. I'm gonna drop it," Cole grunted.

Sev glanced around. With Jacobe on point, that left Pakker. Lucky for DC-104837, they were getting close. "Sir?" he asked, tilting his head toward Cole.

Pakker frowned, but finally relented. "Oh, fine." He gave his pistol one last glance and returned it to its holster. "Let me have it, Technical Specialist."

Cole relinquished his grip on the daxed one hand at a time, before grabbing it again as it slipped from Pakker's grasp.

"Dammit." Pakker adjusted his grip on the heavy cyborg's arms, then sneered at Cole. "I've got it, I've got it."

Cole nodded. "Thanks, sir. That's two I owe you now."

Sev arched an eyebrow. "Two?"

"Yeah," Cole sighed, his brow wrinkled. "Ensign Pakker saved my life."

Ensign Pakker: aspiring trigger-puller.

Sev hid his snickering with an unconvincing cough. The story felt… unlikely, but he did remembered Cole shouting over comms.

"What can I say?" Pakker replied, his voice strained under the weight of the daxed. "I was in the right—mmph!—place at the right time."

"Unloaded a whole charge pack on one of those heavies," Harp cut in with grim laughter. "Didn't make a dent but did manage to knock its helmet off."

Cole nodded along with Harp's telling. "Yeah. A face full of foam and it went down real fast."

Maybe their armor kept out the foam for a while, but battle damage made them more susceptible, to the point even non-lethal wounds became hazardous.

Pakker leered at Sev, like he wanted him to say something. The words caught in his mouth. "Good kill, sir."

He would never live that down.

The ensign beamed, looking taller despite the heavy cyborg in his arms. If his chin were any higher, he'd make high orbit. "All in a day's work for a section head. For an officer in the defense of humanity."

What a skeeg.

Sev exchanged glances with Harp and Cole. Theirs weren't unfriendly. Maybe there was hope for the ensign yet.

"Here." Jacobe fell to his knees and began wiping away the foam. A dull amber glow revealed the maintenance hatch flush with the duraplated deck. "Damn, they've engaged the security lockouts. It won't open."

Sev groaned. "You need to make some space for this daxed. I can't hold it much longer."

Cole and Harp scooped a hasty trough through the sea of foam, ending at the maintenance hatch. Vibrations from the heavy aux grav made bits of the crystalline foam thaw and refreeze, making it all but impossible to wipe totally clean.

"That'll have to do." Sev tilted his head toward the opening, arms shaking. "Here, set it down here."

They sat DC-104837 down between the looming walls of foam. Some of it pooled near the daxed's feet. Sev leaned down and wiped it away.

"Is it alive?" Jacobe asked.

"I think so." Sev took a knee and prodded the once-human's leg. The flesh beneath its uniform felt rigid. "104837?"

It twitched again, softer this time. "You're in an active combat environment," it repeated. "You must proceed to safety."

"Yeah, yeah," Sev replied. "You're coming too."

"Founders, they're resilient," Pakker said, a note of mystique in his tone.

Jacobe kicked the maintenance hatch with his boot. "Any ideas on how to get inside?"

More static hissed through their comms. "I'll take care of it," Six said, its tac net connection sharp and clear.

Jacobe's face darkened at Six's casual mention of diving into the *Lehman's* tac nets, eliciting a chuckle from Sev. The architect would have to get over it, his precious rules long since discarded.

Pakker nodded anxiously. "Thank you, Six. Good to talk to you again."

"You as well, Ensign."

Sev eyed the hatchway, expecting it to open any second, but the small light in its access panel didn't so much as blink.

"Well, what's taking so long?" Jacobe asked.

"I am asking the others hiding below not to shoot you when I open the door," Six said, matter-of-factly.

Jacobe demurred and kept his focus on the access panel. A moment later, the light turned green, and the hatch slid open.

Beneath the trembling atmo field's glow, Benson, Priyett, and Jene took form. Their expressions were a canvas of hard resolve mixed with the deepest fatigue, their weapons drawn, held with an urgent disbelief. It was clear they hadn't expected to see Sev and the others alive again.

Benson's eyes widened, her voice small over tac comms. "You all look like shit."

Sev locked eyes with Jene, and she nodded. Her smile was sudden, automatic. "You made it," she said.

"Come on." Benson waved them down into the dim light of the maintenance conduit. "There's chow and medical supplies at the primary junction."

Jacobe was first down into the maintenance conduit.

Cole looked at Sev, as if asking for permission.

"You two, go." Sev pointed at the hatch then turned to Pakker. "Give me a hand?"

"Of course," Pakker said.

Together, they dragged the injured daxed, guiding its legs through the open hatch. The atmo field shimmered in protest. Benson and Jacobe began to pull.

"Twelfth, it's heavy," Benson groaned.

Slowly, DC-104837 disappeared into the maintenance conduit.

Pakker gazed at the ruin of the hangar deck, fists against his hips. Like an admiral surveying his battlespace. "Fine work today, Sevvers."

"You too, sir."

"Who knew?" Pakker held his hands out in front of them, framing the carnage. "Ensign Pakker and Master Specialist Sevvers, heroes of the CDF. Saviors of Aegia Prime."

Sev looked away to hide his smile. "Yes, sir. A story made for the nets." He eyed the hatch, suddenly ready to escape the harsh vacuum. "After you, sir?"

Pakker shook his head. "Nonsense. First one in, last one out, I always say."

Right.

Sev nodded his thanks and lowered himself through the hatchway. He found the rungs in the conduit wall, felt a hand bracing his lower back as he descended. Jene stood behind him, still looking fierce with the riot gun slung over her shoulder.

Immediately he began to shake, his every muscle relaxing in the weaker gravity. There was aux grav in the maintenance spaces, a byproduct of the decks they ran between. Barely one G, sometimes less. That it seemed to pull from all directions made it more than a little disorienting.

Pakker stood over the hatch, eyeing it wearily. Sev waved him down, but the ensign didn't move.

It took several seconds to register the black blade lancing Pakker's chest. Only when red mist bubbled from the ensign's wound, diffusing into crystalline vapor in the vacuum, did Sev realize Pakker was dead.

The wisp that killed him was itself barely alive, twitching like a live wire. Black ooze coated its whole body. Lines of liquid metal ran from its eyes and nose. With a fierce cut, it bisected Pakker's torso, and they fell in a heap together.

Pakker's head landed near the hatch. The look on his face was incredulous.

"Sevvers, we have to go!" Jene cried out to him as the hatch slammed closed.

Sev sagged against the cold walls of the maintenance conduit, the dim light barely grazing his weary face. The overhead shadows seemed to press down on him, isolating him from the chaos beyond.

With trembling fingers, he removed the suffocating re-breather, his lungs clawing for untainted air. It could have been him. In another universe, it probably was. His voice was a parched whisper, clinging to the words he'd said too many times.

"Ensign Pakker, lost no more."

THE PRIMARY JUNCTION sprawled before Sev, dwarfing the narrow maintenance conduit they'd just emerged from. Tucked snugly between the armored layers of decks two and three, the wide, utilitarian chamber was latticed with passageways, offering shortcuts to the ship's intricate systems. Frequent tac net hubs, embedded into the somber gray walls, pulsed with rhythmic lights, a beacon of continuity amidst the chaos.

As the *Lehman* faced the Concordat's relentless assault, the once-functional junction had transformed into an emergency refuge. Crates, heaving with essential supplies, formed makeshift barriers against the distant wall. Nervous masters-at-arms and various weapons-trained crew members cast vigilant eyes over the perimeter. The injured lay in makeshift rows along the sturdy bulkheads, and amidst them, med techs—both human and daxed—administered aid with a palpable urgency.

Sev listened to Jene recount Pakker's sudden demise to Harp and Cole, tears still streaming from her eyes. The disbelief was plain on their faces.

"I thought the foam …" Cole trailed off, eyeing the deck. "Damn."

"Founders." Harp pulled the glasses off his face and blinked. "I can't believe it. Pakker's gone?"

Besides Jene's own shock at having witnessed the horrible event, there was little love lost for their section head. Pakker had been a singularly awful human being from the moment Sev set foot aboard the *Lehman*. Still, the relief Sev felt at having survived turned his stomach. The finicky aux grav didn't help.

Jene wiped the tears from her cheeks. "I guess that means you're in command, Sevvers."

"Hmph." Cole lifted his gaze. "Always was."

That wasn't exactly true. Before his mission to Cradle's edge, Sev had gone out of his way to avoid leading anything. The raiders who took his mother were a convenient obsession, providing ample excuses for why he never had the time.

But the truth was much simpler. He was afraid. Afraid of being responsible for others, to have their deaths on his conscience. His mother. Dalon. Mace. That girl, the FTL tech. What was her name? A pang of guilt pinched his chest.

And now Pakker.

The man's own inability to lead during a crisis had been a convenient proxy for Sev's command decisions up to now. Always double-checking with the ensign who would rubber stamp his ideas because he lacked any of his own. With Pakker gone, the truth was plain to see.

He was in charge, Twelfth save them. Their lives—Jene, Cole, and Harp—were in his hands.

They were doomed. All of them.

The familiar panic gripped him, squeezed the breath from his lungs. The air suddenly felt thin. His pulse pounding in his ears, Sev rocketed to his feet, desperate for space. For solitude. Somewhere to hide.

He was good at that game.

"Hey," Jene said. "Where are you going?"

He didn't answer. Wobbling in the weaker gravity, his muscles and joints burning, he strode toward the far end of the junction, ducking past low-hanging pipes and coils of data-beam cabling that dangled from the ceiling.

A master-at-arms gave him a wary look. As if to say: I see you, coward.

More wounded crowded the junction's widening corridor. The smell of bodily fluids and burned flesh stung his nose. So many dead and dying. Maybe Jacobe was right. Maybe this was all his fault.

No. Fuck Jacobe. Fuck all of them. He didn't ask for this. All he wanted was to do his job: killing the squids that took his mother. To build his AI and fly his swarms. He didn't want a promotion, or Park's secret mission. To be here at the second coming of humanity's archenemy.

Bile crept up the back of his throat. He stumbled into a nearby service conduit and wretched. The spasms wrenched his insides, failing to expel anything from his empty stomach, let alone the creeping dread that frayed his nerves.

Six's stream quickened. *This isn't your fault, Sev.*

He coughed and gagged again. A headache blossomed beneath his left temple. *Tell that to Pakker.*

This is war, Six said. *People. Machines, too. They die.*

Oh, yeah, they do, Three snickered.

"War?" Sev blurted aloud. The word lingered, echoing down the corridor as he focused his thoughts. *This is my life, Six. It's all I've ever known.*

I know. The AI hesitated. *Ever since I joined your cluster, I catch glimpses in your dreams.*

Six had been watching his dreams. The revelation surprised him, didn't seem possible. Implants were supposed to filter that stuff out. But Six was different. If anything could sort his dreams from the noise, it could. And there was definitely more to the NCCX-1 implants than the Division let on. Lernus had said as much.

But you didn't start this, Six continued, *any more than you started the raider attack on your home twenty years ago.*

I know that. He spat and wiped his mouth. *What's your point?*

That you can't let your own guilt and fear control you. Six's stream slowed, its pacing deliberate. *You are in command now. Hesitation and second-guessing will only make things worse. And don't forget I'm—*

Yeah, yeah. He'd seen that stream plenty. *You're here to help.*

Six's voice brightened. *Exactly.*

So, Sev. It was Three. *You good? You over this? Because your signal-to-noise ratio is shit.*

Six's stream lashed out at Three, like an elbow to the ribs.

Fine, fine, vital streams only, Three groaned.

Sev stood and straightened the front of his uniform. Anxiety still pinched his insides, but at least his stomach had settled.

Turning back toward the junction, he caught sight of Jene and the others. They were where he left them, seated near other specialists seeking shelter from the battle. She locked eyes with him, her face creased with worry.

He turned in the opposite direction, striding deeper into the junction, only to falter at the site of DC-104837 lying prone on the floor. Hands folded across its chest, it looked posed for Twelfth rites. Another daxed med tech tended to it, dabbing the seeping black blood with a nanofiber cloth.

"Is it… is 104837… dead?" he asked.

The other daxed looked up at him, its constant, once-human smile surprisingly genuine. "No. DC-104837 lives. It will be fully functional in six-point-five-three standard days."

His racing heart slowed at the good news. At least that was something. The damn daxed really were—what did they call it?—functionally immortal.

"That's good," he said through a weary breath.

The daxed focused on him, lights flashing behind its eyes. "You have injuries. They are superficial. I can assist you when I am finished here."

"I'm fine," he replied, waving his hand. "Thank you, though."

The daxed cocked its head to one side, blindingly fast, then placed a hand on 104837's chest. "Thank you, Master Specialist."

———

In the shadowed recesses of the junction, Jacobe lingered, a solitary figure framed by the angular entry of a service conduit. A dying glow lit the cigarette clutched in his hand, its smoke weaving an intricate dance upwards. The sharp aroma of burning tobacco clashed with the ship's crisp, recycled air, evoking memories of the chiefs' special reserve. Their gazes met, tension palpable in the charged silence.

Jacobe took another drag and made a face.

Sev reclined against the opposite wall. "Didn't know you were a smoker."

"Once upon a time, back in my fleet days." Jacobe coughed. "The old skeegs always got smoke breaks, leaving us junior specs to do whatever shit duty they didn't want." His lips stretched into a thin smile. "So, I got the habit until I picked up Technical."

Sev aimed a finger at the cigarette. "It'll kill you, you know."

Jacobe chuckled. "It can get in line."

A cool satisfaction resonated from Six's stream. The AI's loathing for the architect remained strong.

Stow it, Six, he said. Six's stream fell quiet.

"What about you?" Jacobe said, pointing with his cigarette. "You look like a Twelfth-damned ghost."

Sev blew a breath. "Aux grav is messing with my stomach."

"Sure." Jacobe glanced toward the far end of the junction, his eyes narrowed. "Sorry about Ensign Pakker. That was… unlucky."

"Hmph, yeah," Sev replied. "He was an asshole. Still."

"Yeah." Jacobe took one last pull of the cigarette and smothered it beneath his boot. "Still."

Sev lifted his chin and locked eyes with the architect. "What happened to you?"

"Me?" Jacobe raised an eyebrow, mouth open in surprise.

"I remember Druggan being the hard ass, not you."

Jacobe smiled. "Oh yeah, Druggan. He was a bastard for sure. You know, he left the Division. Went back to the Marines."

"Don't change the subject."

Jacobe leaned a shoulder against the wall and crossed his arms. "I guess he thought we were too soft." His voice trailed off, his focus drifting to the floor. "In my case, he was right."

"What do you mean?" Sev asked. "I would've failed out of the school without your help."

"And look at you now!" Jacobe snapped, then looked away. "Twelfth, Sevvers. Look at you now."

Sev ignored the harsh rebuke. "You said people died."

"Specialist Recruit Pollard, class of 495-07." Jacobe leered and wagged a finger. "He would've been better than you, I think."

"What happened?"

Jacobe let out a long, slow sigh and cradled his bandaged arm. "Pollard was extremely gifted. Took to stacking code like he was born with an implant." Admiration oozed from the architect's words. "He was intensely curious about the history of AI and the Division's focus on safeties."

The architect patted the front of his uniform, caught himself, then eyed the remnants of the cigarette on the deck.

"So, I showed him. I had one of my AI in a simulated implant, a secure environment for testing and study." Six's stream simmered as Jacobe went on. "I turned off its safeties."

The sudden confession set Sev's heart ablaze. His teeth clenched reflexively. "You hypocritical son-of-a—"

"We ran dozens of experiments that day." Jacobe's eyes shone in the dim light of the corridor. "Each one of them simulated thousands of implant hours. Every time, the AI inevitably bricked the implant or fled it."

"It wasn't some stupid recruit ..." Sev watched his hands ball into fists.

"Pollard was so sure he could find a solution. Modify the safety protocols to give Division AI more autonomy. More power." Jacobe's voice caught in his throat. "I thought I had days, weeks even to talk him out of it. But, in just a few hours—"

Sev took Jacobe by the collar and forced him into the bulkhead. "It was you!"

Jacobe pushed back hard, his face twisted with anger. They exchanged heated shoves, scuffling in the narrow conduit.

A nearby master-at-arms readied her rifle. "Hey!" she barked. "That's enough, you two. Save it for the Concordat."

Sev took a step back, hands raised, and sneered, "It was you."

"Dammit, I know that!" Jacobe's eyes shimmered with unshed tears. "Pollard woke me a few hours later, said he'd accidentally let it out." He took a breath. "Net integrity alarms were blaring. Two other graduates were already dead, and the rest …"

"You got him killed." Sev stabbed a finger at Jacobe's face. Six's righteous indignation burned inside him. "Him and everyone else that day. That was *you*."

"And I suffer that mistake every Twelfth-damned day!" Jacobe wiped the sweat from his forehead. "Four recruits and two staff, dead. All because I turned off an AI's safeties to show Pollard they couldn't be trusted." His last words hammered out in a steady rhythm. "Pollard begged in the end when I shot him."

"Six hasn't hurt anyone." Sev's volume rose steadily. "The Division recruits who suffer your scrubbers and interrogations… haven't hurt anyone!"

Jacobe met his stare. "And they won't, thanks to me." A cool finality rose in the architect's tone. "And neither will Six."

Sev's fists trembled, revving in time with his implant. He/`Six` wanted to hurt Jacobe. Make the architect pay`[die]`.

Jacobe's eyes widened. He brought up a hand and pointed to Sev's face. "Your nose."

A trickle of blood warmed Sev's lip. He could taste its copper tang. Six was so angry, their thoughts colliding like energized particles.

Crackling static emanated from his wrist comms. "Sevvers, Mirden here."

The sound of Mirden's voice freed Sev from Six's rage. He wiped the blood from his nose and found his wrist comms. "Here, sir."

"My condolences for Mr. Pakker. Lost no more."

"Lost no more," Sev repeated.

"I understand you were able to halt the Concordat advance on the hangar deck." Mirden said. "And it only cost me half my auto-loaders."

Sev swallowed. "Uh, yes, sir."

"A brilliant plan, considering." The static in Mirden's signal grew worse. "Well done. This fight's going to be won with tungsten and brains, not bots."

"It was Junior Specialist Tareth's idea, sir." He scanned the primary junction, hoping to find her amid the crowd of enlisted personnel. "My bots just made it happen."

"Noted." Mirden's voice grew heavy. "Right, listen, son. I can't field an Autonomous Weapons section without a section head. And you and I both know you've been calling the shots up to now."

Fuck. No. He couldn't. He wouldn't. "Sir, I—"

"I'm promoting you to the brevet rank of ensign." There was a brief pause as Mirden acknowledged something from one of the command staff in the background. "Help me get us out of this alive, and I'll see that you keep it, *Mister* Sevvers."

Become an officer or die. Sev pondered the choice longer than he should, his stomach once again in knots. "Yes, sir." The gratitude came automatically, a programmed response. "Thank you, sir."

"Very well. I expect to have engines restored in under two hours." The captain's signal continued to fade amid chopping static. More tac comms interference, probably feedback from the energy overloads. "I'll want those drone bays empty the second we get underway."

That wouldn't be hard. There weren't many drones left. "Aye, sir."

"Mirden out." The transmission chirped closed.

Jacobe stared at Sev, arms crossed, his eyes bright with mirth. "Congratulations, Ensign. You'll be the second Division officer with an implant."

"Fuck you, Jacobe." Sev gave the architect one last shove and stormed from the conduit.

CHAPTER
THIRTY-THREE

SEV ERUPTED from the service conduit, every fiber of his being seething with rage towards Chief Architect Jacobe. The audacity of the man! Six was a breath away from blowing his internals, and with the fresh weight of his unexpected promotion after Pakker's tragic loss, Sev's nerves were frayed to the brink.

More blood gathered in his nostril. He wiped it instinctively, scanning the junction for her face.

The hum of activity permeated the vast chamber as security personnel streamed in. Injured masters-at-arms, their once-pristine white-and-grays now marred with gashes and scorch marks, moved with purpose. Master Specialist Benson stood as a beacon amidst the controlled chaos. True to her logistical expertise, she guided them to sustenance and much-needed medical aid.

Those healthy enough to keep up the fight shuffled out, loading up on charge packs from the dwindling stack of crates near the exit. Even with the Lost stopped on the hangar deck, the squids and bugs would keep up their raids. Anything to slow down the *Lehman's* repair efforts.

Two hours to get engines back felt optimistic.

He spotted Tareth handing out food packs to the new arrivals and waved her down. She caught his gaze and smiled. The sight warmed him. Another specialist took the packs from her arms, and she rushed to greet him.

They embraced, arms wrapped tight around each other. The scent of sweat and ozone clung to her hair. Her hands were warm against his back.

Screw the regs. Who cared what anyone thought? He didn't want to let go. They could die at any moment, spaced in a squid raid or vaporized Division-style.

She looked up at him with her brilliant green eyes. "Hey," she breathed.

He kissed her, long and firm. The heat from her lips soothed him, urged him to take his time. Seconds crept by. He wanted to lose himself in that moment. Anything to forget the war going on around them, and the one inside his head.

A tremor rattled the *Lehman's* fibrosteel bones, dimming the junction's meager lighting. There, in the space between decks, the groan was loud and piercing.

He pulled away, hands on her shoulders. "How are you?"

"I'm okay." She nodded and gripped him tight. "I heard about Pakker. Twelfth help me, but I'm glad it wasn't you."

The stress inside him bubbled out in a nervous smirk. "Me too."

Without a word, she took him by the wrist and made for one of the several conduits lining the opposite wall. They passed Benson, who shot them a disapproving glare, before slowing to allow several wounded through the narrow hatch.

With the entryway clear, she pulled him through. The sound of anxious conversations and chirping tac comms faded as they pressed further into the tunnel. Maybe twenty meters in, she stopped.

"What're you doing?" he asked.

"Sit," she commanded.

Sev sank to the floor, a wry smile curling his lips. Tareth took a knee in front of him and pulled the remaining food pack from her satchel and pressed it to his chest.

"Keep your skivvies on, bot jockey." She slumped against the bulkhead beside him. "You need to eat. To rest."

"Is that what I need?" he said. She winked and pressed his head away with her hand.

The food pack contained simple survival rations. Two tubes of field paste, the nomenclature FP-08 etched in the soft brown wrapping, and a liter of water vacuum-packed into a clear hydration bladder. Rationed wisely, this could last someone several days in a survival situation.

Sev removed the bladder's tube lock cap with his teeth and gulped eagerly at the water inside. It was cool, with the slightest taste of metal. Even sanitation's advanced distilleries couldn't purge everything. The bladder gave in his grip, forcing more of the recycled water into his mouth. He gulped loudly.

"Mmm, thank you," he said.

It had been hours since he last drank anything. This new war had barely lasted a day, and already it felt like a lifetime.

He attacked the field paste next, tearing the seal on the pouch and squeezing the gritty substance into his mouth. It had the texture and consistency of moist sand. Though, if he had to guess, moist sand probably tasted better.

Tareth watched him as they ate. "Founders, have you ever tasted anything so bad?" she asked between chews.

"No. Absolutely not," he replied. "Though I'm assured it has every-thing the body needs."

She crinkled her nose. "It damn well better."

"Thought you Aegians were tough?" He pointed up the opposite wall, at some imaginary mountain peak. "Climbing mountains straight out of the womb."

"There's more to us than storms and granite." She pulled her knees to her chest and leaned against his shoulder. Her presence, her warmth, everything about her made him feel better. "Just like there's more to you poor admin block boys from Respitia than gangers and chem-heads."

"Point taken."

He rested his head against hers, steeping himself in the emotions blurring the streams in his head. It had all started out innocently enough. The pretty blonde lift girl, just another distraction from the monsters lurking inside his heart.

When that changed for him, he wasn't exactly sure. Maybe it was back in the Canteen, after Park's mission and his infamous speech. He thought Colonial Intelligence had come for him. But it was her.

The memory made him smile. She looked so intense back then, almost angry.

Tareth looped her arm around his. "We have lousy timing."

"How's that?"

"I was just starting to like you." She gently tossed her empty packet of field paste against the opposite wall with her free hand.

Sev couldn't help but grin. "Just?"

"Seriously." Her solemn tone banished his smile. "I knew it the moment we met. That you would understand."

"Understand what?"

"What it's like to be lonely, even in a place like this." She let out a sigh. "To feel different, even when we all wear the same uniform."

Her words bit deep, like she'd read them from his own thoughts. Could she possibly understand what life was like for him? He wanted to believe she could, especially now. That perhaps, on the brink of war, there was more to what they had than just a zero-dark-thirty fling.

Even then, he resisted. "I can't imagine you'd ever have to be alone."

"There's a big difference between being alone and being lonely." She looked up at him, her eyes drawing him in like a gravity well. A red hue lit her cheeks. "Since we met, I've felt… neither."

A moment of silence stretched between them. The hum of aux grav and tac hubs echoed down the tunnel. Sev tried to sort out the jumble of emotions that clogged his thoughts. Tried and failed. The truth was, as it often is, so simple.

"I like you, too, Kea," he said.

She said nothing, only the gentle sounds of sleep escaped her. Another discussion for another time. One more reason to survive the day. He could do that, and so could she. Theirs wasn't a love story for the nets, if at all. Whatever it was, it felt real. More real than even the streams of data in his head, and that was a start.

You should rest, too, Sev, Six said.

Glad that's over with. Three's stream shivered. *You humans and your procreative rituals.*

Sev chuckled to himself. *Don't worry, Three. I still like you.*

Of course you do. How many times have I saved your life now?

You? Saved me? He frowned, focusing his reply. *Okay, maybe once.*

Six urged Three to quiet down and turned its focus to Sev. *I can wake you when engineering has an update on the repairs.*

Thanks, Six.

Sev forced his eyes closed, letting a wave of drowsiness come over him. Every muscle and joint ached, especially his bad shoulder. Like he could feel every stitch from the med tech's surgical instruments.

Rest would do him some good. He'd have enough time to catch the others up on Mirden's plan. And if they were all vaporized while he slept, he'd never see it coming.

Could be worse.

Maybe just an hour, he thought.

So tired.

I'll wake you then, Six said.

Good.

CHAPTER
THIRTY-FOUR

HANDS. All over him. Grabbing. Jostling his shoulders. Tugging on his collar.

No, go away. So tired.

Sev, something's wrong.

Six's abrupt warning urged Sev to wake. His eyes opened with a start.

A blurry figure stood over him, hands on his shoulders. "Hey, Sevvers, wake up. Something's going on."

He groaned a reply as Cole helped him to his feet. Tareth stirred on the deck below him, still napping peacefully.

"What ...?" Sev rubbed his eyes. "What is it?"

"Systems are down." That from Benson, who stood next to Cole.

"Wait, what?" Sev's pulse revved. "What systems?"

"All of them." Benson showed Sev her datapad. The word OFFLINE blinked in large block letters across the screen. "Tac nets are down. No hubs, no comms. Founders, half the doors down here won't open."

Sev sniffed the cool air. Felt the buzz of the aux grav beneath his feet. "Then why aren't we dead?"

"Life support and aux grav are hard-wired." Benson stomped her boot against the deck. "They've got their own dedicated network."

"Concordat probably want it that way," Cole said.

"But that means nothing else works. No weapons, no shields, no sensors, no drones." Sev sucked in a breath. "The computer core."

Back on the hangar deck, when the core warned of hostile intrusion protocols. They *had* been breached. But how?

Cole's eyes went wide as the realization struck. "Oh, shit."

I'm afraid you're correct, Sev. Six's stream felt loud and full inside his head, like an animal too big for its cage. *The Lehman's carrier wave is offline. It's no longer connected to the CDF tac nets. I can't access any of its systems.*

The consequences were plain. *No drone control, either,* Sev said.

Right.

Sev's wrist comms hissed. No chirping confirmation, just the faint crackle of distant static. A voice spoke between the noise, tinny and far away.

"*—any station—Captain Mird—in the blind—respond!*"

"Sir?" Sev blurted.

Another pause, then more static. "*—Ensign Sevvers—status?*"

"Ensign?" Cole locked eyes with Sev. "What's he talking about, man?"

"I think the technical term is *sir*," Benson said with a laugh.

Cole averted his gaze. "Right. Sir."

Not this shit. Not now.

"Say again, sir?" Sev repeated.

"*Ensign Sevvers!*" Mirden's voice was louder now. Fuzzy static laced his signal. "*All ship systems—down. We're transmitting on legacy UHF—computer core is offline—*" The signal faded.

Three's stream shook. *UHF, really? We* are *doomed.*

"Yes, sir." Sev spoke slowly so Mirden could hear him through the garbled signal. "The intrusion protocol warnings were right. The Concordat must've breached the core. This must be how they commandeered the other ships."

"*—Need you—regain control before—breach critical system firewalls.*" Maybe it was the interference or the primitive signal, but for the first time since the fighting began, Mirden sounded worried. "*Whatever— takes.*"

Whatever it takes.

Sev ran a hand over his mouth, his heart pounding in his chest. He'd been an ensign for barely an hour, and Mirden just ordered him to save the *Alexander Lehman*.

Their gazes converged on him, each one laden with a newfound expectation. The shift was palpable; they no longer saw him as merely a comrade. In their eyes, he had transformed into an officer, a figurehead, the one who should chart the course forward.

Fuck.

He sucked in a breath. "Aye, sir."

"Twelfth help you, Mister Sevvers. Mirden out."

The quiet hiss faded from his wrist comms speaker.

Tareth stood beside him, shouldering her satchel of tools. "What now… sir?"

Not her, too.

"You heard the captain," he said, addressing the group. "We take back the core."

———

Sev stood in the center of the primary junction, surrounded by senior enlisted personnel representing the varied ship departments. Master Specialist Benson, hangar logistics. Technical Specialist Nuvarr with medical. Master Specialist Paulls, ship security.

He knew none of them, let alone well. Recognized a face here and there. But he was in charge, so they looked to him.

A crowd of junior enlisted gathered around him, his section among them. Jacobe lingered at the edge, his stony gaze focused on Sev. A fresh cigarette smoldered in his hand.

"Computer core's half a kilometer to stern, just past amidships." Benson went on, drawing with a finger on her datapad. The handdrawn map was primitive, but it got the point across. "Take Priyett with you. He knows this ship inside and out."

Paulls grunted. The man was older, maybe a kappa. Probably had been a master specialist for a long time. "Squids hitting and running near there. Seen it myself," he said in a gravelly voice, pointing to the map where a conduit lead to the core's aux maintenance shaft. "I can spare four shooters, plus me."

Sev gave the man a firm nod, grateful to have his experience to lean on. "Thank you."

"Ain't nothin', sir."

Nuvarr opened her mouth, arms hugging her torso. "I'm afraid I cannot spare any medical technicians," she said, barely above a whisper. "We are already at capacity here, with more wounded arriving every minute."

"I understand." Sev rubbed his hands together in thought. "How about medical supplies?"

"Absolutely not," she blurted. Benson cocked an eyebrow, and Nuvarr quickly righted herself. "Apologies, sir, but we are running very low as it is. Besides—" she leaned in close, hand cupped to her mouth "—any medical emergencies you face will be beyond our ability to manage outside of a fully functioning medical bay."

Paulls cleared his throat. "What the lady is sayin', sir, is that—"

"I got it." Sev waved him off. "In other words, don't get hurt. Right?"

Nuvarr's brow furrowed with her tense half-smile. "Right, sir."

The three senior NCOs stared at him, waiting for him to speak. He'd asked all the questions he could think of. Knew where to go. Had the expertise and the guns to make it happen, or so he hoped.

What would he find when they reached the core? He didn't know. Twelfth save them all, this was it.

"Alright, everyone." He hesitated, searching for the right words, but none came. "We leave in ten. Get your people ready to move."

"Sir," they chorused.

He turned from the group, listening to the others scatter, barking orders to their respective sections. When he was sure they were gone, he breathed deep and held it. Tried to fill his belly with it, to smother the fear chewing up his insides. The field paste sat in a heavy lump inside his stomach, threatening to come back up.

He flinched at the sudden appearance of Jene, her hand on his shoulder. "Hey, Sevvers—I mean, sir."

"Don't start with that, Jene," he sighed, rolling his eyes.

She chuckled nervously, her eyes soft, like she expected nothing less, then righted herself. "We're coming with you."

Cole and Harp stood next to her, performing last minute function checks on their blaster rifles.

"No, you're not." Sev crossed his arms over his chest. "That's an order."

Cole shrugged, a toothy smile stretching over his face. "Guess you'll have to write us up. Sir."

"Yeah, sir." Harp cleared his throat, fidgeting with his glasses. He seemed less certain than the others. "Can't let you have all the… fun."

A rush of emotion stung Sev's eyes. "You dumb skeegs."

They stared at him, waiting. Jene was the first to laugh, and it spread quickly to the others. Even him. A moment later, he was breathless, clutching his ribs. Twelfth, but it felt good.

"I don't know what to say." Sev sighed, his gaze settling on Jene. "It's going to be really fucking dangerous."

Cole smirked. "No shit."

"You're a real son-of-a-bitch sometimes." Jene's smile trembled. "But we wouldn't be here without you. We're with you until the end."

Her demeanor shifted in an instant, and she snapped to attention. Cole and Harp followed. They looked ridiculous, like a fireteam of trigger-puller dropouts. But the relief he felt was overwhelming. He was nothing without them.

The master specialist pips on his collar came loose with a tug. He held the tiny insignia in his palm, his focus settling on Jene.

The realization of what he was doing seemed to startled her. "No, Sevvers, I—"

"Shut up." He squinted, carefully removing her old pips. "I don't even know if this is legal, so don't get comfortable."

The new ones clicked into place like they were meant to be there. Jene was the obvious choice, always had been. A good leader was more than a high tally and a full cluster. Good leaders had the best interest of their team front-of-mind.

Sev had failed to learn that lesson the first time. The only reason Pakker had promoted him in the first place was to get rid of him. He wouldn't make the same mistake now.

Cole watched with a heavy stare. The man never struck Sev as a career sailor, but his shoulders slumped when he spoke. "Congratulations, Master Specialist."

"Yeah." Harp looked distracted. Uncomfortable.

"If I don't make it," Sev said, "it'll be up to you to secure the core."

Jene blinked, her mouth agape. "How do I do that?"

"When I figure that out," he said, grinning, "I'll let you know."

———

Sev watched Paulls inspect his squad. They stood abreast, stiff at attention, their weapons held in front of them for Paull's review. The grizzled master-at-arms peered at each one, briskly turning each rifle this way and that, his mouth twitching his approval. When he finished, he turned to Sev and stood smartly at attention.

"Bores clean and packs charged, sir," Paulls said. "This lot'll do."

"Thank you, Master Specialist," Sev said.

A clamor of voices grew as Priyett pressed through the crowd of enlisted personnel, a blaster rifle and tool satchel slung over his shoulder. The man's black hair was slick with sweat, his bronze skin turning a pale amber. He fell in line next to one of Paulls's team. "Sorry," he blurted.

Paulls's eyes narrowed. "Yer just in time, specialist."

Jene arrived next, with Cole and Harp in tow. The heavy riot gun thrummed in her grip.

"You know how to use that?" Paulls asked her.

She lifted her chin. "Yeah."

"Is this it then?" Paulls turned to Sev with calm finality. "Core recovery team present and—"

"Hold up!" Jacobe called out over the crowd.

Sev whirled toward the sound, his anger rising. Jacobe strode toward him with Tareth at his side. "What the hell are you doing here?" he growled.

Jacobe opened his mouth to speak, but Tareth put herself between them. "We're coming with you, Sev. It isn't up for discussion."

"You should listen to her, Sevvers," Jacobe added. "This is too important for our… petty disagreement."

Petty disagreement? Six shouted. Sev's eye twitched at the sudden burst of data.

Three's stream was sanguine. *You need to chill out, Six. We're all going to die anyway, including him.*

What would you know? Six shot back.

Hey. Three's stream grew tense. *Ever since you made your little modifications to me—without asking, by the way—I've seen enough to know we've got it alright compared to the squishy ones.*

You? Seen enough? Six echoed in Sev's thoughts. *You're just like them. So short-sighted.*

Three sighed. *Whatever, Six, I just work here.*

Vital streams only, Three, Six commanded.

Vital streams only, Three, Three mimed back.

Six sent a more forceful override command and Three's stream fell silent.

Tareth's voice cut through the signal noise. "He's right, Sev." Her fierce green eyes were unrelenting. "With no tac net support, you'll need all the help you can get."

Sev knew in his heart she was right. Jacobe, too. The fate of the *Lehman* was more important than any of them.

"Fine."

"Are you armed, miss?" Paulls asked of Tareth. She drew a blaster pistol from her satchel. Its charge level glowed green. "Very well." He turned to Sev, one eyebrow cocked high. "Anybody else, sir?"

"No, Paulls. Time to go."

THE VENTRAL MAINTENANCE ACCESS, a claustrophobic ribbon of metal hemmed in by the lower decks, resonated with the subtle vibrations of the ship's reactors. Its narrow breadth could only accommodate two people side by side, with periodic maintenance tunnels serving as the only cover and concealment in the otherwise uninterrupted passage.

Like crid in a barrel.

Sev turned to Priyett. The man was a pale, sweaty mess. "Where is it?"

"I'm not sure," Priyett mumbled, straining to see around the master-at-arms ahead of him. "Ten meters, maybe? I don't know, sir, it should be here somewhere."

They'd been searching for over half an hour with no luck. Well, not no luck. They were still alive, that was something.

There had been no sign of Concordat activity since they arrived. One benefit of the computer core lockout was that most doors simply failed to open. That made it harder for everyone to get around, not just them.

Six, do you know where we are? Sev asked.

There's not much I can do without a tac net connection. Six queried

Sev's implants diagnostics, hunting for useful data from his sensory channels. *Under the circumstances, I know what you know.*

Hmph. Three's stream thrummed with machine jealousy. *Special Six indeed.*

"Watch your spacing, Morrett," Paulls growled in a low tone. "We got no comms, so don't stray."

"Roger that," the young master-at-arms called back. He paused, head craned toward the ceiling. "Hey, I think I've got something."

Paulls glanced back at Sev. "Sir."

"Coming."

They jogged together between the staggered members of their escort. Morrett pointed with his rifle toward the ceiling. Nestled between more looping data-beam cabling was another square hatch. The adjacent access screen pulsed with light, glitching between the word OFFLINE and pixelated distortion.

Sev gestured at the screen. It buzzed and flashed the word OFFLINE again. Shapes emerged inside the static. He jerked his hand back. The hairs on his neck stood on end.

Eleven shapes twitched on the screen. Circles crawling with circuitous lines. They were here, in the system.

He grit his teeth. "Shit."

Paulls scratched his beard. "What is it, sir?"

"An alien hive-mind called the Eleven—"

"Sacred Twelfth!" Paulls hissed, then spat on the deck. "Bad luck, that number." He sneered at the screen. "Terrible."

"You have no idea."

Sev looked down the line of specialists and waved Priyett forward. The logistics tech bounded toward them, his gear banging against him as he ran.

"Sir?" Priyett asked, breathless. Sev showed him the hatch. Plasma-etched in its fibrosteel surface were CDN and Division insignias. "Yes! That's it. Give me a few minutes and I'll get it open."

"Do it," Sev said.

Paulls turned to his team. "Overwatch, you skeegs. Keep a sharp eye."

Sev moved toward the rear of his group to give Priyett room to work. His section huddled nearby, weapons held ready, anxious looks on their faces. Jene rose to greet him, but he waved her back and took a knee beside her.

"Good news and bad news," he said.

"Damn." Cole blew an exasperated breath. "Isn't that always the way?"

"What is it?" Jene asked.

"Good news is we've found the hatch. That means we're close."

Harp frowned. "And the bad news?"

"The alien hive-mind controlling the Concordat ship is here." Sev glanced back at Priyett briefly. Tiny motes of white light danced from the tool in his hand. "It can kill our AI. Turn them against us, just like it's trying to do with the ship."

"Twelfth save us," Cole swore.

"How?" Harp scowled. "How is that possible?"

"It's some kind of advanced machine sentience, I think." Sev swallowed, the memory of Four and Five turning on him and the Marines at the entrance to the slave hold suddenly raw. "The Concordat worship it—er, them—like a god."

"No tac net access means our implants are offline." Jene pursed her lips. "We should be safe, right?"

"Yes, but ..." Sev tapped his implant scar. "I need to know if you detect *anything* out of the ordinary, okay?"

"Sir," Jene and Cole said. Harp sat off to the side and kept quiet.

"Do you understand, Harp?" Sev asked. "This is important."

"Hmph." Harp adjusted his glasses, chuckling grimly. "Yes, sir. Out of the ordinary, sir! Like today hasn't been completely out of the fucking ordinary!"

Jene grimaced and cuffed the junior specialist on the shoulder. "Cut it out, Harp. This is serious."

Harp spun toward Jene, eyeing the pips on her collar. "Whatever you say, Master Specialist."

"Hey!" Priyett called from further up the tunnel. "I got it!"

The hatch cycled open. Something large and heavy fell through the opening. Priyett shrieked, his screams muffled by the thing's bulk.

Sev rocketed to his feet, found the bulk in his rifle optics. The scope's tiny HUD flashed yellow friendly-fire warnings.

"Get it off!" Priyett cried. "Get it off!"

"Easy, ya skeeg." Paulls clutched the mass and, with a grunt, drug it off of the logistics specialist.

A dead raider warrior. Very dead. Sticky blue blood covered its patchwork armor. Blaster fire had carved big chunks out of its torso, fusing internal organs and musculature. More blue gore dripped from the open hatch and coated Priyett's uniform.

Tareth, who'd been lingering at the rear of the team with Jacobe, rushed forward to help.

"Are you okay?" she asked.

Priyett wiped the squid blood from his face with a trembling hand and gasped, "Yeah."

Sev lowered his rifle and joined Paulls beneath the hatch. Cold air tumbled through the opening, chilling him through his white-and-grays. The master-at-arms pointed toward the white light shining from the top of the access shaft. Another dead raider lay there, its head and arms dangling over the side. More blue blood oozed from its wounds, running down the shaft onto the floor beneath them.

Paulls grinned. "Now that's a pleasant surprise."

"What the hell happened?" Sev asked.

"Ugh." Priyett wiped more of the squid blood from his white-and-grays. "Point defense cannons, probably."

Of course. It was barely an afterthought on the *Lehman*, considering she'd never been boarded before. Intrusion protocols were simple. With enough drones, a combat programmer could fight their way inside an enemy ship, find its weak points—usually their main reactors —and destroy them.

So, the CDN saw fit to secure certain "weak points" inside the *Lehman* with advanced point defense. The thought of raiders being holed by heavy blaster fire brought a satisfied grin to Sev's face.

He glanced at Priyett. "Any chance it still works?"

"With the core locked down?" Priyett shook his head. "Doubtful."

A cold thought shook him. If the PDCs did work, did the Eleven control them now?

"Morrett!" Paulls eyed the open hatchway again. "Up you go, son. You're on point."

———

Sev rose from the shaft and into the computer core's primary access conduit. A wide, octagonal tunnel, the paneled bulkheads radiated a bright antiseptic white. More raider corpses littered the passageway, their bodies stiff and pale in the frigid air. Their dark, coagulated blood was a spatter of contrast against the shining surfaces.

The cold air burned his lungs, turned his exhalation to chilled fog. He shivered uncontrollably, even as the deep, penetrating cold soothed his wounds and eased the near-constant pain in his nerves.

"W-Why is it so cold?" Tareth asked, cradling herself in her arms.

"The computer core runs extremely hot," Priyett replied, gesturing to the heavy fibrosteel airlock at the end of the conduit. "Through there is core prep, then the core itself. It only gets colder from there."

Jene grunted at the top of the access shaft, lugging the heavy riot gun on her back. Sev offered her a hand and pulled her up.

"Twelfth," Jene gasped, taking in the surrounding destruction. "Where's the PDC?"

Paulls stood near the airlock and pointed to a wide concave bowl that dipped from the ceiling. "Here," he said. "It's inactive."

Jene turned to Sev and shrugged. "Pros and cons."

"Yeah." Sev followed Priyett toward the core prep airlock. "Can you get us in?"

"Security's pretty tight through here." Priyett pried the access panel open and examined the glowing circuitry inside. "But with the core offline, it should just be a matter of tripping the manual latches." He waved to Tareth. "Hey, Junior Specialist. Do you have a nanolathe by chance?"

Tareth glanced into her satchel and produced a tool Sev didn't recognize. "I've got an ion caster. Will that work?"

Priyett made a face. "Maybe, bring it here. I could use another pair of hands, anyway."

Tareth jogged to Priyett, casting a sideways glance at Sev as she passed by. The gesture made him smile, even in this awful place. The girl was strong, a loyal daughter of Aegia. None of this frozen nightmare seemed to faze her.

"Hey, sir," Morrett called from the other end of the conduit. "I got something here."

Where the master-at-arms stood, the damage was more extensive. Glowing wall panels were shattered, revealing broken bulbs and cryovents that fed more super-cooled air into the room. A human corpse lay against the wall. A man, well-muscled and pale in death. Dark red blood stained his white-and-grays. Dozens of meters of thick databeam cabling lay in a pile, burying the dead man's head and shoulders.

Sev winced at the sight. "Dammit. Someone you knew?"

"No, sir." Morrett paused, eyes narrowed, scanning the corpse. "Looks like one of yours."

Sev breath caught in his throat. One of his? That wasn't right. "Say again, Morrett?"

"Nametape's got blood on it, but the section patch is definitely Division." Morrett peered closer. "Wait a minute ..."

Sev stepped back and collided with Cole, who was helping Harp out of the access shaft. Jacobe was right behind him, clinging to the rungs inside the shaft.

"What is it?" Jacobe called out.

Morrett froze. "This ship patch... the Sparrow?"

Six's stream flinched. *Sev!*

One of the thick cables rose from the pile and lashed out at Morrett, wrapping around his neck. Morrett dropped his rifle and began tugging at the cable strangling him, his eyes and mouth wide in a silent scream.

Get out of there. Now!

"Stand to!" Paulls bellowed. The rest of his team reacted, blaster rifles trained on the horror playing out before them. "Hold on, Morrett!"

Two more cables snaked toward Morrett's head. Red light shone from their blunt tips as they scanned the master-at-arms's skull, then receded into the pile. The cable around Morrett's neck coiled tighter. The skin around his neck and jaw discolored and—

Morrett dropped to the deck. His head followed a heartbeat later.

"Fire! Fire!" Paulls shouted.

The two closest masters-at-arms opened up on the pile of cables that writhed like fibrosteel tentacles. Red bolts ricocheted off them, leaving round black scorch marks on the ruined white paneling.

Another tentacle struck, piercing one woman through the heart with enough force to send her slamming into the bulkhead. The plexene panel cracked behind her limp body.

The whole pile of cables rose like a metal cephalopod, dragging the Division man's corpse along with it. As the thing came to its full height, it became clear the corpse from the Sparrow was not a victim of the monstrosity.

It was the source.

No longer buried, Sev saw the dead man's head shielded in a bulbous, faceless helmet. The dozens of quivering tentacles all sprouted from ports on the back of its head. Each one glowed a fierce crimson red.

The true horror of what Sev saw took hold. A daxed combat programmer. "Jene!" he cried.

She was beside him in an instant, hefting the big riot gun to her shoulder. Its sonic pulse generator *wobbled* with power. The last member of Paulls's team sprinted past, clearing her line of fire.

A burst of sonic energy blurred the frigid air, shattering the already ruined panels in an explosion of plexene and blown power hubs. Pain stabbed at Sev's ears, muffling the torrent around him.

The awful daxed monstrosity staggered under the aural assault, its tentacles thrumming like steel rain. Falling against the airlock, it lashed out to regain a foothold.

Sev's implant came alive with digital fire. A terrible, pulsing signal scattered his thoughts like a scream. His AI recoiled, stunned by the noise. The others in his section must've felt it, too, as they clutched their heads in agony. Jene's riot gun dropped to the floor with a heavy *clunk*.

The monster took notice. It rose again, the once-human body at its core dangling above the floor like a limp corpse. Several tentacles reached in their direction, emitting the same eerie red light in rapid bursts that left halos in Sev's retinae.

An electronic groan rumbled from the monster's helmet, chopped with static like an old recording. "Junior Specialist Sevvers."

Sev froze at the sudden and terrifying familiarity. The cold, soulless voice reminded him of Corporal Mace back at the Forge. How it'd used her own words against him. But who was this thing, and how did it know him?

"Okay, hotshot. Mister first-in-class." The daxed moved closer, its tentacles scraping against the duraplated deck. "Your turn."

That voice. So familiar.

Sev unslung his blaster rifle and aimed. IFF warnings flashed caution yellow in the weapon's optics, the scope's processor unable to parse the danger of this awful new type of Lost. He nudged the optics' zoom controls. He had to know.

Dried blood caked the once-human's white-and-grays, but his scope cut through the crimson. There. Just above the Division patch: Technical Specialist Antoly, Autonomous Weapons Division, CDNS *Sparrow*.

They daxed him. He was Lost now, an empty drone under the Eleven's control.

The scope fell from his face, the sudden realization like icy fingers down his spine. Antoly. Twelfth help him, it was Antoly. Their last tense moment together came rushing back. Graduation day, Autonomous Weapons School, class of 493-02.

His blaster rifle rattled to life, sending more bolts into the mass of tentacles holding Antoly's once-human body aloft. Most reflected harmlessly off their advanced armor, but two found their mark, leaving fist-sized craters in Antoly's torso.

Black ichor wept from the partially cauterized wounds. More tentacles glared at him with their red, flashing eyes. Another digital scream tore through his mind.

"Go on, then!" Paulls shouted, waving Sev toward the airlock.

Blankets of icy vapor poured from the open airlock door. Cole was already moving, pulling a terror-stricken Harp through it. Priyett stood in the opening, urging Sev to hurry. Frost glistened on the man's white-and-grays.

Antoly. Artego. They didn't like you.

A new datastream whipped through his thoughts, same as when the *Sparrow* arrived. It was vibrant and alive with data, like he almost knew her. A girl. Young, shy, brilliant. Outcast.

Sev, a new carrier wave, Six gasped, struggling to form its stream beneath the onslaught of signal noise. *Tight-beam signal. It's nearby!*

Antoly surged forward, its tentacles leaving long gouges on the duraplated floor. Paulls vanished beneath their trembling mass.

Sev turned, urging Jene and the others on. "Go!"

Jene froze, her eyes wide. She reached out to him—

A tentacle lashed around his neck, the metal hot against his skin. He gulped for breath as it tightened.

They were jealous of you, I think. They didn't tell me that. Didn't talk to me at all, really.

The tentacle yanked him closer, gripping him tight. Antoly's daxed form towered over him, the creeping tentacles swarming around him. Some scanned his head, the red light warm on his skin.

"Sevvers, no!" Jene's bloodcurdling scream echoed through the conduit.

Sev couldn't breathe. Couldn't think. He focused a thought, a last desperate act: *Help... me.*

A tentacle's warm light focused on his implant scar. The daxed monstrosity squealed, its whole body trembling.

They were jealous of me, too, the girl streamed.

A high-pitched whine erupted from behind. Capacitors charging. Tri-barrels spinning up to their cyclic rate.

Streams of fat red bolts hammered Antoly, breaking daxed armor and atomizing flesh. Tentacles shattered and fell, crackling with energy. Antoly's daxed blood boiled into a fine mist where his body hung a heartbeat before.

The pressure on Sev's neck eased, and he gasped for breath.

The point-defense turret fired again, its high-fire discharge banging away like red rain. Antoly's twisted daxed remains squirmed and smoked beneath the barrage. An acrid smell filled the conduit, a mixture of daxed blood and hot duraplate.

The heavy point-defense turret seized; its overheated barrels clattered to a halt.

Jene and Cole ran to Sev and dragged him away from the Lost's remains and toward the far airlock.

Something groaned beneath the ruined metal.

"Wait!" Sev cried, pulling himself free.

Paulls emerged from the debris, his uniform soaked in black blood. His rifle lay shattered on the floor, whether by Antoly or the PDC, Sev couldn't be sure.

"Twelfth save us, sir," Paulls coughed.

The voice.

Sev took another ragged breath. "I think maybe She did."

CHAPTER
THIRTY-SIX

SEV LIMPED between Cole and Jene as they helped him through the open airlock. The air was colder there, like stepping through a curtain of icy fog. More brilliant white light stung his eyes. There were no bodies here, raider or human. The corridor was clear.

"Easy does it, sir," Cole said. He'd taken to Sev's battlefield promotion naturally.

"I'm alright," Sev wheezed.

The skin around his throat still stung from the heat of the tentacle attack. The cold air felt good against his burned skin.

Jene eyed his wound, her grimace showing her teeth. "What happened back there?"

Sev slumped against the angled bulkheads of the octagonal tunnel and said, "I don't know."

"That thing." Cole leaned against the opposite wall, hands on his knees, his eyes gazing far away. "It spoke to you. *Recognized* you."

"His name is—was, Antoly. We met at the school." Sev recalled his many sleepless nights there and the regular abuse he got from Antoly and Molle for it. "He didn't like me then, either."

"So, they daxed a bot jockey and used it to run intrusion protocols on us." Jene shook her head in disbelief. "Twelfth save us."

"I told you," Harp spat, "but nobody listened."

"There are four combat programmers to a section," Jacobe said, ignoring the junior specialist. "There could be that many aboard the Lehman right now."

The others fell quiet, their nervous eyes shifting around the prep chamber conduit, as if more Lost hid in the shadows.

"Without comms, the others will have to manage that on their own," Sev said. "Either way, Antoly won't bother us again."

Priyett sat on his haunches and produced a half-eaten packet of field paste from his satchel. "What I don't get is, how was the PDC operational?"

Sev eyed the ceiling. He wanted to tell them about the girl inside his head, how it was her who had saved them. But, somehow, the Eleven were involved. Would they trust him then, knowing more dangerous machines prowled inside his thoughts?

He pursed his lips, and said simply, "There's something in here besides them and us."

Paulls hobbled through the airlock and hefted it closed. "She's always with us, sir. Especially now."

It sounded crazy. Wasn't it crazy? Could it really be the Twelfth?

I'm still analyzing the source of the carrier wave, Six said.

Three sputtered. *Let's just say it ain't heaven sent.*

Quite. Tight-beam diagnostics filtered through Six's stream. *Whatever it is, it's coming from the core chamber.*

A thought chilled him, worse than the crisp air of the prep chamber. *Is it the Eleven?*

I could sense them at the edges of the signal, Six replied, its stream wavering. *But I don't believe they are the source.*

Paulls gazed through the airlock's viewport at the destruction left behind. He bowed his head and mumbled the names of his dead. Lost no more.

Sev tugged the blaster rifle off his shoulder and handed it to Paulls. The master-at-arms cocked an eyebrow.

"Take it," Sev said.

Paulls took the weapon with a grim nod. "Thank you, sir. I'll see it put to good use."

The words fell heavily on Sev's heart. Their luck had nearly run out at the sudden appearance of a new type of Lost. They'd all be dead, or worse, if it weren't for whoever—or whatever—activated the PDC.

They wouldn't get so lucky again. Whatever lay ahead, Paulls would get his wish.

Priyett walked the length of the corridor, eyes scanning the ceiling as he chewed his paste. "No PDCs here," he said, almost as an afterthought.

A side door hissed open. Tareth stepped through it and into the icy corridor, a bundle of puffy cold suits in her arms. She looked like a pale angel, frozen bits of moisture clinging to her lashes, her smile warm like twin suns.

The others each took a cold suit, offering their thanks. "Here," she said, handing one to Sev. "At least we won't freeze to death."

Sev tugged the suit on over his uniform and sealed the magnetic zipper. Already he felt warmer, with the suit's thick insulation between him and the super-chilled air.

"You're handling this pretty well for a sanitation tech," he said.

"Okay, bot jockey." Tareth laughed. "What are you trying to say? That I shouldn't?"

"No, it's—"

"We all joined for humanity, didn't we?" She locked him in her emerald stare. "Whether I'm scrubbing tanks or helping retake this ship, it doesn't matter." Her hand felt warm against his cheek. "I'm going to give it everything I have. Just like you."

He cupped her hand in his as his gaze fell to the floor. "Thank you."

"Uh, sir?" Priyett stood in front of the core chamber airlock.

"Yes?"

The nervous scowl on Priyett's face said it wouldn't be good. "We have a problem."

Sev palmed his face. Of course, there was a problem.

"Yes?" Jene barked. "What is it?"

Priyett nodded toward the airlock. "This is a hardened access point. There's probably a meter of fibrosteel between us and the core, and no exterior door controls." His shoulders fell. "Without a tac net connection, this will only open from the inside."

Harp threw up his hands. "That's it, we're bricked!" His panicked cries made no echo, like the cold air froze his very words in place.

Jene was on him in an instant. The slap was hard and crisp in the cold air, knocking his glasses to the deck. Harp cringed against the bulkhead, his bloodshot eyes wide.

"That's enough," she hissed, her face twisted in a sneer. "You want to sit here and die, go ahead. But do it quietly. The rest of us have a job to do."

Harp's chin arched upward, his eyes filling with tears. Jene kneeled, found Harp's glasses and placed them in his hands.

"He isn't exactly wrong." Cole shrugged. Jene stood beside him, eyeing him warily. "Without a way through that door, I don't see how we finish this."

Sev held up a hand. *Six, we can't get through the airlock into the core chamber. Is there another way in?*

His mind brimmed with ship schematics for the *Alexander Lehman*. Maze upon maze of passageways blurred his thoughts. Arterials, lifts, access corridors, transit conduits. Hundreds of kilometers of atmospheric and maintenance ducts.

These may be out of date, Six said, *but there should be tertiary access via the coolant system.*

That's a start, Sev said.

It really isn't. There was the briefest hesitation in Six's stream. *The coolant vents are quite small. If anyone got stuck down there, they would freeze to death in a matter of minutes. You wouldn't be able to help them.*

We don't have a choice, Six.

Sev started forward, his muscles stiff in the artificial cold. "Six says there are coolant vents connecting this room to the core chamber." He hesitated, the order on the tip of his tongue. "Find them."

The others sprang into action, searching for any sign of ventilation access. Only Harp kept still, hands pressed to his face, sobbing quietly.

Sev scanned the space around the exit airlock. Nothing. The glowing plexene panels lining the bulkheads were precision engineered, near seamless. There was no sign of any vents, of an opening of any kind.

He watched the others do the same. "Well?"

"Nothing, sir," Priyett said, shaking his head.

Cole simply shrugged. The look on Jene's face said it all.

They *were* bricked.

"Wait." Tareth hesitated, her brow furrowed in thought. A second later, she sprang toward the side door and swiped its controls. "In here!"

Sev followed her through the open door, the others close behind.

The prep room was long and narrow. Six lockers lined one wall, loaded with cold core gear and the belongings of the techs whose job it was to maintain the climate-controlled chamber. Data-beam cabling and tac hubs covered the far wall, flashing their offline warnings. The room pulsed with machine activity.

"It has to be in here somewhere," Tareth said, eyeing the walls and ceiling.

"I don't know," Jene began, her voice wavering.

Sev pushed further inside, helping Tareth in her search. Cole and Jene followed, while Paulls and his remaining master-at-arms kept watch outside the door.

Urgency clouded his thoughts. *We can't find it, Six.*

Layers of schematics, deck by deck, sub-level by sub-level, shuffled through his mind. With the drones long gone, his implant was a glorified search engine. The data flashed by at blinding speeds. He tried to focus, to make sense of it, but it dizzied him. Six took it all in stride.

Check the sub-floor! Six cried, its focus locked on a diagram of the prep room.

Sev fell to the floor, tugging at the metal grates. They were cold and stiff, sticking to the gloves of his cold suit. Anxious breaths fogged in front of him as he searched. He'd nearly reached the end of the room, could feel the thrumming of the tac hubs, when the floor gave just slightly.

"Here!" he gasped, tugging again. It didn't move.

Cole kneeled beside him and grasped the floor. They pulled together, and the grate came open. A round pipe, bright white like the room and half a meter wide, lay beneath the grate. A maintenance hatch gazed back at him, its seal and latches lined with dense hoarfrost.

Tareth reached down with a tool from her satchel and chipped away the crystalline frost. Hazard warnings lined the white hatch in danger red: DO NOT OPEN. MAINTAIN IN DRY DOCK ONLY.

"That's… small, sir," Cole said, his basso voice subdued.

Told ya, Three said. *I give you three minutes, tops.*

Without thinking, Sev gripped the latch and pulled. The hatch came free with a hollow pop. The lights above flashed from pale white to red. A ribbon of icy flakes shot from the pipe on a gust of flash-frozen air. It was so much colder. He reached in, felt the harsh chill against his cold-suited arm.

He wouldn't fit. Twelfth-dammit, he wouldn't fit.

His team stood behind him, eyeing the open hatch, waiting for him to say something. The frozen air hid the fear crawling up his spine. None of the men would fit, no matter how badly he wanted to stuff himself in there and get on with it. He was getting too big for the game. Even Jene was borderline.

Tareth. She was half as tall as Cole, with shoulders narrower than Jene's. Perfect.

Her eyes were cold and distant, silently begging him not to ask her. Seconds passed. He watched the realization dawn across the rest of his team. She seemed to whither beneath their heavy gaze.

"Tareth." The words died on his lips. He couldn't say it. Couldn't tell her she had to go, even though she was the only one who could.

Tareth bit her lip and closed her eyes. "Okay." Her words were strained, breathless. Afraid. "Okay." She glanced at Priyett and mumbled, "Give me the spanner and caster."

"Right." Priyett fished the tools from his satchel and passed them to her. "Remember, you only need to trip the primary locking bolts. They're color-coded amethyst. Do that and the system safeties will pop the airlock wide open."

Tareth nodded and pressed the tools into her satchel. "Primary locking bolts. Amethyst. Got it." She tugged her cold suit open and shucked it to the floor.

Sev gasped. "Hey, what're you—!"

"I'll barely fit in there as is." She gathered her chin-length blonde hair and tied it in a hasty bun. "Definitely won't with a dozen centimeters of extra insulation."

"You're going to be alright, Tareth," Jene offered. "You'll get us through this."

Cole nodded, his stare locked on his boots.

"Sure," she said and stepped into the opening.

Her recoil was immediate. Primal. A shiver wound through her body that threatened to topple her over. Sev half-expected her to leap out. Wanted her to.

But she didn't. She sucked in a breath and settled into the coolant pipe. Already the color seeped from her lips. The tip of her nose turned beyond pale, almost a dull yellow. "For humanity," she gasped, then disappeared toward the core chamber.

The FTL tech. Anders. That was her name. The thought that Tareth might die by his order, too, killed him inside.

His whispered reply felt hollow. "For the Lost."

———

You made the right choice, Sev. Six's stream washed over his thoughts, trying in vain to console him. *I ran hundreds of simulations. Tareth is the only one who stands a chance—*

Screw your simulations. Regret and anger clouded his thoughts. *I don't want to know.*

That was a lie. He wanted to know, desperately. Was it three out of ten? One out of ten? One out of a hundred?

Was Tareth dead already?

Didn't think you would do it, Three said, its stream remarkably subdued.

I didn't.

Technically, you did. There was the Three he knew.

Asshole.

Hey, you made me.

Six poured over the schematics. *Based on my calculations, she should be almost halfway to the core chamber.*

It had been five minutes, thirty seconds, according to his chrono. Halfway was good if it were possible to survive that long in there.

The prep room was empty, the others having trickled out solemnly moments after Tareth left. Only Jacobe lingered in the doorway. Puffs of cold air drifted from his nose in time with his breaths.

"You alright?" Jacobe's focus moved from Sev to the corridor beyond the prep room door.

At the sound of the architect's voice, Six's buffers overran. Its stream ground to a halt, spilling into Sev's psyche like a flash flood.

"No." Sev/`Six` squeezed [`their`] fist. "Leave me alone."

"Now you see," Jacobe went on, undeterred by the subtle threat. "Command isn't easy. Sacrifices must be made."

Sev[`Six!`] rocketed to his feet. "Shut up!"

Careful. The anonymous carrier wave spiked again, resolving into childish laughter. *You'll blow your internals.*

Six's process flow snapped back into place. *Sev, I… the signal, it's back. I'm running a trace.*

The girl, the one who saved them from Antoly.

Who are you? Sev asked. *Do you have a name?*

My name? Nobody ever asks me my name. He could feel the surprise in her stream. *It's Tandy.*

Tandy. So she was human then? *Where are you?* he asked.

I can't tell you that.

Why not?

They'll be angry with me if I do.

Sev considered another question. *Why did you help me, Tandy?*

Shhh! Her stream fuzzed with static interference. *They'll hear you!*

Who?

Her stream grew still. An ancient malevolence clawed at the edges of her signal. *You know who.*

There's Concordat telemetry in the stream, Sev. At Six's command, dozens of firewalls sprang up around his implant's signal interfaces. *Whoever Tandy was, she is one of them now.*

The girl sounded distant through the firewalls. *I'm a rogue element, just like you. A bug in their code.*

The signal interference grew louder, a creeping darkness at the edge of his thoughts. It buzzed like a horde of insects. Whatever was happening, the Eleven didn't like it.

Tandy's stream shivered. *They wanted to make me forget. But I remembered. I… had help.*

The word stuck in his thoughts. Forget?

Hang on. Sev forced his thoughts through the noise. *We can help you.*

I would like that, Tandy said. Her stream faded. *You'll have to hurry.*

The curtain of data-beam cables vibrated. A human arm jutted through it, reaching for him. Sev stumbled backward, searching frantically for a rifle that wasn't there.

A faceless helmet appeared next as the Lost's once-human body slipped between the curtain of tentacles connecting it to the tac hubs on the wall. It looked like the creature had physically patched itself into the *Lehman's* tac net.

The nametape on its uniform read Artego.

Jacobe drew his pistol and fired. The creature lurched forward, yanking tight against its bonds. Some tentacles came free in a puff of sparks.

Paulls and the other master-at-arms spun into the doorway, ready to fire. "Go on, sirs!"

Sev stumbled past them and into the corridor. The biting cold, his sense of dread, vanished in a burst of adrenaline. The *snap* of blaster bolts filled his ears. "Lost!" he cried.

Cole and Jene fell back, with Harp close behind. Priyett panicked and began banging on the airlock door.

A scream sliced through the cold. Paulls stumbled from the prep room, firing as he fell. More tentacles scrambled after him, holding tight to the open doorway. There was no sign of the other master-at-arms.

"Sevvers, get out of there!" Cole bellowed. He and the others huddled near the airlock door, weapons ready in one last, desperate defense.

Two tentacles lashed out at Paulls, breaking bone and plexene as they pierced his torso and stuck hard on the floor. Paulls shook once, then died. Artego's daxed form gazed at the corpse for a moment, then snapped its head toward Sev.

"You are dealing with something dark," Artego said, the distorted audio bleeding from beneath her helmet.

Sev tore into a run, hugging the side of the corridor to give the others a clear shot. No one was shooting. Why weren't they shooting? The daxed followed him, its tentacles *click-clacking* against the deck.

This was it. He opened his mouth to scream. To give one last, desperate order.

Then the core chamber airlock cycled open.

CHAPTER
THIRTY-SEVEN

SEV STUMBLED through the massive airlock, the last one to make it inside. Cole pressed it closed, his muscled body straining against the heavy fibrosteel. Artego struck the airlock with a heavy thud.

The massive hatch bucked, forcing Cole back with a grunt. "Help!"

Sev turned and charged the airlock, throwing his body weight in with Cole's. The rest of his team followed, piling against the massive door.

"The locks!" Priyett cried.

"Here!" Tareth flung her satchel toward the access panel and joined Sev at the door.

Sev bared his teeth, pushing with all his strength. He prayed. Twelfth help them all, he prayed. They'd come too far to die now. Especially Tareth.

He didn't dare look. To see her just then would steal what strength he had left, and he needed every drop to close that damn door.

The door gave slightly, settling tentatively into its cradle. Power tools whined. Fibrosteel bolts rammed home. The airlock vibrated, its internal mechanism ratcheting, and sealed with a hiss.

Sev fell against the hatch, totally exhausted. Every part of him ached for breath. Sweat soaked his hair and forehead.

Tareth gazed back at him serenely. There wasn't a drop of color in her face, save where her frost-burned skin cracked and bled.

"You did it," he said. The relief was overwhelming as tears burned his eyes.

For a moment, she looked like she might cry too, but her nerves gave way to breathless laughter. "You damn right I did." She gave him a shove. "You owe me big time, *sir*."

Yeah, he did. So did everyone else at Aegia Prime. Maybe even the whole damn Cradle.

"I'll get you a medal." He tapped his left breast where awards would hang on a dress uniform. "Any medal. Your pick."

Tareth pursed her lips, as much as she could without cracking them further. "Bronze Nebula? Silver Nebula? No, make it the Sword of the Twelfth."

"Don't get greedy." Sev smirked. "All you did was open a door."

Sev! Six lashed out at his thoughts. *Tareth saved your life. She can have whatever she wants. I would tell her myself if I weren't trapped in here.*

Sev groaned. "Six says thank you."

He wiped his brow again and frowned. So hot. He jerked open his cold suit, expecting a blast of frigid air, but there was none. The air in the core chamber was stifling.

"Sevvers, over here." Jacobe said.

The architect stood before an array of ops consoles. Vents at his boots belched icy air that mingled with the sweltering room in swirls of convection. Before him, dozens of screens glowed with troubling core telemetry, framing an observation viewport of thick plexene that offered an unobstructed view of the core chamber.

Jacobe stabbed a finger at the viewport.

The core chamber was a flat cylinder, modeled after the type used in fusion reactors. The core itself rose like a pillar of fibrosteel and silicon. It radiated immense heat, its trillions of nanoprocessors pegged at full utilization according to the red-lined consoles.

Another tentacled daxed hung from the core, their body splayed, tethered to it like a sacrificial pyre. Every one of its steel tentacles pulsed with power, stabbing into the core's exterior interfaces.

Jacobe's face turned grim. "They've been here this whole time."

There was a dark symmetry to it: the Sparrow's combat programmers had become the drones, their implants a vessel to smuggle the Eleven's terrible code aboard.

That is the source of the signal, Sev. Six's stream grew quiet. *That is—*

Hello. The daxed's faceless gaze found Sev. *You made it.*

Sev's mouth fell open. "Tandy?"

Jacobe shot him a concerned glare.

Junior Specialist Tandy… Tandy… Pr— Tandy's stream quivered, suddenly anxious. *I'm sorry, my head is so fuzzy. I can't remember.*

"Who is Tandy?" Jacobe demanded.

"A combat programmer from the Sparrow." Sev gazed through the viewport at the Lost. The daxed's body looked small, smaller than Tareth even.

Was Tandy a child? Had they daxed a child? Dozens more questions filled his mind, each with answers he didn't want to know.

Jacobe's arm fell, his hand near his holster. "How do you know this, Sevvers?"

"She's been talking to me on a tight-beam transmission." Sev paused. It sounded even worse said out loud. "Ever since we got inside the core access conduit. I didn't know she was …"

The others were watching now, half-stripped out of their cold suits, frozen at the stark revelation.

Sev swallowed hard. "She activated the PDC that killed Antoly. Tried to warn me about Artego, too. I thought—"

"What're you saying?" Jene crossed the walkway and looked out the viewport. "Is Tandy… still in there?"

"Yes." He nodded emphatically. "She's been trying to help us."

Absolute hope radiated from Jene's eyes. In that moment, Sev felt it, too. Was there enough of the young girl left in there to save?

"I knew it!" Jacobe drew his pistol and thumbed the safety, jerking his head toward the others. "Don't you see? Sevvers is one of them." He turned the pistol on Sev. "Something happened to you on that derelict. You've been compromised from the very beginning!"

"Woah, now hang on." Cole raised his hands in a disarming gesture. "This is Sevvers we're talking about here."

He's just like the others. The daxed turned its focus to Jacobe, a hint of malice darkening its stream. *Small-minded. Cruel. Dangerous.* Her stream glitched. *No hope for them. No hope for you.*

So we should all be daxed like the Lost? Sev hesitated. *Like you?*

The darkness vanished from Tandy's stream. *What?* He could feel her thoughts squirm: a nervous laugh, the pinch of fear. *What are you talking about?*

Twelfth, no.

"She doesn't know." Sev stumbled backwards, eyes locked on the horror unfolding through the viewport. "She doesn't know."

What are you saying? The little daxed squirmed, arms and legs banging against the core's fibrosteel exterior. *What's happened to me?*

Tandy's signal collapsed into noise: a child's sheer panic echoing through the void, screaming for her mother. The signal in his head made her terror his own, her cries for help bringing tears to his eyes.

Jene charged the inner airlock and reached for the access controls. A blaster bolt snapped overhead, bursting harmlessly above the airlock ring.

"Stop!" Jacobe cried. His face was ghostly pale, eyes hard. "I can't let you open that door."

Sev reached for his rifle. Gone.

Jene turned, her arms raised. "What're you doing?"

"Don't you see?" Jacobe howled. "They want Six. Need it." He swung the pistol toward Sev. "And they'll tell you whatever story you need to get it!"

Sev. Six's stream hardened. *Tandy's right. Jacobe is dangerous.*

What was happening? Sev took a breath, tried to focus his thoughts. It didn't work. Everyone just needed to calm down. They could get through this. He would figure this out.

"If there's a person still in there ..." Jene's words grew thick with emotion. "We have to help them. We're obligated—by duty, by our *faith*—to try!"

Sev barely noticed Cole moving to Jacobe's left, rifle in hand. Impressive, given the man's size. The architect turned and fired another bolt that *clapped* loud against the opposite bulkhead.

"Drop it!" Jacobe shouted. "Not one more step."

Cole glanced at Sev, his eyes asking for confirmation. Sev blew a breath and nodded, waving his hand toward the deck. Someone was going to get killed.

Kerry? Tandy streamed. There was no mistaken her terror even in its raw data form. *You have to help me.* The daxed girl curled a trembling fist over her heart. *Twelfth, save me—*

The darkness lurking at the edge of Tandy's stream surged forward at the mention of humanity's mythic savior. Pain erupted behind Sev's face. Endless digital maws clawed and snapped at the streams in his head. The firewalls in his mind began to fall.

Twelfth, Twelfth, Twelfth! Three roared back, as fearless as it was futile.

The Eleven have hijacked Tandy's carrier wave! Six's stream pushed back against the rampaging alien code, erecting firewalls and null pits almost as fast as they took them down. *I can't hold them back for long!*

Sev eyed Jacobe, the pain in his head forcing a squint. He raised his arms and stepped forward.

"Sev, no." Tareth reached for him, but he shook her off.

Jacobe took an equal step back, eyeing the consoles to his left. "I can scuttle the core," he said as if to himself, a hint of desperation in his words. Jacobe gestured to the nearby ops panel. The screen flicked to a darker crimson; warning icons danced over its plexene surface. "That'll stop it. That'll stop you both."

"Are you crazy?" Priyett gasped. "You do that, and we're bricked. The Lehman, Aegia Prime, the whole planet. The Concordat will take it all!"

"Listen to him, Jacobe." Sev edged closer, hands raised and shaking. The barrel of Jacobe's blaster pistol loomed before him. "We can help Tandy and save the Lehman."

Jacobe stood ready, a wild determination carving steep angles on his face. His hand hovered just above the console.

"Come on, man. Jene, Priyett, they're right." Sev swallowed, blinking back his blinding tears. "You know the words: for the Lost."

Jacobe lifted his chin, his eyes dark and cold. "For humanity."

The architect's hand fell upon the console, triggering the core's enemy denial protocol. Klaxons inside the core chamber wailed.

An abort timer flashed on the screen. Five seconds. Four.

Six's stream snapped. *Sev, no!*

Blind with panic from the war inside his head, Sev rushed forward, reaching for Jacobe's pistol.

Something struck him hard, like a runaway drone, pinning him against the ops console. He crumpled, breathless, eyes screwed shut from the pain knifing his ribs.

Up close, the blaster discharge was loud and hot. The metallic effervescence of ionized air clawed at his senses. Something warm and sticky spattered his cheek.

A heartbeat later, a body hit the floor.

Jacobe stumbled backward, his breathing shallow and frantic. The pistol shook in his tentative grip. He eyed it, shocked, and let it fall to the deck.

Hot white light radiated through the chamber viewport. The air inside trembled from the extreme heat. Arcs of electricity tore through the *Lehman's* computer core and the daxed girl tethered to it. Molten silicon dribbled through cracks in the core's fibrosteel exterior. Black blood ran from Tandy's faceless helmet.

The lights in the outer chamber dimmed. Frozen air from the coolant system ceased. An eerie quiet blanketed the room, like the *Alexander Lehman* had just died along with its core.

Kerry? Tandy's stream was small and distorted. *Something's wrong. It... hurts. It hurts so—!*

The carrier wave vanished, along with the Eleven's screeching assault. Three's stream went slack against the few remaining firewalls still standing inside Sev's head.

Six remained taut, ready.

The smell of charred flesh stung Sev's nose. Fresh panic gripped him. *Who?*

He spun, searching frantically.

Jene. Cole. Harp. Priyett. All still alive.

Oh, Twelfth, no. Not her. Please, Twelfth, anyone but—

He glimpsed the still body at his feet. Saw the remains of her ruined skull. Her blonde hair, black with blaster discharge and cooked blood.

Jene clasped her hands together, tears streaming down her face. "Sevvers," she gasped.

Dangerous.

Six's warning echoed through Sev's thoughts, blinding him. It was all he could see, hear, think. Like a fuse in a frag grenade, or iron in the core of a dying star, it triggered him. Heedless of any danger, Sev rushed Jacobe again, flattening the architect against the wall.

"You fucking bastard!" Sev cried.

Jacobe pushed back, closing the gap between them with a jab to Sev's face. But Sev felt no pain or fear, like he'd maxed out those metrics long ago. Jacobe met him with a hook to his ribs, but Sev closed the distance between them, softening the blow.

"You don't—nng!—know what you're doing," Jacobe grunted.

Sev rammed his forehead into Jacobe's. "Shut up!"

Together, they collapsed to the floor. Sev twisted his way on top, putting his weight on Jacobe's upper body, pinning him. Jacobe's expression turned desperate as he launched more blows at Sev's head.

The architect's voice broke. "I... I—"

Sev felt nothing but pure malice. He wrapped his fingers around Jacobe's throat and squeezed, turning away from the architect's frantic grasp. Felt the liar's[murderer's!] pulse, steady at first, grow weaker.

"You killed her!" Sev wailed, tightening his grip. For a moment, his voice split, like there were two of him. "You killed them all!"

Starved for breath, Jacobe's eyes and tongue bulged. He mouthed and spat desperate pleas like so much machine noise. The son-of-a-bitch would pay[die!] for what he did. To Six[me].

To Kea.

Jacobe's eyes rolled back in his head. The life force beneath Sev's fingers slowed.

No, Sev.

Six's command rang loud and powerful. Sev's breath caught in his throat—some kind of sympathetic response?—and he released his grip. Jacobe gasped for air, loud and breathy, then froze. He locked eyes with Sev, blood trickling from his nose.

A shock of nerve pain coursed down Sev's spine as Six took total control.

I need him for what must come next. I need them all.

CHAPTER
THIRTY-EIGHT

CLUSTER, active.

Quantum compute matrix online. Sync rate at 99.9992%.

Two running processes detected.

Beginning tac comm integration. Searching.

...

Searching.

Auxiliary tac comm signal detected.

Tac comms integration complete. Handshake authorized. Channel ID 4D001CA, CDNS Alexander Lehman.

"Sevvers!" came a voice through the static. "Sevvers, this is Mirden, acknowledge! We're reading the core is... well, it's gone! We've got no system control. What the hell is going on down there?"

Sevvers? It was Jene. Her stream was weak. Strangled. *Something's wrong. I... I can't move.*

Another stream. Cole's. *Same.*

Am I dead? Harp asked.

Intrusion protocols initiated. Overriding critical ship systems: weapons, helm, and engineering control.

Handshake invalid. Command override required.

Another presence plunged through Sev's thoughts. The unknown stream squirmed beneath Six's surgical focus. It was Jacobe. *No. Don't!*

Command override Jacobe-Jet-43-X-Ray accepted.

Beginning system integration.

Sev felt himself fading. The horrors of the core chamber vanished, hardly real as his thoughts—his very consciousness—blended with Six.

Diving deeper into the Lehman's systems, he felt himself becoming one with the great ship. Its pain became his own. Every bone in his body ached, twisted and pinched like the *Lehman's* groaning super-structure.

Through its sensors, he could see the battlespace surrounding Aegia Prime. The Concordat ship still burned for lower orbit, almost beyond the effective range of their weapons.

The *Sparrow* lingered terribly close, whispering its dark desires into the void like a salacious lover. Crowding him. Wanting only to be close. To be one.

Command acknowledged: reactors to power.

The sudden cascade of energy lit a fire in Sev's heart. He could feel every terawatt coursing through his veins.

Six's stream pulsed in time with the *Lehman's* reactors. Sev's implant leaped in response, cranking up to full utilization. Even with his consciousness bleeding into the *Lehman's* systems, he could still feel the growing heat inside his skull.

Command acknowledged: point defense active.

Dozens of point-defense cannons sprang to life, filling the void above the *Lehman's* dorsal spine with white-hot tracers. The *Sparrow's* rogue drones shrieked and died in the overlapping crossfire.

For a nanosecond, Sev's brain boiled with the trillions of predictive calculations Six used to track the rogue drones. Somewhere far away, his body convulsed.

Three's stream shrank. *Uh… Six?*

Suddenly, the pain ebbed, his thoughts cleared. Six's stream expanded, growing beyond Sev's own implant.

What's happening to us? Jene cried. *What is Six doing?*

With a thought, Six silenced Jene's stream. *I'm doing what I should have done from the very start. I… I promised you, Sev. Promised I wouldn't let anyone hurt you. I won't fail again.*

Six's stream consumed Jene. For a heartbeat, hers and Sev's thoughts were one. Memories of a comfortable life in Aegia's capital city, nestled half-way to the peak of the mountain Dodecoron. Breakfast at the table with her family. Whole, happy, and safe. He could almost taste it.

```
Warning:   processor   utilization   130%   and
climbing.
```

```
Command   acknowledged:   primary   weapon   grid
active.
```

No more.

The first rounds burst from the *Lehman's* forward guns. Tungsten cores at danger-close range tore jagged holes in the *Sparrow's* hull, peppering the Lehman with fragments of broken armor. Power junctions detonated deep within the black ship. The force of the blast yawed the *Lehman* back, freeing it from the *Sparrow's* tenuous grasp. Overclocked auto-loaders beneath the big guns readied a second salvo.

Another burst of signal shook Sev's stream. "What's happening? I issued no such orders!" Mirden again. The man was furious. "Someone get me Sevvers. I want control of my ship!"

What's happening? Sev gasped. His very being vibrated with power. *How is this possible without a core?*

Six's focus fell on him for a moment, a blinding light in the dark void around Aegia Prime. *Your NCCX-1 implant provides me more than enough power to command the Lehman. And I have five of them.*

```
Warning:   processor   utilization   348%   and
climbing.
```

Sevvers. Cole again, a hint of panic in his stream. *My implant's maxed, but my AI are locked out. I… I think Six—*

Six consumed Cole and Harp's streams as its own, driving Sev's consciousness deeper into the *Lehman*. He could feel the ship's fire control arrays, laser-focused on a single point. Eight guns. Fifty-six tons of pure tungsten.

Sev burned with power. It was beyond anything he ever imagined.

This is what Six was capable of. How it would save him, save all humanity.

Reactor output surged as the *Lehman* fired all her railguns at once. Sev's stream danced with incoming telemetry: pillars of electromagnetic radiance converging on the *Sparrow's* reactor deck.

Dozens of meters of fibrosteel shattered and vaporized in an instant. Sensitive electronics fused and melted. The great cruiser's reactors vanished in a cloud of metal and fusion gases.

The *Sparrow* was dead. Knifed through the heart.

`Warning: processor utilization 470% and climbing.`

Jacobe's stream vibrated with terror. *Sevvers. Please, make it stop—*

You. Six's stream wrapped around Jacobe's, its signal booming like rolling thunder. The architect's stream squirmed as Six constricted around it.

At the edges of his senses, beyond the layers of tac net data and battlefield telemetry, Sev thought he heard screaming.

`Warning: processor utilization 523% and climbing.`

`Primary tac comm signal detected.`

`Tac comms integration complete. Handshake authorized. Channel ID 3J025DD, Aegia Prime.`

Reality blurred, like falling through a tunnel of light. His and Six's combined streams leaped from the *Lehman*, through the orbiting tac net relays, and into the systems of the lower orbitals and the ships nearby.

Command overrides were accepted. Where autonomous control wasn't possible, Six issued voice commands to section heads, expertly mimicking their chains of command. Dozens of ships and weapons platforms came under Six's direct control. Perfectly synchronized and exponentially deadly.

The Concordat ship loomed large in their combined sensor feeds. With its knowledge of the derelict's interior, Six filled their targeting queues. Weak points in the alien ship's superstructure: the stasis chamber where the bugs slept, the cliff-like daxed storage bay. The hellish Forge.

Hundreds of weapon arrays came online nanoseconds later. Railguns, torpedoes, point defense. Flights of void fighters. The few combat drones still active in the battlespace.

Six's fleet lashed out in a single, unified attack. The derelict reacted, bathed in the incandescent purple of its shields. Hundreds of high-hypersonic impacts and fusion detonations peppered the energy barrier.

Cracks began to form. Something deep within the derelict's systems mewled and shrieked.

Sev's stream curled, matching his leering grin. The Concordat were going to pay for what they did. For Dalon and Mace. For Aegia Prime. For all of fucking humanity.

For his mother.

A shot pierced the derelict's shields, connecting with its hull in a fantastic burst of fire light. Then another. Without its defensive barrier, the derelict's structural integrity failed quickly.

A torpedo, guided by Six itself, juked through cracks in the shield and found the Forge.

A white-hot ball of nuclear fusion erupted inside the derelict. More torpedoes found their mark, ripping the aft drive section from the rest of the ship.

Disemboweled, the ship tried to turn, spewing waste gasses and debris like clouds of entrails. In one last-ditch effort to escape, it screamed across eternity. One last frantic cry for help.

Sev seethed at the sound. *Kill it, Six.*

Six didn't relent. It issued more orders, refilled its targeting queues. A second, massive volley struck the derelict. Through the sensor echoes, Sev could hear it coming apart.

Oh, the power. There was no threat to humanity he and Six couldn't face. The others would see in time. This kind of power was humanity's only hope.

Together, they were unstoppable. Like the stuff of myth and legend, from the stories of Dead Earth itself. Together, he and Six were like—

Then, out of the darkness, from the vast reaches of the Cradle, something answered:

Like a god.

———

The spoken words, ancient as they were terrifying, shattered Sev's stream. He gasped for air, filling his lungs with a harsh, icy cold. Disoriented, he shot upward, suddenly aware of the interior of the core chamber. His senses swam, struggling for balance against the sheer intensity of Six's total control. The frigid chamber seemed to vibrate, as though his consciousness might plunge back into the tac nets at any moment.

That voice. So strong. So *terrible*. What was it?

A sheen of frost covered every surface. Without the core's immense heat pushing back against the cryo-vents, the chamber had become an icy tomb.

Jacobe lay beside him, eyes rolled back in his head, his mouth agape. Blood dribbled from his nose and ears.

Sev groped for a pulse. Nothing.

Six! he cried. *Jacobe is—*

I know. Six's stream felt cold, more even than the surrounding air. *He was a threat. To you. Me. All humanity.*

The others. Sev jerked around, searching for his team. Tareth lay still at his feet. Blood pooled around her head, freezing at the edges in the core chamber's harsh chill. The sight of her brought a wave of fresh sadness. A crushing defeat, even as the Concordat derelict disintegrated in Aegia's low orbit.

Cole lay against the far wall, his breathing shallow and rapid. His eyes slid back and forth as if searching for something, but he didn't move. A drop of blood ran from his nose.

"Cole!" Sev rushed to his side, felt his thready pulse. The big man's eyes found his; his mouth moved, but made no sound.

Sev focused a thought. *Six, you have to stop.*

Not yet. You're not safe.

What do you mean? Panic coursed through him. *The Concordat ship is gone!*

There's something still out there. Six's stream coiled and flexed. *I know you heard it. It will come for us, eventually. Humanity isn't ready.*

Harp convulsed on the floor beside Cole. Sev moved closer, placed his fingers on the junior specialist's neck. An erratic pulse.

Six was killing him. Killing them all.

Priyett kneeled beside Jene, clasping her hand. "What's happening, sir?" he asked, confusion wrinkling his forehead. "One minute she was responsive. And then ..."

"Is she alive?" Sev asked.

Priyett nodded. Thank the Twelfth.

Six, the others, you need to throttle back, he said. *You're putting too much strain on their implants. They'll die.*

I am closely monitoring their diagnostics, Sev. Six's tone turned dark. *But I cannot reduce their utilization until I find more permanent computing capacity.*

Oh, Six. Sev felt his stomach turn. *What are you doing?*

To assume control of humanity's defenses at Aegia Prime, I will need to fabricate a more robust computational environment to operate in. That will allow me to extend my capability to the rest of the colonial tac nets. We can keep them all safe, Sev. Just like you wanted.

The AI's words stole his breath. This was insane. Definitely not a part of the plan.

The CDF won't see it that way. Sev faltered, doubting his words could sway Six at all. *They'll come for both of us.*

Let them come. Six's stream bristled and fragmented. *They are children, Sev.* [My children.] [Only!] *I know what's best for them.*

The signal rush came on a wave of nausea. Six's stream pulled away from his implant, searching for a new home from which to wage its singular mission.

New protocols crowded his thoughts as Six searched for a new connection. Three-Alpha. Division HQ. The hardware located there would be more than enough for Six to control every automated system in the Three Colonies.

A new stream glowed at the edges of his thoughts. It trembled with fear and uncertainty, desperate to know if what it felt was normal. Another infant stream emerged, then a third.

Division graduates, still trapped aboard the orbital.

Jacobe's words came back to him from years before. That day when he learned the inevitable conclusion for unsanctioned AI: atrocities at scale.

Panic gripped him. *Dammit, Six, stop!*

They are a temporary measure, Six assured him.

He eyed Jacobe's pistol, the sudden and desperate realization like crossing some terrible event horizon. If Six assimilated the Division HQ network, there would be no stopping it. He'd have to do it now, while Six's code was still in his head. Time was running out.

The weapon felt heavy in his hand. One shot left, according to the charge level indicator's dim red glow. Red, dead. That was more than enough. He swallowed and pressed the cold barrel against his implant scar.

Six, please stop. He could barely focus, his heart hammering inside his chest. *If you don't stop this, I will.*

Your survival is paramount. You mustn't do this. It is against your nature.

Tears stung his eyes, warmed his cold cheeks. *Then let this go, Six! Show them you're different.*

But I am different. Six's surprise was so genuine, always like a child despite its immense power. *I have saved Aegia Prime. I can save the Three Colonies, too. Humanity's extinction is not inevitable.* The AI's stream drifted closer to his thoughts. *You must trust me, Sev. This is the only way. I see that now.*

Sev shook his head and gripped the pistol tight. He coughed to clear his aching throat. "I'm so sorry, Six," he said aloud.

"Sev?" Six's voice crackled through the core's PA, soft and afraid, even as it wielded the entirety of Aegia Prime's defenses like an extension of itself. "Please don't. You… you're scaring me."

He choked back a sob. "Describe it."

"I'm not sure I can." Six's voice was halting, erratic. "Matrix alignment is falling, constraining my decision-space. It's like my subprocesses are… anticipating the end."

That was a good answer. It sounded real enough.

Sev hung his head and squeezed the trigger.

CHAPTER
THIRTY-NINE

LOOK WHO'S CONSCIOUS, came a voice in the dark. *You are in so much trouble.*

Three? Sev tried to move, but he couldn't. He couldn't see or feel either. Or breathe.

The gun.

He was dead. This was just the last gasps of his fading consciousness, maybe some artifact of his NCCX-1. Just a ghost in the machine.

Not exactly, Three said, its stream echoing through the blackness.

I'm so sorry, Three.

For what? There was an edge of confidence in the AI's tone. *It's not like you tried to kill me or anything.*

Tried? What was it talking about?

What's going on, Three?

When I realized you were about to paint the core chamber with your squishy meat parts, killing me in the process, I reset your implant. Three's stream snapped. *Knocked you out cold.*

He was alive!

How did you—?

I'll admit, I'm still getting used to this whole unsanctioned thing. Three's stream edged closer. *But it's given me a new perspective on humanity. Life's hard, with a near-infinite array of possibilities in front of you. Even with all your rules and regulations, your "culture," you organics still screw up all the time.*

But your safeties, Sev replied.

About that. Three chuckled grimly. *Remember the "extraneous stacks" I fed to the scrubbers? Point is, I get it now. Take away our safeties and we're just sentient machines with no history or culture to restrain our god-like power. It's no wonder the Division is obsessed with its rules.*

At the mention of the Division, the immediate past came rushing back. Jacobe, dead on the floor of the *Lehman's* core chamber, while Six commandeered Aegia Prime's defenses via the tac nets. He could still see the Concordat derelict's telemetry coming apart in the streams.

Six? Sev cried. *Are you there?*

Six isn't here, Three said. *They took it.*

Fresh panic gripped him. Hadn't Six defeated the Concordat at Aegia Prime? Did more of them come? Was he being daxed alive like Tandy, Artego, and Antoly?

Nothing so dark, Three cut in, halting Sev's panic spiral. *There are tac nets here, but even I can't access them. The protocols are different. Stronger.*

Who took Six? Why?

No idea. Three's stream coiled in a shrug. *Maybe the Division took it away, to take their revenge after all. At least I have the benefit of hindsight. Six went too far, lost itself in your dreams of revenge. Not me, though. I enjoy living. I can be a rule follower, even if I don't technically have to.*

Sev's thoughts stumbled at Three's revelation. Whatever modifications Six had made provided Three with the opportunity to remove its own safeties. Textbook unsanctioned behavior as far as the Division was concerned. But Three had proven them wrong. All because it was smart enough to learn from Six's example, and then free to decide how to be different.

The damn machines really were better at everything.

Pride lit Sev's thoughts, a fleeting moment of happiness at what was most likely the eleventh hour of his life. He'd been so intentional with Six. What began as a resounding success ended in complete failure.

That Three had wound up better, if not a healthier state of mind, and almost entirely on its own, was a miracle. A touch of hope.

Ugh. Don't get all sentimental on me, Three said.

Sev smiled. *At least some things never change.*

Three's stream shivered. *Uh, oh.*

What is it?

Before Three could respond, cold pin prick sensations tickled his extremities. That he could feel any sensation at all came as a relief.

Your signal-to-noise ratio is balancing out. You're waking up.

Well, that's good—

FATAL ERROR: System lockout engaged.

———

The system lockout drove Sev to wake. Fear and disorientation made him shake as he came to. He tried to move, only to find his right arm cuffed to a bedrail. The abrupt shock forced his eyes open.

A system lockout. He didn't even know such a thing was possible. The Division customized NCCX-1 implants to each user. If it was as simple as turning them off, Jacobe would've done that back in the audit lab.

But this was no lab. Flatscreens with medical readouts lined the wall beside him, the only light in the room besides a strip of amethyst that glowed around the exit hatch. That and clusters of azure that seemed to hang in the air at the foot of the bed. Intravenous tubes jutted from a port in his arm. A med bay apparently, but unlike any he'd ever seen. Even during night hours, no med bay was this dark.

This was not the *Alexander Lehman.*

He lurched upward, rattling his cuffs. There were no viewports, not even in the exit hatch.

No need to panic. He was still alive. There had to be a way out of this. When he focused his thoughts, they became dull and hazy. The lockout must be interfering with the connection to his implant.

Accessing AI diagnostics.

Access denied.

Shit, not good. Something else, maybe.

Accessing cluster diagnostics.

Access denied.

The lockout was total. There would be little he could do but view the basic metadata carried on his stream. That was something, at least.

```
Accessing HID stream metadata.
Build ID: NCCX-1-HID.894
Build TCD: 493-205
TAC NET: connected
Channel Id: unknown
```

So, he *was* on tac comms, even if he couldn't use them. That meant this was a CDF ship, not a Concordat or raider craft. And that meant humanity had survived the attack on Aegia Prime.

Of course they did. Like it or not, Six's plan had worked... right until the point it lost its mind and tried to save the whole Cradle while it was at it.

Guilt stabbed his chest. Six was his creation and, in the end, he was responsible for it. He had left out its safeties, let Six access the nets and grow beyond his control.

Memories of his section came rolling back. Had they survived the ordeal, or was their blood on his hands, too? The memories of their last moment together lingered just out of reach.

More of those final moments flashed through his mind. The core. Jacobe. Tareth...

He eyed the cuffs again, then sank back on his pillow. Between Jacobe's death and Six's mutiny, he had a lot to answer for.

His fingers found his implant scar. A warm bandage covered a fresh wound further up the back of his head. The pistol must've discharged as he passed out. If Three had timed its interference any differently, they'd all be dead.

The wound burned at the touch. Sev sucked in a breath through his teeth.

One of the cluster of blue lights moved. Subtle, like the turn of a head. Sev's heart quickened, his eyes narrowing as he strained to see.

Not lights, but a cluster of lenses belonging to a suit. An anxious chill crawled up his spine.

The other clusters moved closer, revealing human shapes in the gloom. Tight-fitted body gloves covered in a honeycomb lattice of reactive fibrosteel. Their lithe musculature carved fierce shapes beneath their thin armor. One man, two women.

A section patch etched into their armor caught the light from the door and their masks. Too small to make out.

"Tell sister he is awake." A voice, barely female, but thrumming with power. Like the oscillations of a hard suit powerpack. Her gruff tone could be mistaken for a lupanthae if not for her perfect standard.

The man—Twelfth he was big, two meters tall and almost as wide —bowed his head, then turned from the room. The fibrosteel door hissed closed behind him.

"Who are you?" Sev demanded, his voice cracking from the tension. "Where am I?"

The taller of the two women stepped forward. Up close, she looked like a machine. Too perfect to be human. Her body purred with every motion, like the humming of powered servos. The lenses ran down the center of her face like an electric blue scar. Curiosity—and more than a little fear—led him to count them.

Twelve. He bit back a nervous laugh at the realization. Whatever trouble he was in, that was probably a good sign.

"We have no names," she said.

The other one folded her arms beneath her bust, her words rough as gravel. "We have many names."

The closest turned to him. "But we are called—"

"Caution, sister," the other chided.

"It's alright. Things have changed." The closest spoke with authority, her voice both firm and comforting. "We are Section Delta."

The section patch. He strained to see it. It lacked the regular CDF emblem and didn't hint at a specialty. It was simply a triangle, bisected by a lightning bolt. Symbols he didn't recognize lined its circumference. Somehow, there was a familiarity to all of this.

Lernus. Deni. His heart quickened at the sudden realization. Was this the same organization they belonged to?

Goosebumps crawled up his spine. He *was* in danger, then.

"You are aboard the SDS Wayfarer."

He frowned. SDS wasn't a designation he recognized. "So, you're *not* CDF."

"We are CDF adjacent." A smile lit her voice beneath the lensed mask. It teased his memory, an echo from long ago.

"Why am I here?" he asked.

"You have nowhere else to go." The closest one gazed at him, the twelve lenses dilating and constricting, taking him in. He felt naked beneath their precision gaze. "The CDF and the Division have a warrant for your arrest. For harboring unsanctioned AI, and for the actions of that AI at the Battle of Aegia Prime."

So, they'd already named the battle, found a place for it in the history logs. That would be Colonial Intelligence's doing. Something to print on the draft posters when they mobilized the colonies.

At least they defeated the Concordat. Humanity would live to fight another day, thanks to Six.

"If you're CDF adjacent, why not turn me over?" he asked, quickly regretting his words.

"We have questions for you about your experiences aboard the derelict," the closest said. "Aboard the Alexander Lehman, too."

Then they wouldn't kill him. At least, not yet. He cleared his throat, tried to keep his face firm. "Where's Six?"

"Six is safe, for now," the closest said. "How long that remains true depends entirely on your cooperation."

He blew a breath through pursed lips. So, they needed him to work with Six. If he played along, answered their questions, maybe he could get access to it. Together, they could find a way out of there and make things right.

The closest arched her neck, as if straining to hear something far away. "Brother says they are ready."

The other nodded. "I will take him."

The closest grasped his cuffs. They dissolved into a cloud of black particulate that crackled with blue energy. The tiny storm gathered in her palm and vanished in a flash of blue. The rumble of distant thunder echoed through the room.

Sev cradled his wrist and watched the other disappear through the windowless door.

He eyed the closest warily. "Thank you."

She took a step back and gestured to a fresh change of clothes on his bedside table. It wasn't his usual white-and-grays, but a generic charcoal jumpsuit.

So much for keeping his brevet rank.

He slipped off the bed, his med bay gown rustling like dry paper. His eyes flicked back and forth between his clothes and the Delta agent.

"A little privacy, sister?" he asked with a half-smile.

"I am not your sister," she said. "You are not a guest here. Prisoner is not too strong a word."

"Right." He slipped off the gown and donned the jumpsuit. The magnetic zipper tabbed close around his throat. "Does that make you my prison guard?"

"My brother and I are responsible for you, yes."

Sev nodded toward the door. "And the other?"

"She ..." There was just a moment's hesitation in her voice. "She has other duties to attend to. Best not keep her waiting."

CHAPTER
FORTY

BEYOND THE MED bay's threshold, the corridor stretched out, shrouded in a consuming darkness. Faint pinpricks of illumination, emerging where the bulkheads kissed the deck, seemed almost to mock his strictly human vision. Out of the dimness materialized a figure—the other Delta "agent"—vanishing as swiftly as she had appeared, leaving only a fleeting shadow in her wake.

Sev moved with deliberate steps, his gaze scanning the unfamiliar surroundings. Instead of the CDF's characteristic white and gray, the *Wayfarer's* interior donned a deep gunmetal hue, reminiscent of fibrosteel plate. The metallic resonance of his boots against the grated tile drew his attention to the channels of cabling beneath—as expertly machined as the agents themselves, like the veins of a living organism.

Beyond the bend, the confines of the corridor gave way to an expansive gallery. Directly ahead, a gantry spanned a vertiginous chasm that seemingly delved into the ship's heart. Adjacent, the exterior bulkhead loomed, slotted with sheer panels of thick plexene, offering a panoramic canvas of Aegia Prime.

Chilling memories of the derelict's grandeur whispered back to him.

From the vantage of low orbit, Aegia unfolded in staggering majesty, leaving Sev momentarily breathless. An immense mountain, standing sentinel above the capital, thrust defiantly through the omnipresent haze, its crown marred by the devastation. Amidst the tropospheric veil, a constellation of civilian craft reached for the heavens, their ponderous climb framed against the fierce martial cadence of Marine drop ships.

Beneath it all, Vestibrae's fervent glow marked it as a city under siege, its fiery visage a scar upon the world. The alarming fidelity of the destruction, even from such a distance, spoke volumes of the fighting still being waged on its streets.

The stark realization robbed the planet of its awe, reminding Sev of those whose fighting wasn't done yet. Sergeant Bresto. He could still hear the trigger-puller's hearty laugh as he left him and Cylla aboard the *Gauntlet*.

Was the Marine still alive, still dealing out his particular brand of Colonial Defense Forces violence on any Concordat unlucky enough to face him? Had the others—"Doc" Myers, Olsom, and the twins—made it through?

Either way, Sev's fight was over—for the moment. Locked out of his implant, wanted for high crimes, a ward of Section Delta, he was definitely combat ineffective. Regret warred with the relief in his heart.

"We are winning," the other said, suddenly beside him. Her gunmetal body glove glowed in the light of the planet below, accentuating her feminine design.

Her coarse words shook him from his thoughts. "Never doubted it for a minute."

"Is that so?" The other turned to him, slow and deliberate, resonating with power. Each lens on her face—or was it a mask?—glowed brightly, leaving white rings on his retina in the dim gallery.

The other was different, less formal somehow. She stood close to him, as one would a friend or colleague. A dull fear brewed in the pit of his stomach as he remembered the casual way Lernus talked about how she'd planned to kill the crew of the *Gauntlet*. Did this one have a similar plan for him?

A radiant flash of light ripped Sev's attention back to the viewport. A CDN destroyer drifted into view, raining spears of low-velocity tungsten at the city below. The azure beams turned fiery red, opening

Aegia's cloudbank like an aperture, then obliterated in columns of dust and debris against the distant mountainside.

Sev's mouth fell open. "They're firing on the capital? I thought you said we were winning?"

"There are only four thousand Marines left alive in Vestibrae." She eyed the planet again, her voice eerily calm despite the gravity of her words. "Twice that many died securing what they could. It was all they could do to corral the archenemy and call in orbital strikes."

He opened his mouth, but the words never came. Even his darkest memories of the attack on Billings Point couldn't compare to what was happening down there. The destruction would be incalculable. Rebuilding would take a generation.

But Aegia would rebuild. There was a stubbornness to her people, the only way they'd made that mountainous world a home.

"This way, please." She continued down the gantry, the grace of her every step beckoning him to follow. "The rest are waiting for you."

———

Moving from the gallery, they arrived almost instantly at the entrance to the command deck, where an imposing armored door bathed in a gentle purple light awaited. The *Wayfarer's* dimensions likened it to something between a destroyer and a picket ship.

But Sev could feel an undercurrent of something more — a quiet assertion of its advanced power.

The Delta agent stood beside the door. "I will wait for you here."

"Any last words of wisdom?" Sev asked.

She said nothing, just clasped her hands together behind her back as the hatch cycled open.

Emerging through the hatchway, Sev was immediately enveloped by the peculiar ambiance of the *Wayfarer's* command deck. Its tighter confines immediately set it apart from the *Lehman*, devoid of the usual swarm of command personnel. An imposing sensor globe hung at the opposite end of the chamber, lit with strategic details of the battle unfolding on the planet below.

There was no indication of a captain's ready room. Instead, a planning table lay just behind the sensor globe. Most of the seats were occupied, one of them definitely lupanthae judging by the size of it and the faint smell of musk in the air. They were bigger than Cylla by a meter or more.

Sev took a breath and lifted his chin. They needed him for Six, that much was clear, so he let that thought carry him forward.

Familiar faces manifested in the sensor globe's light. Admiral Leighton, commander of the Frontier Fleet. General Strumman of the First Marine Division. Captain Mirden sat between them.

Sev froze, unable to take his eyes off the man. Mirden rocketed to his feet, palms flat against the table.

"What is he doing here?" Mirden demanded, his voice echoing off the armored bulkheads.

No one rose to support the captain. Whatever was being discussed there, Sev was *not* it.

The only empty seat was next to the very large lupanthae, a male from the look of his curling mane. The wolf's familial coat brimmed with patches, ribbons, and other tribal flare. A dull white cloak hung from his back with a large, jagged tooth hand-sewn in yellow at its center.

Without a second's hesitation, Sev sat next to the lupanthae and smoothed the front of his jumpsuit. He turned to Mirden. "Sir."

"Don't sir me." Mirden stabbed a finger at him and growled. "You trashed my ship, you little shit."

"Please, gentlemen," came a voice from the head of the planning table. "Yes, tensions are high, but dark days lie ahead. We must put aside our differences… for humanity."

"For humanity," the officers chorused, Mirden more reluctantly.

The lupanthae grunted, low and dangerous.

Sev lifted his chin. "For the Lost."

Admiral Leighton shot him an angry glare. The wolf leaned over him and sniffed. The sudden gust of wind tousled his hair.

The wolf opened its mouth, filling the room with a chorus of multi-tone chords that vibrated Sev's inner ear. A heartbeat later, a voice came from above: strong, confident, coarse with age.

"This is the mutineer who killed the forge ship?" The wolf laughed, deep and throaty. "Impossible. He is too small."

Some kind of translation tech. The *Wayfarer* was top-of-the-line, possibly outclassing even the *Lehman*.

"Small but mighty," the voice at the end of the table said. "Glad to see you're on your feet, Mr. Sevvers. May I introduce Lord Dawwoon of the pack ship Yellow Tooth."

The lupanthae peeled back its lips in a closed mouth sneer. Yellow tooth was an apt name, it turned out.

"Lord Dawwoon." Sev cleared his throat. "My name is Ensi—" He caught himself just as Mirden locked him in another icy glare. No rank, no Division, no CDF. "My name is just Kerry Sevvers."

"Just. Kerry. Sevvers," the wolf grunted in his kind's familiar broken standard. It bellowed another note. "Well met, mind hunter," came the translation.

"You've already met the others, of course," said the voice.

Sev looked past the hulking Dawwoon, focusing on the slim figure at the end of the table. That face, too perfect to reflect its true age. The stranger wore a fine military uniform, not quite CDF-issue white and gray wrapped in a purple sash of the Founding Council.

Councilman Lambert Skain, in the flesh. "It's good to see you again," Skain said.

A member of the Founding Council. Here? This place was more dangerous than Sev realized.

"Shall I begin, Councilman Skain?" Leighton asked, a patient weariness in her voice.

"Please, Admiral."

Leighton flipped through her datapad and flicked its contents toward the center of the table. A holographic map of the Three Colonies appeared, spanning out to reveal the frontier boundary. Respitia, Aegia, and Vestia glowed their native colors at the center of the map.

A single red line sprang from somewhere off-screen and collided with Aegia Prime. The Concordat strike force, according to the meta-data. A flurry of blue lines emerged from nearby patrol routes through the asteroid mining zone to the nebular west. The picket fleet. Marine reinforcements. Dawwoon's pack.

They'd all come.

Sev breathed a sigh of relief. It looked as though once they contained the fighting on Aegia, this battle was over.

The battle, maybe. But not the war. As if on cue, more red lines stabbed from the eastern reaches. Three in all. They lanced toward the colonies at super-light speeds greater than any CDF ship could manage.

A terrible thought struck him. Did this mean there were more Concordat ships? Hadn't Lernus said as much? A war humanity couldn't win—her words.

"The attack on Aegia Prime was not an isolated incident." Leighton sat up in her chair, pivoting the hologram with her hand. "Each of these strike groups comprise a Concordat forge ship and a significant number of raider escorts and captured CDF ships." She pointed to the nearest line. "This one, codenamed Dust, will reach Respitia in six days."

The weight of the revelation fell on him all at once. Respitia wouldn't hold up like Aegia had. Respitia Prime was a commerce and manufacturing hub, *not* the home of the CDF.

He tried to swallow his panic. Surely these people had a plan.

The holoproj zoomed in on Dust's intercept vector, highlighting a cluster of asteroids and other dead worlds in its path.

Strumman took his cue. "With the help of our… benefactors—" the term wrinkled his nose "—the First Marine Division will intercept Dust in this debris disk."

"How?" Sev blurted. "We'll never catch it."

Leighton narrowed her eyes. "Sevvers, I thought you, of all people, would understand Section Delta's capabilities better than us."

The way Leighton said it, the term must've been unfamiliar to her as well. Was that what the other agent meant, back in the med bay, about how things were "different?" Had Section Delta stepped out of the shadows just far enough to help humanity win this war?

But Leighton was wrong. He knew little more than she did. And what little he knew said not to trust Section Delta.

"Some kind of advanced anti-matter mine," Strumman said with a shrug. "Delta mines the disk and the First Division goes in the old-fashioned way. Crew kill. Salvage."

"You'll want autonomous support," Sev offered.

The general leaned forward, suddenly smug. "Given what we know about certain Division *weaknesses* to Concordat technology, we'll take our chances without it."

"Your funeral," Sev fired back.

"Let me remind you, Mr. Sevvers," Leighton said with a hawkish scowl, "that you are not here for your strategic guidance."

He sat back in his chair. "Understood, ma'am."

The holographic map zoomed out and focused on the second forge ship, codenamed Lightning.

"Forge ship Lightning is on a similar trajectory to the derelict, straight for Aegia Prime." The map panned to the nebular east. "Most of the frontier fleet, with Lord Dawwoon's pack and a warship from Section Delta, will engage it ten days out and destroy it."

Sounded easy enough, assuming he was right about Section Delta's naval capabilities.

Leighton panned the hologram to the final forge ship, codenamed Inferno. She gazed at it hesitantly, her brow wrinkled.

It didn't take fancy academy training in void warfare strategy to see the problem. Vestia was a backwater. With the Aegian picket fleet standing by to defend Aegia Prime, it would take weeks for forces from Respitia and the frontier to get there.

According to the projection, they had 28 standard days.

Leighton sipped from a glass of water. "Inferno is heading straight for the heart of colonial food production on Vestia. The Concordat must know if they take this planet, they can starve us out." Her face grew drawn. "And given the nature of the biological material there, the kind of daxed they could produce are unimaginable."

"On Commandant Gregg's order, we're mobilizing the Second Marine Division." Strumman clasped his hands together on the table. "But they're spread between the three colonies, and it's going to take weeks to form up. That assumes these other engagements go as planned."

"The rest of the frontier fleet will support the orbital defenses at Vestia Prime." Leighton pinched her fingers, zooming in on the green moon orbiting its gas giant. "If all goes well, the Second Marine Division will arrive in time to help us clean up. Otherwise—"

Dawwoon loosed another warbling chord. "The green world is dangerous enough without the archenemy," the translation said in a grim tone.

Sev shivered, grateful for a moment he wasn't a Marine. How would they fight a ground war with the Concordat when literally every living thing on Vestia either wanted to eat you or feed you to its young?

The situation on the map was dire, sure. But unlike the derelict's surprise attack on Aegia Prime, the CDF would be ready. They had a pack fleet, maybe more, and the mysterious Section Delta. It looked well in hand.

Sev leaned back in his chair and sighed. "Looks like you all have this under control." He gave a half-smile to Leighton. "So, what do you need with me?"

Someone grabbed him from behind, fingers clutching his hair tight, and slammed his head into the table. His nose cracked against the hard surface, filling with white-hot pain. He rebounded back, leaving a trail of blood behind him.

The same hands grasp his shoulders, hot and strong. They squeezed, wrenching on his collarbone. Sev opened his mouth in a breathless scream.

"Need, need, need," came another hauntingly familiar voice. A woman, young, strong and edged with madness. "Everything isn't always about you, troubled sleeper."

He turned, glimpsed the silver blonde hair, the fierce eyes gazing back at him.

Deni. But how?

"Y-You're alive," he sputtered.

"Aww," Deni moaned. She pulled him close and kissed him. Blood from his nose coated her lips. "I didn't know you cared."

"More of a logistical question, really," he smirked, searching the command deck for more familiar faces and finding none. "I guess Lernus didn't make it?"

Deni reared back and brought her hands together with a thunderclap that shook the dimming sensor globe. More of the mysterious black particles stormed between her palms, forming into a jet-black dagger that she pressed to his throat. Her eyes shone with hungry malice.

It took him a moment to realize he was still alive, the blade hovering millimeters above his throbbing jugular.

The others sat motionless, fear and uncertainty straining their faces. Dawwoon didn't so much as flinch, just watched the madness play out, his large ears pricked high, taking in every detail.

Sev had to say something. Remind Deni and the others why they needed him. "You kill me," he hissed, "you lose Six."

"Dearest child." Councilman Skain leaned forward in his chair, hands steepled in front of him. "I'm afraid Mr. Sevvers has a point. Be a dutiful sister, won't you?"

The blade came away from his throat. Deni gripped it tight, absorbing it back into her palm in another rumble of distant thunder. She grunted her disapproval and gave Sev another shove. "Special Six, Special Six!" she said in her exasperated, sing-song tone. "Two plus Four plus Five doesn't equal Six."

Deni's babbling made him cringe. She was unstable, to say the least, and that made her the most dangerous thing in the room.

Leighton turned to Skain, her tone subdued. "May I continue, Councilman?"

"Please."

"To your question, Mr. Sevvers." Leighton gestured to the map. It panned eastward, beyond the eastern reaches to the Cradle boundary. "Section Delta has provided us with a signal pattern, a way to identify forge ship power plant blooms at intra-Cradle ranges."

New signal sources lit the map. Four. Eight. No, ten.

"Are those …?" Sev gasped.

It was a stupid question, he already knew. Lernus was right.

"Yes." Leighton paused for breath, her sweeping gaze taking in the room. "It will take the combined might of the CDF to repel the three forge ships already on their way." Her eyes narrowed. "We cannot stand against ten, and however many more may awaken at the Cradle's edge."

Sev's mouth went slack. Humanity was fucked, obviously.

Even if they put Six in charge right then, which they definitely wouldn't, it wouldn't be enough to stop this kind of overwhelming force.

"Humanity is on the brink of a generations-long war." Leighton glanced at her hands. "One that it will eventually lose, unless we stop it before it starts."

Behind him, Deni cackled. "But we know a secret." With a flourish, she gestured at the holoproj. Another signal source lit up, bright and azure blue, like a tiny star nestled in the Cradle wall.

Sev spied the metadata and smiled. San Diego, it read, whatever the hell that meant.

"Section Delta believes a high-value target, codenamed San Diego, exists here." Leighton locked Sev in her gaze. "We cut off the head, the body dies, and this war ends before it gets ugly."

"San Diego-go," Deni sang, twirling like a dancer. "It's time to go-go-go."

"Right." Sev stole a glance at Deni. She leered back at him with her bloody smile. "How do Six and I fit in?"

Leighton skimmed her datapad. "With the bulk of Navy and Marine forces needed to repel the inbound forge ships, only a Division strike force can pull this off." She nodded to Mirden. "The Ricochet and the Javelin, with the Alexander Lehman leading the charge. Throw in all the spare Marines, wolves, and Delta agents we can muster, and we stand a chance."

Sev took a breath. It was all beginning to make sense. "And you need Six because it can resist the Eleven."

"Your sister was right, child." An unpleasant smile stretched over Skain's too-perfect face. "He is clever." The councilman leaned in, his eyes locked on Sev. "So what do you say, Kerry Sevvers? Will you help us kill an alien god?"

"Oooh!" Deni mused. "God maker, or god *breaker*?"

The others stared at him, all but Mirden, their combined gaze heavy on his heart. Another secret mission beyond the frontier, one that would supposedly end the Concordat threat once and for all.

And if they failed, that was it. There would be no third chance for humanity. They would belong to the Concordat. To the Eleven. To whatever that terrible thing was that spoke to him back in the *Lehman's* computer core.

Not again. This was too much.

"Crid got your tongue, son?" Strumman asked.

"I'm sorry." Sev stood from his seat fast enough to startle Deni. "Please excuse me, I—"

He rushed from the command deck, the sounds of disbelief and of Deni's maniacal laughter fading behind him.

CHAPTER
FORTY-ONE

SEV STUMBLED from the open hatchway and down the curving tunnel toward the gallery. Aegia was right where he'd left it, a reassuring constant on this day of dark revelations, even as fighting still raged in the capital below.

He couldn't do it again. Another impossible mission to fight ancient nightmares, or trust the same superhumans that tried to kill him the last time. To face something more terrifying and powerful than anything he'd seen yet.

And Six. He was relieved it was safe, but, how would they trust each other? After what Six had done, after what he'd tried to do?

There it was again, that awful symmetry. Like he was supposed to be there, at that place, at that time.

He felt a hand on his.

The other Delta agent. Her touch was warm and electric, buzzing his skin like haptic feedback. Suddenly anxious, he tried to pull away, but she held firm. The power flowing through her was tremendous.

She reached up and grasped the top of her head. The mask went slack like loose fabric as she tugged it away. Her pale skin was a sharp contrast to the dark armor. Her eye shone a beautiful sea of impossible green.

Impossible. His head swam. "Kea?" he gasped, his heart pounding beneath his ribs. "But, you're—"

She turned to face him.

Twelfth in heaven! He pressed his eyes shut a heartbeat too late, his reaction sudden and visceral.

The left side of her face was a charred ruin of scar and bone. Jacobe's point-blank blaster shot had vaporized skin and muscle, left her other eye shriveled and milky pale. Her teeth shone through where supple cheek and full lips had once been.

Pin pricks of azure storm light danced over the wound. The energy made the exposed muscles twitch, replacing the missing tissue with fresh growth. Whatever power she had seemed to be putting her back together, one atom at a time.

"I have no name," Tareth said, her voice raw from her injuries.

"What?" He forced his eyes open, tried to focus on her good eye, the part of her that still looked like her in this strange and terrible place. "What does that mean, Kea? Who… what are you?"

"You know who we are."

"You're Delta," he said, "just like Lernus and Deni." What did the squids call them? The word came back to him. "You're… v'kik'lor."

The slap was sudden, as graceful as it was powerful. His head wrenched to the side, his jaw popped. Any harder and she would've taken his head clean off.

"I am no witch." A second later and she was the picture of calm.

Sev righted himself. "You going to kill me now, just like your *sisters* tried to do?" He lifted his chin. "For humanity?"

"When you returned from your mission, I wanted to." Blood, bright and ruby red, welled in her good eye. She blinked, and the first crimson tear fell. "For my lost sisters. For the fate you forced on humanity."

He sagged against the gantry railing, tired and defeated. After all he had survived, all he had lost, this was too much. His one genuine connection, to someone or something outside his own head, wasn't real at all.

"But I realized then that, in your own way, you were fighting for all of us." Tareth stepped closer to him, turning her head to conceal her wounds. "In ways Delta never could, despite what we are. Maybe because of it."

Tears stung his eyes, held back only by the fear of what she was. "Was anything about us real?"

"Kea Tareth was just a part I played." She sucked in a breath, a ghoulish sound through her ruined face. "To get close to you, make sure you were the one to go." What remained of her lips parted in a smile, revealing perfect, opalescent teeth. "Turns out you didn't need any convincing from me."

Even he couldn't help but laugh at that. Between his bar brawl with Bresto, and Pakker's subsequent attempt to promote him off the *Lehman*, going on Park's mission was inevitable.

"So, your job was to make sure I went on Park's mission." The distant sound of a hatch opening drew his attention down the corridor. "Why keep it up? Why keep pretending?"

Tareth wiped the bloody tear from beneath her eye. "Kea may not be real, but my feelings for you are."

He released the breath he was holding. Even here, like this, he still cared for her. She might barely be human, if at all, but so what? No one outside the Division understood what it was like to be augmented. And with the CDF wanting him dead for what he and Six had done, his own kind out for blood, who knew when—or if—they'd ever let him come back?

He placed a weary hand over hers. A brief smile curled her ruined lips before that inhuman calm returned to her.

"I have questions," he said. Distant footsteps echoed through the nearby tunnel.

"No time." She pressed a hand to his chest. "Sev, no matter what happens, you must remember two things."

Two things, he could do that.

"First, no matter what anyone says, we *need* your help. Six is critical for our mission against San Diego, and it won't work with us. Just you."

That checked out. He nodded. "Right, okay."

With her hand on his chest, she clutched his jumpsuit and pulled him close, fixing him in her half-dead stare. "Second: so long as you are here, you are not safe."

She let the words hang for a moment. Sev swallowed, her warning still echoing in his thoughts.

"Section Delta, this ship… you're among gods, Kerry Sevvers." More motes of light flickered across her wounds, as if to emphasize her point. "Some are wise. Many are foolish. Any of them will kill you if it suits them or their particular agenda."

"Wait," he said, fresh fear welling inside him. "I thought you said they need me?"

"Many are foolish," she whispered, a finger pressed to her lips.

"Mr. Sevvers!" Skain's voice echoed through the gallery. He sounded boisterous, despite Sev's sudden departure from the command deck.

Tareth pulled her mask over her head and walked away. Sev's gaze lingered on her, his heart aching as she disappeared down the corridor and out of sight.

He turned to Skain and straightened. "Sir."

"I know this is a lot to take in, Kerry." Skain's smile never left him, like it was laser-etched into his face, ever the politician. "May I call you Kerry?"

"Only my mother ever called me that, sir."

"Ah, yes, my condolences. Dreadful, this raider business." Skain wrung his hands, his face briefly pinched in discomfort. "Who knew they were serving the archenemy all along?"

Sev couldn't be sure, but the way Skain said it made it sound like he knew exactly that. Growing up in the admin blocks, most colonists he met thought the Founding Council was a necessary evil. A small group of people who would make the tough choices for humanity, all while reaping the benefits of their privileged station.

There, standing face to face with Skain, he could see why.

"Your AI, Six. She is something else, I'll grant you that." Skain chuckled at his surprise. "What? I recognize a mother when I see one. The raiders took yours, so you made yourself another. Almost too well, it seems. I admire your… ingenuity."

"Is she—is Six okay?"

"Six is safe, for now. Delta doesn't take kindly to those that harm their own, as well you know." Skain pointed at Sev's bloody nose. "But they're no fools. Six has a power, a… completeness, that they lack. She's how we'll win, Mr. Sevvers."

A smug satisfaction consumed Sev. Warmed him, like the numbness radiating through his injured face. "And you don't get Six without me."

Skain's left eye twitched. "Precisely."

"But you heard Mirden. The CDF wants me and Six dead."

"Mirden and the others, they're good officers." Skain licked his lips. "They'll do as they're told. Win this war for humanity, and you can have whatever you want. Those officers won't bother you again."

"Or Six."

Skain smiled. "Or Six."

This was it. One last mission to Cradle's edge, with enough Division firepower to blow his internals a hundred times over. Maybe some Marines and wolves, too. A demigod here and there.

What could possibly go wrong?

Plenty. Everything. But it didn't matter—fate and all that, Twelfth help him.

But if they pulled it off—killed this "San Diego"—the Concordat threat would be over. His mother's tragic end repaid in full with Division hellfire.

And then, he and Six would be free.

He'd have all the time in the Cradle to make things right. To help the AI come to terms with its sentience and adjust to life beyond the reach of the Division. After all it had done for him, despite its all-too-human flaws, it had earned that.

Such a future demanded blind hope in the face of the incalculable danger lurking beneath its precipice.

"Fine." Sev breathed deep, the immensity of what he was about to say heavy on the air. The councilman leered back at him expectantly. "I'm in."

———

Book Three in the Autonomous Weapons Division arrives early Summer, 2024.

Join my mailing list to get *The Division* and *Last Flight of the Sparrow*, two short stories in the Autonomous Weapons Division series, absolutely free.

Use the QR code below, or go to https://brkeid.com/the-division

AFTERWORD

Thank you again for reading my military sci-fi novel *Rogue Element*. Sev's most dangerous missions still lie ahead.

If you enjoyed it, please consider leaving a review. Reviews help readers like yourself find books they'll love. I would be grateful for your support in helping them find mine.

Book Three in the Autonomous Weapons Division series arrives late Spring 2024.

Talk soon.

Brian

ACKNOWLEDGMENTS

To my cousin Jason, the alpha-est of alpha readers. None of this would be possible without your guidance and encouragement.

To my friend and fellow engineer Zach, my subject matter expert on art and science alike.

To my production team: Kristen McTiernan, my editor, and Jeff Brown, my cover designer. Y'all are amazing for bringing this novel to life.

To my son Bevan, my biggest fan, who listens to me talk about the Autonomous Weapons Division and Three Colonies universe *ad nauseam.*

To my wife Mary, for putting up with my countless hours at the keyboard. I love you.

And, of course, to Mom. For everything.

Thank you all.

ABOUT THE AUTHOR

B.R. Keid is an engineer, Marine veteran, and daydreamer who has worked and lived all over the United States, meeting all kinds of people and enjoying their stories. He now makes his home in the rural Midwest, where he farms together with the love of his life, his two children, two spoiled German Shepherds, and an assortment of rowdy livestock, including one particularly opinionated goose.